Foreign Devils

John Hornor Jacobs

First published in Great Britain in 2015 by Gollancz
an imprint of The Orion Publishing Group Ltd
Carmelite House, 50 Victoria Embankment,
London EC4Y 0DZ

An Hachette UK Company

1 3 5 7 9 10 8 6 4 2

A CIP catalogue record for this book is
available from the British Library

ISBN 978 0 575 12380 9

Typeset at The Spartan Press Ltd,
Lymington, Hants

Printed and bound by CPI Group (UK) Ltd,
Croydon, CR0 4YY

For Lily and Helen

We outrode today, into the Hardscrabble, just Fisk and I. Father was whining and petulant and Carnelia sulked in the dry heat, but I remained adamant that neither pregnancy nor parentage would prevent me. Lupina, ever solicitous of my health since my not-so-delicate state was detected, nodded sagaciously as I waved off Father's protestations and strapped the Hellfire shotgun to my leg.

Despite the heat, there was a breeze as we took our horses out, away from wagon train, the lictors and legionnaires, as they made their way east toward Dvergar Spur. We rode fast; Fisk knows the ways to lose any tagalongs that may follow.

As we rode, my mind remained clouded. The expected clarity of hardscrabble and horseback did nothing to brush away the dark skein of thoughts shadowing me.

I dreamed of Mother last night.

It was after Father put her aside and I took the *daemon* steamer to Salonica, where she had placed herself in voluntary exile in a villa there, entertaining gentleman suitors, until her family's public shame around the Citlapol event could be either expunged, Imperially forgiven, or ignored. The suitors were well bred, but lesser men; laden with gifts in hopes of winning Octavia Messala's hand – in hopes of winning her purse. Mother always had money, otherwise Father would have never been interested.

It had been a strange few months there. The island was lovely – mostly a fishing community – and at night boys would come to the villa with woven baskets of wild flowers, calling 'Domina! Domina!' and tossing sprigs of *nocteflorius* onto the stone steps. Lavender. Blue agapanthus. Seabloom and butcher's heart. Until Mother would send out a slave with a few small coins to sprinkle about.

She wasn't happy, my mother. But I never knew her to be. And, I think, this more than any other reason was why Father put her aside. He is a creature of jollity – the Citlapol event was just an excuse.

In the dream, we walked on the rocky bluff above the shore one day, standing in the wind-wracked trees there and watching the ships move like toys across the wide face of the Pelagus. I was fourteen and thirty-three all at once in the strange way that dreams have, possessed of both the innocence of my youth and the knowledge of the present.

'You will marry,' Mother said, looking out at the sea. 'And soon, and it will be of your father's choosing.'

I said nothing, locked in the dream, watching Mother.

'You will marry,' she said again, 'And will not love him because how can you? We are strong, Livia. Women are the strength of the world; we bring life into it. We nuture life while our time passes and ease it into the grave when life is done.' She turned away from the shore to look at me. 'We are the stronger sex. Men are but mean and petty things and this is why they rule us. So we must be mean and petty, too, to survive.

'You will never love your husband,' she said. 'But you must make him love you. You must be mean, and petty, and *make* him love you for your own safety's sake.'

In the distance a bell tolled and I found myself struggling to escape. A horror settled on me, and I thrashed and writhed until

I woke, steaming in the darkness of the tent and spent the rest of the night looking upon the sleeping face of Fisk.

And today we outrode against Father's wishes.

'There's someone following us,' Fisk said, looking back over his horse's rump. A rare tenseness there, tightness in his shoulders, his legs, made more remarkable because of his accustomed calm.

'Father sent legionnaires to hound us?'

Fisk shook his head and brought his horse alongside mine, so that our legs touched. Even astride a horse, I felt the raw, physicality of the man and thought of night, in our tent.

'If he sent legionnaires to follow us, they are dead. That is a *vaettir*.' He inclined his head toward the far horizon.

'I have seen nothing,' I said.

He nodded. 'Still. It's there. We must circle back.'

'Could we not hide? Wait for it.'

'An ambush?' He glanced at my stomach. 'No.'

'I am not an invalid, my love,' I said, and pulled the shotgun from its holster.

'Ia-damn,' he said, and his face softened. 'Don't I know it. But there's more than just us to think about.'

'My movement hasn't been impaired. Yet.' I pulled my horse away from his and wheeled it about. 'And I am a match for you or anyone atop a horse.'

He stared at me, breathing softly. 'Don't I know it,' he said again.

'Then let us take care of this creature, shall we, you and I?'

He looked about. 'There. Ride there,' he said, looking at an outcrop of dark rocks pushing through the hardscrabble. 'Slowly. Like we were out on a picnic, or some dalliance.'

I raised my eyebrow. 'Are we not?'

'I don't think we'll have time for the little death since we're doing this for the big one.'

'We shall see.'

We reached the rocky outcrop – cartographers will no doubt name the place The Fingers or some other nonsense in the future, since the rocks *did* look much like gnarled fingers jutting through the earth's surface – and dismounted. The horses were nervous, nickering and stamping as Fisk hobbled them. I untied our woollen army issue blankets, water and food.

'How long until he reaches us?' I asked.

Fisk pulled his carbine and fed Hellfire rounds into it. 'Moments. He could be here already.'

'Then there's not much time to waste,' I said, and found a smooth spot and spread the blankets out on top of it. I lay my shotgun within easy reach. 'Come, my love. Let us give the *vaettir* bait enough to set it to salivating,' I said, patting the blankets.

He came and sat by me, holding his rifle in his hands. After a moment, he unbuckled his gun belt and withdrew the pistols, checking the rounds.

The rocks circled us, dark, crooked pillars and looming shapes. Fisk scanned them, eyes narrowed. I leaned in to kiss him, but he drew his head away.

'Love, I can't see,' he said.

'Then, we must do this without kisses,' I said, and pushed him back, straddling him.

He resisted, but only for a moment. And never let go of his gun.

It was when it was over, sweat discolouring both of our clothes, that the screeching came and Fisk jerked his gun upright and began firing as I rolled away, shotgun in hand. A shadow lanced overhead, like some deathly fast carrion bird, and instinctively I led it and fired, feeling the boom and sinking feeling that accompanies *daemonic* Hellfire.

The shadow plummeted to the ground and writhed, scratching and hissing. The stretcher whipped about and Fisk was up and firing but not before it dashed up the sheer face of one of the black fingers and launched itself up and over, out of sight.

Fisk moved to where it had fallen.

'Blood,' he said and turned to me. A small smile gave the barest crease to his craggy features. 'You winged it. A fine shot, if not a killing one. The Ia-damned thing will be burning with silver for a while.'

'How do you know it wasn't you who hit it?'

'It wasn't.'

'Come, love,' I said, withdrawing Hellfire rounds from my bandolier and reloading the shotgun. I set it down and unpinned my hair.

'Let us lure him back again,' I said.

PART I
Foreign Devils

ONE

Kalends of Quintilius, 2638 ex Ruma Immortalis

To GET TO FORT BRUST from New Damnation you take the Big Rill downstream until it doglegs south and then you're hoofing it overland for the next two hundred miles through hard-scrabble until you hit the Smokeys, what my kin call the Eldvatch. Dry land there, for mile upon countless mile, full of bramblewrack, gulleys, cracked ground sundered from the heat. Nothing for hot, waterless days and bone-cracking cold nights until the Smokeys appear like a pall of blue smoke hanging in a long unbroken line from the northern horizon to the southern rim of the earth.

Cornelius, hanging tongue a-loll, torso half-out of the carriage's window, said, 'Dwarf! My eyes have dimmed due to lack of spirits! How far till the Dvergar Spur?' The senator had been complaining it was too hot to drink in the mid-day heat for the last week. He was right and most of us – legionnaires, lictors, outriders, servants, slaves, secretaries, and family members – had agreed with him. Yet he continued to gripe.

'Day, sir. Maybe two, most like,' I said.

'But Livia said they've been spotted! Like a line of blued-gunmetal, she says.' He held his hand up to shield his eyes. Beyond the senator in the window of the large, draft-horse-drawn carriage, I could see where Carnelia and Lupina, the slave-attendant, sat cooling themselves with enamelled Tchinee fans decorated in dancing *daemon* motifs. Carnelia stared off into the hardscrabble, lips pursed in a sour expression, a book held loosely in one hand.

'Big enough to be visible thirty or forty miles away, sir.'

Cornelius cast his hot, busy gaze around, looking for something else to complain about. 'Where are my son and daughter?' he said. 'Where's my legate?' He'd been calling Fisk 'his legate' for the month. It was a hollow title, conveying Fisk a high rank – a rank high enough for someone wed to Cornelius' daughter – without any of the bellicose responsibilities that rank is heir to. No prefect or tribune would take orders from Fisk without umbrage, Fisk never having worked through the offices of any legion, never shared a tent with a conturbium of soldiers, or blooded himself in battle alongside other members of a cohort. While Fisk never complained, it rankled him, I could tell. I might not know much, but I know Fisk well enough that he'll accept but one bridle, and the one who holds that rein sat a saddle with him – Livia.

'They should be back soon, sir. Fisk took Livia out yonder, to ride,' I said. 'And Secundus, he rides there, chatting with the men.'

Cornelius looked a tad peeved at my near use of Secundus' name: they'd had a row recently regarding it. With Secundus' elder brother Gnaeus' bodily integument now burnt and mixed with gambel ash, scattered on the winds of the White Mountains like pollen and dander, Cornelius wanted Secundus to take a new name – Livius. 'You and Livia will make a brace of Cornelians! No need for you to bear the name of a second son any more!' Cornelius had exclaimed in his boredom during the journey to Fort Brust. Both Livia and Secundus had answered him with outraged silence. When Cornelius pressed the matter, Secundus said, 'My sister and I aren't quail. I had an older brother and he took pre-eminence, Father. As it was and ever should be. But now he's gone, joining our Cornelian ancestors at Ia's great triniculum, I shall remember and honour him and simply remain Secundus.' Cornelius huffed, more at being thwarted in his hasty decisions than the obstinacy of his son.

Cornelius fell into blessed silence, looking back at our train of wagons. He squinted his eyes at his son who rode beside dusty legionnaires marching – now slowed with the weight of silver-threaded gladii and pilum in addition to their Hellfire carbines and pistols; the lictors in an adjacent carriage, holly fasces pricked with silver spikes; the munitions vardo riding a distance behind ringed with armed junior engineers warily watching Engineer Valerus, who scowled and watched them back with a demeanour soured either by the journey or his vocation, it was hard to tell; the slave vardo, where the Cornelian slaves and servants indulged in sleep and the rare occurrence of indolence; the chow buck weighted down with sacks of beans and rice and corn, casks of salt pork and garum, wax-sealed ceramic jars full of pickled ackra and longbean; a passel of sutlers willing to sell almost anything to the marching legionnaires; a rolling smithy; finally, the draft-drawn waterwagon that rode higher on its springs with every evening.

I don't know a lot of former consuls, but judging from Cornelius' wagon train, and my experiences on his boat, they don't travel light.

In the evening, the sun lowering in the west, Fisk and Livia returned, dusty and parched.

Pulling his horse by the senator's wagon, Fisk said, 'Encountered a stretcher today, sir.'

Cornelius sat upright. 'And?' He looked at Livia, then the horses.

'Winged it,' Fisk said. 'Or, Livia did.'

'This is interesting!' Cornelius said. 'Do you think we could break this dreary baggage train and have a little hunt?'

Fisk shook his head. 'There's always the chance there are more *vaettir* out there. But there are no guarantees in the Hardscrabble.'

Cornelius harrumphed. 'My legate, there are no guarantees in *life*. And we are expected at Fort Brust,' he said and called a halt. 'I need a drink. We'll camp here.'

After watering their horses, Fisk and Livia joined us in the massive praetorium tent that the proconsul's wagon transformed into at every nightfall. Somehow, the tent-raising had fallen to me to organize and the slaves and legionnaires balked, sometimes, at taking their orders from me, due to my mixed blood. I may be small, but my voice is loud and with Cornelius' favour, my workers managed to swallow their pride at being commanded by one of my stature and *dvergar* blood. Rumans are one thing, but even their slaves are proud.

First, the hardscrabble ground was cleared and raked, and smooth pine planks were laid down on the dirt. The praetorium tent was unrolled over the planking, legionnaires straining against the weight of the tent and the ash struts and supports themselves were raised with a great heave and ho and clamour as finally the main tent pole, some twenty feet high, was erected at the centre while thick hemp ropes were drawn taut and secured to iron spikes driven deep into the earth by sledgehammer, lines creaking like gambels on the heights. *Daemon* lanterns were unveiled, casting flickering yellow pools of light inside the dim interior. Then, a portable parquet floor was unlimbered from its crate from one of the wagons and assembled in its interlocking pattern – a clever *dvergar*-made artifice – and a makeshift triniculum and meeting area established. Wicker divans, chairs, and folding tables were set up while the braziers and sleeping areas were arranged for Fisk and Livia, Carnelia, Secundus, and Cornelius himself. Cilus, the chief lictor, cast blessings about the place while Rubus, Cornelius' chief secretary, began placing maps of the known world, the empire, the protectorate, and the Hardscrabble Territories on the meeting table so that Cornelius, at his leisure, might peruse matters of state. Along with the map went a Knightboard and many decks of cards so that the senator might gamble or game, as he was wont to do, or use the Knightboard figures as markers on the maps, indicating troop or flotilla movements.

Outside the tent, the legionnaires, their labours just beginning, formed a square perimeter, and began the process of establishing a Ruman military camp on the march – smaller than a permanent camp, yes, but still a considerable labour unto itself with makeshift cook and mess tent, latrines, and tent-dwellings for each contubernium. The soldiers, men of the thirteenth returning to Fort Brust, sang marching and work songs as they went about their duties – *Mighty guns of the great thirteenth! Riches and death, victory and grief! Balls of silver and sharpened teeth! Mighty guns of the great thirteenth!* There being only a complement of one hundred and twenty eight legionnaires with us – sixteen contubernium sent as escort for a legate reporting to Marcellus and now returning as ours – only sixteen tents were needed plus three more; one for the two optios, one for the lictors, and one for the slaves. The sutlers and waggoneers, the waterwagon and engineer vardos, brought their charges within the perimeter and set up rolling camp, sleeping bags laid out underneath the wagons – except in the case of the engineers, who disappeared inside the lacquered vardo and were not seen again until morning.

Inside the senator's tent, the sounds of legionnaires fell away as Lupina and two of her junior household slaves bustled about. Cornelius washed his face in a bowl of water, cleared his nostrils like a cornicen blowing assembly, then paced and fretted until the *dvergar* woman poured him a tall whiskey in a cut crystal tumbler and lit his cigar.

'Ahh, that's better,' Cornelius said, sitting down upon one of the wicker travel-chairs before his desk, beads of water caught in his whiskers and blue smoke collected around his head.

Cornelius propped his artificial leg on the desk. The thing was intricate; wrought from his own severed legbone, gold and silver filigree danced down its length, and on one side there was a neat little ceremonial skean and on the other, a small silver flask. I'd never seen that particular drinking container tarnished. The leg ended in fur and long hinged claws – the paw of the bear that took his foot. 'Daughters! My legate! Attend me!'

Carnelia sulked into the common area of the tent. 'Yes, Tata?'

'Not you, Carnelia. I've been looking at your face all day. You may go.' He waved his hand, and slurped some whiskey, sighing again.

Rumans fascinate me by what they're able to ignore, in this case his youngest daughter's look of outrage.

'Secundus! Livia! My legate!'

Miss Livia appeared, still wearing her riding leathers, a sawn-off Hellfire blunderbuss strapped to her hip. Life in the Hardscrabble Territories had been kind to her, if not clean. There was a rime of sweat-lined dust on her collar and she was wiping her hands on a dirty towel as she approached, but her face was bright, if tanned, and her eyes shone with fierce intelligence. The child she carried in her stomach was just beginning to alter her slim figure after three months, but, if anything, her pregnant state had increased her activity, as if she wanted to do and see everything she could before the child came into the world.

Fisk followed after Livia, his grey hat removed and his hair wet from his post-trail ablutions. My friend and partner for more than ten years now, but life, rank and marriage had been drawing us apart. Before Livia he was pained, and incomplete – there's no other way to say it. The meanness of the trail, the loss of his family, the necessities of living on this wide expanse of harsh earth – all had coarsened him. Wounded him. Once, it seemed, wounded him irrevocably. Yet. There came Livia. Now, Fisk was, if not whole – some things cannot be healed – at least content.

'What of the trail, children? Will there be stretchers?' Cornelius asked as Secundus emerged from his quarters – a partition, really, of the command tent. 'What awaits us?'

Fisk pulled out a wicker seat for his wife, dusted his trousers with his hands, and sat down. Cornelius snapped his fingers at Lupina, motioning for her to be free with the whiskey. Lupina poured a dram or two for Fisk, who cupped the tumbler in his hands and breathed the fumes deeply before sipping. Livia motioned Lupina away. 'I must see to the legionnaires.'

Fisk swallowed a measure of whiskey, and said, 'Tomorrow we go north, a few miles to get around that gulch, and then east again. We should hit the spur by evening of the following night, barring any other gulleys or sundered earth. Or stretchers.' He glanced at me. I knew the look.

'In your opinion,' Cornelius asked, his voice excited. 'What are the chances we'll encounter *vaettir*?' Patricians. Sometimes they don't even have the sense to be afraid.

'Not something I'm willing to speculate on, sir. They are always around. Or never. You just can't know.'

'I would not have thought they would be found so far east.'

I stepped forward. 'We are still in the Hardscrabble Territories. The *vaettir* travel fast, as you all know. Time was, they were seen in the thousand-acre wood. We are not so far east yet to be out of their territory.'

Cornelius glanced at me, sniffed, no doubt slightly perturbed that I had the temerity to pipe up during his first drink, yet Fisk and I were the experts in these lands.

'It shouldn't be much longer, Father,' Secundus said. He caught Lupina's eye and removed a crystal tumbler from a tray. She hustled around the table to pour him a measure. 'If our maps are correct, after we manoeuvre around this gulch it's a straight shot to the Dvergar spur.'

Cornelius harrumphed. 'For years I told Gallius that we'd need a mechanized baggage train line south! Years! He was too intent on scratching all of the taxes he could out of the protectorate and spending all his free time whoring in Novorum.'

'Gallius?' Fisk asked, eyebrows raised.

'Oh,' Cornelius said, beginning to smile. Secundus joined him. 'A little nickname for Rutilius.'

'The commander at Fort Brust?'

'The same.' Cornelius' smile had taken on monumental proportions.

'I imagine there's some shared history between you,' Fisk said, noncommittal.

'An unfortunate matter.' Cornelius' smile grew predatory. 'When we were both legates during Nerva's governorship in Gall, he became smitten with a dancing girl in one of the theatres there.'

Fisk stared, sipping. 'That doesn't quite explain that particular nickname.'

'A Gallish girl, she had flaxen hair and was quite thin and he spent a fortune on her, lavished her with gifts, attended every performance where she pantomimed Loumdima's capitulation to Aemilianus' army.'

'I'd think they'd prefer *Our Heavenly War*, what with all the Rumans getting bloodied in that one,' Fisk suggested.

'No, the Gallish people do not bear us much umbrage for the events of a thousand years ago. However,' he chuckled. 'They take their revenge in smaller ways.'

Secundus laughed out loud. 'Of course, I wasn't there, though I've heard this story enough times to tell it myself. After wooing her for weeks, he had her brought to his villa for a private audience.'

'Private?' Fisk said, shaking his head. It doesn't take a Pandar to know what that means.

'Alone, he disrobed her. Trembling.' Cornelius slurped more whiskey and then giggled, a surprising sound coming from a proconsul who once ruled Rume itself under Tamberlaine's watchful eye. He dipped his index finger in his whiskey, licked the tip, and then made it rise like a growing erection. 'The tension grew.

Rutilius' spear, ever the symbol of the legions, became rampant.'
Cornelius laughed again and drained his glass. 'Imagine his surprise when he realized that the Gallish lass possessed a spear of
her own.'

Secundus slapped his knee, howling with laughter. Cornelius
was overcome with mirth, unable to call for more whiskey. When
the laughter subsided and the senator reclaimed control of himself,
he brushed his moustache, smoothing the errant hairs, and popped
his cigar back into his mouth. 'Afterwards, he had her – I mean
him – crucified.'

'Ia help us, Father, you're worse than a child,' Livia said. 'You
shouldn't be repeating such stories of your peers.'

'Oh, Rutilius is a good chap, reliable as stone. A shame his one
bit of foolishness ended so ... pointedly.'

Father and son erupted with laughter again.

'Well, love,' Livia said, placing her hand on Fisk's. 'I will leave
you to my father and brother's dubious company. I hope they'll
act befitting their age.' She glanced at Secundus and stood. As
she passed her father, she laid a hand on Cornelius' shoulder. 'Or
rank.'

With that she disappeared in the folds of the tent to retrieve her
medical kit and remove herself to one of the optio's dwellings to
offer whatever bloodwork the legionnaires might need. I'd watched
her there before at her labours. Half the men of the thirteenth were
in love with her and the other half in love with the idea of her – a
pregnant patrician woman, a medic, carrying Hellfire at her hip.
She was formidable. She lanced their boils and mixed them balms
and talcums and bound their wounds while they looked upon her
like she was some goddess incarnate upon the earth, holding her
in a talismanic position reserved for revered mothers, gods, and
the legion's eagle. Soldiers are terribly predictable. But Livia has
that effect on people.

After her departure, and when the sounds of the camp quieted, four legionnaires muscled in a large box, removed the lid with crowbars, and very carefully lifted up and stood upright a tall still figure while Cornelius gestured with the tip of his cigar as to where they should place it.

'A beauty, isn't he?' the senator said, looking over the stuffed figure of the *vaettir*.

'He is impressive, sir,' I said. 'But hardly beautiful.'

Fisk remained silent, staring at the figure. Whatever taxidermist had prepared the carcass of Berith, the *vaettir*, they had replaced the eyes with smooth, milky glass, so that the fourteen-foot-tall creature seemed to stare into infinity as an unpainted stone statue might. But frightful he was; tall, his head in the shadows of the tent, the taxidermist had set the *vaettir* in a pose as if he were about to leap – legs flexed, clawed hands open and eager, lips pulled back in a snarl, showing sharp teeth.

'Took the taxidermist two mounts to get the posture right. The damned fool had never seen an elf and I had to explain to him how they leap about,' Cornelius said. 'But I am well pleased, now. It will make quite a stir back in Rume.'

I looked at the mount. Maybe longer than I should have. Whatever they are, the *vaettir* and the *dvergar* are the two native intelligent races here in Occidentalia and knowing Rumans – even Cornelius – I would imagine that somewhere, at some time, he might've been party to the mounting of a *dvergar*.

'Damn straight,' Cornelius said, walking around the mounted figure of the stretcher. 'That jumped-up whore's son didn't realize he prodded the bear in the balls with a pointy stick.' Cigar in his mouth, whiskey glass in hand, he reached up with his free hand and rapped on the *vaettir's* ribcage right where its heart would be: the exact spot where Cornelius had shot the stretcher, punching a fist-sized hole in the creature's chest cavity, killing it.

Rubus, the chief secretary, entered the tent and cleared his throat, lightly.

Cornelius turned, moving smoothly despite the whiskey and artificial leg. 'Rubus! What do you think of this bastard? Fierce, is he not?'

'Terrifying, sir,' he said, and it sounded like he meant it. Rubus' hair was shorn very short and on a metal chain around his neck were a set of ground glass oculars. I'd guess, due to the shortness of his hair, he might've seen some of the damage a single *vaettir* could wreak on the human body. In particular, stretchers have a penchant for scalpings. 'It is the kalends of Quintilius, sir.'

'Ah,' Cornelius said, looking a little grumpy. 'Already?'

'Yes sir.'

Cornelius laughed. 'Back in Rume there'll be a great amount of fornication today!'

'The Ludi Florae?' Secundus asked. From what I heard around the fire, it was some sort of naughty Ruman carnival, but no one in the Protectorate or Territories celebrated it. 'The old gods rear their fleshy heads. The plebs will be fucking in the alleyways.'

Father and son both laughed and then, together, noticed Rubus' scarlet face. The secretary blushed to his roots.

'Well then. Ahem. Place the parchment and device over here then, on the table. I can do the rest,' Cornelius said. He moved around the table, limping only slightly.

An intrigued look crossed Secundus' face and Fisk sat up, quaffing the rest of his whiskey. Rubus left the tent briefly and returned – his blush now gone – carrying a small wooden box wrought with silver pellum wards and threaded with etched intaglios deep in the wood. Waiting until Rubus left the tent, Cornelius flipped the catch on the box's lid, revealing a velvet interior containing a warded silver knife, a stoppered inkwell, a bowl with a curiously fluted mouth, a stone, and an ornate device. The device itself was small, no larger than a human skull, and resembled the filigreed *daemon*-light lanterns and fixtures that decorated the *Cornelian*. Wrought of a detailed webwork of silver, it glowed and the sense of the infernal was strong near it – the device had a sulphuric, charnel smell.

Cornelius removed the items from the box, placing the inkwell at one corner of the parchment, the knife at another, the box itself on a third and the stone in the fourth so that the parchment remained flat on the table.

He held the device in his hand, staring into the low light emanating from it.

'This device,' he said, placing it on the parchment, 'is the reason for Ruman pre-eminence.' He waved his hands toward where the legionnaires bedded down in their tents. 'Not Hellfire guns. Not steamships and mechanized baggage trains.'

'What is it?' Fisk asked.

'We call it the Quotidian, as a little joke. If you used this device every day, well, you'd be bloodless in a month. It is *not* a humdrum little trifle. The way I understand it, it is a sympathetic *daemon* device,' Cornelius said. 'Secundus has seen it before—'

'Yes, but it is always fascinating,' Secundus said.

'It is not a secret, by any means, but it is very valuable and expensive to create.' He looked at the thing sitting there on the desk and then his gaze returned to Fisk and his son. 'Eventually, you both will possess similar devices. Or more than one. Indeed, the higher you rise in life, the more Quotidians you will possess. It's rumoured that Tamberlaine himself has hundreds.' Cornelius sat down at the desk again and lifted the knife. 'Currently, I have five.

'I don't know how it works, truly. I leave those matters to the engineers to devise. But I've been told that inside of this,' he said, looking at the device, 'is a one of a pair of *daemons* that are inextricably linked.' Cornelius looked around the tent, as if reluctant to begin. His gaze fell upon me. 'You, dwarf. Come here.'

Suddenly uncomfortable having a senator holding a silver knife with an infernal device in front of him, I stepped forward slowly.

'You're always loitering about? Eh? Well, this time it's to your loss,' he said, face becoming grim. I've oft remarked how Rumans – and Cornelius in particular – can swing from comical to deathly serious in a moment's notice. And I'm eternally surprised that neither state lessens the impact of the other. 'Put out your hand.'

'My hand?'

His jaw tightened, lips pursed.

'Go on, Shoe,' Fisk said. 'There's nothing for it but to do what he says.'

I extended my hand. Quick as a mink, Cornelius slashed my palm – slashed deep, too – then snatched up the bowl and began to collect the blood pooling in my cupped hand. Rumans will always take deep and fast when offered. I've known that since I was a brawling little brat on my mother's mountain.

When the senator was satisfied there was enough of the red stuff, he unstopped the inkwell, added a measure of the ink into the still warm blood and swirled it about. When it had mixed to his satisfaction, he repositioned the Quotidian device on the parchment, unsnapped a small latch on top of it revealing a mouth to what I could only think was some sort of reservoir, and poured the unclotted mixture of blood and ink into the device. I motioned for Lupina to bring me a wrapping for my hand, and when she was slow to move, I retrieved a cloth napkin from the table and mashed it into my palm.

The glow from the Quotidian became more intense, pulsing, and small wisps of vapour emerged and rose to join the blue tabac smoke hanging above us in the lantern light. Then, with a lurch, the device began to move. It slid across the parchment at a furious pace: in its passage it left a trail of ink and blood. The air of the tent filled with a scratching, hissing noise. The thing was writing.

'This Quotidian is paired with Tamberlaine's own,' Cornelius said, looking away from the device's movements. Lupina came forward holding the decanter of whiskey and poured him another glass. 'In this way are the Emperor's orders disseminated throughout the Empire, almost instantaneously.'

For a while, Cornelius, Secundus, and Fisk simply watched and drank whiskey as the Quotidian smoked and dashed about the parchment. Lupina handed me a wad of raw cotton, a dour look on her face. I mashed it into my palm. Eventually, Cornelius glanced at me and said, 'Take up a glass, dwarf. Lupina!' He pointed at me. 'Whiskey. You've paid for that drink in blood.' Then he smiled, curling his mustachios upwards. 'You're a freeman and a stout little fellow, after all, and a good friend to our family. Have a seat.' With his bear-foot, he pushed out a wicker chair for me to sit in.

Rumans are mercurial. I took my seat, making deference to the senator by bowing my head, but all the while aware he could have me crucified tomorrow, on a whim. My hand throbbed with each pumping of my heart and I held my hand over my head to lessen the flow.

Cornelius watched me, implacably.

When the Quotidian stopped its movements a few minutes later, Cornelius didn't move to pick it up. 'It's got to cool, a bit,' he said, sipping his drink. 'The blasted thing doesn't get hot enough to scorch the parchment, strangely, but it's hot enough to burn your hand. It's as if it's got a taste for blood.'

Finally, he gave the bowl to Lupina to wash and returned the Quotidian and its accoutrements to the box. From a salt-well, he liberally dusted the parchment, allowing the granules to absorb any surplus ink mixture, and then picked up the paper and began to read.

He stopped abruptly. 'Get Livia in here,' he said to me. 'Now.'

TWO

7 Nones, Quintilius, 2638 ex Ruma Immortalis

I FOUND LIVIA WASHING HER hands in a bowl of bloody water underneath a *daemon* lantern. The optios sat near her, chatting in the easy, loose way that soldiers do when not actively on duty and camp has been pitched. She smiled as she noticed my approach.

'Ma'am? Your father requests your presence.'

'I'm almost through here, Mr Ilys. I'll be with him shortly.'

'He was adamant,' I said.

'He's always impatient.' She wiped her lancets, scalpels, and various sharp pointy things and began to place them them in her bloodkit next to the bottles of acetum and tersus incendia. 'You're injured, Shoe. Give me your hand.' When she's distracted, Livia will return to using my nickname. And I'd had that particular one so long – Shoestring – that I even thought of myself that way.

I gave her my hand and she turned it over in her own. 'So calloused. It's like they're made of stone.'

'A gift from my mother.'

She nodded, thoughtful. Picking out the acetum, and some cotton bandages, she cleansed my palm and wrapped it with gauze. 'Aurelius says that one's hands are the truest glimpse into the character of a man.'

"He is loud and portentous, yet his hands are soft," I said, grinning, giving her one of the most oft-quoted lines from Bless' *His*

23

Infernal Demise. New Damnation's *Cornicen* had begun printing that play in serial, and I'd taken an earnest liking to it despite my obvious lack of any sort of education. Much to Fisk's irritation, I'd even taken to memorizing some of the more penetrating bits.

'What's the emergency this time, Shoe?'

'A message from the Emperor.'

'And?'

'I don't know, ma'am. He told me to fetch you. As I said, he was—'

'Adamant. Right.' She lifted her medical case and said, 'All right, let's go.'

'Let me get that for you,' I said, offering to take the heavy case from her. Miss Livia handed it to me – and I realized that she was no longer a 'miss' now that she and Fisk had married and maybe she never was, but that's how I always thought of her and still do to this day. There are some women who can bear the hardship and ignominy of life and remain blushing, fresh all their days. Livia was such a woman. And so her memory has never become lessened in my mind throughout the years.

We entered the tent and Cornelius held the letter in his hands, his face a study in concern. Carnelia had joined them and sat silently at the end of the table, slightly behind her father, as if trying not to draw his attention.

'What is it, Father?' Livia asked.

'A letter from Tamberlaine. You're involved.'

'What?'

'It seems that our Emperor has heard of your nuptials and has decided to use it against me,' Cornelius said.

'What does he say?' Livia's voice remained calm. Even Tamberlaine could not ruffle her composure.

'Secundus?' Cornelius said, proffering the parchment to his son. 'Why don't you do the honours?'

Secundus took the letter and read:

'"To Gnaeus Saturnalius Cornelius, Governor of Occidentalia (Or The So-Called Hardscrabble Territories west of the Imperial Protectorate), Proconsul of Rume, Ambassador to Mediera, Princep of the College of Augurs, and in general a Crafty Old Bastard; from your Emperor, Lord and Master, Tamberlaine Best and Greatest, Ruler of Myriad Kingdoms, Wielder of the Secret of Emrys, Sacred God of the Latinum Hills, Master Debator and Adept Rhetorictician, and in general a Crafty Old Bastard As Well—"'

'Well,' Fisk said, leaning back in his chair. 'That was chummy.'

'Quite,' Cornelius said, tightly. 'He's just getting started. Go on, Secundus.'

'It begins "Snuffy—",' Secundus said. 'Snuffy? That's you?'

'We had the same tutor as lads,' Cornelius said. He did not seem happy with the letter at all.

'That sounds friendly enough, Father,' Secundus said, smiling.

'It most assuredly is not. Read the blasted thing, boy.' Cornelius' moustache quivered. He occupied his mouth with whiskey and tabac.

'"Snuffy, as for the dispensation of the troops in the Hardscrabble Territories, the fifth will of course remain at the fort in New Damnation, and the eighth and sixteenth should be en route by mechanized baggage train to Fort Brust and then on westward, per your recommendations. The thirteenth shall remain with the eleventh at Fort Brust to protect our interests, specifically to ensure the completion of the Dvergar Spur. That avenue of transport must be opened. The Medierans are moving and the blocade in the Gulf of Mageras is building strength. We must be ready should fat old Diegal get his cock hard enough to thrust.

"The news that Beleth has defected is of great concern to me. My advisors here tell me he was high in the college of Engineers, indeed, he was princep of the organization and wielded great power there – and was privy to all the secrets of the summoners.

The events surrounding the Diegal lass are extremely unfortunate. You really screwed the Ia-damned goat in that debacle, Snuffy. In addition to your losing the girl, placing half an empire on war footing and, in general, destabilizing peaceful relations in all of creation, I have been having trouble grasping that this *daemonic* vestment Beleth created could negate the effects of Hellfire. Thankfully, we still have it in our possession. Please explain to me, in detail, how this could be so. I will, however, inform all commanders in the western theatre to recommence training with pilum and gladii, effectively throwing our military two hundred years into the past."'

Secundus paused, cleared his throat, glancing at his father.

'Go on, son,' Cornelius said. 'It gets worse.'

Secundus swallowed, thickly. He took a sip of whiskey and then resumed reading.

'"I am quite vexed with you. I half-way considered issuing an edict demanding your nuts on a platter, Snuffy. However, I am willing to give you another chance to redeem yourself. I advise you to do your utmost to accede to my wishes.

'"By the way, congratulations on your daughter's nuptials – yes, I have other eyes and ears there in the Hardscrabble Territories. And I even have learned some of her new husband. The son of that bastard Fiscelion Cantalan Iulii, is he not? My wedding gift to them both is that I will not have him – or the lovely Livia – crucified. While I was tempted to do so, word reaches me that there's a new Cornelian on the way. I'm sure you must be very proud, Snuffy, swelling the ranks of your brood. My great weakness is that I am a romantic; too kind-hearted, and I still believe in love. Why I did not crucify his father instead of exiling him, I shall never know. A passing malaise, perhaps. The influence of malevolent household gods? Nevertheless, I issued the exile edict and he absconded with three hundred talents of silver. But tell me. Is this Fisk ostentatious?

'"I require some things from you. You, your son Secundus, your daughters Livia and Carnelia, will present yourselves here, in Rume, at my court for Ia Terminalia, to present me with gifts due my exalted station – that's right, Snuffy, exalted – and make obeisance for your failures in the west. Rutilius will act as governor in your stead. We must prepare for war and I need your counsels here, for the time being, so that we can take stock of the resources of the Protectorate and the Hardscrabble Territories. In time – sooner, rather than later – you will have to return there and take command of our legions in the west. I trust Rutilius but he is a peacetime commander, wonderful at training and building legions, but not in commanding them on the field. And Marcellus, while a fine commander, has low blood. So it falls to you. Congratulations. Had you not been such a pedigreed and able commander, your testicles might be adorning one of my altars to Ia.

'"After Terminalia, Secundus and Livia will travel on east, and bear a message to the Autumn Lords for me, becoming my emissaries to Kithai in hopes of finding an avenue toward peace and prosperous trade.

'"Your son-in-law – who I hear is quite able – will remain there in the west and track down Beleth and return him to Ruman custody – or failing that, kill him and preserve his head – appended to this message will be his orders. There will be no more defections from the Ruman Collegium of Engineers. And yet. This must be done quietly and in secret. A blatant and obvious traitor can do more damage to the empire than any loss of knowledge. My heart is heavy that Livia and this Fiscelion must be separated so soon after their wedding but the needs of the Empire are tantamount. And I want traitor Beleth's head. He cannot leave those territories.

'"It is only fitting, is it not? A traitor's son shall hunt a traitor.

'"That is all. I shall expect you at Terminalia. Do not fail me. Your old friend, Tamberlaine."'

When Secundus finished, the tent remained silent for a long while, each of the Cornelians lost in their own thoughts.

'What does it mean?' Carnelia asked, breaking the silence.

'It means exactly what it says,' Cornelius said, outrage pouring off him. 'He's pulling me back to Rume! The venomous old sot! He knows how it will appear to the other benchers – it will weaken my position in senate! It's a public humiliation! As if I wasn't competent enough to govern! And while I'm gone, all of the skim of taxes will go to Rutilius.' He quivered in anger, or fear, I couldn't tell. 'A public shaming. I would rather he just crucify me.'

'I think you might be reading too much into this, Father,' Secundus said.

'I wish you were right, son,' Cornelius said. 'Tamberlaine revels in mixed messages. He pulls me home, but tells me it's because he values my advice. He gives congratulations to Livia and Fisk, yet he separates them. He's a venomous old shit,' he spat, and then waved Lupina over to refill his glass.

No one else had noticed, but Livia and Fisk had locked gazes the moment that Secundus had read the name Fiscelion. There was a sadness there now.

'Can you defy him?' Fisk asked, softly.

'No, love. All I can hope to do is fulfil his orders as best I may,' Livia said.

Cornelius, seeming to realize that others than himself might be affected by the Imperial missive, said, 'Tamberlaine's a shit, but he will keep his word. When we return to Rume, you must get him to agree to allow you to return to Fisk after you complete your task.' He looked at Fisk, pointedly. 'Your reunion with your wife—'

'And child,' Livia said, touching her stomach.

'Your *reunion* will be hastened if you can present Tamberlaine with Beleth. Or his head.'

'So that's it, then? Shoe and I hunt down the Engineer and the rest of you are back to Rume? And then—' Fisk stopped. His voice remained calm but underneath I could tell fierce currents of emotion churned. 'And then Livia and Secundus are to voyage halfway around the world to treat with the Autumn Lords. With my child! Why should we not refuse?'

Cornelius shook his head, sadly. He gestured at Livia's midriff with his cigar. 'You'd doom that lad.' He thought for a moment, his lips pursed. 'You're a good man, Fisk. We know it. Tamberlaine doesn't and whatever his complexities, he won't be thwarted. Should he send me a missive to take you in chains—'

'You'd do it,' Fisk said. 'And if he ordered you to crucify Livia? What then?'

'Let's make sure it doesn't come to that.' Cornelius stood and stumped around the table bearing the maps, to stand between Fisk and Livia. 'In one sense, it's a great honour to our family – Tamberlaine wouldn't trust just anyone to the task of journeying to Kithai. On the other hand, he knows you're pregnant and the rigors you'll endure. Long sea voyage, strange land, all that.'

'I don't like being forced into anything,' Fisk said, staring at the maps before him.

'Welcome to the service of the greatest empire known to mankind,' Cornelius said.

'Neither do I, my love,' Livia said, touching Fisk's hand. Her neck was straight, and firm, but her eyes bore the pain of coming separation. 'I swore never to return there. The mark on my name—' Her voice grew thick and she stopped speaking.

'Secundus will take care of that, darling—' Cornelius said.

'So we jump to this fiddler's tune, is that it?' Fisk asked.

'That's the shape of things,' Cornelius said.

'Damnation.'

'Exactly.'

THREE

6 Nones, Quintilius, 2638 ex Ruma Immortalis

T HE NEXT NIGHT CORNELIUS uncrated cases of whiskey, rum, and claret. He had Lupina, as quickly as she might, pilfer the last stores of sugar and create what sweet dainties she might while Cornelius plied us all with booze and speech-making in the praetorium tent. On the next day we'd reach the Dvergar Spur and, the senator assured us, the *Valdrossos* – a *daemon*-fired steam engine – would be waiting there to take Livia and the rest of the Cornelian clan to Fort Brust and further points east, away from us, if not forever, then for a long while. Carnelia wept and embraced Fisk, calling him brother, not through any overt sentimentality on her part, but because, I imagine, she thought she should. Cornelius gave gifts.

'As I mentioned, you will collect these as you rise through life,' he said to Livia and Fisk, motioning for Rubus to come forward from where he stood awkwardly holding a pair of heavy wooden boxes identical to the one that held the Quotidian. 'You'll need to blood them together and have Rubus show you the way to *send* a message. It's much less pleasant than receiving one, I can assure you, and even if you have a dwarf –' He winked at me '– or slave present, it will do you absolutely no good because it must be the sender's blood to activate the damned thing. So there's that,' Cornelius said, his voice thick with alcohol and slightly unsteady on his one good leg. 'At least this way you'll be able to correspond with each other. "Fill'd her ears with sweeten'd words, dripping from the infernal tongue," or something like that.'

· 'Bless?' Secundus asked.

'No, a new poet I picked up in the printer's shop in New Damnation. Vintus Mauthew, his name is. I have his folio around here somewhere. *The Teats of Fortuna*. I shall gift you with it.'

Livia rose and approached her father. He had the honesty to look surprised when she kissed him on the cheek. 'Thank you, Father. This will make it bearable.'

'A brave face, my sweet. A brave face.'

Fisk thanked him solemnly as well and, after Rubus explained to them the workings of the Quotidians, they retired to spend what time they had left together.

The next day, camp was struck quickly – even the legionnaires and lictors were eager to end the long march through the hardscrabble – and we came within an echo's distance of the Smokeys before turning north. A great plume of dust was cast against the liquid blue of sky and only when we drew nearer did we see that it was a great horde of workers laying the railway line. As we drew near enough to the terminus – the point at which a flurry of labourers wielding shovels levelled the earth and set massive iron bars with spikes, filling the air with the ringing report of sledgehammers on iron – we heard the call and response chants of the men; *be my woman, girl, I'll – be your man – put that silver money – in your hand* – chanted over and over again with one dusky-skinned man leading the chorus, to be answered by the rest of the men, establishing a kind of inexorable, inescapable rhythm that I couldn't shake until long after we had passed them.

Secundus and Fisk, both mounted and in Imperial blues, rode over to the nearest optio, stationed at the spur-head, to inquire about the *Valdrossos*. From where I sat atop Bess, I could see the ranker pull aside the bandana covering his mouth – the dust kicked up from the earth-levelling spiced the air something fierce – and pointed north.

By late afternoon, we'd come within sight of the steaming iron behemoth that was the *Valdrossos*. It stood black as midnight and thirty feet tall and was easily the width of eight horses riding abreast, a massive column of black smoke pluming skyward. Looking at that panting black machine, fuelled by malice, I was reminded that war was coming unless we could prevent it.

I bid my farewells, and even Cornelius was kind enough to shake my hand – though it remained bandaged from when he took my blood. 'You're quite an acceptable little fellow. Your society has given me hope for the rest of your kind,' he said, slipping a silver denarius into my palm.

My first inclination was to say that I wish I could say the same and throw the coin as far as I could into the hardscrabble, but it *was* a silver denarius. And that impotent gesture might've seen me crucified. So I nodded and thanked the senator, silently praising the old gods that it would be a very long time before I'd have to endure his company again.

Secundus was more cordial. He gripped Fisk's and my forearms in turn and, smiling, said, 'And I was so looking forward to a life out on the shoal plains.'

'Never can tell, young master,' I said, answering his grin. 'You could find yourself on the plains again. And if you do, you'll always be welcome to outride with us.'

'There would be far worse things than that,' he laughed.

'Let's not go borrowing trouble, Mr Cornelius,' I said.

He turned to Fisk. 'Good luck, brother,' he said.

'And luck to you . . .' Fisk said, glancing at Livia who stood watching. He swallowed. 'She can look out for herself. But an extra pair of eyes watching her back couldn't hurt.'

Secundus smiled. 'Of course.'

Livia came to me and said, 'I would be absolutely distraught if not for the Quotidian and the knowledge that you will be with my Fisk. I couldn't ask for a better companion for him, save myself.' Then she kissed me on my brow. When she was done, she stood back, one thumb hooked in her gunbelt and the other on the grip of her sawn-off and laughed at my surprise. 'Dear Shoestring,' she said. 'Don't ever change.'

'Don't think that's possible, ma'am,' I said.

Silence then except for the bellowed orders of legionnaires and the steaming anger of the *Valdrossos*. No tears fell from Livia or Fisk. That they loved each other fiercely I have no doubt. Does that incorruptible part of us have to writhe and fret publicly to prove it exists? It's not something that has to be proven to exist except to the one to whom it matters most.

In the slanting, late afternoon light, they stood near each other for a long while, hand in hand, watching as legionnaires, lictors, and porters manhandled the vardos and wagons up rough pine planks onto flat beds and led nickering horses into the livestock pens. Slaves and servants trucked crates and luggage into the ornate passenger car. The whole world seemed wreathed in dust.

Finally, Fisk turned to Livia and took her hands in his raw, big ones, and softly kissed her. Then he fell to his knees, placed his head on her stomach and wrapped his arms around her. When he rose, she turned and with quick steps boarded the train, which had begun to smoke and hiss with dramatic vehemence. We watched from our saddles as the massive locomotive began to move, chuffing and steaming, and we continued to watch as it diminished in our vision, the sound fading and the smell of brimstone dissipating on the air until it was lost with one piercing scream from its whistle, a diminution into an infinitesimal speck on the horizon. Then it was gone.

'Well, Shoe,' Fisk said, when the whole expanse of hardscrabble around us was empty and silent. 'Let's go find Beleth.'

FOUR

3 Nones, Quintilius, 2638 ex Ruma Immortalis

T HE SILENCE THAT FELL UPON us at the Dvergar Spur lasted
for five days as we pushed west, back across the hardscrabble,
travelling much faster than we had with Cornelius' baggage train.
We took on water and feed from the optios commanding the spur's
polyglot workforce and at night we bunked down near our horses
and silently ate hardtack and jerky, rolled cigarettes on our knees,
and spent our time contemplating the number of stars and the
number of coyotes yipping and singing in the distance.

'You got the Quotidian. You could write her,' I said.

'Kalends and Ides,' he responded, and fell silent again. That was
all I could get from him.

Back on horseback, well watered and fed, we pushed past the
hardscrabble plains and into the shoal grasses of the Big Rill
watershed quickly, and soon had game enough for meat and wood
enough for roasting.

He took it out that night from its lavish box and turned it over
in his hands. It caught the light of the fire and shimmered along its
intaglios of silver warding. A soft glow came from it. A *daemon*
churned and fretted inside it, slavering for blood.

'We'll make for New Damnation, see what Marcellus knows
about Beleth,' Fisk said.

'Would he be keeping tabs on the engineer? Seems a small job
for a general.'

'He won't, but his spymaster would. And Cornelius has made this a priority.' He spat into the fire and sat there thinking. 'Beleth's an important piece on the Knightboard, that's for damn sure.'

'You wouldn't remember, since we were hauling you back, but I think we saw him fleeing the *Cornelian* when—'

'The *vaettir* and the Crimson Man, right?'

'That's right. He was trucking north and west. And we were north of here.'

'So, heading to Passasuego, then. Or Hot Springs.'

'Hot Springs is doubtful, since there ain't much left of it after that infernal *shit* burnt it down,' I said.

He nodded, silent for a while. The coyotes yipped and screeched in the distance. With our fire, they wouldn't get close. He turned the Quotidian over in his hands.

'Always something, isn't it?' he said, glancing at me where I was mending a shirt. 'If it's not some damned thing hanging around my neck, it's one lusting for my blood.'

I patted the Hellfire pistol I now carried, given to me by Secundus himself. A nice piece with a gunbelt full of ammunition. While the legion will defray some of the cost of getting Imp rounds replaced by an engineer, it won't cover all of it, and so, when my gunbelt ran empty, it was empty for good. Unless I stumbled upon a silverlode.

'Or these pieces of damnation,' I said.

'You really think that?'

'What?'

'Damnation. That when we die we'll go to the same Hell these infernal creatures come from?'

'No. I don't.'

'Then what do you believe?'

'Most folks carry Hell with them.'

'I don't even know what that means,' he said.

I stilled in my darning. Looked at Fisk close. 'We get to where

35

we are by the choices we make. Everybody's the same in that, right?'

'That sounds about right,' he said.

'Then it stands to reason, if you're in your own little Hell, it's one of your own making.'

He looked at me, grinding his teeth. It was not me he was mad at, I knew this. But he was angry all the same. 'Innocents die, Shoe. Children. Those settlers we came upon before all this—' He waved his hand to indicate the night. 'They didn't get dead by poor choices.'

'Didn't they?'

'So, is there some Hell waiting for us?'

'No. Way I understand it is the "Hell" these things come from is just some—' I thought a moment, trying to remember what Samantha had told me as we climbed to the caldera in the Whites to find the Medieran lass. Or what was left of her. 'Other place. And these *things* have found their way here, summoned. Crawled through some breach between worlds.'

'But with every shot, I feel it. The despair. I feel dirtied. Marked with soot.' He held the Quotidian in his big, calloused hands and looked into it as if trying to divine some answer.

'Don't know, really, why that is, partner,' I said in a soft voice. 'They *are* devils and possibly full of evil. Or maybe they just *are,* like fire. I just don't think they have any claim upon our souls.'

He remained quiet for a long while and then placed the strange device back in its box.

'You see him?' I asked, casting a glance over my shoulder. We were heading south, now, toward New Damnation, following the curve of the river. It was still rocky here, near the Big Rill, and we were on the eastern shore, away from the Whites. On the whole, the stretchers tended to stay on the western shore. But there's no reckoning stretchers.

Fisk gave the barest inclination of his head and said, 'Our little stretcher shadow.'

'Not much little about him,' I said. 'He's fast and knows how to stay out of sight.'

'Why don't we lead him on a snipe hunt, then, one whose ending he might not like.' He looked about. 'We're maybe three miles shy of that brambled gulley we camped in two years ago during the blizzard. Remember?'

I nodded. 'You thinking ambush?'

'Yep.' Now we were away from the Cornelians and back on the trail, the formality in his speech fell away, leaving the Fisk I knew of old. But it was disconcerting that he was so mutable. 'There's that offshoot of the gulley where we kept the horses. Almost grown over. You make your way up and out, I'll duck in there and wait until he passes.'

'That sounds like a plan.'

'You don't sound too keen on it.'

'Tight spaces. Stretchers. Not my favourite things in the world, that's for damn sure.'

He looked at me. At this point, most men would make some crack about my size, my heritage, indigenous as I am. I might run from it, but unlike the Rumans, I am *of* this place. Just like the stretchers.

Fisk remained quiet for a bit. Then, he said, as if considering it, 'You not up for it, pard?'

'No, Ia dammit. I am game.' Something in me twisted. I wasn't for it and calling on Ia – even though it was my own mouth that uttered the words – felt wrong. But we have old habits. My mouth remembers the words of faith when my heart doesn't. I touched the grips of the Hellfire six guns and Bess chuffed her head and snorted her derision. It still felt wrong, the guns, but we live in a fallen world.

We rode hard for an hour, and Bess' flanks foamed when we drew near the gulley and entered. When we reached the offshoot, where we'd kept the horses that week we were snowed in, Bess began to nose her way back to her old spot, among the bramblewrack and brush, where she'd huddle against the cold, but I tugged her away.

Fisk dismounted, pulled his carbine, and levered one into the warded chamber. He swung the carbine into the crook of his arm and then thumbed the six-guns and the Hellfire cartridges on his belt. He tossed his horse's reins to me and I snatched them out of the air before the black could get up to any mischief.

'Lead 'em up and out. He'll be on our trail, close. When he passes . . .'

He left it unsaid. Boom. No more stretcher.

I nodded. We'd worked this sort of ambush before on the *vaettir*, to various results. The thing about *vaettir*, they are old, and know all the wiles of man. Like *dvergar*. We are kin, of a sort. Both natives of this big, fierce land.

I led the horses up and through the gulley. Fisk backed into the offshoot, rifle held loosely in his big, raw-boned hands.

The sides pressed in, as we made our way through, and bramblewrack scratched at the sky, and snagged on Bess and the black's flanks.

Everything hushed. My heart continued to beat, and I could feel the surge of the sanguine stuff through my body with each pump of that desperate muscle.

Stillness except for the movement of horses. Silence except for the falling of hooves.

Then I was up and out of the gulley. No gunfire. The land opened up around us, no trees, just shoal grass, bramble, and wrack and ruin. The sky, unbroken and vast. The wind, cold though the sun beat down.

And *vaettir*. He was standing there, a hundred feet away, grinning, a sword held in his clawed hand, long hair whipping in the wind. A legionnaire's gladius, by the looks of it. Our ambush was his ambush. There was a moment's shock of recognition – a moment it seemed he'd waited for – and then he raced forward.

Bess whipped around, despite my startled yell, putting her haunches between us and the oncoming *vaettir*. I fumbled for my six-guns. I tugged at them, desperate, the back of my neck itching, already feeling the impending blow from the stretcher's sword. I toppled sideways, out of the saddle, onto the hard-baked earth, guns in hand, rolling onto my back.

There was a high-pitched screech and a shadow like a carrion fowl filled the sky and descended. The *vaettir*.

Bess hawed and kicked out, wheeling and bucking. But too slow. The stretcher was on top of us. He raised his sword.

From my left, a blur crossed my vision. Another fierce bird, another screech.

The stretcher fell away, howling. Bess hawed and kicked in a cacophonous ruckus. Pushing myself up on my elbows, through the hardscrabble dust I saw two figures rolling and tearing each other with clawed hands and sharp teeth.

Another stretcher.

They wailed and thrashed about almost too fast to see. And then they parted, hissing, like scrapping cats. The first *vaettir* rose, hands outstretched but empty. The other lashed forward and there was a glint of light on metal. The first stretcher's head fell away with a gout of blood. He toppled and pumped his life into the dirt.

This new stretcher stood tall and was dressed in mouldering garment and furs, but with a look I'd never seen on a *vaettir* face. A series of expressions chased on another across his features – first relief, then outrage, then sadness. He turned to me, red blade held loosely.

Both pistols raised and centred on its chest, I said in *dvergar*, 'I slew your kin, not so long ago. I will kill you.'

The massive creature – a big bull elf – cocked his head, slowly, as if he were remembering. Raising one dirty, clawed hand, he touched his chest.

'Gynth?' it said, the sound thick and oddly pronounced through the forest of teeth in its mouth. Its voice was deep, very deep, yet clear as a massive bell tolling on the heights. 'Gynth' is the *dvergar* word for 'kindred' or 'kin' but can also mean 'brother' or even 'blood.' My native tongue has layers upon layers of meaning.

'Pierced through the brain,' I said. There is no shame in admitting fear and I can admit that I was terribly afraid. But I forced myself to take three steps toward the *vaettir*, both Hellfire pistols levelled on its chest. I would plug him before he took me, all the old gods and new as my witness.

Then the elf did a strange thing. It shook its head, looking puzzled. It acted as if it had been awoken from some long, all-consuming dream. I looked at its clothing again. Maybe it was a shroud and the thing had been buried – though all the whys and hows of that question quickly swarmed and clamoured for my attention. I brushed away the distraction. Being distracted near a stretcher is a quick visit to the undertaker.

The *vaettir* raised its hand and extended a long, clawed finger at me and repeated, '*Gynth. Yan gynth.*'

We are kin. We are blood.

The *vaettir* looked at his gore-streaked hand holding the sword as if he'd found a serpent there. He dropped the blade, held his hands up to me in what seemed like supplication.

A moment passed between us, our gazes locked, and the *vaettir* nodded to me almost imperceptibly.

A clatter of loose rock was the only thing that alerted him. He leapt into the air and dashed away – as fast as only *vaettir* can – as Fisk came out of the gulley, his face a storm cloud and gripping his carbine tight.

He approached where I stood, looking down at the headless body of the stretcher that trailed us.

'What in Ia's name happened here?' he said. 'You do this?' He nudged the gladius with his foot.

'You're not gonna believe this, partner.'

When I had told Fisk what happened, he remained silent for a long while. Finally, he said, 'Bullshit,' and huddled into himself, becoming smaller. Something in him calcified. He would rather think me a liar or a fool than countenance a *vaettir* not a villain.

'So, I chopped off the stretchers head with a sword I pulled from the air?' I said, nudging the gladius with my foot.

'Bears fight other bears. The mountain lion will eat another lion's cubs,' Fisk said, as if that finished it.

I opened my mouth to retort, to describe the *vaettir's* face after the altercation. But seeing Fisk's expression I stopped. It would be wasted breath.

We collected the body, the sword, and rode on.

FIVE

6 Ides, Quintilius, 2638 ex Ruma Immortalis

THE CITIZENS OF NEW DAMNATION feared fire.

It was a city that grew around the fifth's garrison in a mad jumble of wooden buildings; engineer college and munitions, a river harbour and port, slaver's wharf and auctions, millers and dyers, crossroad colleges, bathhouses, barbers, artisans, boatwrights and fishermen, printmakers and engravers, whorehouses and saloons, and one great aqueduct lancing down like an arrow from the springs in the foothills of the Whites. New Damnation's air was filled with the noise and spice of industry: the bustle of tradesmen and the dusky slave-teams chanting work hollers as they pulled sledges through packed-dirt streets, the constant banging of hammers on wood as carpenters built arrogant houses for merchant kings, equites rising, the steaming tenements and insulae near the river teeming with street vendors, the scents of their foreign foods and fragrant worship of obscure gods filling the air, the stink of sewage spilling into the Big Rill along with the chaff of millers and the dross of the smelting forges, the drunken laughter of theatre-goers and the chants and incense of the pious visiting the temples to Ia and the older gods.

Of course, it wasn't named New Damnation to begin with. Its original name was Novo Dacia – founded by Hellenes – but that was a century ago, before the Ruman occupation and then outright ownership of the territories. A wooden town, built from gambel and pine timbers harvested from the skirts of the White Mountains. A tinderbox.

One poorly drawn ward, one ill-guarded lantern and New Damnation would live up to its name, blossoming into inferno.

We crossed the Big Rill upstream at the Miller's Crook ferry and reached the town on 6 Ides, and the whole place was in a tizzy. Vigiles patrolled the streets, wary and watchful – never straying too far from fountains or water wagons. The lanes were full of pistoleros loitering on the planks in front of stores, shops, and the larger homes while the legionaries kept to the campus martius and, mostly, inside its walls.

I picked up a copy of the *Cornicen* as we rode into town from a newsie-lad for a copper denarius. The headline read *Harbour Town On War Footing – All Able Bodied Men Needed*. When I showed it to Fisk he shrugged, as if he expected it.

We made our way through the streets, avoiding the homeless wanton-boys, the slave workers bearing palanquins over the muddy streets, past the shit-slicks and refuse piles near insulae, up the hill to the better appointed neighbourhoods with paved streets lined with white, soft, quarried stone until we came to the campus martius plateau, and showed our papers to the legionnaires posted at the gates. The dead *vaettir* on the back of Fisk's horse drew attention, causing a small commotion, and we led a processional to the stables, where my partner tasked the saucer-eyed stable boys to guard the body until he could figure out some way to dispense with it.

What was once a camp of the Ruman army on the march had, over time, become a permanent encampment. Timber walls were replaced with stone, tents with housing and barracks. The command tent was now a three-storied office complex, adorned with *daemon-light* fixtures allowing worklight at all times. Yet all of the buildings were still plain, devoid of all but the barest adornments. Simple functional buildings crafted of stone harvested from the

Whites and brought here on the backs of countless slaves – most of those *dvergar*, but also Numidian, Aegyptian, and wherever else they came from. But above the command centre a great flag pole stood flying the emblems of V Occidentalia. There was a fifth back in Latinum, but the emperor Ingenuus saw fit to reset the legion counter, as it were, with the discovery of the Imperial Protectorate and the Hardscrabble Territories. The fact that this fifth was the second fifth caused some consternation when officers who had served with the Latinum V Prima were assigned. The Prima galled them, over here.

But it didn't keep them from being proud. The brag-rags whipped in the fresh wind coming down from the Whites and showed holly and silver, cannon and ships, and a curious flame emblem I could only take to mean Hellfire.

We stabled our mounts and made our way to the command.

If there's one thing that Rumans love above all else, it's bureaucracy. It was hard to tell the difference between secretaries and slaves here – everyone ran about clutching papers and wax styluses. But Fisk fixed the pilum-bearing eagle pin to his shirt – showing his rank as legate – and snagged a page by the elbow.

'Take me to Marcellus,' he said.

The boy – no more than sixteen – looked frightened. 'Can't, sir. He's in Harbour Town. Some of his legates have remained here, and so has the camp prefect.'

'Take me to the prefect, then.'

The boy led us through a warren of offices and hallways, neatly lit by *daemonlight* fixtures, until we came to a large room centred around a three-dimensional map of the Imperial Protectorate and Hardscrabble Territories. Many officers and messengers spoke quickly and quietly, prim and officious and efficient. The air smelled of tallow and blood and ink and on a far wall there were six or seven tremendously large slaves – each wearing a torc around his neck – attending Quotidians that hissed and scratched their messages on parchment and were then snatched up by waiting legates.

'I'll be damned,' I said, looking at the slave-manned Quotidians. 'That's a blood-thirsty bit of work, there, Fisk.'

He squinted, eyeing the slaves. 'Those hosses seem like they got enough, though, don't they?'

There was one officer who simply sat at the map, holding a parchment and smoking.

'That'll be our man,' Fisk said to me and then approached the map, the orders Cornelius provided us in-hand.

The camp prefect was a thick, burly fellow with a distracted air. He stared at the parchment he held as if he wanted to strangle it. Or the person who wrote it.

'Pardon me, sir,' Fisk said, slowly. 'We come under orders from Governor Cornelius.'

The camp prefect glanced at us, jarred out of his brooding, and looked surprised to see us there.

'And?'

'We're looking for a man. Beleth. Cornelius' fugitive engineer.'

'I have heard of him. There are wanted posters.' He turned and bellowed, 'Gellus! Where's that munitions report?'

A thin, nervous looking man piped up: 'Coming, Mr Maelli! It will be ready in moments.'

Maelli frowned. 'From Harbour Town as well?'

'Yes, sir.'

He nodded brusquely, and then waved Gellus away.

'A reward?' Fisk asked.

'I believe there is,' the man replied, his thick shoulders set in sort of a defiant shelf of muscle. It'd be easy to imagine that he was half-bear. His corded arms were covered in dark fur and he had a bristling, angry beard. 'Not much for a man of your rank, but it would be a nice bonus, if you bring him in.'

'No matter. If you know of him already, is there any intelligence on the man's whereabouts?' Fisk asked.

Just like that, the prefect's interest in us evaporated and he turned back to his parchment and resumed reading. 'Have a slave take you to Andrae. He's the spymaster.'

Fisk made a curt bow and touched his heart in salute.

A slave led us downward, into the guts of the building, revealing that there were at least as many levels below ground as there were above. The corridors became closer and more cramped and the *daemonlight* fixtures more sparsely positioned – which was odd because down here was where they were needed most. But the slave led us to a small conference room with a large table covered in stacks of parchment.

Sitting at the desk was a long, lean man with hawkish eyebrows and a narrow, patrician nose. He had the full, lush lips of someone familiar with pleasures of the flesh, yet tinged toward cruelty, and his eyes possessed a keen intelligence. More Quotidians sat in neat rows behind him. There was a bottle of wine and a plate with a rime of blood on it perched precariously on a stack of ledgers and papers, a fork and knife at crazy angles. Judging by the Quotidians and lack of slaves, he'd have to eat quite a bit of meat just to have the blood for correspondence. Behind him, a mirror-backed *daemonlight* fixture cast a bright, yet wavering, luminescence about the room, almost like sunlight reflected through water. There were regular tallow candles strewn about the place as well, giving the conference room an air of ceremony and mysticism. I imagined he might want it that way.

'Yes?' he said as we entered.

'You Andrae? Intelligence?' Fisk asked.

A smile hinted at appearing on his lips, little amused flickers at the corners of his mouth. But it was only hints and flickers. The smile never touched his eyes.

'I hope so.' He gaze rested on me for a moment and then back to Fisk, taking in his riding leathers, the six-guns, and the insignia of rank pinned on his shirt. 'Ah. You must be...'

Andrae shuffled through papers until he brought up one and squinted at it, his thick lips pursed in concentration. 'Legate Fiscelion and companion—' He paused for a moment. 'Shoestring? 'No other known name', it says here. Hmm.'

'Yep,' I said, giving a small nod of my head. 'That's me.' Strangely, I felt a small relief that this man didn't know my name just by looking at me. Fisk didn't seem to mind.

'I've been tasked to find Cornelius' engineer. I was told you might have some intelligence on his whereabouts.'

Andrae considered Fisk very carefully. The man's whole aspect was desultory. The slant of his shoulders. The sensuous pursing of his lips. The derisive amusement flitting about his features. In some ways, he reminded me of the stretchers – infinitely bored and desperately craving entertainment.

And here we were, mice for the cat to play with.

'Is that so? Please, have a seat. Wine?' He gestured with one long, pale hand at the bottle on the table.

'No, thank you,' Fisk responded. 'Just any information you might have on our man would be helpful.'

Andrae looked slightly miffed at that. He wanted to play – banter, maybe. Gossip. Might be we should introduce him to Carnelia.

'Let me look in my files.' He rang a bell, and from the other door a young man, his secretary, scrambled in, dressed plainly in a white tunic with a torc around his neck. Looking at his hands and wrists, it was quite easy to see the scar tissue there and recent wounds. Fuel for the Quotidians. 'Go fetch the file on Mr Beleth—' He stopped, turned to Fisk. 'Full name?'

'Linneus Gauis Beleth.'

'Right,' Andrae said and waved his hands at the secretary. 'Go.'

He picked up the bottle and poured himself a glass. 'It will be a while. Our files are . . . extensive, to say the least. Please join me.'

'Water would be nice,' Fisk said, dusting his britches and taking a seat on the opposite side of the table. Andraé focused on Fisk. He ignored Fisk's request of water and poured a small earthen cup – a settler's cup – of wine and then one for himself. Fisk ignored the cup, hooked his thumbs into his gunbelt and put a boot on the table, tilting his chair back on its hind legs.

Andraé now paid me not the least bit of attention. *Dvergar*, of course. Hardly worth noticing. That can be a blessing, at times. The man made my skin crawl.

'Nasty business with the Diegal girl,' Andraé said. 'Nasty business.'

Fisk remained silent. His stillness was a warning to me, if not Andraé.

Andraé went on: 'You were tasked with recovering her from the indigenes, were you not?' He waved his hand negligently at me.

'That's right.'

The spymaster tsked, and shook his head. The sound was loud in the quiet of the room. Fisk did not respond.

'It's interesting that Tamberlaine would saddle you with this task, then, in light of your previous failure.'

To someone who didn't know him, Fisk would've seemed as still as a statue. But I know him. The muscles in his cheek tightened and shifted.

'There was nothing we could do about that,' I said. 'It was the stretchers. You ever seen one? We got one on Fisk's black in the stables.'

Andraé blinked, slowly. A bit of artifice, that, the slow closing of his eyes before turning to look at me. Only his head moved, pivoting on his long – almost gimballed – neck. 'No. I hear they're quite vigorous in their carnal appetites.' The way he said carnal made me uneasy. 'I'm sure you did all you could.'

We all remained quiet for a bit, Andrae sitting there, sipping the wine from his cup, Fisk meeting his gaze placidly.

'I understand you wedded the Cornelius girl.' Andrae tilted his head back and looked at the ceiling, as if trying to remember. 'Livia?'

Fisk nodded. I don't know if the other man realized how treacherous the ground he trod upon was.

'Fascinating,' Andrae said. 'It's hard to believe that a proconsul – the governor of this region, in fact – would allow his daughter to wed such a man as yourself, Mr Fiscelion. If you'll pardon my saying so.'

'Seem to me that you're free to say whatever you like, mister,' Fisk replied. 'You seem to know quite a bit about me. So much that it doesn't seem like I need to do much talking at all.'

'Quite,' the spymaster replied. 'Those are nice guns, I see.' Andrae cocked his head. 'Might I see one?'

'Sure,' Fisk said, whipping it out so fast that it was as if he went from one state to the other simply by thinking. A blur. Fisk popped open the cylinder and emptied the Hellfire Imp rounds into his palm. He then presented the six-gun to Andrae grip first.

The man took it, holding it lightly in both hands. 'Hmmm. Judging by the wear, this has seen some action,' Andrae said. 'And here, "Labor Ysmay".' He ran a finger along the underside of the barrel. 'I'm aware of this engineer. From Harbour Town. Not an adept, but a reliable and expensive provider of munitions.' He offered the gun back to Fisk, who took it, thumbed back in the rounds, and replaced it in his holster. 'How ever do you afford such weapons on a scout's salary?'

Fisk tapped the legate's emblem on his chest with a finger.

'Ah, yes. You have risen quite far, quite fast, as well,' Andrae said. 'That seems a bit odd to me, though. Why should Cornelius allow you to wed his daughter and raise you – the son of an exiled traitor – so high?'

The sound, at first, rose like a cough, dry and wracking. And then Fisk laughed. It was a short, brutal sound.

'That's what all this is about? You'll have to chase down my father, I'm afraid. I don't have Tamberlaine's money.'

Andrae's smile became brittle. 'I had already surmised that, judging from your garb and...' He sniffed and glanced at me, 'your companions.'

Well, this fella was definitely wanting some perforations. A hole right there, above his heart, would look quite fine.

'But that does not mean you do not have information that could be helpful locating it.'

'I haven't seen my father since I was twelve and living on the eastern coast. Last I heard, he was living in Chiba working for the Medierans.'

'Twelve?' Andrae said incredulously. 'That seems hard to believe.'

'I don't give a frog's fat ass what you believe; I left with one hundred aureus and a bundle of clothes.'

'And headed west? Into the brand new world?' He smiled again, the lush flesh of his lips curling with some mockery. 'How clichéd. "The promise of the shoal grasses".'

A half century ago, the Lex Manciana was passed to encourage settlers to move west and Rumanize the Hardscrabble Territories – and counter the growing Medieran presence in Passasuego – allowing any settler who could keep and hold a farmstead west of Fort Brust for ten years to own it. He would be free from Imperial taxation during that time, and only subject to lessened taxation for the next five. All of the papers in the east touted the 'promise' of the west.

'That's right, Mr Andrae. The lure of the shoals,' Fisk said. 'Anything was better than staying at home.'

'We all have sob stories, Mr Fisk,' Andrae said, taking a drink from his wine. 'My mother was a whore and my father a sot. And now I'm stuck in this shithole of a place, sniffing out little secrets of settlers and common folk and natives.' His smile fulfilled its promise. It bloomed into a full-grown sneer.

'My condolences,' Fisk said.

The secretary returned, looking very nervous and scratching at his arm. He held a sheaf of parchments covered in a neat, orderly script.

'Ah,' Andrae said, and there was a little disappointment in the tone of his voice. 'Here are the files.' He took the papers and ruffled through them. 'A fortnight ago an agent in Hot Springs said one of the junior engineers working there in the rebuilding efforts—' He paused, raising an articulate eyebrow and glancing at Fisk, 'was found murdered in his lab, and his reserves of silver taken. A man by the name of Labadon and matching Beleth's description had been seen entering the premises.'

'That old devil,' I said, voice hushed.

Andrae glanced at me, lips pursed. 'You recognize this alias?'

'Yes,' I said. Fisk looked at me and waved his hand in an out-with-it sort of gesture. He'd had his fill of this spymaster and was happy to let me take over the palaver, if only for a little while. 'The name of a *daemon*. Ebru Labadon is the devil that drives the Cornelian's paddlewheels.'

'I see.' He made a notation on the file. 'We will see what other *daemons* Beleth has bound in vessels or engines of war. If he used that alias once, he will have used another. This is a boon.'

A strange sort of satisfaction suffused the man: I realized that whatever else our spymaster was, he was suited to his work, a strange amalgam of gossip and archivist. And if he was the eyes and ears of Rume, possibly murderer.

'Any other details on his whereabouts?' Fisk asked.

'My agent lost contact. But he did not remain in the town. And I can say with certainty he's not here in New Damnation. My contacts in Breentown and Panem have reported nothing and both would be hard to reach in the time since the murder. So that leaves either Passasuego or Harbour Town.'

Fisk looked at me, his eyebrows raised. 'The Medieran Embassy is in Passasuego.'

'That's right. He's got some silver now, too. He's probably trying to find a new patron.'

'I imagine old Diegal would love to know Beleth's secrets,' Fisk said.

'He was privy to Cornelius' counsels for a long while,' I agreed. 'And Samantha mentioned he was arch level member of the college of engineers. That means he's on the council, and what I know of Beleth, he wouldn't be content just being a member of a council.' I picked up the settler's cup of wine and drank it. 'He'd want to be in control.'

'So,' Andrae said, slowly. 'You believe he's in Passasuego, trying to gain new patronage. And deliver all Rume's secrets of engineer and leadership to a new master.'

'That sounds about right,' Fisk replied.

'This is not good,' Andrae said.

Fisk pushed his chair from the table and stood. 'Can't say it's been a pleasure,' he said in the drawl that I knew and not the wary, guarded tones of the legate, the son-in-law of Cornelius and the husband and equal of patricians. Not Fiscelion Iulii. Just Fisk. My old partner. 'But it's been educational.'

Andrae stood as well. The sneer and the smile were gone. Standing, he looked gangly and slightly unkempt. He extended his hand.

'My job,' he said, slowly, 'necessitates some subterfuge and a level of mendacity that has . . .' He shrugged, slightly, as if searching for the right phrase. 'Coarsened me. And my superiors . . . are at the highest level.'

Fisk looked at his hand for a long while. Finally, he took the other man's wrist and they clasped forearms.

'Might I invite you to dinner?'

If Fisk was surprised, he did not show it. 'Many thanks, but my partner and I have to tend our horses, grab supplies from the quartermaster, and then light out early for Passasuego in the morning.'

The spymaster nodded once, abruptly, as if he expected the rebuff. 'Of course. I'll have the list of Beleth's possible aliases delivered to you there by one of my agents.'

'How will we know him?'

He smiled, and this time it was genuine. 'You won't. But the list will be delivered all the same.'

'Many thanks,' Fisk said.

'I'll have Stefan lead you out,' he said.

'Much obliged.'

When we'd emerged from the praetorium centre, blinking in the light of the afternoon sun, I said, 'What fascinates me is how we got out of there without you killing that man.'

'You'd never want to visit Novorum or Felix Sulla, Shoe. Every person you meet is just like him.' He rubbed the stubble on his chin and then spat into the dust. 'He takes his orders directly from Tamberlaine. I'm very lucky I was able to leave at all.'

He turned and walked off, his hand resting lightly on his six-gun.

SIX

5 Ides, Quintilius, 2653 ex Ruma Immortalis

'W E'LL TAKE A BOAT UPRIVER to Bear Leg,' Fisk said that night, after we'd found lodging in a dingy hotel with livery near the docks. He'd removed the legate insignia pin soon after leaving Andrae.

After a dinner of greasy soup and stale bread in the common room, we bunked down in the stable – as is our wont on the trail. Bales of hay might be prickly and uncomfortable, but they're an honest sort of bunk and not prone to bedbugs or the peculiar sort of human stain that often goes with rented rooms. 'Give the horses a rest. From there we'll see what we can see. Beleth might've passed through.'

'Sad the *Cornelian* won't still be there?'

'Sad?' Fisk said. 'I guess so. There's good memories, and bad, tied up with that boat.'

'True.'

In the morning, we found the only barge going up river with room for our mounts that didn't look as if she'd sink the first league away from the wharf. Her name was the *Quiberon* and she was a *daemon*-less slave-driven paddle-barge. Slow, ugly, and low-slung. She carried livestock and casks of salt-pork and piled sacks of hominy and was home to a large glaring of semi-wild cats and captained by a brusque woman, quite young and of a matter-of-fact demeanour, named Maskelyne. There were also a couple of other paying passengers, who looked a bit put out when we clambered aboard. Especially at me.

Maskelyne bit our coins when we gave them over, and looked us up and down. 'You two should be good in a pinch if them stretchers come a'leapin. Clear?'

'I imagine we'll hold our own, ma'am,' Fisk said.

'Don't ma'am me, braw, I was shitting me diapers when you were full grown,' she said. But she handed back a couple of coins. 'You'll use them little devils in the *Quibby*'s defence else there'll be a reckoning come Bear Leg.'

'Agreed,' I said. 'How long is the journey?'

She was an intense-looking woman, bright blue eyes, and a compact muscular form. She wore simple garb, dungarees and a fitted shirt with numerous pockets brimming with styluses and a Hellfire pistol on her waist. 'Water's high and the paddle-teams are rested, braw. Shouldn't be more than five days, barring stretchers or shoal beastie,' she said.

'Much troubles with the *vaettir* lately?'

'Not too much since winter. Very quiet, really, braw, but better safe than slitted or scalped, me mam always said.' She laughed, showing a mouthful of white, snaggly teeth. 'Anywho, if you two gents would be so kind as to get your arses out of the way of my slaves, there you go—' she said as we clambered onto the barge's roof – an area that served as a wide, open-aired berth – away from the workers and livestock. Maskelyne then bellowed at the slaves in the river patois called *Craulia* by the speakers of it but *Brawley* by those who were not. A mixture of Medieran, Gallish, Tueton, and some other indistinct, indefinable linguistic spice that had yet to be determined.

Once the hold was loaded and the stevedores skulked back to the shady confines of the nearest saloon and the slaves returned to the hold of the ship, Captain Maskelyne bellowed once more and one of her burly freemen attendants withdrew a snare drum and two sticks and began a rolling beat. From somewhere inside the hold there was a chanting, *lè a vini nan ranje ranje ti gason,* over and over again in a rhythmic churning and then deep inside the ship a chorus of rich masculine voices answered not in Craulish but in common speech, *roll boys roll*, and the paddle-wheels began to turn slowly and build speed. Maskelyne gave a bright, echoing yawp as her freemen lascar threw off the hawsers and the *Quiberon* moved into the waters of the Big Rill and began churning upstream.

'We are away! We are away, braws!' she called and yawped again.

That we were.

That evening, with New Damnation miles downriver, Maskelyn had her off-team of slaves come up-deck for air. Some were dusky skinned, some fair, but all wore torcs and rippled with muscles. They were lean, but it took a lot of chow and a lot of tugging oars and lifting cargo to sculpt physiques like that. They found seats on gunwales and some joined us on the flat, wooden expanse of the roof while other slaves moved among them with jugs of water or stronger drink and others passed out hardtack or dry corncakes or dried aurouch. They lolled about, lying down, sitting cross-legged, speaking in soft voices to each other.

'Fascinating,' the woman in the brown tweed suit said to her companion in a slightly accented voice that I could not place. 'I don't understand why they don't just jump in the river and swim for it.'

'Winfried, I can think of two reasons, off-hand,' her companion said, removing a small tin snuffbox from his jacket and pinching himself a measure. 'First, they're all wearing collars.' He brought his index finger and thumb to his nose and huffed the dark powder deep into his nasal passages. 'Second, where would they go? We're in the middle of nowhere.'

Some of the slaves watched us from where they took their rest, murmuring to each other. Maskelyne climbed onto the roof, clutching a bladder skin. She approached one of the older slaves, a bald, dark-skinned man with a rangy physique and wooden plates in his earlobes – an Aegyptian possibly, or Numidian – and presented him with the bladder. He smiled at her and nodded in a queer ceremonial fashion and then took the bladder and drank from it. He handed it back to her and she drank, nodding her head. He took it once more, drank deeply and then spat the liquid into a fine spray in the four directions. Finally, he passed the bladder to the other slaves who then drank as well.

Fisk, who had been silent for a long while, said so that Winfried and her companion could hear, 'They don't run because they know, someday, they'll be free.'

'Yes, we are aware of the Lex Parens Parialis, even in Malfena Protectorate. However, that hardly seems a reason to stay enslaved, thralls to a simple riverboat queen.'

Fisk shrugged and turned to look at the odd pair. 'We're all slaves to something, or someone. Sometimes to masters we don't even know.' He pointed to the slaves with his chin. 'At least they know who they serve.'

The man stood from his chair and approached us, extending his hand toward Fisk.

'Well met, good sir,' he said. 'I am Wasler Lomax and this is—' He gestured toward his companion. 'My sisterwife, Winfried.'

Fisk nodded his head in acknowledgement and slowly clasped the man's forearm and then the woman with the manly name.

'My name's Shoestring,' I said, brusquely grasping their forearms in turn. 'I mean, Dveng Illys.'

'Ah, you are *dvergar*!' Wasler said, pleasure and excitement spreading across his face. 'While I've seen many of your kind in ... shall we say ... functional capacities, I've never yet had the opportunity to converse!'

'I would continue speaking on the subject that was broached

regarding slavery,' Winfried said. 'It seems you approve of this custom of owning human beings,' she said to Fisk.

'No, ma'am,' Fisk said, slowly, as if thinking over what he was to say next. 'I don't approve of it, nor the bitter cold. Nor the bloodthirsty *vaettir*. I concern myself mainly with what *is* and what I can affect.'

'So,' she said, eyes brightening, 'You see yourself as powerless to affect loathsome customs?'

Fisk stilled. His eyes narrowed and he looked at her closely. 'I choose to fight where I may yield the best results. There are some that say the Malfena tradition of incest should be abolished.'

The Malfena Protectorate is a small island nation off the coast of Tueton. I know of it only through camp talk about their sexual practices. Because of the limited resources on the island, only certain members of each family, chosen by lottery, are allowed to marry and breed. The others are made sterile. And so, over the millennium, the taboo of incest has faded there for the sterile ones, and unions between siblings and cousins are, if not commonplace, then accepted. And Rume, with its love for all things *other*, especially loved that which seemed forbidden and hinted at perversion.

'Ah, that old logical fallacy. Should a sisterwife or brothermate get in some sort of lively discussion, out come the cries of *incest!* It is, in essence, admitting a weakness of argument.'

Wasler coughed into his hand and said, 'Please pardon Winfried. We've had a long journey with only each other to engage in conversation.' He had a precise accent, reminiscent of the Tuetonic speech yet not having all the hard edges and ugliness of that language. Winfried turned to him, delivering a withering stare. He continued: 'We are here on a grant from the Malfena governor to document the indigenous life of the Imperial Protectorate and the Occidentalis Territories.'

'Ah, so you're journalists!' I said, understanding. 'What paper do you write for?'

Wasler bowed his head in acknowledgement. 'Journalists, of a sort. Our endeavours are funded by a private grant and the results will be our patron's to do with as he pleases. I hope he chooses to publish, in some form.' He looked worried for a moment and then waved the thought away. 'But yes. We are journalists in that we record. We are infernographists.'

'Infernogra—' I began.

'The capturing of portraits through *daemonwork* engineering. It is, in essence, an anthropological exercise.'

'How does that work? The capturing of portraits?'

Wasler smiled, showing brilliantly white teeth. Apparently, in addition to having no problem with inter-familial sex, Malfenese people have exceptional dental hygiene. 'We were hoping to be able to show you the process, Mr Ilys, if you agree to it, since you'd be the first native Occidentalian recorded.' He was like a pup, quivering with excitement. If the man had a tail, its wagging would have thrown him off-balance.

'Only half *dvergar,* myself,' I said. 'My pap was a Ruman soldier.'

If possible, the man's excitement grew. 'Wonderful! Even better. We'll take your name, age, a short biography.'

Thinking of the Quotidian, I said, 'And have a *daemon* commit my likeness to paper?'

'That's the idea!'

I looked at Fisk, who shrugged in response. I wear Hellfire now. My former reticence to involve myself or use the infernal machines all around me no longer had any grounds to stand on. Ia is not some benevolent God but some sort of jumped-up yet meaningless *daemon* and if the Pater Dis was there to judge the sully I'd done my soul in life, he didn't take into account Hellfire, however it made me feel. Yet it still didn't feel right to me, this reliance upon the dynamos of devils.

However, I was curious to see how this process differed from the Quotidian.

'How much blood?'

'Ah, so you have experience with infernography?'

'A tad,' I said, holding up my hand and exposing the cut still healing there.

'Not too much. A cupful, possibly,' he said. 'But we'll replenish your sanguine humours with strong drink and companionship!' Wasler said, beaming. A nice fellow, this Wasler. His sisterwife Winfried, while pleasant enough, was not nearly as ebullient. 'Please sit.'

I sat cross-legged on the far side of their small chest while Fisk sat and then leaned back on his hands, his booted feet crossed and stretched out in front of him, watching now as Maskelyne rousted the slaves and made ready for the night's mooring. Other boats – *daemon*-driven, equipped with *daemonlights* – might travel upriver at night, but not this one. A slow boat is faster than none at all and the horses needed rest after crossing the Hardscrabble back from Dvergar Spur.

After a few barked commands at the slaves, a group disappeared in the hold and then re-emerged, grunting and straining, carrying two large canvas-wrapped objects. They brought them onto the hold's roof, setting them down on the rough wood, and unfurled them, revealing wooden struts, ropes, and more canvas. Tents. Speaking to each other softly, the last bits of sunlight failing, they set up the tents on the barge's roof and returned with folding cots while the freemen hung oil lanterns along the perimeter of the boat.

Maskelyne approached, carrying two lanterns. She handed one to me and then placed one near Wasler and Winfried. 'Braws, I hope this will make you comfortable. I'd offer statesrooms if I had them but I don't.'

'This is just fine, ma'am,' I said, opening the tent flap. 'Better board than we'd have on the trail.'

'Figured as much,' she said, nodding her head. I got the feeling it wasn't us she was addressing, though. Fisk and I are pretty rough and tumble.

Winfried stood and moved to the lantern, picked it up, and entered the tent. With the lantern inside of it, the light-dun fabric yellowed and brightened, becoming a squat, faintly glowing obelisk in the darkness. She returned shortly without the lantern.

'It will do,' Winfried said simply.

'It's all part of the experience!' Wasler exclaimed in his clipped, precise accent. He glanced at Winfried as if checking a clock or barometer. 'This is the Hardscrabble Territories!'

'It is that, my *canvelet*,' Maskelyne said, not bothering to explain the unfamiliar phrase. She turned to Fisk and me. 'Moment or two, one of my boys will be cooking some fish and hoecakes near the paddlewheel, braw.'

Fisk nodded. My stomach rumbled. It had been a while since my last meal.

'There'll be guards set, *cherkme*, but if you hear some sort of alarum – bells, a'whooping and a'hollering – that Hellfire will be needed.'

'Understood,' Fisk said and I echoed that sentiment.

Maskelyne, seemingly satisfied, gave a little half-bow and departed.

'She seems especially worried with the guards,' Winfried said.

'Nope,' Fisk replied, slowly standing up and stretching out the kinks in his long frame. 'Like your brother, er, husband...' He paused, putting both his hands at the small of his back and bending backwards. 'Like he said, this is the Hardscrabble Territories. Always the chance of stretchers.'

'Are they really as terrifying as the papers say?' Wasler asked, like a child hearing of the great wyrms for the first time.

Fisk looked at me. 'Shoe? I'm gonna go get cozy in the tent.'

I nodded. If there's anything Fisk didn't want hear it was tales spun to greenhorns about *vaettir*.

When he was gone, I said, 'You mentioned something about strong drink?' Wasler laughed and after a moment of digging in a satchel, handed me a flask.

'Well,' I said, taking a sip of some sort of burning liquid. Insects – mosquitos, moths, mayflies – swarmed the lanterns. The ship's cats prowled about, looking for rats and other vermin. Even here, moored on the eastern shore of the Big Rill, the sound of coyotes yipping and screeching reached our ears. Wasler and Winfried looked at me with faces open and eager for tales of the shoal plains. These two could use a little local lore. Or colour. 'Let me tell you about them stretchers.'

Later that night, after I'd eaten some dinner and fielded many questions and listened to statements of disbelief from the two Malfenians, I returned to our tent. Maskelyne's watchful freemen had armed themselves with gigs, then lowered the lanterns close to the still surface of the river and waited, still as statues, as fat, smooth-bodied lickerfish rose to the surface to examine the lights. No exclamations as the gigs lanced out, hooking the thick, muscular fish with such force and surety that many only struggled weakly as the men hauled them aboard. Others, when the gig went slightly awry – enough to hook but not to stun – erupted in furious thrashing and splashing while the other freemen scrambled over to assist in the harvesting.

I entered the tent in the dark, my *dvergar* sight was keen even under a starless sky and this one was brilliant and sprayed with wavering pinpricks of light.

Fisk sat on his cot, holding the Quotidian in his hands, turning it over and over. He did not acknowledge me when I entered, nor did he say anything as I piled onto my bunk and closed my eyes.

I don't know how long he sat there, pondering the infernal thing.

In the morning there was lamb stew; one of the sheep had expired in the night and before we woke, Maskelyne's burly freemen had flayed and filleted the creature. The smell of the meat, mixed with the scents of coffee and chicory, perked up everyone – even the Lomaxes, who looked as if they had not slept well.

The pacemaker began drumming, the wind picked up, and the *Quiberon* moved upstream, against the current.

Fisk, unused to waiting or the wasting of time, busied himself in our tent in the maintenance of gear and guns, checking the integrity of wards, oiling the action on his carbine and disassembling his pistols and ammunition on a chamois cloth and inspecting all the warding very closely.

The Lomaxes beckoned me to join them at their tea. For folks in a rough foreign country, far away from their own home and carrying limited supplies, they were quite nicely accoutred both on their persons – dressed neatly in sombre woollen suits, tailored in similar style that highlighted neither Wasler's masculine traits nor Winifred's feminine ones – and their gear, which was well maintained and quite clever. Light-weight folding chairs and tables, a chest that doubled as another table with interesting access points on the side and back for when the top was in use, folding umbrellas and stands that they'd arranged outside their tent, and a miniature portable stove which really captured my attention.

As I joined them, Winfried pulled a teapot off the tiny stove and banked the flames. 'Would you care for some tea, Mr Ilys?' she asked, and gestured for me to sit, placed a curious metal device in a cup, and poured near-boiling water over it.

I wasn't much of a tea drinker, honestly. Coffee, whiskey, water and some cacique in a pinch when my spirits were low, and that's about it. But I didn't want to offend so I took her up on the offer.

'That is clever,' I said indicating the small stove, holding my tea a tad nervously. The steaming liquid was in a small, delicate little porcelain cup and hard to keep level on the ever-shifting deck of a boat, even one plying the relatively calm waters of a river. I sipped the tea – it wasn't too bad, really – and chucked my head at the device. 'There's no *daemon* in that, is there?'

Winfried laughed. 'No, Mr Ilys, there's no infernal presence here. Just an incredibly strong alcohol, under pressure. One of the Malfena college of engineers is a mountaineer as well.'

I was puzzled. 'How do you mean?'

'Well,' she said, slowly, in a slightly school-marmish voice. 'On any mountaineering expedition, everything – every bit of gear – must be multifunctional.' She indicated the stove with her hand. 'This is a stove, but it is also a heater in cold weather. The alcohol inside it is fuel for the device, but also a cleansing agent and, while horrible to the taste, quite intoxicating.' She smiled, showing teeth nearly as white and gleaming as Wasler's. '*Daemons* are cheap, yes, but in many ways they are cumbersome and not very versatile.'

'Cheap? I've only had a few dealings with engineers and the word "cheap" never entered my mind.'

She nodded. 'Well, they are cheap if you consider the time a summoned *daemon* can last. Barring any unforeseen consequences, a *daemon* in, say, a steamship or mechanized baggage train can remain bound for hundreds of years. *Daemon*light fixtures will last millennia – we think, at least. So, if you amortized the initial cost of the engineer's work over the life of the infernal object . . .'

I could see what she was getting at. 'Ammunition is another matter.'

'This is true. Hellfire pistols, with their Imp rounds, are a different proposition all together.' She sighed. 'I don't believe on a reliance on any single technology. So, little things – like this stove – are important.'

'I wouldn't mind having one of those stoves myself. How pricey are they?'

'I can send a letter at the next post we encounter. It might be a few months before Persa receives it and then months more before he can answer. Where shall I have him send his response?'

'To the Postmaster General in New Damnation. He will hold it for me there.'

From one of the pockets in her jacket, she withdrew a charcoal pencil and small bound notebook and took that down. When she was finished, she smiled again.

Wasler, who had remained silent all this time, clapped his hands lightly, and said, 'Are you ready for your portrait, Mr Ilys?'

'I reckon so,' I said.

Wasler made a great fuss about how he wanted me to sit and the comportment of my body for the portrait while Winfried busied herself setting up the infernographical device that would record my image. It wasn't very large, the image-making machine – only slightly larger than the Quotidian – but the wooden contraption they had to mount it on was quite big. Like most of the Lomaxes' gear it was a collapsible folding wooden artifice, which when fully deployed came to about eye level on a man and had a horizontally-aligned board suspended behind it.

It took Winfried quite a long time to set up the damned thing and, finally, she withdrew a portfolio and removed a thick piece of smooth, bleached-white parchment, very expensive if my rough eye were any judge, and fastened it to the board.

'Mr Ilys,' Wasler said, looking at me thoughtfully and rubbing his chin. 'Do you have a saddle?'

'Sure,' I answered. 'In my tent, since Bess is stabled below.'

'I think it would be good to have it here, in frame.'

'Why? We ain't got no mount for it.'

'For sociological detail,' Wasler said.

'I don't even know what that means,' I said.

'Can you get it?'

'Sure.' I rose, went to our tent. When I entered and grabbed the saddle, Fisk looked at me with raised eyebrows.

'For the portrait,' I said.

The barest hint of a smile touched his mouth. 'You'll need to take up the girth quite a bit to get that saddle to stay on your back.'

'You're a cruel man, Fisk. I've always known that about you,' I said, and left the tent.

After he had artfully placed my saddle at my feet, I had to endure more of Wasler's fussy positioning and posing before he was satisfied.

'Ah!' He said, as if realizing something. 'I know what's missing.'

'What's that?' I asked.

'Your pistol! Please hold it in your hand.'

I drew my pistol and sat there, the bore pointed skyward, as if I was going have a duel.

'No, no. Hold it in your lap,' Wasler said. 'But casually!'

'Like this?' I held it in a way it was pointed off, toward the shore, so that if it discharged it would do no harm.

'No!' He came forward and positioned it himself so that it was pointing down, at the roof of the hold.

'That could hurt someone,' I said, not liking how this portraiture had developed.

'Then we shall be quick. Winfried?'

She came forward with a small bowl and knife. 'Your hand?'

It was the wounded one she sliced and bled into the bowl. Not too much blood. Quickly she returned to the device and unstoppered a larger bottle of ink and mixed the two together and then, with a tin funnel, poured the mixture into the device. Very much like the Quotidian.

'You will need to shut your eyes, Mr Ilys,' Wasler said. 'It is important. So that the *daemonic* link can be established.'

'*Daemonic link?*' I asked.

'Now, Mr Ilys!'

I closed my eyes.

It was a bright morning, so the sunlight filtered through my eyelids, making everything seem bloodred and veined. Then the redness faded and there was, behind my eyelids, a churning smoke that seemed to envelop me even though I could feel the fresh wind of the Whites on my skin and ruffling my hair. It was disconcerting because the sensations of my body belied the dulled sensations of my closed eyes. A tenebrous smoke churned and breathed in vaporous exhalations and I was contained and surrounded by it and had a sense of its massive size. I was just a spark in the darkness. The smoke swelled and grew in some dynamo of combustion. I could easily imagine some rough beast, panting, slavering, watching me from its smoke-wreathed vantage. It crept forward on tremendous claws and readied itself for a leap. And then...

'Good! Mr Ilys. Very good,' Wasler said, breaking the moment. The tension was gone. I opened my eyes. There was a furious scratching coming from the board. Winfried watched it closely.

Once the infernographical device paused for a moment, Winfried said, 'The proof is good! One take makes my day, Wasler!'

The reality of what they were saying sunk in. 'You mean, if something went wrong, we'd have to do that again? The blood?'

'Well,' Wasler said, uncomfortable. 'It would be entirely up to you. But I'm glad to say, it won't be needed.'

The device scratched and shuddered on the board. Winfried watched it closely while Wasler went to make another cup of tea. When the device stopped moving, the Lomax woman unclasped the parchment from where it was affixed and then brought it to the makeshift table. She dusted it with salt, and held it face-up in the sun for a good long while so that the ink would dry. Once she was satisfied with it, she whipped out a pair of scissors and cut away a strip of the parchment from the edge and handed it to me.

'Your proof, Mr Ilys,' she said.

The scrap of paper held my image. Eyes closed, I sat uncomfortably holding a Hellfire pistol in my lap. Behind me, the White Mountains were shrouded in gauzy scratches and lines, indicating clouds. It was me, made from tiny detailed ink strokes. A strange sensation to look upon yourself and not have you peering back. My visage was disturbing, eyes closed, like a death mask.

'This is absolutely incredible,' I said.

'It is a clever, clever device,' Winfried said, smiling.

'May I see the larger one?' I asked.

Wasler shook his head. 'Not until I tint it, if you please. Tonight I will carefully gouache the final image and it will need to dry, so that it will be ready in the morning.'

I was a little disappointed.

'But the proof is all yours, Mr Ilys.'

Later I showed it to Fisk, after the Lomaxes had disassembled the infernographical device.

All he said was, 'You blinked.'

SEVEN

3 Ides, Quintilius, 2638 ex Ruma Immortalis

T HAT AFTERNOON BAD WEATHER blew in over the mountains and we took to our tents to wait it out. A shelf of dark clouds rolled in like gravy poured on a blue plate and the light patters of falling droplets soon began deluging us in earnest. There was a quick scramble to get the Lomax gear inside their tents before it could get drenched. The wind picked up and made the dun-coloured fabric of our tents bluster and whip, but Maskelyne's slaves had done a fine job in their assembly and we had no issues with the wind. But the temperature dropped and I pulled on my oilcoat and remained in the tent with Fisk, sitting upright, watching the foggy shore pass dreamlike beyond the slightly open slit of tent. I whittled a branch I plucked from the Big Rill. Softened by water, the wood curled away under my knife like seconds from a clepsydra. Fisk sat hunched, his shoulders tense at the opening of the tent, his breath coming in hurried puffs. He didn't have to say it for me to know he was thinking upon a certain engineer. While spring was nearly finished and summer close at hand, we still travelled in the shadows of the White Mountains. It could get cold and even snow a long ways into summer.

'Ia dammit, Shoe. Ia dammit all to Hell and Damnation,' he said, softly.

I said nothing.

By afternoon, the sky cleared and the rain stopped, though it remained cool. Wasler came by our tent to apologize.

'I'm sorry, Mr Ilys, but I won't have the tint finished on your portrait until tomorrow. With the rain, I chose not to expose our rendering to the moist air. By tomorrow, I think, I'll be able to complete it.'

'That's fine, Mr Lomax. It was your picture to begin with,' I said.

'Yes, but many people are very . . . shall we say . . . fixated on their own image. It becomes important to them beyond all measure,' he said.

'That 'cause of the *daemon* jiggery that goes into the likeness?' I asked.

He looked at me closely. 'There *is* something of that to it, Mr Ilys. You haven't been feeling any overwhelming need to look upon it, have you?'

'Nope,' I said. 'Got my proof in one of my satchels, I think. It's interesting, but I ain't had any trouble sleeping.'

'That's good,' he responded and looked a tad relieved. 'It's just—' He stopped, chewing his bottom lip.

'It's just what?'

'Nothing,' he said, and then smiled wanly. 'Nothing.'

I placed my hand on my Hellfire and made my eyes go hard. 'Mr Lomax, if it is nothing, then there's nothing stopping you from telling me.'

A startled expression crossed his face. Fisk turned from where he'd been sitting, sharpening a longknife, and raised an eyebrow at Lomax.

'It's just that there've been a few—' He stopped again. Swallowed. He clasped his hands in front of him, realized he was doing it, and then stuffed them in his pocket.

'A few what?'

'A few possessions,' he said, nervously removing his hands from his pockets again. 'That's all.' He turned to go.

'What?' I said. I may be small, but I'm not slow or weak. I snatched his elbow and turned him back, pulling him inside the tent. 'What do you mean, "possessions"?'

'Well, it's complicated,' Wasler said. 'I should not have said anything since it is not even an issue here, Mr Ilys!' He looked at us like that ended it but when we said nothing, he sighed and then gave a little nervous chuckle. 'The *daemon* and the subject become linked – for just a moment – during the sanguine phase of image capture. Sometimes, when the person opens his or her eyes, it's not them staring out of them any more.'

Fisk sat up. Alarmed. 'You mean there's folks toddling about out there with *daemons* inside of them?'

Both Fisk and I have a little experience with this. But in our case, the *daemon* – a real pesky sonofabitch – was bound in a severed hand. And even then, it was enough to almost destroy all of Hot Springs.

'I daresay there are,' Wasler said. He straightened his jacket. 'But not by my – or Winifred's – hands. Persa, the engineer who developed this technology – and also my brother – said that there were some unfortunate occurrences in the development of the device.'

Fisk whistled. 'That's not good. How did he figure it out?'

'The possessed often had an undeniable compulsion to view its portrait. When it wasn't killing or eating or, well, laughing.'

Fisk remained still. But I remember the mirth and hideous glee of the Crimson Man. They were a cheerful bunch, those devils that made it into our world.

'I assure you,' Wasler continued, 'I have never had any such thing happen. And I assure you, it will *not* happen.'

'Better make sure of that, mister,' Fisk said.

71

'And you might want to let folks know, up front, that they're at risk,' I said.

'But they might not agree, then,' Wasler said. 'To the portraiture.'

'That's right. But at least you won't get shot, afterwards,' I said.

'Surely you aren't that angry—'

I chuckled. 'I'm not, though it's not my favourite news. But other folk of the territories?' I placed a thumb at my crotch and drew it upwards. 'They'll split you from crotch to collar just as soon as look at you.'

He swallowed. 'I will remember your advice,' he said, and scurried back to his tent.

The next morning, we'd reached the wide, open shoal plains where foothills softened and levelled and the Big Rill widened and became shallower. Lomax beckoned me into their tent. Winfried was studiously maintaining their gear, the infernographical device on the table in front of her, while Wasler opened a leather portfolio and riffled through parchment until he came upon my portrait.

He'd painted in my eyes – artfully, no doubt – but they were slightly off. On the rest of the portrait, he'd applied a thin wash of colours, blue and pink in the sky, blue-grey for the snowless bits of the White Mountains, a burst of orange and gold for the blooming gambels on the shore. And browns for me. Taken wholly, it was quite a rendering.

'I'm honoured, Mr Lomax. You and your sister will do well, I think, in this endeavour. For my part, I am glad to have seen it,' I said, and gave a slight bow.

Wasler beamed and even on Winfred's face a half-grin made an appearance.

From without, a bell clanged. Maskelyne's bully-boys had gathered on the lower deck, where the captain stood.

'Hark me, braws! We're nigh on Bear Leg. Tend your animals

and buck or see me if you'll river on with us!' Maskelyne bellowed, loud enough to rival any centurion's holler. 'We'll see smoke by the sixth hour! That is all.'

Bear Leg hadn't changed much since we'd left it three months before: still muddy but there were more wooden shacks and buildings than tents now. And there was a proper wharf – before there'd only been the *Cornelian*'s swing stages. The *Quiberon* muscled into position with the incessant beat of the snare-drum and the bleating of sheep. From below, I could hear Bess haw in anticipation.

As Fisk and I readied our gear and tack, I noticed Wasler and Winfried speaking together quite intently, as if arguing. Eventually, Winfried threw up her hands and re-entered the tent. Wasler cast his gaze about, found Fisk and I standing below, and trotted down to join us.

'A word, if I may,' Wasler said, a tad breathless. 'I've discussed it with Winfried and we would ask a service of you.'

'A service?' Fisk asked.

'I have been thinking,' Wasler said.

Fisk, holding a translucent rolling paper flat in his palm and stuffing it with tabac from a pouch at his belt, said, out of the corner of his mouth, 'Congratulations,' before twisting the smoke and thumbing a match into flame. The scent of sulphur and brimstone filled the air.

Wasler blinked, glanced at me. Then continued on: 'As you so aptly pointed out, Mr Ilys, the Hardscrabble Territories are dangerous. Yet it's our job to document as much of it as we can. We, my sisterwife and I, would ask if we could continue to travel on with you?'

'Not really a good idea, Mr Lomax,' Fisk said, drawing on the smoke. 'We travel light and fast.'

'We have money. And you would be surprised at how compact Winfried and I can be.'

Fisk looked to me and shook his head. 'No. We've got our own business to attend to. We can't be weighed down with baggage.'

'I'm sorry, Mr Lomax. We're for Hot Springs to the north and west of here. It's rough travel and not for the likes of you two, if you pardon my directness.'

Wasler swallowed thickly. He nodded, unsmiling. 'Well, thank you for considering it,' he said and hastened off to find Winfried.

Maskelyne's bully-boys began bustling sheep out of the hold onto the wharf and the livestock pens there with a great clatter and bleating, while stevedores cursed and strained, rolling casks and hefting sacks from the holds. Fisk and I bid our goodbyes to Maskelyne.

She clasped forearms with us in turn. 'I'm damned happy that we had no tussles with stretchers, braws.' She smiled mischievously. 'But I'm Ia-damned sad I discounted yer money before the voyage.'

Fisk let a smile touch his face in return. 'You're young yet, and bits of you still wet.'

'Ah!' She exclaimed. 'Not that kind of captain, Mr Fisk! Go on with you,' she slapped his arm in a playful gesture more masculine that feminine, and shoed us off the deck. 'There's a break in the bucking, braws. We'll moor here for the night and press upstream in the morning. If you change your mind, we'll be here.'

We disembarked, leading Bess and Fisk's black onto the rattling planks of the wharf and into the street. Fisk spurred his horse on, and I nudged Bess to keep up. We were half-way up the skirts of the Whites when Fisk stopped and looked on our backtrail.

'I'll be rolled in shit,' he breathed.

'What's that?' I asked.

'Your strays, Shoe. Your Ia damned strays.'

The Lomaxes followed. They had two ponies, the sturdy Hard-scrabble breed that was almost more mule than horse. And they were riding fast and not too far behind us, maybe an hour or so. Behind one of them was quite an interesting contraption drawn by a horse. It had the look of a two-wheeled jaunting car, yet narrower and taller, giving it the aspect of a miniature mortician's hearse. Yet it wasn't having a difficult time traversing the Whites, and their horses appeared – at least from this distance – to be quite fine.

'They're well accoutred,' I said to Fisk.

'If that contraption isn't stolen or firewood in a fortnight, I'll eat my hat,' Fisk replied.

'I think that's why they wanted to tag along with us, pard.'

'Let's put them behind us then. Daylight is burning,' he said, and spurred his horse on.

We rode hard for the rest of the day and hours into the night. Fisk rose before the sun on the following day, kicking my boot to rouse me, his jaw working and a fierce expression on his face. For a moment, I expected to see a desiccated black hand hanging there from a silver clasp, his expression was so intense. 'Come on, Shoe. Come on. Up.'

Fisk set a gruelling pace. We were hours on the trail when he said, 'Damnation,' and peered back over his horse's haunch.

'What? Stretchers?' I asked.

'No, Ia dammit. There,' he pointed.

In the valley below us, the Lomaxes and their odd, narrow wagon emerged from a copse of trees and crossed the stream through the same ford we used only hours before.

'How in the Hell are they keeping pace?' Fisk asked no one.

We waited a while, watching. 'The strange wagon of theirs is quite fleet, pard,' I said. 'Surprising.'

'And the woman has a firm hand on the reins. The man though—'

'He's staying mounted,' I said.

'Look at him.' Fisk spat. Then, after a moment, gave a short humourless laugh. 'He'll be sitting funny for a fortnight.' He turned his horse. 'Let's go. Beleth isn't just sitting around, that's for damn sure.'

As if to put our tails behind us, once and for all, we rode hard until the trail was almost black before us and the wind had kicked up, skirling down the flanks of the mountains. In the dark, I found wood for the fire and we had a late, cold supper. Our fire had burned low when I heard the rustling and whispered words off in the darkness.

'Them Lomaxes,' I said. 'They're out there, looking for us.'

Fisk, who had his head resting on his saddle and a cigarette in his mouth, stirred slightly. 'Amazing they made it this far.'

'And this quickly,' I said. 'They wouldn't slow us down that much. Might as well take their money. With them stumbling around in the night, they might draw the stretchers to us.'

'You're lining up your arguments like a little cohort of soldiers, Shoe,' he said, and spat out loose tabac. 'We don't need their money and never had any issue killing stretchers,' he said. 'But I've been thinking about that device of theirs.'

'The Infernograph?'

'That's the one.'

'What about it?'

'Remember the last time we were in Hot Springs?'

'You had a passenger around your neck and the town burned down around us. So yes, I remember.'

'Well, maybe some of the citizens do, too.' He was quiet for a long while. 'Those Lomaxes. They stick out, don't they?'

'You could say that.'

'We roll in with them, nobody'd be looking at us, would they? They can blather on about their *daemonic* portrait machine and all eyes would be on it and not us.'

'I think you have the right of it.'

'Go on and fetch them, Shoe. But you'll do all the coddling.'

'Right,' I answered. 'Don't I always?'

'Now, that ain't fair, Shoe.'

'But it's true,' I said, standing. I went to find the Lomaxes in the dark and lead them back to camp.

The Lomaxes travelled well. Their jaunting-hearse (as I began to think of it) was quite narrow and had clever, articulated joints where the axle was affixed to the body that absorbed any jars and shocks. It was drawn by a massive draught horse of inexhaustible stamina both the Lomaxes affectionately called Buquo. Where Winfried sat on top of the jaunting-hearse, reins in-hand, she seemed to be quite comfortable, though she had to dismount a couple of times as we passed through overhanging brush and bramblewrack.

Fisk led us on the trail, pushing us all hard and Bess had taking to hawing at streams and gulleys, voicing her discontent at the pace. There was no frivolous talking in the day. We rode, we rested horses, we ate hardtack, we rode.

We bunked down that night in the lee of a gulley, around a small fire, eating hardtack and drinking the Lomax's tea that they were so eager to share. The designer of the jaunting-hearse had not forgotten anything, it seemed. Wasler pulled two small posts from underneath and stabbed their metal-shod ends deep into the rocky earth and then unfurled a tailored canvas tarp that converted the buggy into a tent where they made themselves cozy.

We were climbing higher on the Whites' skirts so that we could come at Hot Springs from behind, and the vistas were opening up: the Big Rill gleamed like a silver ribbon in the valley below; gambels and birch and pine wreathed the mountain-side; great lichen-covered abutments of rock jabbed through the earth, here and there, in great dramatic heaves.

'Mr Fisk,' Winfried called from her perch on the jaunting-hearse. 'Mr Fisk!'

Fisk stopped, looking back, hand on the black's rump.

'Ma'am?'

'When would you like to have your portrait taken?'

'Let's see,' he said, thinking. 'How 'bout when we reach Harbour Town?'

'But we're not going to Harbour Town,' Wasler interjected.

'That's right,' Fisk said and turned back to the trail.

I hunted in the afternoon, bringing down grouse and quail and rabbits with my sling and afterwards Fisk made us push on until far after dark. His urgency wasn't as pressing as it was when he wore the *daemon* hand around his neck, but he was riding us hard and pushing our mounts to their limits. Nevertheless, when he did allow us rest for the evening, the game I bagged earlier made for a fine supper. Fisk, when the Lomaxes' society wore on him, went outriding or walked the perimeter, even in the dark. 'All this Ia-damned talk and we're no closer to the blasted engineer,' he said, spitting loose tabac from his cigarette. The Lomaxes didn't hear, or even notice, but I marked his restlessness.

It had only been a short while since he had worn the *daemon* hand around his neck, had the Crimson Man in his head. It's the still, silent times when that comes back.

I think of Agrippina, sometimes, at night. And that fierce kiss of fire.

Can't imagine how it affects Fisk, when his experience was so much worse.

They get into you and make wreckage of your heart.

The Lomaxes had retired early and when the pop and crackle of the fire banked low, I could hear the slapping of their flesh against each other, their moans and heavy breathing. Brother and sister, mating furiously. For a long time.

When they stopped, it was only then I was able to find sleep, myself.

Next day, we came down from the higher ridges and followed a virulently green-hued, steaming stream down out of the heights toward the back side of Hot Springs, far enough away from the rough road and rail-line to the silver mines so as not to be seen. Spread out below us was the town, a loose gathering of timber and stone buildings, washed out and muddy-grey, long dark lines of sooty smoke emanating from chimneys and rising to join the plumes of steam coming from the spring pools around the little hamlet. The sounds of carpentry and hammers falling echoed through the air. To the north-west, along the miners' road to the Brujateton Silverlode, was a rough-hewn century camp, the kind of garrison you'd often see in smaller, out of the way places where Tamberlaine and the Empire had an interest. And in Hot Springs, the interest was silver.

'Mr Lomax,' I said when we all came to a stop. 'I was wondering if you'd do us a small favour.'

Wasler brightened. 'Of course! Anything!'

'If you'd walk on down into town, maybe get yourself a room at the hotel. I imagine it's been repaired by now.'

'Repaired?' Wasler asked, curious.

'There was a fire,' I said, not glancing at Fisk. 'Looks like they're rebuilding pretty good.'

'I can do that,' Wasler said.

'That's not all,' I continued. 'Need you to look around for a fella that we're trying to find.'

He looked confused, possibly realizing he never asked us why we were travelling.

'You're bounty hunters?' Winfried asked, half outraged, half pleased.

'You could call us that,' I said. 'But there ain't no bounty. We're tasked with this by Marcellus, commander of the fifth.' No need to tell him about Tamberlaine, Cornelius, and the rest.

'Who are you searching for?'

Fisk looked at me from where he sat on horseback.

'A traitor by the name of Beleth. Might be going by the name of Labadon. Short, well-fed fella. Wears suits like yours, neat and tailored. Thinning hair on top. Smart man. Wears spectacles.'

'That could be any merchant or shopkeeper,' Wasler said, 'But I will do as you ask.'

'This one has a smug, superior air. He was here, while back. Probably isn't still around,' Fisk said, finally joining in the conversation. 'But he knows us, and we can't just go barrelling in there if he's got eyes out.'

'I understand,' Wasler said, solemnly.

'Don't do anything foolish,' I said. 'The man's a menace, despite his looks.'

Wasler swallowed, thickly. 'Should I be worried?'

'It's the territories. You should always be worried,' I said.

'I should go with him,' Winfried said.

'Don't think that would be a problem, ma'am,' I said. 'And you're free to do whatever you'd like. But if one of you spots him, you'll need to hustle back up here to tell us. If not, just stay there, and we'll come down after dark.'

A suspicious look crossed Winifred's face. 'Are you wanted, here?'

Our last visit to Hot Springs ended up with us in jail and the whole town on fire, courtesy of the Crimson Man who was riding Fisk like a bronco. But that was when the town was owned and run by the Hellene, Croesus, and his Argenta Mining Company bully-boys. Now, Hot Springs was firmly under the Imperial thumb.

'No. We're members of the Ruman army and have papers to prove it.' I dug in my satchel and removed the orders that Cornelius had given us, waving them in the air. I was thankful neither of the Lomaxes asked to inspect them, revealing our patron. I don't know why I didn't want them to know – and, even in silence, could tell Fisk didn't either – except that it would simply complicate matters.

Better we remain rankers, minor functionaries performing a menial (if exciting) task.

'Should I procure rooms for you both?' Winfried asked.

'That might be in order,' I said. I glanced at Fisk and he nodded. 'I could use a bath, and the hot springs promise a good one,' I said, dug around in my pouch for enough sesterces to cover a night's stay and handed them to him.

After a bit of nervous preparation on Wasler's part, and prim efficiency on Winfried's, the Lomaxes rode down the trail to Hot Springs, the jaunting-hearse in tow.

'You don't think they'll end up in no harm, do you?' I asked my partner.

'No. Beleth is long gone,' Fisk said, staring at the town. 'But who knows what mischief he's left behind for us.'

'I hope you're wrong about that,' I said.

'I do too, Shoestring. I do too.'

EIGHT

Ides, Quintilius, 2638 ex Ruma Immortalis

WHEN IT WAS DARK, WE walked down the mountain, alert and watching for any who might be alarmed at our prescence, past the graveyard which had grown large, and came into Hot Springs proper. The gallows were gone, I was thankful to see, and much of the town had improved from its former state of corporate despotism. Plain ole Ruman despotism had worked wonders. If there's anything the Rumans know how to do, it's build and organize towns. The new Hot Spring's streets were open and wide – while still as muddy as any frontier town – and the sides were well planked for walking, patrolled by Hellfire-toting legionnaires and vigiles bearing *daemon*fire lanterns. A year past, the streets had teemed with Argenta bully-boys in the employ of a Mr Croesus. Storefronts were restored and looked profitable – a few sported plate glass windows that, in a Hardscrabble town, were begging for trouble. Couples walked arm in arm along the plank-walks on their evening *passagiatta* as store clerks unbanked *daemon*lights, swept porches, and performed their last chores for the day. Faint sounds of piano and guitar and laughter emanated from the largest building in the town, the Aurelian Hotel – a three-storied wooden structure whose planks still oozed sap. The whole thing was golden if you squinted in the dying light.

All of Hot Springs smelled of sulphur and the sickly-sweet odour of fresh cut pine. A town swiftly on the mend.

Fisk's shoulders rose and hitched as we rode down the main street. He had his hat on, low, covering his eyes, even in the dark. The events caused by the Crimson Man – and consequently Fisk – would remain long in the townsfolk's memories.

We stabled the horses in the Aurelian's coach house, tossed a couple of extra sesterces at the stable boy to give a little tenderness and loving attention to our tack, and hoisted our personal effects and satchels over shoulders while Fisk hefted the ornate box of the Quotidian.

'Pard, you want me to get the room key from Wasler?' I asked. 'Or you gonna sit the lobby?'

Shaking his head, Fisk said, 'Ain't gonna hide. But I'm not gonna rub these folks' noses in it either. We go in, find the Lomaxes, and then I'll retire.' He rubbed his stubbled cheek with a rough hand. 'The hot spring bathing and ablutions will have to come tomorrow. It's the Ides.'

'Livia!' I exclaimed. 'She must be somewhere in the middle of the Occidens Ocean, if all is well.'

Nodding his head, Fisk said, 'I'm not eager for the bloodletting, but I am desperate for word from her.'

He turned and clomped down the plank-walks toward the hotel's front doors. So it was understandable he didn't see the boy.

The child was remarkable because of his stillness. He stood on the suspended plank surface, across the wide main thoroughfare, between two buildings. Beyond him, behind the main street of Hot Springs, a smithy or smelt of some sort burned, filtering flame-coloured light in radiant patterns out on the street and making a silhouette of the child. The child himself was one of those miscreant urchins all towns have, ill-dressed and barefoot, chasing dogs for sport or spite or food.

Homeless, possibly. Parentless, most likely.

Near feral, assuredly.

This boy watched us. His poise, his posture all indicated that we had his attention, though his face was cast in shadow. The tense inaction of his flexing hands made me think he might fly at us, screaming, at any second.

'Fisk,' I said, before he could get to the hotel doors. 'We got an audience.'

Fisk stopped, turning. 'What?'

'Yonder. A boy watching us.'

Fisk squinted, ducking his head a little as if that would help. I turned back to look at the boy once more just in time to see him launch into motion, running down the swaying, bobbing plank-walk, away from us, and turn into another alleyway.

'He was moving like his ass was on fire,' I said.

'You think he recognized us?' Fisk asked. 'From last year?'

'He sure was peering at us good, that's for certain.'

'We come looking for Beleth, and we're the ones getting peeped.' He shook his head and spat into the general muck of Hot Spring's street. 'I don't fucking like it.'

Fisk went silent for a long while before running his hand around the brim of his hat, drawing it down tighter on his head, lower over his face. Fisk is many things: a killer, a nomad, a noble, a martial man, a loyal friend, and mate. Subterfuge doesn't sit well on him.

He spat again and turned back to the hotel's front doors.

The Aurelian Hotel was a grander affair than its predecessor, Ruby's – it boasted an extra floor, a fancy dining room separate from the more homespun bar, and was decked out in brass geegaws and doohickeys. It seems that the owners of the hotel sprung for a furnace *daemon*.

Infernal lantern light flickered in front of mirrors while house *coercitors* hefted Hellfire and wore short, silver-threaded stabbing swords on their belts above their aprons. Ex-legionnaires, from their bearing, and familiar with *vaettir* judging by their shorn heads.

Whores, sweetboys, and other characters of negotiable virtue lolled indolently about the bar. We found the Lomaxes sitting quietly in the dining room, where they had enjoyed a repast of what looked like venison, some sort of stewed greens, and fresh bread. And wine. Wasler's face, at this point, was flushed and he was smiling. Winfried just seemed tired.

'Ah, Mr Fisk! Mr Ilys! We were wondering if you were going to come into town or you had abandoned us in an elaborate ruse!'

I winced a little as he spoke. While nowhere near full, there were still enough diners in the room to take notice of our names. Between Beleth's spies and shell-shocked – and possibly vengeful – townsfolk, Wasler's enthusiasm for our company could prove dangerous. We sat, and the waiter, a thin, moustachioed man in black and white garb presented us with wine glasses and a menu. Fisk waved off the menu, but Wasler poured wine into our glasses.

'I spoke with many storekeepers and patrons of the bar. None knew of the man you mentioned. He hasn't been here recently, as far as I can tell.'

'He's been here,' Fisk said. 'Just covered his tracks. I'll speak with the *vigiles* in the morning.' He knocked back the wine in his glass and looked at Wasler. 'Did you check in?'

Wasler nodded and began digging in his pockets. He produced two keys and gave one to Fisk and one to me. 'We're in connecting rooms, should you need anything. Winfried and I will most likely be doing infernographs most of tomorrow, but we'll canvass the bar for suitable subjects tonight,' he said, smiling. He was excited, that's for sure.

'Don't go too heavy on the drink,' I said. 'Folks around here will roll you.'

Winfried snorted. 'Do not worry. I will manage him,' she said, nudging her brothermate in the side with an elbow. I was happy to not have to hear their lovemaking, tonight. Old gods and new, I hoped they wouldn't get wild enough to hear through walls.

The waiter reappeared and placed a small, lacquered tray in front of Fisk bearing a folded piece of parchment.

'The cheque's for him,' Fisk said, indicating Wasler. 'I didn't order any food.'

'No sir,' the waiter replied. 'The gentleman over there ... well, that's strange—' He looked puzzled and glanced around the room. 'A gentleman gave this to me to give to you, sir.'

Fisk, very slowly, picked up the paper. It was heavy stock, rough edged, and looked bleached and expensive. He did not open it.

'What did this man look like?' I asked.

'A courier of some sort, I think. Like the vigiles and army folks use.'

'What did he look like?' I repeated.

'Oh. He was young,' the waiter said. 'And had a courier-cap on. A smudge of dirt on his face. I had the impression he'd been working. Slim, I think.' The waiter shrugged. 'That is all I can tell you.'

Fisk's jaw protruded a little, like he was about to chew on something. And maybe he was. He settled into his chair, holding the unopened paper in his hand. 'My thanks,' he said, dismissing the waiter.

After a moment, he tucked it into his shirt pocket, unread. Then he stood.

'Goodnight, folks,' he said, inclining his head toward the Lomaxes. 'Stay out of trouble.'

Winfried, her eyes sharp and watching Fisk curiously, said, 'Thank you. I will make sure of that.'

I bid my goodbyes and followed Fisk up to the room.

The room was small but well appointed, with a banked *daemon-light* lantern and a couple of single beds with expensive-looking coverlets and large eiderdown pillows. It had a boothorn and there was a large ceramic ablution-bowl affixed to the wall with spigots feeding it hot and cold water, in addition to a small writing desk squared away in a corner. There was a large, paned window that looked out onto the White Mountains that now appeared just as far-off shapes in the dark, cutting a jagged line into the star-sprayed vault of heaven.

Fisk twisted the window's handles and pushed them open to let in some air. The scent of fresh-cut pine was powerful, here.

After a moment of looking out into the dark, he turned, tugged off his boots and sat on the bed.

I sorted my gear and tromped back downstairs to order us both some dinner in the room. And a bottle of whiskey.

When I returned, Fisk had begun unlimbering the Quotidian from its box, and setting out the bowl and knife and a large piece of parchment.

'The note?' I asked.

He withdrew it from a pocket and handed it to me.

It read: *Beleth bound the smelt daemon in Harbour Town. Its name is Unchleigh. A man going by the name Unchleigh has checked into the Pynchon Hotel in Passasuego. He's been seen with the Medieran ambassador's son, Honore Quintanar. My agent will make contact once you're there – Andrae*

'So, we head to Passasuego in the morning?'

'Yes. Nothing for it but to haul ass.'

'I speak truthfully here in saying that I'll miss the Lomaxes' company.'

Fisk looked at me. 'Truly?'

'Yes.' I kicked off my boots and hung Hellfire on the end of the headboard. 'You're quite the conversationalist, pard.'

'Their night-time ruts are a mite bothersome.'

I laughed. 'You heard those? I thought you were asleep.'

'Hard to sleep when you got a brother tupping his sister not ten paces away,' he said, his face very serious, until a sly smile cracked the facade. He laughed. 'Malfenians! Oh shit, Shoe, I thought us Rumans took the cake.'

Laughing felt good. It had been too long.

A knock sounded at the door and when I answered it, a liveried porter deposited a platter of cold meats, stinky cheese, pickled onions and olives and bread – joined by a whiskey bottle and two glasses – on the small credenza by the door. We took turns washing our hands and faces in the ablutions-bowl and then fell upon the food like the ravenous household gods that the old rustics around New Damnation worship; jealous ghosts, hungry numina. Fisk and I remained silent for a long while as we put away the victuals. Afterwards, Fisk rolled two cigarettes and I poured whiskey and we sat looking out into the night, through the open windows, sipping the fire of liquor.

'I'll clear out for a bit,' I said, pointing at the Quotidian with my chin.

Fisk nodded his head. 'Much obliged. After, I'll give you the news,' he said.

When I finished the whiskey, I dropped the butt in the bottom of the glass, pulled back on my boots and buckled on my guns, went downstairs to see what I could see in the bar.

Wasler sat at a car table holding a handful of trumps, a look of consternation on his face. Surrounded by men with faces like sides of beef, bodies to match, he seemed dwarfed by his companions. They were either soldiers on R&R or auxiliaries looking for work with the century, maybe. Didn't matter, really: the bully-boys were large, ugly, and toting Hellfire and longknives.

Winfried stood behind Wasler, looking on the game with a furious expression on her face. When I came in, she spotted me. She raised a hand, beckoning me over.

I took a deeper, more serious gander at the place than I had when I first toddled in, fresh off the trail and hot for Beleth.

'He had a drink,' Winfried said, low and through her teeth. 'And then the fool decided that joining a game would be the best way to meet possible subjects for portraits.'

'He lost his ass?'

'No,' she said. 'Not yet. But every time he moves to get up, they tell him to sit back down.'

'And he does?'

'Wasler is not a fighting man.'

I shook my head. 'I'm not either, ma'am. But this is the Hardscrabble Territories. If you're not prepared to fight, you'll always be at the mercy of bully-boys.'

Putting my hand on my six-gun, I went around the table until I stood next to Wasler. Loud enough for the knuckleheads to hear, I said, 'Commander Marcellus has sent a message, sir, regarding his portrait.'

Wasler jumped in his seat and then looked at me closely. 'We have no—' he began. Seeing the look on my face, he swallowed. 'Ah, Marcellus. I should answer him, immediately.' He looked at the other men at the table. I looked too, my hand on Hellfire.

'Gentlemen, you'll have to excuse me,' Wasler said. 'I have business to attend to.'

Wasler began to rise and one of the men said, 'Trust a dwarf to sour a game.' A couple of the men guffawed at this, showing a surprising number of gaps in their teeth.

'Yes,' another one said. 'The squat men are shites. But dwarf pussy is like no other.'

'Aw, Bert, you only likes them because their little hands make your tiny cock look all the bigger.'

Bert, a great pile of a man with a broken nose and lopsided face, put his trumps face-down on the table. 'Go on, you cunt. You know the real trouble with the *dvergar* women is they're so Ia-damned squirmy when you stick them.' He gave a short, ugly laugh. 'You really got to hold 'em down when you dip your prick.'

I'm old, it's true, a hundred years older than the oldest person in the room, but it still surprised me how anger could bloom like the sun exploding over the shoal plains. My hand tightened on the pistol's grip.

'Come, Mr Lomax,' I said. Wasler stood and went to join Winfried. I remained behind, just in case.

Bert looked at me. 'Shave him, and I could've sworn I fucked his sister last summer near Tapestry,' he said, and the table erupted in laughter.

Bert tilted his chair back on the two hind legs, brought a shot to his mouth and drank it, hissing loudly. He hooked his thumbs in his belt and stared at me with a cruel smile on his face.

There was a long moment where I considered shooting him in the belly.

I didn't.

As I retreated, my face burned with the sounds of their laughter.

I joined the Lomaxes at the bar. I ordered cacique, which the Aurelian had a bottle of, surprisingly.

'Wasler,' I said, blood still high. 'Stick to merchant men, whores, and sweetboys for your portraits.' I knocked back the cacique and ordered another. 'Unless you got the stones to get yourself out of your own messes.'

Wasler looked both surprised and ashamed, all at once. Winfried, her face dark, nodded grimly, her arms crossed on her chest.

'Mr Ilys,' he said, hesitantly. 'My apologies. I merely wished to—'

'I know what you wished to do. You're a good man, but godsdamned green as grass,' I said.

He looked like he wanted to cry. Winfried took his arm and led him away, saying, 'We'll retire, now, Mr Ilys. Thank you for your assistance.'

'Stay in your rooms and keep watch. This is the Hardscrabble,' I said. 'Don't you understand that?'

Speechless, Wasler stumbled out, accompanied by his sisterwife.

I drank. Thinking of my time in Tapestry, when I was a young man and all the world was new. It was a *dvergar* village – a 'tinkers' village – renowned for producing, guess what? Tapestries. There'd been a girl who later became my wife. Illina – my black-haired beauty – bore me sons and a daughter, and worked by my side until the devourer's disease ate her from the inside out.

It was late, then, when the bar cleared and the bartender bellowed '*Last call!*' and would serve me no more.

Bert and his three companions rose from their table and unsteadily made their way out into the night. Auxiliaries might bunk down in stables, in flop-houses or hostels, or even at the century garrison, but that crew wouldn't be able to afford a hotel as expensive as the Aurelian. Once they left, I waited a bit, stood, tipped the bartender, and followed them out into the night.

I could hear them, laughing, their heavy treads making the plank-walks groan and creak. The sky was brilliant overhead and became more so as I moved away from the hotel's *daemonlights*.

Dvergar, when away from man- or *daemon*-made illumination, have exceptional darksight. I clearly saw the soldiers, ahead of me.

Time was, I was finicky about the use of Hellfire for fear of the taint done my immortal soul. I'm not so fastidious today, but some habits die hard. I withdrew my sling from a pouch at my waist and loaded an iron shot.

The first soldier fell face-first into the plank with a great thud and then rolled into the mud. This was greeted with catcalls and blustery suppositions regarding Marius' ability to hold his alcohol.

'Let him sleep it off in the street, boys!' Bert bellowed. Somewhere in the darkness, a dog barked.

I pegged the second soldier behind the ear, twisting him about so that he fell silently off the plank-walk and the other two soldiers never noticed. Bert was gesturing wildly with his hands, saying, "Ere's the meat of it, Bots, the damned praefect's a gorm cock-sucker and don't know which end of a horse to feed. 'Ows he 'erposed to give us orders when—'

I popped Bert's last companion in the centre of his back, making him cry out and fall over and had another iron shot in the sling within seconds, striking him directly in the forehead, felling him.

Bert, realizing he was alone, and in jeopardy, whirled about. 'Boys! Mithras' balls, boys, yer all fallin' out!'

I came forward. Bert stopped, peering at me in the dark.

'The fucking *dwarf*? 'Ere, little one,' he said, withdrawing a longknife from its sheath. 'I'll prick thee like I pricked your kin, you cunt.'

I let the shot fly. It whistled through the air and made a dull *thock* when it impacted Bert's cheek, crushing the bone there. He flopped backwards, making a garbled sound. When he rose again, I launched another shot, hitting his jaw, shattering it. He spluttered, sending loose teeth flying. Blood poured from his face, spilling through cupped hands. He moaned and stumbled away, desperate.

I did not follow.

The other soldiers would wake with terrible headaches. Maybe even be dullards for the rest of their lives.

But Bert?

He'd spend the rest of his days eating soup.

I don't know why I looked up as I returned to the hotel. Maybe it was to take in the glory of the night sky. Maybe it was to remember Illina. Maybe it was to place our room's window on the second floor of the Aurelian. I don't know. We should've been more watch-ful.

The hotel's *daemonlights* had not obliterated my darksight, not then, and the small, ragged figure was clear in my sight, standing on the pitch-plank roofing, just outside our window.

For an instant, I thought the figure might be *vaettir*, it held itself with such tense fury. But even from where I watched, I could see that it was smaller than those giants. They aren't called stretchers for nothing.

I ran forward, cursing all the cacique I drank earlier. It hadn't affected my aim, but my breath came in great heaves as I dashed forward, pulling my six-gun from its holster.

I burst through the hotel doors to the surprise of the concierge and raced up the stairs to the second floor. The hotel was still and nearly quiet except for the muted sounds of coughing and the moans of people having sex in their rooms. The sound of something heavy falling pulled me forward. I leapt down the hall and nearly broke down the door to mine and Fisk's room.

Fisk looked up from the desk where the Quotidian sat. The knife and bowl was out, but the parchment was clear. The bowl was full to almost overflowing with blood. A large stoppered bottle of ink stood next to it, ready to dilute and swell the amount of blood for the Quotidian.

I scanned the room in a flash.

'What in Ia's name, Shoe—'

From the next room there was a scream and something crashed. Fisk had his six-gun out in a flash, despite the cut to his hand, and I was already moving to the door that connected the Lomaxes to ours. A well-placed boot kicked it inward. Fisk right on my arse, I moved into the room.

Things slowed, like swimming in molasses, and I began taking in details of the room: Winfried huddled near the hallway door, her hands in front of her face, eyes wild and terrified. The clever devices of their jaunting-hearse arranged neatly in a corner. Wasler laid out on the floor, blood everywhere. On top of the dresser, a boy crouched, hands like claws, a gleeful expression animating his face. His eyes were huge, and black – blazing, smoking, yet totally black. His skin was pale yet his lips and mouth were blood-red and as he smiled, it displayed his many teeth. Sharpened teeth.

'You,' the boy said, stretching out a long, clawed finger at us. 'The dwarf and his keeper.' Its voice was cold and blood and spittle flew into the room with the plosives. 'I was sent to find you.' It cackled like a witch then leaped across the space as a cougar might. We tracked it with our pistols. It landed on the credenza near the door, sending a *daemon* lantern and crystal glasses flying.

Not a boy. No longer. Whatever animated it was a thing of hatred and glee.

Daemon.

'Beleth sends his regards,' the thing said again, and leapt for us, hands outstretched.

The sound of the guns in the enclosed space was deafening. The smell of Hellfire and brimstone filled the space and I felt a wave of despair and sorrow. The boy's body slammed into my chest, bowling me over backwards. It thrashed some, cracking my chin with a flailing arm, and then went still. I tasted blood and couldn't be sure whose it was.

Fisk pulled me up and we went to check on Wasler.

Dead. His face half-eaten and his throat ripped away.

Poor soul, having ended like that. I pulled a blanket from the bed and draped it over the ruins of his face.

Heavy footfalls sounded in the hall and two vigiles burst in with the hotel manager close behind.

It was a while before we could make them understand the boy was the intruder. In death, his countenance returned to one of youth. Only his teeth remained sharp. I pulled back the thing's lip to show them. The biggest vigile cursed and warded himself and immediately went to find the manager.

Winfried shook off her shock at Wasler's death to corroborate our story. I fetched the whiskey from our room and poured her a healthy measure. She drank it with shaking hands.

'Why don't you come sit in our room?' I said to her. She seemed lost now. Always before, she'd been forceful, straightforward. Now, everything was different. 'We've got to examine the boy.'

'Why?'

'To be sure.'

She shuddered, but then straightened. 'I will remain.'

Fisk, turning the boy's body, pulled his shirt off and tossed it to the side.

'Here, now,' one of the vigiles said. 'You think you should be doing that?'

Fisk withdrew his legate's eagle pin from his pocket and showed it to the man.

'Right, then,' he said. 'Carry on.'

They stood, silent and dumb, as Fisk squatted on his hams and searched the boy. There was blood everywhere. When he turned him over, I saw the mark.

'There. Shoulder,' I said.

A small circular burn mark, strangely familiar. Beleth once drew it on a napkin. A ward for binding *daemons* into a human 'vestment'.

'He left a little present for us,' Fisk said, sucking his teeth. 'Who knows how many more of these devils are out there?'

I looked at the vigiles. 'You have any children or citizens go missing?'

One of them – a man with a beard and deep, sunken eyes – shrugged and said, 'Always got missing persons. We're in the arse-crack of nowhere, out here. There's always whores and thieves, gamblers and outlaws, come sniffing around for silver.'

'All right,' Fisk stood. 'You can remove him to the undertaker.'

'What about the other fella?'

I looked to Winfried, who stood staring at the sheet covering

Wasler, now spotting with crimson. After a moment, she said, 'Yes. Please take him as well. I will make all the arrangements at dawn.'

Once the bodies were removed – and the hotel manager had sent round a slave to dump sawdust on the bloodstains – I said to Winfried, 'We can stay here, with you, if you want.'

'You are very kind, Mr Ilys.' Her voice was strong, but part of her was very far away from all of this. The thousand-mile stare of the bereaved. 'I will remain here.' She moved over to the writing table and sat down, slowly. She placed a single hand lightly on the ink-blotter. She looked at the sawdust.

I pulled one of my pistols and placed it on the desk. 'Just in case,' I said. 'I'll shut your window, ma'am.'

'Thank you.'

I shuttered the windows and Fisk and I returned to our room, leaving the door between them slightly ajar. There wouldn't be much sleep tonight.

'Ia damn, Shoe. A boy,' Fisk said, once everything was quiet. I poured us both whiskeys while he rolled cigarettes.

'Always knew he was an amoral, avaricious son of a bitch, pard,' I said.

'That man wants a killing.'

Not much to say to that. For the second time that day I pulled off my boots. I lay down on the bed with the whiskey glass perched on my belly and a cigarette in my lips.

'Hell of a thing. We're going to have to be on watch, now, everywhere we go.'

'Should've been doing that to begin with. A boy? We saw him earlier, and I thought he was only a set of eyes for a larger master.' He unslung his gunbelt, tossed it on the bed. 'What I can't figure is why Beleth didn't pick the biggest bastard he could find and stuff a devil in him.'

'He's on the run. Doesn't have all his doodads and nice

equipment. A big fella might draw attention. A boy or child can go unnoticed,' I said.

'And the man's natural inclination is toward cowardice,' Fisk said. 'He'd have to overcome a man and that wouldn't be as easy as a child.'

I expelled a cloud of blue smoke toward the ceiling. 'Andrae said he murdered a junior engineer here. Probably took his stuff. Used it to set the boy as a trap. You think we should ask around about the engineer, tomorrow?'

'No. We know where Beleth is now. And the name he's using. We ride for Passasuego in the morning.'

'Don't intend to stay for the funeral?'

He was silent for a long time. 'Ia dammit, Shoe. You and your strays. We don't have time to waste.'

'He was a good companion, Fisk.'

'No.'

'We stay. Won't leave Winfried like this.'

'No.'

'Go on, then. I will join you later.'

'Ia-dammit, Shoe.'

'That's settled then,' I said.

I lay thinking for a while.

'That boy. His face and eyes. His whole damned demeanour. You know what he reminded me of?'

Fisk didn't answer at once. 'What's that?' he said after a while.

'Stretchers,' I said.

It was then that the Quotidian began to move, hissing and scratching, on the parchment.

NINE

*Ides of Quintilius, Fifth Hour, 2638 Annum ex
Rume Immortalis, A Thousand Miles west of
Latinum in the Occidens Ocean*

My Love,
First, let me allay any misgivings you might have regarding the
health of your unborn child. He is well, if his daily gyrations
and warlike exercises are any indications. A strong boy, I believe,
judging by the kicks; though I fear when he is grown he will be
a terror in the saddle, prone to a love of the spur.

I have thought for a long while upon this missive: I have so
much to tell you. The Quotidian itself seems the perfect vessel
for this endeavour. With the sacrificial knife, I freshen that
wound that joined our blood as our blood is joined within me.

I understand now why the Quotidian is called thus. Daily
I think of it; daily I consider writing to you, despite the
blood-cost. I have even gone so far as to question Valerus if the
messages will be... I know no other word than *delivered*...
if more frequent messages will be delivered to you and he
assures me (after a careful examination of the warding on the
Quotidian device) that all messages will be received but that,
if there is a backlog of missives, the blood-cost to you could
be quite high and so it is common practice to have surrogates.
Secundus and Carnelia have generously offered to provide our
sanguine ink, and while surely an imposition on his friendship,
possibly Mister Illys would let red on your behalf? How strange
to think that with each word of love I send to you, it will cost

98

you a part of yourself. In this, our nuptial correspondence mirrors the wedding wound itself. Yet I love you and wish to share my thoughts, the events of this journey, and hope, when you have a moment's respite searching for Beleth, you could respond, though I realize being on the trail makes it difficult. Should you ever find yourself in a situation that allows you to utilize the Quotidian, Valerus informs me that you can mix five parts ink to one part blood and still be assured that the device will function as designed.

Leaving you was near ruinous to me. My mind kept returning to you, your mission, your well-being. Never before have I felt such a connection, neither between family nor silly juvenile loves when I was but a teenager, before my father had arranged my doomed first marriage. I feel the connexion between us like an invisible filament of gold, beaten to airy thinness.

I have let the blood. I have mixed it with the ebon stain from the Indus river valley. So much blood, my love, and ink to swell its amount. I have naught but ship, sea, swells and time to commune with you through blood and thought and pen.

I will begin.

Five days confined in the luxuriously appointed cabin of the *Valdrossos*, bypassing Fort Brust and any other hamlet or town along the way, stopping only long enough to take on water for the *daemon*-fired engine of the locomotive. We passed through landscapes day and night, moving beneath skies of empyrean; stupendously pure, but small and always framed in an ever-moving window. Always moving, always swaying and vibrating as the great mechanized beast of a baggage train hurled itself forward, the sound of it reverberating across the endless fields and forests of Occidentalia. With nothing to do but watch the rocks, then mountains, then trees pass in stately procession, away.

My father, Secundus, Sissy, and I all withdrew into ourselves, as any person is wont to do on long, ceaseless journeys. I don't know if you've ever had the experience, my love, of a confined journey, but it is an exercise in indolence. As the train moves through the world, so too do the passengers begin to explore the landscapes and countries of their own minds in private, internal reveries. Conversations still and die on lips. Books and poetry remain unread. All endeavour becomes still as one is arrested in perpetual forward movement. It's a curious sensation and one I am ill-suited to over long periods.

So it was to my great relief that Father called us to him from our various berths and explained his vision for Ia Terminalia and our audience with Tamberlaine.

'Secundus and Livia, you two will, of course, attend him and bear our presents, as it would be unseemly if I bore them myself. Yet it would be an insult to him if I had a slave or some servant present them to him. Sadly, you'll have to debase yourselves some so that I might save face.'

'What will we give him, Tata?' Carnelia asked.

'I have not yet decided. But,' he paused as my father likes to do when making proclamations, 'You shall be in charge of presents, of course, my dear, as of all of us, you are most suited to such activities.'

This, of course, pleased Carnelia very much as it does every year. She is, among other things, very particular when it comes to presents and she and Father are of the same mind when it comes to the Ruman pastime of snark. While Father is a practitioner, Carnelia is a master.

A few words on Carnelia, love, if I may. I fear she did not impress herself well on you and I can understand why that might be, for she is a creature ruled by desires and a need for attention. Somehow, the assurance and poise of Cornelian blood did not manifest itself in her with any measure of strength. I fear she will always be a cunning woman, prone to outrageous histrionics and half-imagined slights. She is pretty; she is bright. But she is not abundantly pretty or remarkably bright and often unwise. And so she is often snagged by the hidden thorns of her own blooms. I pity her. And love her. And detest how she acts sometimes.

But the news that Father placed her in charge of the Ia Terminalia gifts lifted from her the travel-malaise and made her companionship spritely and gay. Secundus – taking himself far too seriously – scorned it.

Sitting with a wax tablet and stylus, Carnelia made notes.

'To Metellus,' she said, glancing at me, 'We shall send a cask of garum, namely because that is all he deserves and also because the wife he's replaced you with, while immensely wealthy, has a face like a fishwife. '"To Quintus",' she wrote on the tablet, '"A fine fish-pickle for you on Ia Terminalia. It is sour! But you should be accustomed to that!"'

Secundus stood from the cushioned chair he'd been lounging in, making his own notes – most likely for his own coming suit against Metellus – and said, 'These are but frivolities. Give our valued servants and slaves gifts befitting their station, and give our friends and allies gifts to cement bonds of friendship and loyalty. Do not waste time with spite and petty cruelty.' He looked at her crossly. 'This negativity is unbecoming a Cornelian.'

'Are you not, brother,' Carnelia said, raising an eyebrow archly, 'intending to besmirch Metellus in the courts of law?'

'Besmirch him? No,' Secundus said, shaking his head. 'I'm intending to have the man recant his accusations against our sister and restore the Cornelian name. I am removing a taint.'

'I am doing the same work, Secundus,' Carnelia said, smiling at him. 'In my own way.'

'It seems to me that you are only being childish and spiteful. That does nothing to satisfy our honour.'

'Yes, but it does pass the time,' Carnelia said.

He did not respond, but went down cabin to join my father at his cups.

Carnelia, fazed not in the least, went on. 'To Marcus Claudius we shall give sardonyx from the Indus Valley and a crate of oysters.' She smiled at me, for I was looking bemused. 'For him to keep up his . . . strength.' She made a notation on her tablet. 'To Mincus Drusus, the foal of a wild ass, if available. If not, a *small* ass.'

'To what end?'

'His hawing on the senate floor. Word has it he voted to remove Tata from his Governorship after the . . . after what happened to Isabelle.'

Carnelia was quiet for a moment. Of all of us, she was closest to Isabelle. My sister is uncomfortable with her own emotion, like most of those who live on impulse. Life is simply falling into one situation after another amidst a storm of desires. After a short bit of silence, Carnelia went on. Clouds passing across the face of the sun on a summer's day.

'To Sabella Maximus, sweet onions from Covenant – his wife was known for her chastity at school so this might loosen her legs. To Senator Gillesus, some lovely murex shells to set off his eyes!'

'Carnelia! That might be going a little too far,' I said, frowning. 'It's one thing to joke with our friends, our family, and poke fun at our rivals, but Gillesus is one of Father's staunch supporters.'

'He minces a bit, though, doesn't he?'

'Not that gift.'

'Very well,' Carnelia said, scratching at the board. 'A Gallish mirror for Gillesus.'

'You're still doing it, sissy,' I said.

'So I am. I just can't help myself,' she said, and then giggled. 'Our household, then. For Lupina, some nice whiskey – don't think I haven't noticed her knocking back the dregs of our cups! For Rubus, pornographic etchings, either from Aegypt or Accre, to facilitate his epic masturbation sessions. For Cilas, sow's womb stuffed with figs and Lucanian sausages – the man truly is grotesque at the table.'

'Isn't that a little cruel?'

'None of them are bright enough to be offended,' she said, bringing the stylus to her lips. 'Even if they are, the gifts are what they'd want for themselves, anyway.'

'And for Father?'

'I've spoken with Valerus. While he doesn't have the artistic bent of Beleth, he's confident he can create the *logos* of a single legged-bear on a silver phalerae.'

'Ah, that will please Father greatly.'

Carnelia nodded. 'We'll add to that Pannonian birds and pomegranates, some nice Falernian amphorae, garlands of thrushes, mushrooms, and possibly some truffles. I shall visit the Lampurdae Market on our return to Rume.'

'This is good.'

'I have a terribly wonderful idea!' Carnelia whispered, her hands covering her mouth. 'To Tamberlaine, we will give the mount of the *vaettir*.'

'He will be pleased,' I replied. 'Our father, quite the opposite.'

'He is strong, Livia, and will endure it.'

'Let us hope so,' I said, letting some of my fears creep into my voice. 'The alternative isn't one I relish.'

Carnelia put down the tablet and stylus. 'Are you scared?' she asked, in the small voice she would use when we were children and she'd sneak into my bedroom.

'For myself? No,' I said. 'But I worry about my son.' I placed my hand on my stomach, testing for the life contained there. A strange feeling, my love, containing something within myself. In some ways, this must be the polar opposite of what you endured with the *daemon* hand around your neck. One suffused with love and growth, the other with hatred, madness, death. I love you, Hieronymous, for who you are. And what you bore.

'I wish that I could come with you, sissy,' Carnelia said, suddenly welling with tears. 'I don't want to be left behind while you and Secundus leave for Kithai.'

For a moment I thought of the issues that might arrive on a long sea voyage, captive, with Carnelia. But it was very likely that the baby would come while we were away in the far reaches of the known world. I would have more family with me than just Secundus.

'I will speak with Father,' said I, smiling. 'I want you to be with me when the baby comes.'

'We'll need a midwife!' She looked about. 'Do you think Father could part with Lupina?'

'Never. Who knows his drink better than her?' I said. 'And these years gone, I don't know any of the slaves from the family villas. Any suitable ones?'

'After Vaella died from wasting, I stopped learning their names.' Vaella was our childhood nurse, a thick-chested and loving slave from somewhere beyond Aegypt.

'I'll want an accomplished midwife. Preferably not a slave, if we can help it.'

'She'll be expensive. And taking her to Tchinee!'

'Yes. Will you help me find one?'

Carnelia squealed a little in excitement, and clasped my hands. 'Oh, sissy. Do talk to Tata.'

I would wait, though, until a more opportune moment.

*

The *Valdrossos* took on water at Centre Spike, and then made
the last stretch to Novorum without stopping. There was rain,
and the world outside the windows grew clouded and full of
fog; the fields and vast forests became shrouded and mysterious.
The rain, pattering on the window, hypnotized me and I spent
long hours in my seat, staring at the land passing, amazed at the
fertility and wildness of Occidentalia.

But Nova Ruma, if you haven't been there, is different.
It's a city made in the mould of Latinum townships – neat
and orderly; wide streets with a place for everything and
everything in its place. And it had grown since my last visit.
As the train pulled into the station, we passed the fabulous
new amphitheatre on the Anteninium Hills, beyond the Sub-
Urba. The streets, as we passed, teemed with pedestrians and
horsemen, surreys and carriages, wagons and teamsters and
tradesmen – all heedless of the rain, pursuing their industrious
commerce with vigour.

I love the Hardscrabble and its wild fierceness, but
cobblestone streets are appreciated in travel. We disembarked
and were met by one of Tamberlaine's attachés stationed
in Nova Ruma. He was clad in a black suit that was almost
glossy, and he held himself with a great ease, even languor. Yet
something about him broadcast danger. Of course, Carnelia was
immediately smitten.

'Senator,' he said, waiting on the station platform holding a
large umbrella in a big hand. 'I am Marcus Tenebrae and I will
be your escort to the *Malphas*, and further, back to Rume.' He
managed to perform a neat bow while keeping the umbrella
stable. A bow that was the exact right amount of deference to
Father's gravitas (or lack of it, but that is a family matter). And
that is a rare bird in the course of honour, an underling giving
the right amount of deference without obsequiousness. He wore
a longknife – like the ones you and Shoe seem to favour – and

a small pistol on his left hip. Neither interfered with the slim cut of his suit. Perched atop his head was a sheened billycock, dewed with moisture.

'Welcome to Novo Ruma. If you, and your family, will come with me, I will take you to the wharf, where our ship awaits.'

Father, a bit taken aback, balked. 'Not even a single night in Novorum?' he said, using the elided name of Novo Ruma in the east parlance. He'd villaed here early in his governorship. 'I had hoped to visit Ventolo's for a bit of braised beef.' He didn't add anything about Ventolo's famed wine cellars.

'No, I'm afraid not, sir,' Tenebrae said, regretful but firm. 'Captain Juvenus wants to be off on the turning of the tide. I have porters waiting to convey your personal effects, and transport slaves and servants. A party of twenty-five, is it not?'

Father looked somewhat confused. The number of our party was a detail he was not likely to consider. I stepped in. 'Lupina here will organize the household affairs, and Rubus will provide you with a complete accounting of all members of our entourage.' In my experience, the problem with Father – and proconsular imperium in general – is that the constant deference by those of lesser rank eventually denudes the honoured of any ability to deal with straight, unvarnished talk. Which is why, possibly, I have butted heads with Father on occasion. The night I cut off his leg comes to mind. But this Tenebrae was forceful and that force came from the authority of Tamberlaine behind him – which Father knew well.

'Lead on, man, lead on,' Father said, regaining his composure rapidly. 'Don't keep us standing out in the weather all day.'

Tenebrae gave another curt bow and said, 'Of course. Right this way. Step lively.'

He trundled us into a spacious cab, leaving Lupina and Rubus to direct the rest of our entourage. We came to the wharf almost too quickly.

'Everything's happening so fast, sissy!' Carnelia said, glancing at Tenebrae who sat opposite us, at ease, a half-amused expression on his face. Not mocking, not self-absorbed. The best I could describe it would be content. A man absolutely content with himself.

The *Malphas* was a sleek ship, girded and banded with a steel hull. 'She's nearly a frigate, and could level a small town with her guns,' Tenebrae said, as our coach drew down the long wharf and pier. 'Four pivoting Hellfire cannons on deck. And thrice-damned.' The smell of sea and salt filled the air, spiced with brimstone from *daemon*-fired stacks, while seagulls cried and swooped out on the Novorum bay as we exited the carriage and stood standing on the continent's edge looking at the vessel. The wharf, half cloaked in mist, clanged and rang with bells and the raised voices of porters and stevedores, of tradesmen and harbourmasters and customs agents. Wooden cranes lifted cargo onto and from the holds of ships. The sea was wind-whipped and breaking, sending a spray up to dampen our hair. A multitude of boats lined the piers, and hung moored off-shore: skiffs, skipjacks, ferries, sodden coracles, dories, naphtha launches, sloops, frigates, racers, barquentines, Ruman nemi transports and frigates, even shikaras. And of course, the *Malphas*.

'Thrice-damned?' Secundus asked.

'Damned for the *daemon* that turns the screws,' Tenebrae said, the rich timbre of his voice carrying over the wind. 'Twice damned for the devil that cooks the food. Thrice damned for the lascars beneath the blue.'

Father looked at the gloom of the sky, the wind-wracked waves. He sighed. 'Well, that's a damned depressing nursery rhyme.'

And so we boarded the *Malphas*.

*

And here we are, my love, two days at sea. The *Malphas* thrums and shivers. The stateroom I share with Carnelia is large – relatively – and well appointed; full of clever storage cabinets and thoughtful fastenings for the inconstancy of high swells. I can reach out my hand and feel the shudder of the great dynamos of *daemonic* fury, driving screws, pushing us through the water. And the speed! It's hard to tell exactly how fast we travel for lack of markers, but Tenebrae and Juvenus tell me that we're travelling far faster than a horse can gallop.

The sea itself is vast and unforgiving. The shore is but a memory and the thought of stable land impossible. Seagulls screech and dip into our silvered wake. Lascars let out massive tin hooks with flashing metal spoons behind us, dragging in the swells, and yell when they hook some great leviathan and haul it in. We eat fish and drink fine claret and whiskey and Falernian wine, watered only slightly. The skies remain slate grey and the swells are like great valleys where the *Malphas* dashes down one watery mountainside and up the other to hang on the wave's peak and then, like a child's teeter-totter, tip over and race down the next valley. It took days for me to become used to the constant shifting of my weight. Our first passage to Novo Ruma was not this rough in my memory. But we travelled then by sail in a magnificent barquetine.

Secundus, in his daily visits, tells me we were paced by a Medieran vessel of some sort for a while, but they fired one of the Hellfire cannons – under the watchful eye of Valerus and the *Malphas'* engineer, a man by the name of Tricomalee – and the Medieran ship turned tail and ran. I had no awareness of this other than feeling the hollow boom that shuddered the bulkhead. I was holding Carnelia's hair back as she vomited into a porcelain washing-bowl, sea-sick. She's losing quite a bit of weight and I'm worried for her.

Father is drunk. Secundus plots. And I hold my sister's hair.

Our son grows within me.
It is enough.
You are thrice loved. Once loved for your kiss so fair, twice
loved for your son I bear, and thrice loved for the cut we share.

Ever your loving wife —
Livia

TEN

W E WERE SADDLED AND READY for the trail before the sun was up.

'I'm going with you.' The voice came from the stable door.

She was dressed, her face pale and severe, and she held her personal bags in her hands.

'What about the funeral—'

'I've arranged for Wasler to be buried. I can pay my respects and mourn properly later. When our business is settled.'

'Our business?' I asked.

She glanced at me. 'The business of catching this man, Beleth. I will not be left behind.'

Some folks spill their grief. Some folks tamp it away, deep down inside. Some folks are born without knowing how to even express the most common emotions. I don't know where Winfried fell in this, but she had cried, I knew that. She wasn't a person who felt the need to act out her grief publicly to validate it.

Fisk nodded, chucked his head at Buquo. He wasn't without sympathy, Fisk. Especially at the death of a mate. But he would not wait. 'Shoe, help her harness her wagon.'

We made good time for five days without much talk, camping in piney breaks and gulleys with no sign of stretchers, not that they leave much sign to begin with. We rode through the forested skirts of Brujateton, descended some, into the thickly wooded foothills to pick up game and follow the Big Rill, which flowed below us on the shoal plains, upstream. The river was narrow now, not quite in a canyon, but the banks were twenty feet at least above the surface of the river. We could hear the roar of the Terminus Falls miles before we reached them and began to climb upwards again.

It took a day to rise above the falls, to take the trail there to Passasuego. The Terminus Falls dumped water from a great height in thunderous amounts, half of which seemed to sublime into the air as it fell, wreathing the moss-slick rock face leading to the escarpment above in water vapour and mist. A switchback trail that had been hewn into the living rock centuries before by my *Dvergar* brethren, before the Rumans had come, led the way. When I was a lad, it was said that there were hidden, in the White Mountains, a lost tribe of *dvergar* warriors, called the *Illivatch Seva*. *Dvergar* children loved stories of this heroic race, these *Illivatch*, taming the mountain wyrms and riding massive bears instead of horses and fighting with the *vaettir*, their mortal enemies. The *Illivatch* were masters of rock, and stone, and the metal sap of the earth, and could forge anything. Their weapons, according to storytellers, were wrought of a mythical metal called *brillignatha,* what we today know as steel, and the weapons had their own personalities and wilful minds, and often sang and argued with their wielders. Once, in a losing battle with *vaettir*, the legendary hero *Dveng* – from whom my mother took my name – raised his greathammer *Vringbretha* to do battle with the stretcher host, but the hammer told him not to smite the leaping *vaettir,* but the earth itself, from which, seemingly, *vaettir* and *dvergar* sprang. And so *Dveng* smote the earth. From that mighty blow rose the White – or *Illivatch* – Mountains.

But no one has been able to find their smelts or dwellings. And so the *Illivatch* retreat into legend.

Once on the escarpment, we camped and I spent the rest of daylight spearing the fat, brown speckled trout that teemed in the waters here, beyond the falls. That night, I fried them up nice with some onions and spuds. We bunked down, Fisk and I, by the fire, Winfried close-by beneath her jaunting-hearse.

Later, after an hour or more of silence I heard a stirring and smelled tabac. Fisk, restless.

Then Winifred's voice, soft. 'Might I join you?' she asked.

Nothing from Fisk, though I imagine he nodded. Fisk's many things and generous with words isn't one of them.

'Smoke?'

'Thank you, Mr Fisk,' she replied. There was a long time of silence then and I fell back asleep for a while, like a fish diving and then returning to a stream's surface. When I came back up, I could hear the fire crackling again.

'You'll be fine,' Fisk was saying. 'Hurts now, like the world's full of pain and loss. If you're anything like I think you are, it won't overcome you.'

'You have lost someone—' I could hear the grief in her voice, but I'd wager a silver pig that she was dry-eyed.

'Wife. Daughter,' he said, and fell silent once more.

'I'm sorry.'

'It was a long time ago.'

'I'm still sorry.'

'My thanks.'

'This man you seek?'

'Name's Beleth. A real piece of work.'

'He is the man responsible for Wasler's death, then?'

Fisk was quiet for a long while. 'Yes. Stuffed a *daemon* into the boy. Left him here to ambush us.'

'A part of me wants to blame you,' she said.

'A part of me is to blame,' he said. 'And a part of the blame is yours. Beleth wants us dead, and you got in the way. But we never asked you to ride with us.'

'Yes,' she said, slowly. 'But I *will* ride with you. Until we find this man.'

'To kill him?'

'I don't know,' she said. Her voice sounded puzzled then. 'I want to see him. To try to understand how someone could do that...'

'You look at him, all you'll see is a sober little fella, looks like a book-keeper. You'll gain no understanding there.'

'I need to see him, then. Only then will I be able—'

'Bullshit,' Fisk said. 'What's knocking around inside of you is vengeance. You've been hurt. You've had something taken away from you. You want to even the scales,' he said. The words were harsh, but his tone wasn't. It was as if he was trying to get her to understand what was going on in the currents of her own heart.

'Revenge, then.'

'That I can't give you. My orders are to return him to Ruman custody,' he said. He neglected to tell her about returning his head, if capture wasn't possible. Fisk was a hard man, but maybe he was trying to spare the woman something.

'I would look upon him.'

'As would I. In chains.'

A rustle then, and a whiff of tabac. Fisk stood, or Winfried. Hard to tell.

Winfried's voice came from further away. 'I will retire, now. And—' She paused as if wanting to say more. 'Thank you, Mr Fisk.'

'Don't mention it,' he said. 'If you try to get your revenge on him, before I can get him back into custody,' Fisk said, voice flat now. Hard. 'I'll have to stop you.'

She said nothing.

In the morning, we moved on after chicory and coffee and by afternoon we reached the division point of the Big Rill and the White River. It was a churning, torrid affair where the two rivers split on either side of what we always called the Sundering Rock, in tremendous sprays of foam and lashing water, the White River racing east to descend in a dramatic series of waterfalls into the

Great Chasm that passed near Broken Tooth and Breentown and flowed outward then to the Mammon and eventually to spill into the Gulf of Mageras by way of Covenant; and the Big Rill, flowing out from the escarpment to descend from the Terminus Falls down to the shoal plains to be swelled from the springs and creeks coming from the Whites and eventually make its way to the same Gulf by way of Harbour Town. From what I understand, this is one of the few places in the world where rivers do not obey the natural order of things: Water does not split, it comes together, like fire calls to fire. Yet here, the White River divides into two.

It took almost two days to get beyond the division point because we rode the south side of the White River, away from the Great Western Road that ran from Passasuego all the way to Fort Brust. Like the arrival in Hot Springs, we were staying away from the more populated approaches. The land here was rough and no mythical *Illivatch* trails led the way – the only roads were on the north side of the river. At some points we led the horses through piney-woods and gambel thickets choked with bramblewrack. Other times we had to dismount and help push the jaunting-hearse up and over some obstruction – rocks, deadfall, narrow gulches – and only once did we require ropes and Bess' assistance. At night, we spent more than the usual amount of time brushing out the burrs and checking the hooves of our mounts. Bess couldn't have cared less.

The next day we passed broke-dick derelict tenement camps in travertine quarries, long ago deserted when the Talavera Silverlode was struck and seamed. Passasuego, one of the oldest Medieran settlements in Occidentalia (in addition to Chiba, Harbour Town, and Encantata) grew fat and prosperous on travertine and silver, and with each moment, we drew nearer the town.

Passasuego had always put on airs. Built with the pink travertine that had been mined nearby, the town had the soft, lush hues of a conch pulled from some southern sea, rotting in its luminous shell. Built by Medierans, and guarded by Medieran Castillejo cavalry until the last twenty years – when the Rumans had pushed them out and taken over silver mining rights and profits – Passasuego was the home of the sole remaining Medieran Embassy west of the Dvergar Mountains.

I didn't like the town. It was large enough, but small of spirit, a petty town, trying to be more than it was. Many of the citizens were of Medieran descent and proud of their blood – and outraged by the Ruman control of what they felt was theirs by right. There was an air of barely concealed contempt and possibly rebellion in the pastel streets. I think the only reason the Rumans allowed the Medieran Embassy (once the 'governor's' house) to still exist was the fear of uprising. Uprising itself would be dealt with at the point of a sword, a spear, and the stink of Hellfire, but the silver mines would slow and possibly stop production. And Rumans would not countenance that.

The town's population was in support of the silver industry; the smelts and forges, the arrastras where the silver ore was crushed, and the slag haulers and tenders, the engineer college and workshops, the engineer's munition factory, and the itinerant *pistoleros* and the Ruman cohort that guarded it all. Silver was precious. Silver was life. Silver was poison.

This country is big, and for the most part, pristine. Passasuego sat like a canker on the prick of the west, pink and oozing infection.

We came up over a rise and in view of Passasuego nine days after leaving Hot Springs. The walls shone roseate in the light, but the slag heaps in the fields on our side of the river stood tall and obsidian, some still smoking. We waited until evening and the light was beginning to fail.

'No point in trying to disguise ourselves,' I said. 'Because I'm the sore thumb.'

Fisk raised his eyebrow, looking at me.

'I imagine the description goes something like this. "A hard-bit man, grey-weathered, and his dwarf".'

Fisk said nothing but nodded, slowly.

'I'll circle around and come in on the East Gate, alone. You remember the Icehouse Hotel?'

'Yes. The surveying escort contract.'

'I'll meet you there,' I said and then took Winifred's reins and looked up to where she sat perched on top of the jaunting-hearse. 'You'll need to ride Bess in,' I said.

'What? Why?'

'You might not look remarkable,' I said. 'But your baggage does. And anyone watching will mark you, a woman, and the fancy wagon you drag along behind.'

She blinked and then dismounted. We switched mounts, but not before I draped and tied off an old canvas tarp around the jaunting-hearse.

'Best I can do on short notice, I figure. Gimme your hat, Miss Lomax,' I said.

She hesitantly handed the brown bowler over and I gave her mine. 'I'll want that back.'

'This seems extraordinarily silly, Mr Illys.'

Fisk said, 'Folks look at hats more than you think. It's a shape thing, if you understand. A profile.'

She set her jaw but nodded her acceptance.

They took the *Drenellos* Bridge over the White River – constructed of more pink travertine – and I waited until full dark and then followed.

At night Passasuego smelled like barbecoa and exotic spices. Whatever Passasuego's flaws, it had good travertine paved roads and excellent Medieran food and fresh water drawn by aqueduct down from the headwaters of the White. When I came through the East Gate near the sledge-rails, a legionnaire questioned me and I provided the man with my papers and he waved me through without even the intimation of a bribe, for which I was grateful. He must've been new.

I stopped to buy a meat-filled torta from a street vendor on the *Plaza de Rhiboza* and as I stood there in the shadow of the statue of Capitan Alonz Rhiboza, the first Medieran who encountered the *vaettir* with any semblance of victory (he survived) the torta vendor, a *dvergar* half-breed like myself, said, 'Brother, you have come a far piece, judging by the looks of you.' He said this in the common tongue, heavily accented with Medieran. I could not understand why he didn't use the *dvergar* tongue.

'Yep. Long ways. All the way from Fort Verrier on the edge of the Big Empty.' I lied easily. It's a problem I have, but not one that keeps me awake at night.

He shook his head. 'We all do the Ruman work, eh?'

'Seems so,' I replied, and then took a large bite of the hot meat-filled torta.

As I ate, the vendor seemed to gain courage or realize my mouth was currently indisposed. 'People like you and me, we've had *their* boots on our backs all our lives, no? Would that I could do something about that.' The way he said 'their' was a hint and a half he was getting to something. I figured the best way to draw him out was silence. And the torta was good. When I said nothing, he continued. 'And some men intend to.'

I swallowed, then said, 'Intend to do something?'

'Yes!'

'And who might that be? You?'

He laughed, nervously. 'Me? I am just a street vendor! But I will do my part. We all have a part to play,' he said. His eyes narrowed. 'Neruda will speak. At the Plaza del Monstruo he will speak! At sundown, two days hence!' His expression became ecstatic, almost as if going into some numinous or old-goddriven madness or glossolalia.

'The Plaza del Monstruo, is that right?'

'Yes!'

'I don't know if my errand here in Passasuego will be complete by then, but I will try to make it,' said I.

'You haven't heard of Neruda? He is the greatest philosopher of this age! Not afraid to spit in the eye of the Ruman legions and the corrupt old governor Cornelius!'

I nodded then, frowning. I didn't care much for Cornelius myself, but it was surprising to hear his name on the tongue of this bilious torta vendor.

I left him there, drawing the covered jaunting-hearse after me.

Passasuego is divided into three loose districts. Because the town sits on a slope of the White Mountains, it obeys the rule that shit rolls downhill. In the higher neighbourhoods, or Rosa Distrito, you have the luxury markets, the counting houses, haberdashers and dressmakers, bathhouses and gymnasia, the Adolpho Theatre bracketed by two of the nicer hotels, the Pynchon and the Manteras, along with the homes of the wealthier tradesmen, slave mongers, and captains of industry – most of these buildings and domiciles in the Cantabrian style, full of airy arches, painted shuttered windows, with ochre-hued clay tiles on the roofs and pink stonework, the finest example of this being the Medieran Embassy.

Go downhill a piece, and there you'll find the Centro Distrito, where the working class lives, crowded with smaller homes done in Cantabrian style but on a smaller scale. The neighbourhoods teem with bodegas and parks and miniature plazas so that at any moment, walking the streets there, you might find yourself in a shaded, tree-covered space, cool and quiet, dedicated to some Ruman-hating Medieran nobleman or hero. The neighbourhood schools ring with bells and the peals of children's laughter, the markets are full of brightly woven fabrics and fragrant meats and spices. Vigiles walk the streets warily, always ready for a well-aimed piece of horse-dung flung by a *pilluelo*. There is an artisan's district, where the College of Engineers keep a great behemoth of a building near the south wall and sculptors work to create elegant shapes from the pink marble, and stonemasons cut the travertine blocks for building and export, placing the stone on the rail-sledges that run with the White River down from the heights to where the land levels some and merchants continue porting them on the Great West Road overland to the Mammon River.

In the lowest section, commonly referred to as The Slough or, more affectionately, as Shitsville, lie the tenement houses and tanneries, the abattoirs, the foundries and smelts and slag-wagon fleets, the whores and sweetboys and dealers in stolen goods. The dross of society ends up here.

The Icehouse Hotel was, thank Ia, in the Centro Distrito near the North Gate. I stabled the jaunting-hearse – tipped the stable boy a few sesterius to keep an eye on it until I could return – and went to find Fisk and Winfried. I found them sitting in the corner of the bar.

Winfried sat staring at the wall – more pink travertine.

'I absolutely despise that colour,' she said.

'Better get used to it. It's everywhere.'

'It's like they *want* this town to look like a lady's handkerchief or a baby's toy.'

'Not much they can do about it. It's the colour of the stone around here.' It was good to see her lively about something. She'd been very silent on the journey.

Fisk ordered a whiskey and after a moment, Winfried followed suit.

'So, will you schedule some portraits for tomorrow?' I asked her. She grimaced as she drank the whiskey.

The Icehouse got its name from the blocks of ice stored beneath it. Great hunks of the frozen stuff were cut from high mountain lakes and brought down on sledges and wagons drawn by teams of massive draft horses. I ordered a whiskey with an ice back, and I soothed the burn of the alcohol by dropping chunks of it into my glass and swirling it about.

'No,' she said, her eyes crinkling at the edges as she thought about it. 'Right now I don't think . . .' She stopped, drank some more, glancing at Fisk. 'I am not in a calm enough state to spend all day taking portraits.'

Fisk said, 'Beleth. Ideas?'

I glanced at Winfried and then back to Fisk, curious. He must've spilled the information we received from Andrae.

'One of us should visit the College of Engineers,' I said. 'I don't think Beleth would be able to stay away, honestly. Even if it was for a bit of petty larceny or to recruit some junior engineer to his task. I imagine there are summonings that require more than just a single person.'

'And,' Fisk added, 'Beleth thinks quite highly of himself. A man of his stature requires an assistant.'

'What will you do?' I said.

'I'm going to spend a bit of money,' he said. 'Can't just go barging into the Pynchon, or the Medieran Embassy, half-cocked. Doubtless Beleth will have more *daemon*-possessed watchers about.'

'What about me?' Winfried asked. 'He doesn't know who I am. And it's doubtful the boy that killed—' She stopped. Took a sip of whiskey. 'That killed Wasler would have had time to report back to him.'

'She's right, Fisk,' I said. 'She could work as our agent, enter the Pynchon without tipping our hand.'

Fisk nodded, though his face was pained. To use her desire for revenge as bait rankled him, surely. He would not *want* to put her more at risk. But he would, anyway.

Because Beleth was near.

'Your machine.'

'What's that?'

'The Infernograph. We can use that as our ticket in.'

'He is an engineer.' She smiled. I could tell the whiskey had begun to affect her. She dug around in her coat and withdrew a wrinkled and stained card. It read:

Wasler & Winfried Lomax

In Pursuit of Anthropological Information Regarding
The Denizens of Occidentalia, including the Imperial Protectorate,
Dvergar, The Big Empty, and the Hardscrabble Territories

Are taking Portraits with their

INFERNOGRAPH

On the day(s) of _____ from the _____ hour   To the _____ hour.
LOCATION: _____

Subjects will receive a copy of the infernograph
Contact the Lomaxes to make an appointment

I looked at the card and handed it to Fisk. He scanned it, gave it back.

'He won't be able to stop himself,' Fisk said. 'He'll come like a pig called sooie to a trough.'

'We can get a suite, possibly, if you think your purse can afford it. You can listen in an adjoining room, if necessary, when he comes in...'

'We nab him,' I said.

'I think it's a workable plan,' she said, smiling.

It did sound good, but one thing bothered me. 'What if he's not alone?'

'There are two of you.'

'But there's no telling if they'll be human or have devils at the reins,' I said, tapping my temple. 'And there's only one of Winfried.'

Fisk sucked his teeth. 'All this is just talk. Beleth might've already ducked out of town.'

'We need to find him first, then,' Winfried said. 'And I am *still* the best person for that task, unless you have disguises prepared?'

'She's right, Fisk,' I said, picking up a piece of ice, popping it in my mouth and crunching it. 'We definitely can't be barging in there without some sort of assurance he's here.'

Fisk thought for a long while. Then looked at Winfried with narrowed eyes. 'All right. Why don't you check in at the Pynchon.' He placed a handful of coins on the table and pushed them to her. 'Don't put out the calling card just yet. Let's see if Beleth is bold enough to be toddling about with his face bare,' he said. 'Use some of that money to tip the servants and barkeeps. He'll be going under the name Unchleigh.'

'Unchleigh? That's bizarre.'

'It's the name of one of his favourite devils.'

She frowned.

ELEVEN

7 Kalends, Quintilius, 2638 ex Ruma Immortalis

E ARLY THE NEXT MORNING, Winfried took a room at the
Pynchon – with the understanding she'd send us a note if
she discovered anything.

After she left, Fisk and I discussed our situation in the room.

'I'll make a visit to the College of Engineers,' I said. 'Cornelius'
sheaf of orders should be good for entry. I can talk to the head
poohbah there.'

'Poohbah?'

'Don't know what they call themselves. They're pretty closed
about what and who goes on in there.'

He flashed me his legatus eagle. 'I'll chat up the vigiles.'

I took the Ava Obergón through the Centro Distrito, passing
through residential neighbourhoods and markets, gambel-shaded
plazas and open, cool, paved thoroughfares. Looking to the east,
out over the smoking, jumbled mess of Shitsville and the smelts,
beyond the eastern wall where the White River continued its journey down the mountain, rill after white-frothed rill; the clouds
hung low and dark in the sky, on the same level where I stood,
and in the muted light of the half-obscured sun, everything stood
out in sharp relief. Turning, I saw a shadow dart aside, into some
alleyway or passage.

Followed.

I continued on. My legs are short. I would never be able to outpace whoever was following.

Turning west, heading up-mountain, I found myself on the Calle Llázaron, amidst the hubbub and bustle of tradesmen and shop-keepers and workers making their way to whatever employment filled their days, until I reached the Distrito Artisan and passed the travertine workshops, dusty and rimed in pink, the saddlers and wheelwrights and carpenters' open workshops, the seamstresses and engravers and potters, until I came to the College of Engineers.

It was a tremendous building, built in the Ruman style, flat and unadorned with the exception of a motto above the great brass-doored entrance – *machinor collegium inferi*. Entering, with only one glance back to see if I could spot my tail, I found myself in a massive rotunda, with towering ceilings supported by awe-inspiring columns, covered with chiselled intaglios and skeins of warding. Sound echoed hollowly with each step on the polished marble floor, and looking down, I saw the faint tracery of blackened silver threading its way through the stone. I stood upon an absolutely massive *pellum* ward. It was reassuring, that. No *daemon*-possessed body could enter here. One less thing that I had to worry about.

'Can I help you, sir?' said a voice off to my left.

It was a very small stone desk near the base of one of the travertine columns. A man sat at the desk dressed in a simple white tunic, with shorn hair and a neat, pleasant manner.

I walked over. 'Maybe. I need to speak to the person in charge,' I said.

I have to hand it to the man. He didn't smirk or look outraged. Engineers are little lords among us regular folk, and engineer or Ruman, they all hold themselves higher than a simple native Occidentalian as myself. My blood does me no favors.

'Praefect Saepientia doesn't see walk-in visitors, I'm afraid.' He ruffled some paper and lifted a pen. 'I have an opening in her schedule on the third hour, two days from now. Will that suit?'

'I'm sorry, I need to see her today,' I said. To preclude any officious nonsense and protestations of busyness, I opened the stamped orders that Cornelius had provided me and handed them over.

The receptionist looked at the seal, untied the missive, and began to read. 'I Gaius Cornelius, Governor of ...' His eyes scanned forward in the document, reading quickly. 'It seems—' He checked the document. 'Mr Dveng Ilys, I am to render unto you all possible aid and support – including resources both monetary and military – in the pursuit of your task. Can you prove you're the aforementioned Dveng Ilys?'

'I believe it describes me in one of the later clauses, Mister—'

'Drassus,' he said, negligently, flipping through the sheaf of orders. "A short, half-breed of a man – part native *dvergar* of the tinker stripe – brown of eye and hair, ill-kempt, yet possessed of a spirit of intelligence far beyond the normal intellect apparent in most of his indigenous race. Answers to the nickname Shoestring." He frowned. 'That is a bit unkind.'

'Maybe to other dwarves, sir.'

'And to you.' He looked me up and down. 'You *are* a bit unkempt, though I imagine you spend more nights under the stars than a roof.'

'Keen of eye, sir.'

'Well, it all seems to be in order here.' He rang a bell and very quickly two women dressed in tunics and carrying carbine rifles trotted into the rotunda with a military air.

Drassus wrote a note, folded it, and handed it to one of the women. He said, 'Please take Mr Ilys to Praefect Sapientia's waiting room.' He glanced at me. 'Good day, Mr Ilys. I hope the Praefect can assist you in your task.'

The women escorted me quickly out of the atrium and through a maze of corridors, finally placing me in a drab room ringed in stone benches. One of them entered an inner door, presumably to deliver the note to the Praefect. I sat down, looking about. The walls were heavily warded, though luxuriously appointed with oversized *daemonlights*. There was an ornate carpet on the floor, and one of the curious steam-driven fans rotating on the ceiling. Two small slatted windows were cut into the travertine walls, giving a narrow view of the eastern view of Passaseugo. Once again I noticed the blackened silver of a *pellum* ward in a circle on the floor. The amount of silver in this building must have been staggering.

I waited for what must've been two hours before a burly woman entered the waiting room carrying a wicker basket and said, 'Praefect Sapientia will see you now. Please place all of your weapons in this.'

I dumped my Hellfire revolvers in the basket, followed by a few knives.

'You want my sling?' I asked the woman.

She shrugged and led me into the office. It was a homey affair; more rugs, some ancestral statues, a shelf full of arcane looking books, a scarred and scorched worktable replete with urns and engraving tools, a banked torch, a swivel-mounted ground glass ocular, various knives and cutting utensils. Enamelled wooden frescoes adorned the walls.

'What can I do for you Mr Ilys?' she asked in a rich voice.

'I need some information, ma'am.'

She looked at the woman standing near the door. 'Drusilla, please shoot Mr Ilys the next time he refers to me as "ma'am".'

'Yes ma'am,' she replied.

Sapientia rolled her eyes, then, turning back to me, smiled.

'What sort of information?'

'I'm looking for a man named Gaius Linneus Beleth. He's wanted by the Governor—'

Her smile failed and she frowned.

'You know him?'

126

'Everyone knows Beleth.'

'Sounds like there's some history there.'

She looked at me closely, narrowing her eyes. 'Much of the collegium's current organization and prominence is due to Beleth's influence. He was *princep* in the college until very recently, when the governor Cornelius became his patron.'

'What are the perks to being the *princep* of the college?'

'There's a salary – though it's not lavish. Research is rewarded by patents on processes so that if you can develop a new way to bind inferi into munitions, you will receive a portion of the monies made from that.'

'Did Beleth work on munitions?'

'Early in his career, as we all do. Binding Imps into Hellfire rounds, the larger arch-*daemons* into turbines.' She pursed her lips.

'You didn't like him.' I didn't state it as a question.

'No. He was a shoddy engineer. Talented, yes. But the mechanics of what we do – the actual working parts of gears and weight distribution, heat dissipation, stress tolerances, all of which is so very *important*, he found tiresome. He focused his energies on what he could control.'

'People.'

'Yes. A born politician. Which explains why a poor engineer could rise to *princeps*, I suppose.'

'Why would he leave?'

'Money? Influence? Prominence? Pick one.'

'I have met the man.'

'Then you know.'

I nodded.

For a while I sat thinking.

'So, he wasn't good with the physical side of things,' I said. 'What was he good at?'

'Bindings. Investing *daemons* into physical objects. It's a little understood aspect of summoning because of the mischievous and mercurial nature of *daemons*. In general, engineers want to use the inferi simply as a power source. But Beleth wanted more.'

'More? Like what?'

'He had a scheme to create soldiers.'

Maybe she saw the alarm on my face. She raised her hands in a soothing gesture. 'We never let him get that far. He might have been *princep* but he answered to the collegium.'

That didn't put me entirely at ease. I recalled the boy in Hot Springs, grinning in the dark. *Beleth sends his regards.*

Sapientia noticed my shudder.

'You are not telling me something, Mr Ilys,' she said.

'No, ma'am, I'm not.'

She placed her hands on her desk, palm-down. 'What aren't you telling me?'

'I was ordered to keep this hushed,' I said. I glanced at the guard standing by the door. 'But I can't see any way around getting my job done without letting go some of Cornelius' secrets.'

'Do tell.'

'Beleth, in addition to some murders and a case of arson, has turned traitor and gone into cahoots with the Medierans.'

Sapientia whistled. 'I can see why Cornelius wanted this hushed up. That's a major blow.' Her face grew worried. 'He'll tell all of the collegium's secrets!'

'And Rume's military strategy.'

'They are the same thing, essentially,' she said. 'As you know, very little *pure* research goes on here and it's mostly munitions production and process refinement.'

'War footing, now that Mediera and Tchinee are sword rattling?'

'That's about the size of it.'

'So,' I said slowly, thinking about all she'd revealed. 'Our intelligence tells us that he might be here in Passaseugo. I take it Beleth hasn't contacted you?'

'Not me,' she said, tugging at her bottom lip. 'Nor anyone else in the collegium that I know of. But there are many guilded engineers here and I don't keep tabs on all of them.'

'Anyone gone missing lately? Or left?'

'No, but I'll have to have my secretary check the roster for sure.'

'Please do so. You can have them send any information to me at the Icehouse.'

'I will also alert the members of this college of Beleth's treachery and find out if he's approached any of them.'

'I'd appreciate it if you didn't. We don't want this getting out.'

'Mr Ilys, there is no organization more secretive than the College of Engineers. We are where secrets *begin*.'

I thought about that for a little while.

'You know the names of any *daemons* Beleth might've summoned?'

She raised an eyebrow.

'He's been going by the names Unchleigh and Labadon, which turns out were also *daemons*. We're thinking he likes to consider himself clever. If we can find some other names of *daemons* he's bound—'

'You might get a line on him. Yes, I understand.' She thought for a moment. 'I heard about him getting a contract to bind a *daemon* in a steamship—'

'That would be the devil Labadon.'

'Ah. Other than that, I have no information. But when I'm querying the collegium members about the other matters, I will investigate this, as well.'

'All right,' I said, standing up. Sapientia rose with me. 'Thank you for your time, ma'am.'

'A pleasure,' she said, smiling. 'And I won't even have Drusilla here shoot you,' she laughed.

We shook hands, Drusilla presented me with my weapons and I secured them about my body. Sapientia was kind enough to walk me to the rotunda atrium. We were standing on the massive *pellum* ward when a thought occurred to me.

'Why doesn't this ward dispel Hellfire Imps?' I asked. 'Shouldn't my ammo be duds now?'

'You are a perceptive man, Mr Ilys.' She looked at me closely. 'But mistaken. Each round is protected and whole so that its warding is inviolate even if within another ward.' She thought for a moment. 'These *pellum* wards are strictly for *daemons* who find corporeal vestments. More, I cannot say.'

I nodded. Engineers will discuss theory, but dig too far and they will begin speaking in generalities. I thanked her for her time.

'Do please let me know what you find out. I will render any assistance I can,' she said.

'Well, we're working on something,' I replied. 'Something that might draw him out.'

'What might that be?'

I told her about the infernograph, and as I did, her expression brightened. 'Extraordinary! That's a device I'd like to examine!'

'We can probably arrange that.'

'It is something that would, most assuredly, be of interest to Beleth. I think the idea has merit.'

'I was afraid you'd say that.'

'Afraid?'

'Most traps need bait.'

'Ah, I understand your reticence.' She took my hand in hers. It was warm and strong. 'It has been a pleasure, Mr Ilys. Do stay in touch,' she said, giving a rather impish smile and then turning to walk back into the interior of the building.

The sun was high in the sky when I stumbled into the bright air of the mountain side and Distrito Artisan. I realized I hadn't eaten in hours so I stopped at a small open-air restaurant near the Plaza Cordova and had some coffee and some buttered corncakes and sausage. The name of the place reminded me of a girl, then, the girl that started all this. The White Rose of Cordova, Isabella, who died at the hands of stretchers. The food was good but a strange mood settled on me and I felt as though I was being watched. There was no one at the cafe except for a fresh-faced young matron in an expensive-looking dress with her nose in this week's copy of *The Passasuego Gazetá*. The headline read 'Talavera Silverload to See Arrival of Mechanized Drill.' Engrossed in the story, she paid no apparent attention to me. I paid my bill and wandered back down the Calle Llázaron toward the northern side of Passasuego. There was no sign of the tail and since he or she already knew where I went, it was reasonable to assume they knew where I came from. Stopping in the Icehouse's stables, I checked on Bess, and Fisk's black, and waited for a while, tossing the stablehand a couple of coins to keep him quiet as I climbed into the hay-loft to settle down with a view of the open door.

The stable boy piddled about below – feeding horses, shovelling shit – and no other soul entered, no shadow crossed the threshold. After an hour, I clambered down the loft's ladder and toddled back into the hotel proper and our room. There was a note on the floor by the door. It read: *Checked into the Pynchon. Tipping heavily. No one knows of U. Will continue making inquiries. – WL.* I left the note on Fisk's bed.

With the afternoon growing long, I set myself up in an out of the way corner of the bar and occupied my mouth with a glass of cacique.

Fisk strolled in a little while later, spotted me, and sat down.

'A man's gone missing. His name is Buster Brell,' he said. 'Family man, three or four kids. Good fellow, apparently. Big guy, worked as muscle for one of the wealthier tradesmen in town. He stopped coming home, the family reported him missing to the vigiles.'

'Big guy, then?'

'A bruiser. Hiramis – the chief of vigiles – said that Buster's kid came by the other morning and reported seeing him. Called out to him. Buster didn't respond. The boy said that he "looked funny".'

'That doesn't sound good.'

'No, it doesn't.'

I filled in Fisk on what I learned from Sapientia about Beleth's history, his penchant for *daemonic* investment.

'Figures,' Fisk said, frowning either with the memory of the Crimson Man who rode him so hard, or Beleth himself. 'Seems like he leaves a world of shit behind him wherever he goes.'

'Seems so,' I said. I thought about it for a while and said, 'I might've been followed.'

'Followed?'

I told him about the shadow and the sense of being watched at the cafe.

'You ever had a feeling like this go wrong?'

It's true that *dvergar* have some senses keener than most humans – we can see well in the dark, we have a great affinity for stone and mountains and finding paths, we take to crafting things with our hands. Once I had to find a dead man in a bear cave and felt something then I thought was *vaettir* coming for me in the night as I stood taintless, without weapon, in the mouth of a cave. I was wrong then. But, on the other hand, it could've just been the damned stretchers *fucking* with me.

'Maybe.'

'I told Winfried I would look into getting her a piece.' He said this rather sheepishly.

'What was that about me picking up strays?'

'Ia-dammit, Shoe, her husband died.'

'Yes. And now you're going to arm her and get her close to the man she wants to kill.'

'Beleth's stuffing *daemons* inside people now. And they're damned deadly. She has to be able to protect herself.'

'That's true. But she's bloodthirsty. She can keep it tamped down – *hell,* we all keep it tamped down – but she's like to do something stupid.'

'I'll watch her.'

'You'll have to.'

Fisk grew quiet, raised a hand to beckon a waiter over. The bar had only a few patrons; the card sharps and hustlers who usually ensconced themselves at the tables as the night grew old, the whores and sweetboys that worked the crowd, none had made their appearance yet.

'We'll go ahead with Winfried's plan.'

'You've got your legate pin. Andrae said that Beleth had been seen with the ambassador's son. We could go get twenty legionnaires and just raid the embassy. Go in, swords and guns out. Surprise him.'

'And if he's not there, then what?' Fisk said, scowling. 'Tell Ambassador Quintana, 'Sorry, mister, just looking for a traitor to Rume and we suspected you might be harbouring him'?'

'Ah.'

'"Ah" is right. We go ahead with Winfried's plan.'

I drank my cacique, called the waiter back over and asked him if he could fetch a small piece of parchment from the main desk and a writing utensil. He returned with a writing tray with pen, inkwell, blotter, and a single piece of paper. I jotted a note to Winfried – three little words *Proceed with plan* and took it to the main desk and asked to have a boy run it to the Pynchon.

We arrived at the Pynchon the next morning at the first hour and inquired after Winfried at the front desk. The fussy man with an inkstroke-thin moustache looked at our clothes – his upper lip curling into an oily sneer – and asked our business with her. His stare lingered on me for a while. When you're *dvergar* amongst wealth and not serving, toting, or building, you get some looks.

You get used to it but it never gets easier. Thing about being half-*dvergar* is that wherever you go, surrounded by human and *dvergar* alike, you're always on the outside looking in.

Fisk placed both of his large hands on the desk and very quietly said, 'Our business is our own, mister,' and I thought he was going to threaten the integrity of the man's skin in some way but when he drew back his hand, there was a coin laying on the wood where one of his hands once had been. The fussy man smiled then and was far more accommodating. He nodded his head at the far end of the desk. A small card stood on a stand at the end of the expanse of desk indicating that the Lomaxes would be taking appointments for infernographs throughout the day in suite 215.

'You can see there her suite number,' he said. 'Would you like me to have a porter announce your arrival?'

'No sir,' I said.

'We're just a bit of muscle to make sure everything goes smoothly,' Fisk added and tipped the brim of his hat.

The lobby of the Pynchon hotel was a study in degrees of red. From the polished pink travertine floor to the rose drapes, from the carmine carpeting to the burnished amber of wood. It was as if we had stepped inside a titan's asshole and found it well appointed. Expensively accoutred guests in fine suits and custom dresses took coffee and tea in the restaurant, smoked Medieran tabac and chatted in the lobby. Some, even at this early hour, drank claret from crystal glasses and cold beer drawn in tankards from a cold room.

'Cornelius would fit in just fine, here,' I said out of the corner of my mouth.

Fisk didn't respond. He walked past the concierge and receptionist's desks and took the stairs. Some heads turned to watch us, many of them with blank expressions. If Beleth had set a watcher here, we would know it soon.

Winfried answered our knock, quickly. I had grown accustomed to seeing her in a more rough and tumble garb on the trail – her dusty suit and britches, the bowler hat – so seeing her now in a more professional outfit was slightly alarming. She was dressed in an exquisitely cut suit, black, and had pulled back her hair in a way that made her face seem much more severe and delicate. She was an attractive woman physically and in some ways, her habit of dressing like a man – which I have heard is an affectation of those Malfenian women who have endured the sterilization process – did nothing to allay the fact that she was well-formed, and might even have exaggerated it by contrast. If she could survive her time in the Hardscrabble Territories and this lust for revenge, she would have her pick of willing men and women suitors and would find any suit she might make welcome.

'Why are you staring so, Mr Ilys?'

'You look different,' I said.

'Is there something wrong with how I look?'

'No, ma'am.'

She appeared as if she was going to smile.

'If I need to be aware of some flaw in my appearance—'

'Nope. You're just all *fancy*,' I said, waving my hand at her get-up. I looked around. Whistled. 'This place is cush.'

Indeed, the suite she'd taken was quite opulent. We were in the parlour, where thick, ornately woven Parsuan rugs centred the room, and the walls were lined with expensive teak and mahogany furniture – a burnished credenza, a dry bar with an army of leaded cut-glass tumblers and three decanters of various liquor, a ceramic bowl of crushed ice, a platter of pomegranates and blood-oranges, two massive sprays of fragrant apple blossom branches, a red-velvet couch with arms ending in artfully carved oliphant heads, paintings of whimsical monkeys dressed in formal wear with oculars, tinted glass *daemonlights*, an ornate ablution-bowl and three lavishly framed mirrors. In addition to all of this, there was the blood bowl and a gleaming steel knife along with a good amount of folded cotton bandages.

The infernograph was set up in the centre of the room, pointed at a divan and a nearby chair.

'Wasler was always the one who could arrange the portrait space,' she said, softly, looking at the chair and divan. 'He had the artistic eye.'

'How many portraits do you have scheduled for the day?'

'Five.'

Fisk walked around the room, opened the door to the bedroom. 'Shoe and I will wait back here,' he said. 'Listening.'

'Can I look at the names of the folks who've scheduled portraits?'

She handed me a small, leather-bound book, marked at a page. I opened it. It had five names written in a neat, tiny hand.

Bestus 2 hora, Houszmein 3 hora, Sacedón 5 hora, Raüm 6 hora, Sullust 7 hora.

'No Beleth or Unchleigh, then,' I said.

'Apparently not,' she agreed.

'He's no fool. Hoping he'd sign up using his own name – or one of his aliases – was foolish. But he still might show. Not being able to help himself.'

'Do any of those names sound—' I paused, thinking. 'Suspicious?'

'None,' Winfried replied. 'Er. All of them.'

I laughed. 'We'll be here. Right behind the door.'

'It won't be closed, will it?'

'No,' Fisk said. He moved inside the bedroom, banked the *daemonlights*, and began swinging the door shut. 'If we keep it open, just so,' he said, stopping when there was just a hand's span before the door was fully shut, 'we'll be able to see almost all of the room in the mirror, there. Go to the door.'

She moved to the entrance.

'Can you see me here?'

'No,' she said. 'The door is obviously slightly ajar, but with the lights banked in there, everything's cast in shadow.'

'Good. We'll set up a couple of chairs.'

While Fisk moved about in the bedroom, I stood near Winfried.

'Nervous?'

'No,' she said. 'Though there is a bit of an excitement I've never felt upon me.'

'Fear?'

'Anticipation.'

'I imagine you've got the piece Fisk got for you secured around here,' I said, and her eyes flicked to where the infernograph stood. 'Fine. That's fine. You need to protect yourself.'

She said nothing.

'Beleth is smart. But he's no brawler. He lets other folk do that for him. If he comes in, we'll see. Move to the infernograph and get your piece,' I said. 'We'll take care of the rest.'

'I understand,' she said. Her face remained blank.

'Don't make me say it.'

She looked puzzled. 'Say what, Mr Ilys?'

'If he comes in, let us know and we'll take care of things. If he – or one of his minions – gets rough, don't hesitate to draw and shoot. Put one in his heart. I imagine you've thought about it, before now, anyway,' I said. 'That's how pain works on a person. It festers and you don't even know it's there. It grows and grows silently until it can't be contained.'

'You sound like you know from experience.'

'It's a monster of a world,' I said. 'Not Ia, nor the gods, not *daemons*, not the old gods nor numen, none of them ease the pain of passage through life, ma'am. They are just forces to be harnessed or justifications for our actions.'

'I would never have pegged you as an atheist,' she said.

'I'm not. I believe. But I do not love them. I save that for those that deserve it.'

We were both silent then.

Fisk came from the bedroom. 'It's closing in on the second hour. We should take our positions.' He looked around the room. 'We'll be ready and watching.'

With a few breaks, we spent the day sitting in the dark, peeking through the hands-breadth gap in the door at the reversed image of the sitting room in the nearby mirror. Julius Bestus was a fat butcher with enormous jowls and a florid expression who initially balked at the sacrificial cut for the portrait. Eventually, he screwed up his courage and allowed Winfried to make the wound on his palm and fill the bowl with blood. He watched, wide-eyed, as Winfried mixed the crimson stuff with ink and filled the infernograph. However, he soon calmed himself and the portrait proceeded without incident.

Houszmein, a well-to-do Teuton physician's widow, dressed in mourning garb and carrying the urn of her late husband's remains, was next. She sniffled interminably during the infernograph and picked at the bandaging on her palm after her blood was taken. Willem Sacedón was a Gallic scrivener employed by the legionnaires as an intelligence man, and Raüm was a centurion from the garrison. They arrived together, heads close, either lovers or bosom friends. Their infernographs were taken separately and once Sacedón's proof was complete, they immediately exchanged the images. And laughing, they pressed their cut palms together in imitation of a wedding ceremony's nuptialis sectum. Lovers revealed.

Gaius Sallust was a cadaverous civil engineer in charge of the aqueducts flowing into Passasuego and salaried by the Ruman governor, as all civil engineers were. He said barely two words during the whole process of blood taking but watched avidly as the infernograph took down his likeness on parchment. When Winfried gave him the small proof as payment for his likeness, a toothy grin cracked his visage, making the crags and wrinkles of his face become almost masklike. He uttered one word, 'Marvellous!' and then, thanking Winfried, exited the room.

'You'll need to go to The Slough if you want to see the real grit of the occidens,' Fisk said. 'Or at least the Distrito Centro, where you'll find the backus boys and baillies, the cobblers and hansars, masons and rubbishers.'

'Normally, that's where Wasler and I would be. However, I'm not so invested in the anthropological documentation at the moment, Mr Fisk.'

'No, I reckon you aren't,' he said. He stretched and worked the kinks out of his back, shook his legs to get some circulation going. 'I'll find the back way out of the hotel and head to the Icehouse. Shoe, coming?'

'I think I'll take a walk, stretch my legs some,' I said. 'A long day hiding.'

Fisk's face clouded. 'That's the worst part of it,' he said. 'I'm for being on horseback, gun in hand if need be. This skulking about's got me off my stride.' His mouth puckered and he looked around as if he wanted to spit but finding no spittoon was forced to swallow. 'Shitfire. I need a smoke and a drink.'

'Buck up, pard,' I said. 'Welcome to your first honest day's work in a long time.'

'Honest? Go on with you,' he said, and waved away my teasing. 'If that's honest, I'll eat my saddle.'

'And me? What should I do?' Winfried asked.

'Go to the Pynchon's bar. Talk with people. Check the prissy gentleman at the front desk to see if anyone has left cards for a portrait,' I said. 'How's the money holding out?'

'There's enough left for the next couple of days, barring any unforeseen expense.'

'Send a note if you need more,' I said. 'I hope this won't take days upon days.'

'So do I, Mr Ilys,' she added.

Fisk tipped his hat to us and left while I remained in the suite for a little while, drinking some of the good whiskey from the decanters and eating a blood-orange. After performing some obscure maintenance on the infernograph and annotating and storing the large portraits she had taken during the day, Winfried bid farewell and went downstairs. I followed shortly after, found the servants' stairs near the rear of the hotel and made my way outside.

It was still light and I found myself walking down the mountainside, through the cobbled pink travertine streets. Matrons bustled their wards and called wayward children to dinner, shopkeeps swept storefronts while waiters at cafes set up lanterns and *daemonlights* in hopes of drawing evening crowds. I stopped in a tavern in the Distrito Centro, off the Calle Cuélebre, and had a few beers as the light outside went from pink to dusky blue to a deep azure as I listened to the constant, low-pitched mutterings of a team of waggoneers having just delivered a cargo of wool from Covenant. Afterward, I left with the rolling gait of someone who had drunk a good amount of alcohol but not nearly enough.

I can't say if I was headed there all the while or if my feet had a mind of their own, but I turned off the street I walked onto a side street, followed it downhill aways through the Distrito Centro until I came to the Calle Reyes Basoalto and then from there into the western neighbourhoods of The Slough.

Shitsville.

Along the Calle Lurbira, I found the building I wanted, the one with the sign of a dagger half-out of its scabbard upon a pillow with the word 'Welcome' in common tongue written at the bottom and 'Kvinthé' below it, indicating *dvergar,* too, were welcome. Red *daemonlight* filtered onto the stone street below. From inside there was laughter, the squeals of female voices and rumbling sounds of men. I entered and there spent an expensive long time in the pleasures of the flesh.

*

It is very easy to judge one on what acts they commit of necessity. At that time it had been over four years since I had indulged in the labours of the flesh. I am old, and I was old by human reckoning then due to that blood that set me apart from all society of man, and all society of *dvergar*. Except that society I paid for. But physical desire works differently in *dvergar*. As we age, our body-lust occurs with less frequency, but when it occurs, it's every bit as powerful and pressing as the young might experience. Moreso, truly, because we have the desperation of those who know and have known death.

When I left, night was fully upon the mountainside. I followed the Calle Lurbira out and took a wide stone-walled passage until I came to the Calle Tartaló which I thought might bring me back near the Icehouse Hotel but instead ended up leading me into a warren of tenements. There was a hushed stillness to the air, everything was quiet, and I found myself on a dimly lit street walking along with a group of indistinct labourers who seemed to accept me as one of their own. We came into a wide-open plaza dominated by a statue, this one out of place because it was carved out of dark basalt. In a rough hand, not as refined as you'd find in *Dvergar* or Rume, a large *vaettir* male was sculpted from the basalt in a fierce visage. A fourteen-foot-tall stretcher, its hair messy and its eyes intense and rapacious, holding a longknife in one clawed hand. The rows of sharp teeth were visible beneath its sneering stone lip. At its feet lay a huddled figure curled in a foetal position, with a single word chiselled into the basalt base: *Monstruó*. My gaze was immediately drawn to the leering face of the *vaettir* and for a moment I thought of Agrippina. Her razored teeth. The sulphurous taste of her mouth when she kissed me.

The intensity of the statue's expression caught me so that for an instant, I didn't perceive the crowd gathered around it, or the man standing in the statue's shadow on an overturned wooden potato crate.

The crowd was strangely quiet, listening intently, and as I moved through them, I recognized the garb of labourers and miners, horsemen and tanners and laundresses, of alewives and point-makers, leathercutters and dyers, knackers and kedgers. There were Medieran faces, and some *dvergar* too.

As I approached I was able to see the softly speaking man standing on the crate. He was as I am, part *dvergar*. Between us, we had enough *dvergar* blood to make one whole dwarf. Or one whole man.

He wore a strange high collared suit, discoloured with white or pink dust, and there was a dark smudge of dirt on his chin. He had a thick, compact build and though his suit hid some of his form, from his ropey, gnarled hands I could tell he was possessed of an almost unimaginable strength. He had a wide face with a long nose and a thick expressive mouth full of irregular teeth. As I drew nearer, his wide set brown eyes seemed to recognize me and there was a moment he paused in his speaking and inclined his head, acknowledging my presence, or acknowledging our brotherhood. Afterwards, I could feel the eyes of some of the crowd upon me.

'. . . Something began growing in my soul then, and no simple thing, no shoe, no sock, no drink of cacique, no freshly laundered shirt, no kiss, no bite of the flesh-apple, no full woman's womb could deny that growth. I was lost in some wood and the recognition of being lost was growing.'

He paused, and a murmur swelled in the crowd and then died away.

'We have come to this garden,' he said, raising his hands in a manner to indicate that he did not mean this plaza, or Passasuego itself, or even the Talaveran Mountain on which Passasuego sat. He meant *here*, the Hardscrabble territories. And maybe even all of Occidentalia itself. 'Some of us,' he said, looking at me, 'are born of it of old. Our bones are the bones of the earth, our breath the wind, our blood and ejaculate the molten sap. We are of this place.'

Someone in the crowd yelped, '*We are of this place!*' and another in the crowd echoed, '*Of this place!*'

'And yet. They would war over it. They would plumb its depths and cut down the mountains with their infernal machines to harvest every last bit of silver to bind their *daemons*.'

Of course, *they* were the Rumans. But he never said it.

'And before them, it was *your* ancestors, who built this town and carved the stone from quarries, who first tarnished their hands with silver, who first tainted themselves with the notion to possess this land.' He bowed his head. 'It is hard, yes, to look at this, that we are part of the evil wrought upon this place. Yet we are still *of this place*.'

A woman cried, 'I claim no mastery!' to a great chorus of agreement.

The man – the torta vendor had named him Neruda – bowed his head as if overcome with emotion. 'I claim no mastery,' he said, quietly. 'I claim no mastery,' he said again. 'No mastery over this land. I claim no mastery over any of you. I own no slaves. Where I see injustice, I do what I may to counter it. Is this not so?'

'Yes!' came from many mouths, both men and women.

'As you should do.' He stopped, turned to face the statue behind him. 'We are not *vaettir!*' he cried. 'We do not predate on our people. We do not claim what is not ours. I created this statue,' he said, placing a powerful hand on the basalt surface of the stretcher. His voice rose and fell, projecting out over the crowd, 'To remind us! In the *vaettir's* face you can see the faces of those who would claim mastery over us!'

Something was wrong here. At the edges of my awareness, I could hear a rattling and some muted voices raised in outrage.

Neruda went on. 'In the supplicant body, you can see the aspect of all who have borne subjugation. But some day, we will have to be both! The supplicant and the *vaettir*! For they are of this place! We shall take back our heritage!'

Exclamations, now, of fear and alarm. A groan came from the crowd, swelling. There was the synchronized exhortation of a cohort of Ruman legionnaires in formation. *Hup hup hup hup*. The rattle of carbines and the clatter of gladii in their sheaths. For now. A cornicen blew his horn, piercing the night, and optios bellowed 'Disperse! Disperse or you will be shot!' while the crowd that had been gathered before the statue began to scatter with bleats and desperate shrieks of panic and alarm.

I glanced back at Neruda and for one instant, his face contorted in a private fury, he clutched his hands into fists. Then he hopped off his wooden crate and dashed down the open mouth of an alleyway.

The legionnaires were coming closer and, all in all, if flight was good enough for Neruda, it was good enough for me. They would make no distinction among *dvergar,* I was sure. I ran north, angling away from the approaching legionnaires, and into an entryway and down a close cobbled passage until I was on the next calle and running north and west.

The city was quiet and my heaving breaths came in plumes by the time I reached the Icehouse and stumbled up to my room.

TWELVE

8 Kalends, Quintilius, 2638 ex Ruma Immortalis

I WAS GROGGY THE NEXT morning – and my legs ached from the running – but Fisk and I were at the Pynchon before the first hour. Winfried greeted us, looking much the same as she had the day before, clad in her glossy black suit, hair drawn back, and her face looking severe and a little wan.

'Sleep okay?'

She glanced at me. Surprised, maybe, I would ask such a familiar thing. But we'd been on the trail together.

'No,' she said and no more. Two bellhops maneuvered the copper bucket of chipped ice while a third bustled about placing a magnificent potted hothouse orchid in the spot where the apple blossom had stood, unboxing some small loaves of dried bread on a cutting board with cheese and putting a ceramic bowl full of nuts and dried fruit next to it. Winfried tipped them and they left.

'How many on the list today?'

'Six,' she said. 'Four had left their cards with the concierge. I spent a small part of my evening scheduling and answering them, and then spoke some with the patrons of the Pynchon's bar. I heard a very curious thing.'

'What's that?'

'The Medieran Embassy has been shuttered, and the staff dismissed.'

'Has Ambassador Quintanar fled?' Fisk looked alarmed. 'That would mean—'

Winfried shook her head. 'The woman I spoke with had not heard that the Ambassador had left Passaseugo. And why would he flee?'

'Because he knows something.'

Winfried raised an eyebrow. 'Or because he harbours the murderous traitor Beleth, as we speak. Could that be so?'

'I don't know,' I said. 'It's possible.'

'We'll investigate,' Fisk said. 'But not until after these portraits. Only then we'll pay a visit to the Ambassador. Abandoning this gambit now is foolish.'

'One of us could do it,' Winfried said.

'One man against Beleth and his ilk? Leaving only one of us to protect and apprehend him if he appears for a portrait? And if we cancel portraits, and Beleth is alerted by our absence . . .' Fisk chewed his lip. 'No, I think whatever has happened, it will have to wait until this evening.' He turned to Winfried. 'Do you have your schedule?'

'Yes,' she said, and handed him the notebook the list had been written in the previous day. When he was done, he handed it to me.

Pomponius 2 hora, Dimia 3 hora, Vorinas 4 hora, Xalvadorus 5 hora, Hafaleil 6 hora, Grantham 7 hora

'Xalvadorus is a strange name.'

'All their names are strange, save maybe Pomponius,' Fisk replied. 'Did you meet Xalvadorus? Or was he one of the ones who left his card?'

'Xalvadorus is the owner of the Pynchon, I discovered. Dimia is a well-to-do trader of luxuries – saffron, spices, silk and tabac, and high-quality liquor. He is . . .' She frowned. 'Quite fond of himself.' She paused for a moment. 'The last, Regia Grantham, is the woman I spoke with about the Embassy.'

'All right. We're looking at Pomponius, Vorinas, this Hafaleil person. The rest, I think, we cannot worry about.'

'Will we take portraits again tomorrow?' Winfried asked.

Fisk shook his head. 'No. If Beleth hasn't come out of the woodwork by now, he's not here. And the news about the Embassy makes me think there's a possibility they've pulled up stakes.'

We spent the next little while breaking our fast. When it was time to hide in the bedroom the coverlets on top of the massive four-post in the sleeping area looked unmussed and unused. I nudged Fisk and pointed with my chin. He took in the room, looked back at me. 'We can't guard her all the time, especially not from herself,' he whispered.

'You gave her a gun,' I responded, voice hushed.

'Would you stop with that noise? We've been over this.'

We settled down to wait and watch.

Pomponius lived up to his name; a puffy, overfed contractor for the Ruman legions here, he insisted on his infernograph being taken with a barrel of salt-pork, emblazoned with his own name, and his prize Molossian dog that promptly shat upon the carpet. Pomponius found this extremely amusing and chortled that the dog was as vigorous indoors as out. There was a considerable wait as Winfried rang for room cleaning and a *dvergar* maid came and removed the stinking scat and lit some fragrant candles but the floral scent mixed with the odour of faeces caused Winfried to open both sets of Gallish doors to the balcony. Once the cold mountain breeze had swept away most of the stench, Pomponius had his infernograph taken but something during the process, most likely the *daemonic* sympathy between subject and inferi, caused the Molossian dog – named Kuko – to thrash wildly in his owner's grip and bite his master on the hand, viciously. Pomponius cried out, falling to the floor in a great quivering pile of flesh as the enraged Kuko bore down on the fat man's hand until it was a mangled mess.

Fisk leapt from the hidden confines of the bedroom, placing a boot into the dog's rump and sending him rolling away to yelp madly, scramble to its feet – the poor dog's eyes showing entirely too much white – and dash toward the balcony where it flung itself over the ornate wooden railing to crash in a bloody heap on the travertine stones of the Calle Rhiboza far below. Pomponius lurched to his feet and waddled to the railing to look down at the ruins of his pet. The blubbering sound began then. He wondered aloud, 'Kuko? Why would you do such a thing?' and cradled his mangled hand. Winfried rang for service and requested a physician or barber to bind the wound and there was an uncomfortable wait as Pomponius wept loudly on the divan about the loss of his Molossian.

When Pomponius was gone, Dimia, a tidy little man in a well-tailored and stylish suit, quietly had his infernograph taken and seemed very pleased at the result; so pleased, in fact, he offered Winfried ten gold denarius for her to take a portrait of his whole family, as long as he would receive the larger archival print. Winfried responded that she would think on it and he left her with his card with the invitation to call upon him at her convenience.

Once he was gone, Fisk whispered, 'This next one has the ring of a devil.'

'Vorinus?'

'Yes,' Fisk replied.

'Or a cobbler's son.'

Esa Vorinus turned out to be a heavily perfumed madame – so heavily perfumed that Fisk and I could easily smell her in our hiding spot – of one the more affluent whorehouses in the Distrito Centro. Before her infernograph, she insisted upon disrobing.

'That is not necessary,' Winfried said, a bit nervously.

'Nonsense!' Madame Vorinus answered, pursing her heavily reddened lips. 'I am still young enough to take men to my bed, my breasts do not sag. There is nothing more pathetic than an old whore lamenting the beauty of her youth. I will have *proof!*' she said, and disrobed quickly. Winfried took her blood with a little explanation regarding the necessity of it and then the majority of the hour was spent in conversation with Winfried about the most artful and seductive pose Vorinus might strike on the couch (they settled for her laying demurely on her right side, her left leg brought across the knee to hide her sex, and her torso raised to best expose her breasts). The portrait proceeded quickly and once the instant of *daemonic* sympathy was established, the infernograph scratched and hissed frightfully.

Xalvadorus was an older gentleman, white-haired yet still very hale, looking very dapper in an off-white suit and who, after the blood-letting and portraiture, was very interested in convincing Winfried to take drinks and dinner with him in his private suite. I was surprised at how artfully Winfried turned him down without angering or insulting him.

After Xalvadorus left, there was a few moments of breathless waiting for Hafaleil. Since Grantham was the woman that Winfried spoke with the night before regarding the Medieran embassy, if one of those scheduled for portraiture was going to be Beleth, by elimination Hafaleil would be him.

'Be ready,' Fisk said, low and through his teeth. He rested his hand on his six-gun and watched the room in the mirror, hawk-like.

But Hefeleil, when she knocked on the door, was a rich, horse-faced matron who balked at the letting of blood necessary for the infernograph and apologized profusely for wasting Winfried's time as she quickly made her exit.

That gave us all a moment's respite where we enjoyed a drink, a visit to the honey-pot, and took a little food. We were back in position when the Grantham woman arrived.

Winfried greeted her by name – Servillia – and they positioned her on the couch. I had a momentary jolt of recognition. Grantham was the woman whom I had noticed in the Medieran restaurant the day before, during my visit to the college of Engineers. I was about to bring this to Fisk's attention when Winfried spoke.

'Tell me again about the Medieran embassy,' Winfried said as she readied the bleeding-bowl and knife for the letting. 'Has there been any new information?'

Servillia Grantham gave a throaty laugh. 'No, I'm afraid not. No more information will be coming from the embassy.'

Winfried paused, considering. Then she said, 'At this point, I will require a small amount of your blood. You see, the *daemon* within the infernograph requires a sanguine link between itself and—'

'Yes, yes. I am fully aware of the need,' Servillia said. She stood, approached the device and cocked her head, observing it, her black eyes glittering. 'It is a cunning enough device, this is true,' she said. 'Who did you say invented it? Ysmay?'

'I did not say,' Winfried said, taking a step back.

'Do you know, perchance?' Servillia asked.

'No,' Winfried lied. She took a step toward the infernograph, as if to keep something between her and the Grantham woman. 'If you'll take your position I will be there momentarily to take the necessary blood.'

Servillia turned, her dress swinging like a bell, and went back to the couch. She sat down, crossed her legs almost as a man might, and said, 'Why don't you have Fisk and the dwarf come and join us here?'

Fisk's gun was free of its holster and he was moving into the parlour area before Winfried had time to even open her mouth. I had my guns out and was right on his back.

'Who are you and what do you want?' Fisk said, his pistol pointed directly at the woman's heart. His hand did not waver. His voice was calm.

The woman laughed again, a deep, rich laugh. 'You don't recognize me. We have shared meals, *pistolero*.'

Fisk's eyes narrowed. 'Beleth.'

She laughed again. 'You don't seem happy to see me.' She looked around the hotel suite. 'And where is your blushing bride?' she asked, showing white teeth. 'Is Livia here as well?'

Fisk closed the distance between himself and the woman and pressed the barrel of his six gun into her chest.

'Don't say her name,' Fisk growled. 'I don't know how you're doing this, you old devil, but I will kill you.'

'Beleth?' Winfried asked. 'This is the he who killed Wasler?' she asked.

'Yes,' I said, putting up my hand to indicate silence. 'Quiet now. Don't say anything.'

'How can he be in . . . her?' Winfried asked.

Servillia – or Beleth inhabiting her body – began to chuckle. She waggled her fingers at Winfried's face. 'Ooooh! Magic!'

This did not sit well with Winfried who, placing her hand in the satchel that held the sheaves of parchment, withdrew a revolver.

'Oh my,' the woman said. 'How frightening! So many pistols and not a single one of them can harm me.'

Fisk withdrew his gun, lowered it.

'Why are you here?'

'I wanted to make sure I knew what bumblers were on my trail.' She smiled. 'I thought it might be you two. I take it the little playmate I left for you in Hot Springs was at least an evening's diversion?' she asked.

A small, strangled sound came from Winfried and she drew back the hammer on the revolver.

'Who is this slattern?' the possessed woman asked. 'And why does she glare at me with such hate?'

'You killed my—'

'Quiet,' Fisk said, making a chopping motion with his free hand.

'Tell him nothing.' Fisk turned back to the woman. 'I'm going to ask one last time: Why are you here?'

'I wanted to witness the wonders of the infernograph, of course.'

'Bullshit.'

Servillia laughed again. 'I wanted to play.' Then her face lost its jovial aspect and became very serious. 'Thanks to you two, I've had a very uncomfortable year.' The expression on the woman's face was awful. 'Very uncomfortable. At one point I was hiding in *Ia-damned* barns.' Spittle flew. The anger was becoming titanic. Monumental. 'And you are going to pay for that.' She looked from Fisk to me and back again. 'You all are going to pay for it.' She paused, thinking. 'I wanted to start the game with you two halfwits. But now I am done playing.'

Servillia Grantham stood. Winfried answered by raising her gun.

'If you shoot me, madame, you'll be killing this woman. By now, my body is miles away from here.'

Winfried's jaw clenched. Her hand gripped the pistol until her knuckles were white. She put her finger in the trigger guard.

Fisk turned to Winfried. 'Forget it. It's not him. This is just his puppet. He's pulling the strings elsewhere.'

'I don't care,' she said. She stepped forward and placed the pistol's bore on the woman's cheek. 'He's in there,' Winfried said. 'And he will feel it when I shoot.'

There was an instant of stunned silence. Servillia's eyes went wide in surprise and she muttered something, *tulu ondu girum diavolo ondu,* or so it sounded and then her eyes rolled back into her head. Her breath became foul like carrion and the Grantham woman's skin began to pale, as if leeched of colour. She shut her eyelids and canted back against the cushions of the couch so that her whole body became rigid. A sound – a terrible sound – issued from her mouth. It was ancient and its tone hinted toward hideous glee and abominable horrors. When her eyes snapped open again they were so bloodshot as to be totally red. Winfried began backing away from the transformed woman.

It happened quickly then. The Grantham woman scrabbled backwards on all fours, over the back of the couch and up the wall where she launched herself across the parlour area at Fisk, who moved neatly aside. He was still quick. The woman – now fully possessed by something other than Beleth – hissed in ferocious anger, flexing her fingers like claws, whirling in the enclosed space. She opened her mouth to bellow, hellishly, and her black tongue wormed in the discoloured confines of her mouth.

'A *pellum* ward would dispel it!' I yelled. I had my guns out but the *daemon*-possessed thing had maneuvered Winfried between us.

Fisk glanced at me, an irritated look on his face. That was a mistake. The *daemonic* thing pounced the moment Fisk's gaze was drawn away. She slammed into him, sending his revolver spinning, and drove him across the parlour, knocking over tables and chairs, sending watery cracked ice and fruit spilling. The infernograph tumbled and fell.

When they came to a rest, the woman was on top of Fisk, tearing at him with her claws and he drew his arms up and crossed in front of his face. 'Shoe!' he bellowed.

Winfried came forward, her gun extended, but the Grantham woman's head pivoted about on a gimballed neck, lightning fast, to peer at her with wide red eyes, her mouth open, panting and dribbling blood. The smile that came then was slow, like a rift in the world growing, and it spread across her face like oil spilled from a cracked amphorae.

Caught in the hellish thing's gaze, Winfried seemed paralyzed with inaction, her gun held to the side.

The sound coming from the thing's mouth was hideous. A song maybe. Words sung to some infernal tune. Her thick tongue stirred the air, her throat worked up and down. Like a large puma or

Nemean lion, the *daemon* possessing the woman's body tensed as if to leap. Fisk bellowed again.

The gun barrel, when it fell with all the force I could give on her cranium, sent her tumbling to the side. She did not rise.

Fisk moaned. I offered him a hand and pulled him up. A long furrow traced its way down his cheek and across his neck.

'Thanks, pard,' he said. He looked at the woman lying on the ground. 'Damn thing was strong.'

I looked to Winfried, who had a shocked expression on her face. 'Rope. We need some.'

She looked at me as if she didn't understand what I was saying.

'Rope. We have to tie up...' I waved my hand at the Grantham woman's body. 'Her. She'll come to in a minute.'

Fisk, wincing in pain, said, 'Damn, Shoe. I meant for you to shoot the blasted thing. You're too kind-hearted.'

'Don't know if that's a weakness,' I said. 'Or a strength.'

Winfried, seeming to come to her senses, dug about in some of the jaunting-hearse's compartments and produced a length of thick hemp rope, suitable for our needs. I trussed the Grantham woman like a hog and stuffed a handkerchief half-way down her throat so we wouldn't have to listen to her infernal vocalizations.

'Well,' Fisk said. 'What in Ia's name are we going to do with her now, Shoe?' He shook his head and gingerly touched his face. The wound there welled blood. 'Another one of your strays?'

I ignored that. 'You ever hear of anyone doing something like this? A person, I mean, not a devil? Possessing someone?'

'No,' Fisk said.

'You, Winfried?' I said, turning to the woman who stood looking at the destruction of the parlour.

'What?' she replied. 'Oh. No, I have not. Help me with this.'

We righted a table and began picking up the spilled fruit and foodstuff. The hotel maids would need to be called to clean the carpet and sop up the ever-growing pool of water emanating from the melting pile of ice. Winfried began scooping up the frozen stuff with her hands and returning it into the copper bowl.

'Why do you ask that, pard?' Fisk said, looking at me.

'Because Beleth seems to be doing stuff normal folks shouldn't be able to do.'

'He's an engineer,' Fisk replied.

'That's true. But he was kinda . . . I don't know. Glib, I guess, when he called it "magic". You ever hear an engineer call what he does "magic"?'

''Course not. It's always science to them. Engineering.'

I pulled a Medieran machine-rolled cigarette from my pocket and matched its tip, drawing the smoke deep into my lungs. 'Got me wondering.'

'Wondering what?'

'Maybe we can find out what he's doing.'

'How we going to do that?' he asked.

'Sapientia,' I said. 'If there's a match for Beleth's "magic", I imagine she'll know it.'

Winfried provided me with paper and pen and I wrote a note to Sapientia and sent it by messenger to the College of Engineers.

We waited for dark and hired a cart, rolled the Grantham woman in a canvas tarp I retrieved from our hotel and carried her out the servants' stairwell. Passasuego was particularly quiet at this time of night. Fisk wore his legate pin to preclude interference from the vigiles and legionnaires patrolling the streets, and we slowly made our way to the Distrito Artisan and the College of Engineers.

The building was dark but Sapientia waited for us on the front steps leading into the rotunda, holding a portable *daemonlight*. At our arrival, she ordered two engineer bullyboys to hoist the Grantham woman up while Drusilla took our weapons. Fisk and I gave ours up very easily. Winfried balked.

'You'll need to turn your weapons over to Drusilla,' Sapientia said.

'I don't understand why I should relinquish my pistol,' she asked. 'Our cargo was exceedingly dangerous.'

'You give up arms to enter,' Drusilla said flatly. 'That's the way it is, lady.'

'Might want to stay here, anyway,' I said to Winfried. I *am* the one who picks up strays, after all, and Winfried had proven alarmingly uncontrollable, especially in respect to Beleth. It might be better for her to not enter.

She glared at me, her lips tight with anger, and withdrew her pistol from inside her suit coat and handed it over.

'I will need to frisk you,' Drusilla said.

'Why? You aren't frisking either of them.' Winfried gestured at Fisk and me.

'They didn't balk at giving up their guns.'

An outraged expression settled on Winfried face, but she endured the pat-down.

'You're clear,' Drusilla said. 'That wasn't so hard, was it?'

Winfried said nothing.

There are times you should fight. There are times you have to let go. The older I get, the easier it is to tell the difference between the two. Winfried, however, was young, and in the grip of powerful emotion. So I could forgive her her obstinacy.

Drusilla led us through the collegium to a large sort of laboratory that stank of burning metal and sulphur. The walls and tables were covered with tools: burins of all sizes, copper plates, mountable ground glass oculars, coils of rope and stacks of unbleached parchment, miniature smelts, flasks and casks, salt and inkwells, knives and blood-bowls, pitchers and crystal glasses, titration flasks, mortars and pestles, traditional candles and *daemonlight* lanterns, vices, braces, gears and bins full of metal parts, clay moulds, drawn wire. If it wasn't all so ordered and neatly stored, it would have been too much to take in all at once.

Sapientia directed the bullyboys to place Grantham on one of the tables and hold her down. Having no fixed restraints, she sent Drusilla to find some more rope and we all waited for her to return. Servillia Grantham panted through her nose, masticating the handkerchief in her black maw as I told Sapientia what had transpired at the Pynchon.

'You're telling me Beleth inhabited this woman?' Sapientia said, pulling back the woman's eyelid to get a better view of the bloodshot eyes. They had darkened so now they looked nearly black and inhuman. The eyes of a shark, or large carnivorous fish; unblinking.

'He spoke and acted through her,' Fisk said. 'It was him.'

Sapientia looked worried. Drusilla entered with the rope and we proceeded to modify Grantham's bindings so that she could be examined. Once her legs and arms were fixed individually to each leg of the table, Sapientia said, 'She'll be marked on her body somewhere. We'll have to disrobe her.' She looked at Fisk and me. 'Will you two be all right with that?'

It was a strange question but I was nervous about it. I had an instant's remembrance of Agrippina, the captured *vaettir*, naked and splayed out on Beleth's torture board. It is not a memory I cherish.

I nodded.

'Can you get the thing out of her?' I asked.

'We'll know once I can see her markings.' She opened a nearby drawer and withdrew a gleaming pair of shears and began cutting away the woman's clothes. Grantham was bare within moments.

Fisk sucked air through his teeth while Winfried was noisily sick in a rubbish bin.

The Grantham woman's body was a cartograph of pain and injuries. A landscape of what appeared to be wardwork wrought with a scalpel or burning pin covered her body from head to toe. The time and effort it would've taken to inflict such detailed pain must have been extraordinary. I will describe no more of it here. It is something I've tried for years to forget. There were already many reasons to hate Gaius Linneus Beleth, but now there were many more.

'He called it Lingchi,' I said, my voice raw. 'He lectured me about it as he tortured a stretcher we'd captured.'

'Ah. I heard about that,' Sapientia said, looking at me critically. 'I thought it was just rumour.'

'No.'

She turned back to the woman before her. 'This isn't torture, though,' she said, bending down to examine a bloody intaglio on the woman's breast. It was relatively fresh and oozing blood. 'It seems a glyph-based language I cannot fathom, though I would hazard a guess it is Tchinee in origin.'

'A language?' Fisk asked.

Winfried, wiping her mouth with a handkerchief, rejoined us. Her face was masklike.

'Yes,' Sapientia replied, her fingers lightly touching the woman's skin. 'I will tell you something most people don't know, though it's pretty obvious once you spend any time considering it – engineering is language based. The summoning, the binding, the *daemonic* investiture, it all occurs through ideography that represents sound and thought.'

'You mean all those wards—' Fisk patted his six-gun. 'They're words?'

'Wards are comprised of glyphs, yes. And glyphs are symbols for thoughts, names, sounds. It's more complicated than that, really, but that's an easy way to understand it.'

'Beleth said he'd studied in Tchinee,' I said. 'He seemed to have a great affection for it.'

'Yes,' the head of the College of Engineers said. 'He was

somewhat mad on the subject for a while. But it didn't fit within our mission. To develop technology. Not *daemonology*.'

Grantham thrashed, bucking and hawing and moaning through her gag.

'This is interesting,' Sapientia said. 'It's hard to read through the scabbing, but I will bet a silver pig that's a *corpus locus* glyph.'

'*Corpus locus?*' Winfried asked, puzzled. 'The location of the body?'

'Exactly,' Sapientia responded. She shook her head, looking frustrated. 'I'm an Ia-damned engineer. I can design a turret gun, I can maintain a mechanized baggage-train.' Her face soured. 'But this is beyond my ken. Beleth is playing a very dangerous game here.'

'How so?' I asked.

Sapientia walked over to a cupboard, withdrew a tray holding an earthen bottle, several pewter cups. Whatever she'd seen in the wardwork carved in the Grantham woman's flesh did not sit well with her. She brought the bottle and glasses over to a nearby table and poured herself a drink, knocked it back, and then, almost as an afterthought, poured more of whatever liquor it was into the other cups and gestured that we were welcome to it.

'*Daemons* enter our world through a rift,' she said. 'Did you know that?'

'Engineer Decius said as much,' I said, remembering a painful conversation I'd had with Samantha once.

'The rift doesn't precisely exist in space – you couldn't point it out on a map, per se.'

Fisk nodded, walked over and took a cup. Winfried and I followed suit. The liquor was hot and sweet and totally foreign to me.

'This tear in the fabric of the universe, it exists everywhere at once. Yet it does have a centre. Or a point of origin.'

'Let me guess,' said I, thinking back. 'Terra Umbra.'

Sapientia nodded gravely. 'The Shadowland, where Ia slumbers.'

'Ia? You mean Ia Best and Greatest? Ia?' Fisk asked, pointing up to the ceiling with an incredulous look on his face. 'Him what sits at the heavenly triclinium and feasts with—'

Sapientia raised her hand in a silencing gesture. 'Yes.' She looked at me. 'It seems Mr Ilys is initiated into this knowledge. Let him explain it to you when there's more time. Right now, you need to call the vigiles and legionnaires. Immediately.'

'What?' Winfried said. 'Why?'

Taking a large, exaggerated patient breath, Sapientia said, '*Daemons*, when they enter this world, can enter at any location. There is a fission that occurs when they enter the world and the incompatibility between the two realities causes them to combust. Do you understand?'

There were general mutterings of assent, but not very assured.

'Bound in warded silver is the safest way to summon the inferi. They cannot expand and the glyphs hold their combustion in check. Should they break loose, there would be a great conflagration and expenditure of exceptional force but it would soon dissipate,' she said. She held up her hands, fingers splayed and pointing to each other. Then she jerked them apart. 'But if you bring something over and seat it in a living host or a vestment that it can inhabit, something organic, maybe—'

'Like a severed hand?' Fisk said.

'Anything human or animal,' Sapientia agreed. 'The natural fission process – the antithetical stresses between our universe and the *daemon*'s – is somewhat mitigated. Somewhat.'

A phrase struck me from William Bless' *Our Infernal War*. 'Sheathed in flesh, the dagger still wars,' I said.

'Exactly. But slower.'

'So, when the devils come over and are stuffed in people, they're harder to get rid of.'

'Yes.'

'But why do we need to get the vigiles?' I asked.

160

'Because,' she said, pointing to the Grantham woman's chest, 'this *corpus locus* glyph is fresh and bears Beleth's name. He'll have to bear a similar mark. He is not a *daemon* and can't enter someone from any location.'

I was beginning to understand.

'He's got to be right by them when he does it,' I said. 'In the same room.'

Sapientia nodded.

'Beleth is still in Passaseugo,' she said.

THIRTEEN

5 Kalends, Quintilius, 2638 ex Ruma Immortalis

'THE EMBASSY,' FISK SAID, eyes widening. 'My guns!' he shouted at Drusilla who, after glancing at Sapientia for permission, ran to fetch our weapons.

We barrelled out of the College of Engineers and down the steps at a run. The race through the streets of Passasuego was blurred and blood-spiked. Fisk found the nearest patrolling legionnaire, commanded him to find a cornicen to blow the alarm and fetch mounts from the nearest watch station. Within moments a horn was sounding through the night air. Fisk pulled himself up on the borrowed mount and raced up-mountain toward the Distrito Rosa and the Medieran Embassy. Winfried and I followed along behind as quickly as we could.

By the time we had arrived, Fisk and two vigiles were standing outside the Embassy, smoking cigarettes with sick looks on their faces.

'Too late,' Fisk said, looking at me and shaking his head. 'Beleth killed them all and ran.'

I went inside. Nothing seemed to be amiss until I found the greatroom. The stench of the blood was overwhelming.

The next morning, *The Passasuego Gazetá* headline read '15 Dead At Medieran Embassy including Ambassador's Family', and the Icehouse pre-dawn lobby was choked with businessmen taking their coffee and brandies and discussing the imminent and on-coming war. Many of them – especially the gentlemen of apparent Medieran descent, wearing waxed mustachios and suits cut in the Chiban manner, high-waisted and with tapered legs – wondered aloud at Rume's involvement in the massacre and barely suppressed their outrage.

We checked out early and were tacking out Bess and Fisk's black when Winfried found us.

'I'm coming with you.'

Fisk shook his head. 'Sorry, ma'am. But we're gonna be moving fast. There's only one way Beleth can go, east, and you'd just slow us down with your jaunting-hearse.'

'I've left the infernograph with Sapientia. She will safeguard it until I return,' she said.

Fisk said nothing. He moved to pick up his saddle. Winfried placed herself in front of him. 'Without the baggage, I can travel on Buquo at least as swiftly as Mr Ilys,' she said, lifting a hand to indicate me where I stood next to Bess. 'Forgive me, Mr Ilys, but it is true.'

Now, she might have been right, but my Bess can move fast when she's of a mind and she never tires. I didn't much appreciate Winfried's sentiment.

Fisk stepped around her and slung saddlebags over the black's rump. He placed the small box that contained the Quotidian in the sack and strapped it down, tight. His sleeping bag and personal effects followed. I loaded Bess with oats. We'd stop at a provisioner as soon as the stores opened.

'I *will* come with you,' Winfried said.

Fisk stopped what he was doing and turned to look at her. 'Why?'

'I would see him dead.'

'I told you, that's not the plan I have for him.'

'I would be part of the hunt.'

'Not your job, ma'am,' Fisk said.

Something in her cracked, then. The expression on her face was fierce and wounded, all at once. A welter of emotion contorted her features. Then, with monumental effort, she controlled herself and her expression went blank, almost placid.

'I have money, Mr Fisk. I have Buquo, who is every bit up to the job of bearing me on this journey at whatever pace you set,' she said, each word falling from her mouth like a stone. From her jacket, she withdrew Hellfire. 'I am armed,' she said, letting it hang. 'I am not asking.'

Fisk looked at her for a long time and their gazes held. Finally he looked away.

When Winfried was ready, we mounted up and exited the stable. Winfried walked to Buquo, the massive draught horse, and clambered up on his back. He chucked his head and stamped, steaming in the dawn light.

'Ia-damn you, Shoe,' Fisk said, spitting. 'Ia-damn you and your strays.'

We rode out the north gate and took the Talavera Road east, down-mountain. The White River came in and out of view to our right as we descended. We were making good time and Fisk – his legate's badge openly displayed – questioned every legionnaire we came across regarding Beleth. None had seen him.

We rode into the night, camped late and rose early. After two days we reached the Sundering Rock where the White River and the Big Rill separated.

'This is the sticking point. Either Beleth went east, on the White, or south, on the Big Rill. Which is it?' Fisk asked.

'Either way would lead him toward Ruman legions,' Winfried offered. 'To the east is Fort Brust. To the south, New Damnation and Harbour Town beyond.'

I thought about it a while. 'He'll want to get off the continent.'

Fisk looked at me, considering. 'Don't know who Beleth is working with, now. Could be the Medierans, could be the Tchinee.'

Winfried looked puzzled. 'But he killed the ambassador and his family!'

'No Medieran will know that,' I said. 'He's cunning, Beleth is. Fat old Diegal in Mediera will view this as an outrage. Beleth knew that. He's pushing us toward war.'

'War brings confusion,' Fisk said, his voice disgusted.

'And that means he'll be able to travel more freely,' I said.

Winfried, sounding awed, asked, 'He would have countries move toward death and destruction solely for his own convenience?'

'He's cunning,' I said. 'And his knowledge is powerful. But Beleth himself is petty. He would murder hundreds if doing so would ensure that he slept in a feather bed, dined well, and smoked fine cigars.'

'All that's neither here nor there,' Fisk said. 'Which way would he go?'

We fell silent for a little while. Off in the distance, shrouded by pines and gambels, the White River roared, splitting upon the Sundering Rock.

'Can't help but think of that day, last winter, when we spotted him fleeing the *Cornelian*.'

'And?'

'He was trucking hard north and west.'

'So?'

'North and west was Hot Springs and Passaseugo.'

Winfried turned Buquo so that the horse faced me. 'You are saying he is direct?'

'In Hot Springs, he set the boy-*daemon* to kill us without even knowing for sure if Fisk and I were on his trail. In Passaseugo, he came right to our hotel, bold as brass, and laughed in our faces.'

'I see where you're going with this,' Fisk said.

'The shortest way to get off continent, away from Occidentalia and the Ruman forces here, is south. To Harbour Town, catch a ship bound for New Mediera in the Gulf of Mageras. There he can wheel and deal with the Medieran governor or admiral. Or he could book some sort of passage to Tchinee, remote as it is.'

'He doesn't dick around, that much is true,' Fisk said, turning his black. 'You're right, he's heading south.' He kicked his horse into a canter and called back, 'We'll make the ford after the White Falls! From there, south on the shoal plains until Port Caldo.'

It was a good plan. On the plains, we could give the horses their heads.

Winfried, on Buquo, stomped and churned the earth and then took off after Fisk and his black.

Bess looked back at me, showing green teeth. She was not happy with all the cantering going on. She hawed and nipped at my trouser legging.

'I know, girl,' I said. 'I know.'

She hawed again and after some coaxing, I got her to pick up into a canter.

We forded the White River at a crook where the water widened over an area half a mile in width and it was a short half-day's ride south until the shoal grasses began tugging at our legs. We rode into the evening, until the light gave up entirely, and camped under the wide expanse of sky.

The next day, we came upon shoal auroch and Fisk took one with his carbine and I butchered it for its tongue and liver and tenderloin. The plains were hushed, as if waiting for something. We ate it that night over a driftwood fire on the banks of the Big Rill. Fisk said, after we'd eaten and Winfried was asleep, 'You see them, today?'

'The stretchers? Yes. Why didn't you mention them?'

'For the same reason you didn't,' he said. 'Didn't want to scare Winfried.'

166

'Doubt she'd have been scared. Alarmed, maybe. But she's not one for fear.'

He nodded. 'Maybe I didn't want to have to explain their behaviour. They're hanging back for some reason.' He had his carbine in his lap and fed Hellfire rounds into it one by one.

'The one out on the hardscrabble. During the ambush,' I said.

'Don't start with that again, Shoe.'

Almost of its own volition, my hand made a chopping motion, cutting him off. 'You've known me more than a decade now. How many Ia-damned times have I lied to you?'

'A few.'

'Fisk—'

'I got your point, Shoe.'

'It's hard to take in, pard, but that *vaettir* was different! It dropped its sword after what it had done to its kin.'

He shook his head but I could see I was getting to him. 'Hell, Shoe, I thought I understood them. But now . . .'

'Damned puzzling thing, how you can know something and then not know it at all.'

Fisk spat. 'There's that.' He thought for a while. 'Maybe they're hanging back for another reason. Maybe it has something to do with the hand.'

That puzzled me. 'How so?'

'I don't know, but the same thing that was in me was in Agrippina.' He shook his head, tossed a small piece of driftwood into the fire. 'Just a feeling I've got.'

'Ain't never been one to discount feelings, but that's a strange one, pard.'

He did not answer immediately, and when he did it was a conversation we'd had thousands of times around thousands of campfires in stretcher territory.

'I'll take the first watch. You take the second,' he said. That's our normal arrangement. I can see quite well in the small hours of the night when others can't.

He looked off past the glow of the fire.

'It's the Kalends, Fisk. She'll be writing.'

'I know,' he said, opening his hand to look at the scar on his palm.

'You gonna set up the Quotidian?'

'Yes.'

'Maybe I should take the watch.'

'Get some rest.'

'Naw. I'll watch until you've done your deal.'

He looked at me, pulled out a Medieran machine-rolled cigarette and tossed it over. Tasted good, the tabac smoke under the stars. And maybe even the possibility of *vaettir* watching made it taste even better. That's one of those strange things about living under the open vault of sky in *vaettir* country: everything tastes better when there's stretchers about.

Fisk took out the Quotidian, opened it, unlatched the lid. It cleverly unfolded into a flat surface. He laid it down on the levellest bit of dirt near the fire he could find, withdrew the blood-bowl and knife, inkwell and parchment.

On his knees, half illuminated as he was by firelight, for a moment he seemed some sort of augur or priest to a nameless god about to give sacrifice. He raised his knife to open his palm and begin the blooding.

'Hold on, pard,' I said, moving to join him. I opened my hand and held it out. 'You're stingy with words, pard. But Livia isn't,' I said.

He nodded, once, took my hand, and cut it deep, letting the blood flow.

PART II
Foreign Devils

FOURTEEN

Kalends of Sextilius, Eleventh Hour, 2638 Annum
Ex Rume Immortalis, Near the Aethiopicum Shore,
Bay of Aribicum

Dear love,
Your son within me is still well and thriving, though not much
has changed. Carnelia constantly opines on the growing size of
my stomach and Lupina keeps me stuffed with food. I daresay
I've gained two stone since we last saw each other and not all of
that is baby.

During quiet times in our journeys – we are back on the
Malphas and steaming past the dark shores of Æthiopicum – I
allow Carnelia to press her head against the taut drum-head
of my stomach and listen and feel for young Fiscelion's martial
kicking and gyrations. She squeals and exclaims, touching her
cheek in amazement when his tiny foot connects.

The *Malphas* steamed into the port at Ostia on 13 Kalends,
the twentieth day of Quinitilius, and only three days before
Ia Terminalia. We had been almost thirteen full days at sea,
which seemed an amazing speed, even to my father, who was
extraordinarily pleased. 'Mithras' swollen nutsack!' he said.
(I shall not spare your delicate sensibilities, my love.) 'We've
crossed the Occidens in half the time it would take to sail!' The
captain, Juvenus, explained as we prepared to disembark that
the shipwrights at the College of Engineers in Ostia had made
some improvements on the design of the ship, making it lighter

171

and stronger all at once. But mostly it was the two *daemons* bound in the *Malphas'* belly. The first, Malphas himself, was an incendiary arch-*daemon* of incalculable ferocity and strength. The fiery energy he poured forth was solely dedicated to the turning of the ship's great screws. The other *daemon* – one that no one seems to mention, though I have heard the ship's mess-cook calling his ovens affectionately as *Captain Caiodé,* a strange name for an oven to be sure – remained unheralded, though as passengers we reaped the benefits of his infernal presence with far more immediacy: hot water for our ablutions, hot meals at the Captain's table, staterooms warmed against the damp chill of the ocean swells. And of course the ship is thrice damned, the last for the sailors lost to sea and war. The *Malphas* is a warship, after all, albeit a small one.

Moments after making dock in the shipyard in Ostia, Mister Tenebrae – who, by the way, is quite an exceptional man and who has become very close to Secundus – had arranged for carriages to take us right away back to Father's villae on the Cælian, so to be nearer Tamberlaine's palace for Terminalia. I, personally, had grown quite comfortable on the *Malphas*, and would have preferred to remain there.

Here I will be honest with you, my love.

I swore once to never set foot in Rume again. Part of that was a rebellion against my father and the society that would treat me as chattel; part of that was a fear of the vicious rumours Metellus spread about me to justify his divorce. I was afraid. It is something I rarely feel; I care not what others do and very rarely have physical fear for my own integument of skin. But Rume, for all its history and formalized society, its collegiums and forum, its aediles and vigiles, its laws and libraries, is in its own way as wild and lawless as the Hardscrabble Territories. Power is law, and men – and women too – scrabble just as hard to get it here as they do in New Damnation.

I felt very protective of our child, and fearful of his safety as
we climbed aboard the carriages, Secundus gallantly offering his
arm, and caromed up the Ostian Way, the Tever River winking
muddy brown on our left and the hulking stonework arches
of the Ostian aqueduct passing silently on our right. It was a
journey of only two hours and the rocking of the horse-drawn
carriage made me drowsy. Tenebrae said, 'The sailors tell me
that a swaying carriage ride might make one sick after a long sea
voyage.' He smiled, flashing well-formed white teeth first at me,
then at Secundus. Carnelia moaned. 'Yet, it is the best thing to
end the unsteady sensation one can have after disembarking.'

'Where will you go, now that we have returned? We are no
longer your charges,' I said.

'We shall see,' he said, unworried and quite pleased with the
world. 'I am at his Imperial Majesty's disposal and he will do
with me what he will.'

Father, who had been dozing fitfully, snorted and began
brushing his mustachios vigorously. 'I'm quite chomping to show
off my new leg.'

'Or lack of it,' Secundus said, raising an eyebrow.

'Here now, lad, don't be your sister's mouthpiece when she's
out of commission,' Father said. 'And all of Rume will want
to see my mounted *vaettir*!' He crowed. 'I could charge for
viewing!'

'About that, Father,' I said, coughing delicately.

'What?' Father dislikes being interrupted when excited.

'My sister and I have decided on the only appropriate gift for
Tamberlaine.'

'This is good news, then, child! Don't keep me waiting.'

'Your *vaettir*,' I said.

It is an amazing thing to see a patrician's world crumble. And
Father has never been one to keep his emotions tamped down

hard in his chest. His face, first stunned, became calcified in an expression caught somewhere between shock and misery.

'No—' he said, his eyes shifting in his sockets as if looking for some lifeline or exit from this personal catastrophe.

'Yes, Father,' I said as gently as I could. 'Once you stop to think about it – consider Tamberlaine's current displeasure – nothing else will do.'

'But...' He faltered then. 'Mithras' cankerous prick.'

'Father, no need for such profanity.'

'There is much need. Ia dammit, I need a drink.'

At that, Carnelia called for the carriage to stop and not waiting for any slowing or cessation of forward movement, leaned forward, wrenched open the door, and let fly a thunderous stream of vomit.

Father, looking vaguely disgusted and leaning away from her bilious breath, said, 'Where do you keep it all, 'Nelia?'

We reached the villa at dusk. A watchful footman with a militant aspect and hefting a carbine considered us closely and after a moment opened the barred gates.

The carriage rolled into the courtyard, surrounded by sandstone walls. Father – possibly having used his one of his own Quotidians to alert Fuqua, his manumitted head of household, that we would be returning – led us inside into a bright atrium that smelled of lemon and myrrh. The slaves and servants stood in an expectant line, waiting to greet him.

Fuqua bowed, deeply. 'Father,' he said. 'We are ready to serve you.' As a group they bowed until Cornelius walked past, tapping each servant lightly on his head.

'I am well pleased, Fuqua,' Father said, spreading his hands as if giving a benediction. My father is many things: childish, abrasive, impulsive, drunken, wise, bellicose, foolish, addled. But he always obeys the traditions and I think *that* has kept him well, through the years. He has risen higher than more intelligent (or moderate) men. His natural choleric demeanour belies a greatness of spirit that you may not have seen, my love. He can be mean, he can be menacing, he can be maudlin, he can be mawkish. How many men have so many aspects warring within them and rise so high? I do not think many.

I recognized none of the slaves' or servants' faces. It had been years since I had spent any extended time under my father's roof: first due to my marriage; then due the divorce and my mother's illness; last, due to the three and a half years I spent in the west during Father's governorship in Occidentalia. I have become a stranger in the place I once called home.

We dined in the small triclinium, waiting for our personal effects, luggage, and cargo, to arrive from Ostia under Rubus' watchful eye.

Father, popping an olive into his mouth and then washing it down with a swig of wine, said, 'All right, son, you are prepared? I have put the senatorial gears into motion and set my own personal *daemon* in the form of Messalla Corvinus to light the benches on fire for you. He has successfully lobbied to allow you a time to say what you will. You will have the floor on the fifth hour.'

Secundus looked up from his reading material and smiled, a genuine one. On his return home, he'd immediately disappeared to Father's office and wasn't seen until dinner where he sat poring over an old, musty tome, watering his wine heavily and eating only the barest amount.

'I shall be ready, Father,' he said, brightly. 'Since I am no senator, as yet, it is quite an honour you have done me.'

'Nonsense. It is our honour – and your sister's – you preserve.' Father's eyes brightened with interest. 'How is your speech coming along?'

'Well, Father,' Secundus replied. 'Very well. In fact, I had planned to go to the library at...'

A soft cough came from the door. Fuqua said, 'A Mister Tenebrae to see young master Secundus, sir.'

Father raised his eyes. 'Tenebrae? Here? I assumed...'

Secundus hopped up, tossed his napkin onto the near empty plate he'd been pecking at, and said, 'No, we're to find one last little nail in Metellus' coffin in the Trebinal Quarter's library. Are there horses in the stable?'

Father nodded, pride suffusing his face. Either from Secundus' pursuit in the reclamation of my (and consequently the Cornelian) honour, or his love of horses, I could not tell. 'I imagine your Phrineas is still bucking about. He may be a bit more creaky in the moving bits, but I took him out the day before we left.'

'That was almost four years ago, Father.'

'Well, he may be a bit creakier. Fuqua's reports indicate he's still in fine dander.'

'I shall see,' Secundus said, moving out of the triclinium.

Father smiled and occupied his mouth with more of the Falernian. Carnelia, now that she was able to keep down solid food, said, 'Those two have become quite close.' She raised her eyebrows in an arch manner and glanced at Father.

'Tenebrae is a fine young man,' Father said.

'Very close,' Carnelia restated.

'Yes, yes.'

'That's enough of that,' I said to Carnelia.

'What?' She looked at me, batting her eyes, full of innocence. Since that fateful day, last autumn, when we rode out onto the shoal plains for the auroch hunt and Gnaeus was mortally wounded, my sister has not been able to keep her weight. I imagine that most of her sustenance comes from unwatered wine: when she smiled at me, her teeth were roan. 'Have I said something?'

'Sister, have you ever been to Gall?'

'You know I have not, sissy.'

'In Gall, they have a wonderful way of fattening ducks. They call it *gavage*. Are you familiar with the term?'

'No,' she said, only half paying attention to what I was saying and burying her nose in her wine-cup.

'They take the ducks and shove a funnel down their throats,' I said. Carnelia giggled. 'Then, holding the ducks firmly, they pack its stomach full of herbs and feed. In a short time, the birds grow grossly obese and their livers are positively gargantuan.'

Carnelia put down her cup and looked at me, the smile on her face growing wan and failing altogether.

'I am married with child. Secundus is who he is—'

'Damn fine lad,' Father said, oblivious to what I was saying to my sister.

'Hush, Tata,' I said. Turning back to Carnelia, I said, 'Secundus will someday will take a wife, despite any of his other . . . affections, because he must. And *you*, my sister, now that we're back in Rume – if only for this short while – will be made available for any men of acceptable birth and political connection.'

A strange expression crossed my sister's face then, comprised of equal measures of excitement and wariness. She knew I was taking the long route round the villa.

'Quite right, Livia,' Father said. 'Quite right. I still intend to speak with Tamberlaine about Marcus.'

'Should that fail, we will have to pursue other measures.' I paused, took a large breath. 'You are too thin,' I said, briskly. 'No suitor would believe that you will be able to bear children. If you do not put down the wine, finish everything on your plate, and eat all of that lovely tart—' I looked at her as sternly as I was able. 'I will order two of the burliest slaves to hold you down and I will fetch a funnel and a pail of goat's milk.'

'You wouldn't dare!' Carnelia said, outraged. 'Anyway, I would order them to let me go! Where would you be then?'

'Who do you suppose they would obey?'

Father laughed, wiped his mouth with a napkin and then clapped his hands. 'This is getting interesting. Fuqua!'

Fuqua came in, peering at a piece of parchment with a half-distracted look on his face.

'Yes, sir?' Fuqua said.

'The girls are going to see which one of them has more control of the servants! I'll wager ten thousand sesterces that it'll be Livia.'

'Respectfully, sir, you don't pay me enough for that kind of bet,' Fuqua said. Then he peered first at me and then Carnelia. 'And even had I that amount and was willing to risk it, I do not think that would be the bet I would take. My pardons, madame,' he said, bowed to Carnelia, and exited.

Father chuckled and said, 'Ia's blood, that man has no sense of adventure.'

I looked steadily at Carnelia. 'Eat, or I shall call them.'

Carnelia picked up a hunk of crusty bread and shoved it in her mouth and began sullenly masticating. When she had a moment to breathe she said, 'I don't understand you, sissy. I hope you're not like this on the voyage to Tchinee.'

Father, alarmed, sat forward. 'What's this? Carnelia? Tchinee?'

I shot Carnelia a withering stare – it was far too premature to bring Father into the discussion – but there's no unbreaking an amphorae once it's been dropped.

'We were, once we'd settled back here in Rume, going to speak with you about this.'

He frowned, his whiskers shifting into a greyish slump. 'I don't like being alone, Livia. A father's solace is his progeny. A father's joy is his children.' He looked about. 'Lupina! Whiskey!'

When Lupina did not appear that instant, magically bearing

a glass of liquor, he *harrumphed*, shifted, and settled into his chair like a disgruntled dog might on finding himself sleeping outside.

'Lupina and Rubus are with our luggage, Tata.'

'I know that, child. Do you think I don't know that?'

'Possibly,' I said. 'As I was saying, we wanted to wait to speak with you regarding this but I would ask that you allow Carnelia to accompany me to Tchinee.'

'Whatever for? Won't she just be underfoot?'

'Father!' Carnelia said, indignant.

'No,' I said slowly, placing my hands on my belly. 'I am with child and this is a diplomatic mission. I do not want to be half-way around the world with no family near me when it's time for the baby.'

'You'll be back before then,' he said, shaking his head.

'There are no guarantees of that.'

'You'll have Secundus,' he responded, picking up his wine-cup and looking miserably at the dregs. 'I don't want to be *alone*.'

'Secundus? I need my sister. A woman. And you won't be alone, Father. You'll have all of Rume at your disposal.'

'It's not the same,' he grimaced. 'No, I won't allow it.'

I looked at him steadily. Sometimes, my stare will cause him to flinch or look away. Sometimes it won't, especially when he is being particularly obstinate.

He glanced again at his cup.

'Let's not fight about this, Father. I think it is best if I have a woman of my family with me in case the baby comes when we are away. I will respect your decision, but I wish you would think of your grandson.'

His eyes softened. It was my apparent capitulation that allowed him to be magnanimous.

'Of course,' he said. 'She should be with you.'

Carnelia squealed and clapped her hands lightly.

'I do, however, insist that she be a veritable dumpling on her return.'

Carnelia, beaming, said, 'Of course, Tata,' and picked up the tart from the dessert tray and crammed it into her mouth.

Word had spread about our return. The next morning, there were a crowd of suited gentlemen and women – Father's clients – standing in the courtyard when the cock crowed. I rose early, before the sun, and spent my morning sitting on a balcony watching as the rising sun poured its light into the streets.

I have conflicted emotions regarding Rume itself, her denizens and leaders. Her customs. There is something rotten at the heart of it, and I cannot tell how much culpability I have in that. We live inside monsters, sometimes, and cannot wholly see the evil they do because our senses have grown used to monstrosity. But the city! The city itself! My love, I do not know if you remember it, but Rume is a study in contradictions and I have, and always will have, an ardent desire to *know* it. Life teems here. The insulae brim with peoples from every nation of the earth, and the early morning is a riot of sensations: the streets are flocked with vendors cooking sizzling sausages, lamb, hemdrælla, pork, shrimp, chingale, while the air hangs heavy and luxurious with the exotic spices of Indus and Cythia; the bells ring as the refulgent morning light falls across the domes and spires of the Cælian Heights, the ranked soldiers lining the weathered walls of old Rume's city like cypress trees; the plumes of kitchen smoke and household *daemon*-fires rise like accusations over the rooftops; the sluggish Tever in the distance catches the light and stinks of Rume's effluvium; the brays of donkeys and clatter and nicker of horses drawing wagons through the lightening streets; the light itself, a hazy golden liquor, motes hanging in the sluggish air; children laughing and singing; a waggoneer yelling profanities; the heavy clomp and tread of vigiles; priests moving

toward their devotions, chanting Ia's Precatio – admonishing the
living to live well before their journey and final judgement by
the Pater Dis. It is a great panoply of life, the centre of all of
the world.

Rume. A terrible beauty.

At some point Fuqua opened the main doors and allowed
Father's clients into the atrium, took their names, and
announced them one by one, to enter his study. I knew not
where Secundus was, but I assumed getting ready to make his
suit.

Carnelia and I, after a short amount of time speaking with
Fuqua and the slave Selwina, the female head of household,
and Fuqua's paramour (as far as Carnelia and I could tell)
determined that the slave market nearest Tamberlaine's palace
proved the best hope of finding an educated midwife for the
trip to Far Tchninee and the area offered other shops and stores
where we might purchase enough presents for Ia Terminalia.
As we prepared to leave, a soft knock at our bedchamber doors
revealed Lupina, looking a bit out of sorts.

'Madame Livia,' she began, her hands clutching one another.
'Master Cornelius has got Rebus and Fuqua and them house
slaves tending to him. So I thought might be I could...' She let
the unasked question trail off.

I realized then that the half-*dvergar* woman was experiencing
Latinum for the first time. In Rume, all of life is a spectacle
and many spectacles spring from the rare and the exotic. Being
half-*dvergar* like Mr Ilys, she could command quite a fee for
appearances or... other unmentionable things... should my
Father consent to allow her to keep the money. I daresay he
would. But now that Father was showered with the attention
of multiple slaves and servants, the attention of his clients,
Lupina had found herself if not usurped, then not immediately

required. She was entirely out of her element. I wonder what thoughts were churning behind her eyes.

'Of course,' I said, gesturing her to enter. She began picking up Carnelia's clothes that were strewn about the room we shared.

'Sissy,' Carnelia said, ignoring the slave woman. 'I'll be ready in a trice,' she said, as she fiddled interminably with her hair. 'Maybe we could lunch at Rimbenus'?'

'Possibly,' I replied. A thought occurred to me. 'Lupina, have you ever served as a midwife?'

'For a master or master's wife, ma'am? No.' She shook her head.

'Ah, that is unfortunate.'

'Though I've got five sisters and three brothers, all with wives. Done my share of birthing babies.'

I raised an eyebrow at her. 'Let me ask you this: would you feel competent to deliver my baby?'

She narrowed her eyes, looked at my waist. She came close and said, 'May I?'

I nodded.

Lupina took my hand and felt at the wrist. Then she placed her hands on my stomach. 'When the boy kicks, he kicks hard or does it got a flutter?'

'Right now, a flutter. But it feels quite martial.'

'That's 'cause you're thin. If you had some meat on you, you'd barely notice it. It's early yet. You in your fourth month?'

'Yes.'

'I don't think I'd have a problem delivering your 'lil one, ma'am. But it'd help if you fatten up some.'

Carnelia laughed. 'Serves you right!' she said from the vanity.

I laughed. 'The world wishes us to be quite fat, sister,' I said. And even Lupina grinned. I looked at her. I'm ashamed to admit that I never really had considered her closely, though she'd been owned by Father for nearly four years now. 'Even though you are my father's property, I would not take you away from him, or into harm's way, without your express permission.'

She looked at me closely. She had a plain, blunt face, a compact frame like most *dvergar* and arms as strong as any man's. Her large brown eyes were intelligent, though, and filled with curiosity.

'Would you come with me to Tchinee as my midwife?'

She thought for a long while, her eyes shifting in their sockets as she studied my face.

Eventually, she said, 'I will, ma'am, if Master Cornelius allows it and has no more need of me.'

'That's that, then,' I said, standing. I moved toward the door. 'I will speak to my father.'

The atrium was still full of clients wishing to ask or give favour to my father, their patron. The conversation was hushed and the fountain made a soft tinkling sound. Slaves delivered water and lemons and trays of toasted nuts and fruit for the clients that must wait a long while. Father valued his own comfort and the comfort of others. In a more sly and typically Ruman fashion, his food offerings to his clients – a practice not all patricians followed – sent the message that Father would take care of their needs, even the most small and inconsequential. It reinforced the covenant between them.

'I hear he's brought back a tame elf from the new world,' I heard one woman say as I walked toward my father's office.

'Nonsense. The *Rume Pandect* reports that they're quite bellicose and that none save one had been taken alive.'

'They bring back lions from Aethiopicum, do they not?'

'Rarely.'

Another man with a lazy eye said, 'I hear our patron has also brought one of his dwarf lovers from overseas. *Dvergar*, they're called. And this one is like rutting with a little wolf. What I'd give to have a go at such exotic—'

I stopped to look closer at the man with the lazy eye. While affluent looking, he had a distasteful oiliness to his character I didn't care for. And that kind of talk – the gossip of Rume – needed to be nipped at the branch.

The trio of gossipers stopped, taking notice of me watching them. The woman bowed stiffly and the men inclined their heads. I simply stared at them and then brushed past the rest of the supplicants and into Father's office.

Father looked surprised. Fuqua stood nearby and Rebus was seated next to Father as they pored over a thick tome of what looked to be expenses. A neat little man in a dandy suit sat in front of Father's massive desk.

They all stood as I entered.

'Good morning, Livia,' Father said. 'As you can see I'm occupied right now with Pithicæ and the trade—'

'A moment, Father,' I said, and nodded my head at Father's client Pithicæ. 'I will be quick. First, Carnelia and I need some money to make the appropriate purchases for Ia Terminalia and your list of clients, servants, and slaves to be included.'

Father, blinking, said, 'Understood. Fuqua will handle that. How much do you need?'

'I do not know,' I replied. 'Ten thousand sesterius at the very least.'

Father looked to Fuqua who nodded. 'That is no problem.' He left the room.

Watching Fuqua go, Father waited. When he was sure he couldn't hear, he said, 'Get Fuqua something nice. He's done a commendable job keeping the family finances in order.'

'What do you suggest?'

'Wine, maybe?'

Rubus said, 'Possibly an assistant slave?'

Father frowned. 'Now you're just shopping for yourself, Rubus. No. He's epically thin, so get him something sweet – and that goes for Carnelia as well – and maybe a nice Cythian rug or something ivory. It needs to be expensive. He's a very important part of our household.'

'You could free his paramour so they could wed,' I said.

'No, not that yet. In time,' Father said, rubbing his chin. 'Possibly.'

'You'll hold that over him as long as possible.'

Father looked hurt. 'Of course not, Livia! You think I'm some sort of tyrant.' Then, realizing we were in company, he stood and said, 'If you'll excuse us for a moment, Pithicæ?'

I watched Pithicæ leave. When he was gone I said, 'I know you, Father.'

'This is unfair of you, Livia,' he said.

I ignored that. 'Second, Father, one of your clients – an oily looking man with a lazy eye – is spreading vile rumours about your sexual predilections in Occidentalia.'

Father brightened. 'Oh? What did Nicopælus say?'

'That you've brought your *dvergar* lover back with you.'

He looked surprised then. 'Lupina?' He began to laugh. 'How rich! Anything else?'

'No,' I said. 'Though that brings up a final issue.'

Fuqua returned with a heavy bag of coins and handed them to me. 'Should this not suffice, tell the storekeeps that they may call here and I will take care of any other debts you generate.'

I thanked him.

'The last issue?' Father said. 'I have work here to do.'

'It's in regards to your "lover", Lupina.'

He smiled at that. 'What of her?'

'I want to take her with me to Tchinee as my midwife.'

'No! Absolutely not. First Carnelia and now my Lupina? You'd strip me of everyone and everything.'

'You have Fuqua, Rubus, and all of your household slaves.'

'No!'

'Do you really want to foster the rumours that she's your lover?'

'What does it matter? As long as I'm the one doing the fucking.'

'Gods, Father, that's something I never want to hear come out of your mouth again. And it *does* matter. Look what Metellus did to *my* reputation!'

'That will be fixed this afternoon, Livia, once Secundus speaks at senate.'

'It doesn't matter. The damage is done. If there's one thing I know about Rume, it's that people love nothing more than salacious gossip.'

'I can't do without her.'

'Father,' I said as seriously as I could. 'Do we really need to go through all of these motions? Both you and I know that I will take her with me and it's just a matter of us spending the time having a fight and you capitulating.'

He looked shocked. 'I am your father, miss, and I'll not have you speaking . . .'

'I was thinking about naming him Gaius Saturnalius.'

His whiskers began to quiver and his mouth opened and closed again. 'A fine name.'

'*Your* name.'

He said nothing.

'You wouldn't deprive your grandson of having a trusted family slave with—'

Father made a chopping motion with his hand. 'Oh fucking hell, girl. Take Lupina. Take the money. Get out and leave me in peace.'

I smiled as sweetly as I was able. 'I love you, Tata. You are as generous as you are wise.'

'Get Pithicæ on your way out.' He waved his hand for me to leave.

I opened the door and motioned Pithicæ to return to his seat.

'Pithicæ, do you have children?' Father asked.

'No, sir.'

'Good. They grow up to be pirates and rogues and totally uncontrollable.'

'Your daughter does seem quite formidable.'

'You should see her shoot. She's a match for any woman or man.'

'You should be proud, sir,' Pithicæ said.

'Oh, I am, friend. I am. When she's not robbing me blind.'

Hand on the doorknob, I said 'Oh, and Father?'

He looked at me, frowning.

'Now that Carnelia and I will be gone for the foreseeable future,' I said, sweetly, 'You should consider taking a new wife. If only to stop the gossip in its tracks. I imagine there's some eligible daughters or widows who would make valuable political arrangements.'

His jaw dropped. Fuqua and Rubus barely concealed their smiles.

I turned and left.

'Ia damn her to Hell,' I heard Father say from behind me.

FIFTEEN

Carnelia is in her element when shopping. Lupina and I trailed behind as she went from store to store, buying gifts, arranging for their delivery to our villa. I contented myself with simply paying the shopkeepers and watching Lupina's reactions to the more outlandish aspects of the Cælian. In the Mezzo Market, she did not bat an eye at the vendors and spice sellers, but when we passed two of the seven- or eight-storey insulae, booming with noise and industry – women banging rugs from balconies, dandling babies on their knees, children dumping waste-buckets into the stone sluiceways leading into the Tever, mobile merchantmen pushing wagons full of trinkets or smouldering food carts, labourers hammering and stonemasons pushing wheelbarrows full of lime – her jaw dropped and she said, 'How many people live inside?'

'Three, maybe four hundred. They're some of the larger buildings in this neighbourhood.'

Carnelia sniffed. 'Used to be, the plebs couldn't build on the Cælian, until Græchhus – a rabble rouser – was able to push through the Lex Libertini, which allowed freed slaves to own property anywhere in Rume, within or without the walls. Our neighbourhood went downhill from there.'

Lupina's expression did not change, but she blinked slowly.

'So,' I said, 'our great-grandfather, Marcus Cornelius

188

Aquilonis, passed the Lex Aquilonis which required that all
buildings on the Cælian must be built of stone.' I laughed.
'Little did he know that by forcing them to build with stone
instead of cheap wood it allowed them to take advantage of the
solid bedrock of the Cælian – as opposed to the softer areas
nearer the Tever – and the newer building techniques. Suddenly
tenements weren't two or three stories any more, they were six
or seven, holding far more "undesirables".' I laughed. 'To this
day, Father gets grumpy when the Lex Libertini and Aquilonis
are mentioned.'

'It brings down the property values, sissy,' Carnelia said,
aping something she'd heard Father say.

'So?' I said. 'Everyone has a right to live and at least these
insulae aren't great fire hazards.'

Lupina cleared her throat. 'How many people living in
Rume?'

'According to the last census in 2350, somewhere near two
million people, including slaves.'

Lupina's eyes widened. 'That is more people than in all of the
Hardscrabble!'

I nodded. 'More people than all of the Imperial Protectorate
and Occidentalia.'

'In one city?'

'Yes.'

I could see her struggling with the idea and the sheer size of
it. 'Sissy, let's take her to The Spire.'

Carnelia shrugged. 'It's out of our way.'

'Nonsense. We're not walking.' I instructed Father's carriage
driver of our new destination. The driver turned and after a
short while, we began to rise above the rest of the Cælian,
passing through residential areas on the hillsides until we came
to a steep switchback road that led up to a level area with a
thick copse of cypress trees like a cluster of verdant spearheads,

surrounding a long rising tor of sandstone surmounted by a
crusty altar to Ia. The blood of auguries stained the living rock,
it being so near to Ia Terminalia. There are small sacrifices
each day, growing larger and larger – nothing compared to the
tauroctony that occurs during the Mithranalian Games, of
course, but still substantial. We led Lupina through the cypress
trees and up upon The Spire's tor, overlooking the city itself.

From this vantage, the breadth of Rume was visible. A
multitude of dwellings, congregations of teeming spires and
domes and temples, myriad blocks of villaes and warehouses
and factories. Munition plants and colleges, and cobbled roads
threading throughout. Towering stone insulae on the Cælian.
The dark shape of Rume's original wall encircling some of the
grandest white marble pillars and forums. The theatres and
stadiums and markets. Thousands upon thousands of pillars of
smoke – from homes and industry and *daemonic* combustion
– rose to join in a pall that hung shroudlike over the city, yet
below our vantage, only slightly obscuring the view in almost
dreamlike haze.

'Oh—' Lupina said, her voice catching. 'I have never seen the
like.'

'And you never will,' said Carnelia, strangely grave. 'Behold
the might of Rume, westerner, and despair.' Then, glancing at
Lupina's stunned expression, she covered her mouth and giggled.

At lunch we stopped at Rimbenus' – a small restaurant
frequented by wealthy equite wives and patricians who want
good food rather than a social event. We were ushered to a small
table and had begun to dine upon peppered oil and hot bread
with wine, when a great horse-faced skag of a woman, dripping
with jewels, approached our table. She greeted Carnelia by name
and introduced herself to me and ignored Lupina entirely, at
first.

'I am Vespasia Polla, wife to Octavius Petro Polla,' she offered her hand.

'Livia Fiscelion,' said I, taking her hand.

'I have heard of you,' she said, and a knowing smile touched her lips. 'Rough,' she remarked, feeling the skin of my palm. A small look of distaste curdled her expression. 'There's a marvellous little shop around the corner that sells lotions of all sorts. And they even have a burly Teuton slave who'll scrub your callouses away.'

Carnelia looked terrified, glancing from me to the horse-faced Polla and back again.

'I see no need to rid myself of them,' said I, looking at this woman, with her unfortunate face and even more unbecoming demeanour. 'I came by them honourably.'

'In Occidentalia? Your sister, Carnelia?' Polla asked. 'The one who—' She gestured with one hand in an offhand manner.

Carnelia grimaced, glancing at me.

I raised my eyebrow at the woman. 'The one who what?' I asked, though I knew full well what she referred to.

I did not cow her, though. She gazed at me levelly, her expression not in the least bit intimidated. I thought for a moment of my shotgun sitting cozy and nestled in my chest back at Father's villae.

Polla sneered. 'The one who reputedly ruts with animals.' She glanced at Lupina. 'Ah . . . and collects perversions. While many in Rume would pay for a go at her, most good women of standing are outraged.'

Lupina didn't blink.

'Perversions?' I asked.

'This native *thing* you brought from the west.' She waved a negligent hand at Lupina and then casually indicated my belly. 'And whatever monstrosity you have in there.'

Lupina remained blank. A lifetime of slavery – slavery to

Rumans in the Occident – had inured her to the worst things my kinsman could say. Yet, at the look of her dead eyes and blank countenance, I could only feel a great shame at my heritage and a great sympathy for her plight.

I centred myself. Had I my gun, I might shoot Polla. (My love, that is one of the things I miss desperately of the Hardscrabble Territories: constant danger. A civilization full of physically dangerous men and women makes for tolerance, self-preservation, and a very polite and respectful society.) Still. I had my tongue and it has always been dangerous.

'Thank you, Polla,' said I.

She looked genuinely surprised at that. 'Why?'

'You have said something that I very much needed to hear.'

She looked lost. Carnelia said, 'Polla, I don't think—' but I silenced her with a gesture. Carnelia popped one of her long tresses into her mouth and began chewing it, nervously.

'I can't imagine how I could have said anything to *you*—'

'No, you can't imagine at all. And that is very much the point.' I turned and sat back down at our table and beckoned the waiter with the amphorae of wine over. He poured me a small glass, due to my pregnancy. 'Maybe the gods sent you here to me today, Vespasia Polla. I do not know, but you have performed a very necessary service to me.'

When she did not respond I went on. 'You have reminded me how miserable this beast of a city is. How miserable it is and how miserable are its citizens.'

I took a sip of my wine.

'You,' I said, indicating her with my glass in my best imitation of Father, '– are a great horse-faced *bitch* and I would very much enjoy splattering your brains across the cobblestones of the Via Cæliana, yet I failed to bring Hellfire with me on this little shopping spree. Had I known I would encounter something so needing to be put out of its misery – and you *are* miserable, Polla – I would have done so.'

Polla stood there spluttering. When she finally regained her wits, I had already beckoned Rimbenus Minor – the owner's son – over to our table.

'Mister Rimbenus, this woman is disturbing our lunch and insists upon making a scene. Could you escort her out? Or, at least, prevent her from pestering us further?'

Polla's spluttering continued. What finally caused her to shut her mouth, turn on heel, and leave was the notice of the other Ruman matrons in the restaurant. They were beginning to stare.

Carnelia said, 'Sissy, that was harsh.'

I looked at my sister. 'Yes, it was. I think it had probably been better if I had shot her.'

Carnelia frowned. 'You know what I mean. She is an *important* woman. Her husband has as much *gravitas* and clout as Father. You've made an enemy today,' she said, looking at the stewed lamb in herbs on her plate.

'Make no mistake, Carnelia, I did not make an enemy today, I *discovered* one. And I am disappointed in you being unable to discern those who would harm our family and those who would help us.' I looked at her pointedly. 'I remember now why I never wanted to return here. Now, eat your lamb.'

The incident with the Polla harridan killed any enjoyment of the rest of the day. Carnelia was subdued and Lupina silent. We bought the rest of the presents for Father's clients and household, arranged for their delivery, and returned home. The villae was empty and quiet.

I realized it was now that Secundus was speaking before the Senate. I felt another surge of outrage that I wouldn't have been allowed to listen to my brother's suit against my ex-husband even had I wanted to: no women were allowed on the floor of the senate when it was in session.

Carnelia and I retired to our rooms. Rume – the city, its citizens – had worn me out far more than a day in the hardscrabble on horseback might have done. I find myself growing tired, now, often at times I never felt so before and I must assume it is my body making the great changes necessary for the birth of our son.

When Father and Secundus returned, it was already dark and they entered the villa with a great furore and clatter. They were singing a song of the legions and had obviously been at the wine.

'Daughters! Daughters!' Father bellowed from below, in his office. When roused, his voice could carry throughout the whole expanse of his estate. 'Come!'

We made ourselves presentable and hurried downstairs.

Father sat behind his desk in a sort of exhausted yet victorious languor and Secundus, smiling, stood talking softly with Tenebrae. They all held glasses of whiskey and were filling the room with the smoke from Father's Ægyptian cheroots. The atmosphere was thick enough to slice.

'I assume that Secundus' presentation before the senate went well?'

'Well?' Father said, his whiskers quivering with inebriated excitement. 'It was glorious! Masterful!'

'Congratulations, brother,' I said, kissing him on his cheek and greeting Tenebrae warmly. 'I am excited to hear.'

But Father was going on. 'He took the floor like a lion, Secundus did. And fully stating his intention to bear suit upon that shit-for-brains Metellus. Your brother—' he said to me, 'was so forceful, that it took five minutes before Metellus' cadre of asslickers realized that he was presenting evidence before them.'

'It was masterfully done,' Tenebrae added. 'Presenting

evidence in front of the senate is especially frowned upon and it went on so long, I think that they were caught by surprise.'

'So, we won, then?' Carnelia asked.

'Won?' Secundus said. 'Sissy, this was only a speech in which I announced plans to bring suit against Metellus, a member of the senate.'

'Of course,' Carnelia said, negligently. If there's one thing about my sister it is that she cares very little for specifics.

Tenebrae, his rich voice exultant, said, 'It was a resounding victory, Miss Carnelia, in that it alarmed Metellus and his hangers-on greatly. It announced a new Cornelian in the political arena and, I daresay, stirred up the other senators who have less than above-board economic dealings.' He took a sip of whiskey from his tumbler and followed that with a pull off the cheroot. 'I will wager ten silver denarii that Metellus will be knocking at that front door first thing in the morning in hopes of making a bargain.'

'What sort of bargain?' Carnelia asked absently as she poured herself a large cup of wine and faded it with the barest hint of water.

'He'll want us to not bring suit against him.'

'In exchange for?'

'Making a public announcement in the Rume Pandectium regarding Livia's honour. And possibly a few other concessions in some of his interests in Occidentalia.'

That was interesting and a piece of information I had not been privy to earlier. 'What interests?'

'When we were studying the College of Cartographers and Surveyors' records of Anatolia, Tenebrae saw that Metellus had funded a surveying mission to somewhere around *Dvergar*. The findings were quite interesting.'

'What were they?'

'There was some acanhite and galena discovered in the Smokey Mountains south of *Dvergar*.'

'And that means?'

'Silver.'

'Ahh.'

'But with this suit, we'll be able to place a legal prohibition against Metellus from having any dealings in ore,' Secundus said. 'And the rest of the benchers will vote for it. If Tamberlaine doesn't get involved.'

I was beginning to see the plan. 'But you won't, will you?'

'No,' Secundus said. 'We only intend on having him sell us half of his interest.'

'It's solely about money, then.'

Father snorted. 'Everything is about money, Livia.'

'What about the Cornelian honour?'

'It – and your name – will be restored with Metellus' announcement in the Pandectium.'

I looked from the smug face of my Father to Secundus to Tenebrae.

'Congratulations, again, brother,' I said, and turned and left. The words tasted like ashes on my tongue.

In my room, I fell upon the bed. And, love, I can admit to you here in blood and ink, that I wept. For myself. For you. For our son that was to be born in such a small, petty world.

SIXTEEN

Metellus and his personal retinue appeared at the front gate at dawn. I avoided meeting with him, as you might expect. From the smug and expansive mood Father and Secundus were in for the rest of the afternoon it was safe to assume that they extracted from my ex-husband all of the concessions they required. My name would be cleared. The Cornelian family's honour would be restored and its fortunes would rise should a new silverlode be found in Occidentalia.

How desperately did I wish to be gone from Rume.

That afternoon, I spent some time reading what materials Fuqua had to hand on the far lands of Kithai and was much disappointed with the dearth of information in the booklet he gave me. Written by one I. Minea, all of its content was hearsay – sadly, the author had never set foot on the Kithai shore. So, with Lupina and one of Father's guardsmen in tow, I trotted over to the Cælian Pandect and the bookshops nearby and with the help of the attendants there, found some more acceptable reading material. Our time in Rume was to be short, and I had not the luxury of spending weeks puttering about in the dusty halls of the Pandect, so those books I could find on Tchinee that I could buy, I did, and arranged for slaves to deliver them to Father's villa.

As we returned, there was a great clatter from down the Via Mezzo and a cohort of legions trotted by us, all in blue, carbines rattling, their optios calling out '*hup hup hup*' so that each ranker's footstep fell in rhythm. 'War's a'comin' boys!' yelled a centurion, trotting alongside the soldiers, glaring at them. 'Ye'll either be dead or a killer by the end of it, what? *Hup hup hup hup!*'

Lupina and I were silent after their passing. For a moment I smelled the dry dust of the Hardscrabble, the desperation of Hellfire. All the pompatus of war. It would come.

We hurried home.

On the next morning, much of the Cornelian household put on our finest clothes, clambered into carriages – after carefully packing our gifts for the Emperor, and allowing Father enough time to mourn the loss of his stuffed *vaettir* – and ventured forth to Tamberlaine's palace within the walls of old Rume itself. A rainstorm had swept through the city early in the morning and passed, leaving behind a boiling sun to make the air thick and humid, reeking of the multitudes of sin Rume had on offer. My hair, which I'd worn down, clung to my neck and even though I wore one of my lighter dresses, my sweat traced runnels down my sides and back.

Tamberlaine's palace was built in the reign of Silvanus III almost two hundred years ago on the backs of Teuton slaves and reflects that emperor's love of scale. Towering columns and arches, twenty times a man's height, hold aloft a great limestone roof that spans most of the square length of a *stadium*. Tremendous bronze doors decorated with finely wrought creatures of myth stood open when we arrived, and great sprays of sweet smelling Ægyptian jasmine and lychnis bouquets erupted from Cythian stonework urns in bright purple and yellow explosions. As the slaves unlimbered the crate containing

the *vaettir* – while Lupina, Rubus, and Fuqua arranged for the
conveyance of the daintier presents that we would place at
the mounted stretcher's feet – the faint sounds of music came
trilling out of those great bronze doors.

Passing inside, we were greeted by the sight of half a hundred
of the noblest houses in Rume – Tamberlaine's cousins and
relatives, members of the most august houses of Latinum;
scions, senators, military officers, consuls, praetors, legates;
husbands and wives, sombre children, awkward teens standing
in their Ia Terminalia finest. Praetorian guards dressed in
their formal black uniforms, each wearing sword and Hellfire,
immaculately ringed the atrium. A large bronze Minan bull,
head rampant and tail artfully captured in mid-swish, stood
in the centre of the massive chamber as nude acrobats leaped
and turned flips over the beast, yipping and giving small
exclamations with each feat to a smattering of polite applause.
A trio of musicians played innocuous music as slaves moved
through the crowd with wine and water.

Many of those assembled turned to watch our family's
procession into the palace. Father walked at the head of us,
empty handed as befitted his rank, followed by Secundus
who carried a gift – a small onyx cask full of saffron. Both
were dressed in black, finely tailored suits, though my Father
wore his ridiculously weathered hunting cap from our time in
Occidentalia and had his false bear leg – the silver one with
flask, dagger, and bear paw – on prominent display. It clicked
and clattered and gleamed conspicuously in the *daemonlight* of
the hall.

Carnelia and I followed, each bearing smaller gifts – Carnelia
a bottle of fifty-year-old whiskey distilled near Covenant in the
west, I a small picture I painted myself of the White Mountains
and Big Rill during our time steaming upriver. It was a very
small gift, and a very personal one. Behind us followed Rubus,

Fuqua and Lupina, who all kept watchful eyes on the porters who carried the *vaettir* crate.

Beyond the atrium, a matching set of bronze doors stood open, giving us a view of the dazzlingly lit throne room. Standing to one side stood Tenebrae in the black uniform of a Praetorian.

'You are one of Tamberlaine's guards?' Father asked.

'Of a sort,' Tenebrae answered. 'I am his agent, and his point.'

'But . . .' Father's whiskers shifted. 'You did not tell us this. You've had ample opportunity!'

'My apologies, sir. I am, and remain, a friend to you, Secundus, and your family.'

Father ground his teeth but nodded his head. 'You were to watch us and report.'

'I was—'

'No,' Father raised his hand to cut him off. 'I've known Tamberlaine since our youth. There is nothing you can say that I don't already know.'

Tenebrae pursed his lips and inclined his head. I looked at Secundus. He did not seem surprised. Possibly he'd figured it out on his own, possibly Tenebrae had revealed it in whatever pillow talk occurs between two grown men.

'Announce us, sir,' Father said, not looking at Tenebrae.

Tenebrae glanced from Father to Secundus and, back turned, took a few formal steps into the throne room and announced in a ringing voice, 'Gaius Cornelius, Governor of Western Occidentalia, Hero of the Cantaline Rebellion, Laureled Champion of Rume.'

Father clomped into the throne room and limped across the polished marble floor to the raised dais upon which Tamberlaine sat, reclining on a great marble chair. Tamberlaine himself is a thin, wolfish looking man with intense eyes, a sharp nose, and a thick shock of white hair. He disdained the toga minima and instead wore a rumpled tan linen suit, without tie or cravat. As we approached, the servants and retinue following in train, I could see him better. Once, when I was a girl, I was presented to him and remembered him as a whip-cord thin man with red hair and an easy – if somewhat toothy – smile. He was now a man a few years short of sixty, hale and hearty, still quite trim of waist; he held himself with great ease, belying someone of an athletic bent. His white hair was the only outward sign of the ravages of time.

Before the dais, Father took off his ridiculous hat and knelt awkwardly, his bear leg forward and his good leg supporting his weight.

'Hail Father and Emperor! I come bearing gifts for you on this day of Ia Terminalia,' Father said, giving the traditional greeting. 'As ordered,' he added, under his breath.

Tamberlaine stood and walked down the steps to place his hand upon Father's lowered head. 'I am . . .' Tamberlaine said, pausing. He had a light, happy voice with a hint of music in it. His close-shaved face seemed quite young, despite his years, except for the wrinkles at the corners of his intense eyes. '. . . Well pleased.' He clapped his hands together and helped Father to rise. 'And what have you brought me, today?'

Father waved us forward and we each presented our gifts in turn. Two stewards bustled forward, one to write down the gifts (and possibly assess each one's value) and the other to place the gift on the table allotted for them.

Tamberlaine smiled at the onyx cask and whiskey and paused long enough to actually look at my small framed painting of the White Mountains.

He looked at me. 'And what is this?'

'A picture, sir,' I said, keeping my head down.

'Of mountains? Why would a picture of mountains interest me?'

'They are the White Mountains, your majesty. Also known as the Illivatch by the *dvergar*.'

'You have not answered my question.'

'I thought, your majesty, you might wish to see a representation of the far known edge of Occidentalia.'

Slowly, he reached forward and took my chin in his hand and tilted my head back as to see my face clearer.

'You are a bright one,' he said, considering. 'I am trying to decide if you are having a joke at my expense.'

'Your majesty?' said I.

'You present me with a picture of the terminus of my domain on Ia Terminalia. Surely you must have been aware of that.'

For a moment, everything stilled. Father looked at me, alarmed.

'Your majesty,' I said, in the calmest voice I could muster. 'Unlike most of your subjects, I prefer my gifts to say something about me rather than the person I give them to. Snark is one of the great games of Rume. It is also one I do not play,' I said.

He cocked his head, looking closely at me. His eyes had the unblinking quality of some feral thing on a hunt.

After a moment, he removed his hand from my chin and looked again at the picture.

'It's quite a nice picture,' he said.

'Thank you,' I replied.

'You painted it yourself?'

'Yes, your majesty.'

'Hmm. You have some talent,' he said.

He handed it to his steward who paused as his companion tried to figure out some way to notate it. 'Your earnestness will hold you in good stead in the Autumn Lands of Kithai,' he said. He smiled then, revealing bright white teeth. Quite a lot of them. 'The Tchinee value simple honesty. I am pleased you will be one of my emissaries,' he said and glanced down at my stomach for just an instant.

And that, my love, frightened me more than almost anything I've ever encountered. That one glance toward my stomach.

Father waved the porters to bring forward the massive oblong crate. They stood it on end and carefully removed the lid and with many hands carefully exhumed the mount from the crate, pulling away the gauze wrappings and cloth swaddling and backing away.

The *vaettir* stood revealed. Rampant. Ferocious. A bloody knife in one clawed hand, a scalp dangling from the other, teeth bared. It towered over the crowd.

The imperial attendants gasped, moving into the throne room to gain a better view.

Tamberlaine looked up at the stuffed stretcher, unsmiling, his hands clasped behind his back. He walked around it, slowly, looking it up and down. His survey complete, he smiled.

'You brought me one of the bloody elves,' he said, and then he clapped his hands together in a curiously childish gesture. 'What do they call them?'

'Stretchers, your majesty,' my father said.

Tamberlaine looked at Father appraisingly. 'Looks like you've lost some weight, Snuffy,' he said, eyeing the ornate silver leg. 'Did one of these creatures pull your leg?'

Father forced himself to smile. It almost looked genuine – no one other than Secundus, Carnelia or I would be able to tell. 'A bear, Great Father,' he said. 'A particularly nasty bear.'

'Why didn't you bring back the bear as well?' Tamberlaine asked.

'I did,' Father said. 'Or part of it, at least.' He moved so that the massive claws of the beast clacked on the floor.

Tamberlaine laughed. 'Oh, you Cornelians, how you *please*

me.' He clapped again, this time with some authority, and servants rushed forward and presented us with wine. 'Oh,' he said as an afterthought. 'My condolences on the loss of your son in the west. It is unfortunate, surely, and the Empire will be lessened by his absence.'

Father said, 'Thank you, Great Father. Our families are our succour as we age.'

'Or our dooms,' Tamberlaine said. 'And you've acquired a new son to even things out,' the Emperor said. 'So, there you are!' He cleared his throat. 'Welcome to my home, wayward children,' Tamberlaine said, raising his hands wide and gesturing expansively. 'Momentarily we will dine and afterwards I would speak with you, for there are things moving in the world that must be discussed.'

With that, he clapped one more time, as if to indicate he was through with the conversation, and a bevy of servants, stewards, and secretaries rushed forward to usher us into the grand triclinium, a gargantuan marble space ringed with statues of previous emperors – some who even shared blood with the man currently ruling most of the known world. Their white stone faces watched us implacably as we filed into the dining room and found seats on one of the three oversized group couches that lined the feasting hall table. The table itself held massive floral arrangements, purple heliotropes, pink discordants, bright yellow chrysanthemums, red mignonettes. Somehow the artist arranging the flowers had been able to group the flowers so as to not block our view or cause any sort of nausea by the clashing of colour: each arrangement worked in its place and within the room.

The same could not be said for the guests. The Cornelians occupied one couch, opposite Tamberlaine who was joined shortly by Marcus Claudius Pertinax, his cousin and adopted son – a great hairy brute of a man, extremely muscled, and with almost no intelligence whatsoever illuminating his features. I must say now, my love, that should Father be able to arrange a marriage between Carnelia and Marcus, things will go very badly for the empire. While Tamberlaine is still quite hale, I hope he has the sense to adopt another heir, or that he finds some other, more serious mate for Marcus. As much as I love Carnelia, she would make a very poor mother of Rume.

We were joined by Messala Corvinus – one of Father's staunchest allies – and his lovely wife Vesalia, while Tamberlaine was joined by Tenebrae, who greeted him warmly and kissed his cheek – obviously familiar with the Great Father and on intimate terms. On the third couch sat two priests of Ia and one of their acolytes, a fetching Gallish woman, judging from her accent, and a young boy, apparently her son. I surmised she was the wife of the elder priest, though I could be wrong – she could be some honoured guest or even paramour of Tamberlaine's: he was rumoured to have one, despite his widely known homosexual affinities.

After we were all seated, the meal began in earnest. A different trio of musicians – this time with a Medieran guitarist, a drummer, and a violinist, played softly near a statue of Vitellius XI and servants wheeled in carts bearing stewed apricots and candied pears, cherries, pomegranates, grapes, honeycakes, sugared nuts, quinces, and pastries stuffed with crushed almonds and figs. There was ample wine, though nothing extravagant. Everyone waited until Tamberlaine settled himself, picked up a small dried apricot, handed it to his nearest steward who took a bite. When the man did not expire on the spot, frothing at the mouth and convulsing, Tamberlaine took his own apricot and nibbled at it, signalling the rest of us it was time for us to begin. More dishes followed the sweets – tunny steaming in onions and gravy, mullet fried to crisps, a massive turbot broiled with herbs and vegetables. Casks of oysters bedded on fields of crushed ice and shrimp and octopi and other fruit of the sea steamed in broth laden bowls. At one point, there was a whole smoked boar – wild cingale – garnished with pears and other sweet fruits. The guests oohed and aahed appropriately at each dish.

As other guests chatted quietly amongst themselves, Father said 'Quite a wonderful feast, Great Father. We are blessed by Ia and your Imperial majesty to have been included.'

Tamberlaine raised an eyebrow. 'Go on, Snuffy. Tell me more about how wonderful the feast is . . .'

Father opened his mouth, shut it, and began again. 'It truly is scrumptious, your majesty. This turbot –' he said, raising his fork as if to punctuate his words '– is absolutely delectable.'

'That, I believe, is tunny, Cornelius,' Tamberlaine said. 'However much my asshole enjoys the brisk tonguing you're metaphorically giving it right now, I do not need or require it, Snuffy. We all know that I plucked you from your governorship from overseas and demanded you here.' He popped a piece of bread into his mouth and chewed thoughtfully. 'Being Emperor is a curious thing,' he mused and took a small sip of wine from his glass. 'It is hard to forget the lessons that Proculus the Fifth and Gallia the First offer me.'

Father, glad to be relieved of his 'tonguing' duties, took a great swallow of wine and said, 'And what would those be, Father?'

Tamberlaine said, 'The power of Emperor is absolute. I could have you all crucified in a moment, should I wish—' He raised a hand in peace. 'That being the most obvious aspect of my authority. However, there is a power greater than me in Rume and one I must always be mindful of,' Tamberlaine said.

'And what would that be, Father?' Tenebrae asked, as he picked over the oysters from their bed of crushed ice.

'Rumour is Empress in Latinum. Gossip her crown. Great men have been destroyed by wagging tongues.'

It seemed a very small thing for him to be worried about, in my opinion, yet he went on. 'All of my vices—' he said slowly, looking at my Father, 'and there are many, as you know, must be expressed publicly. So, I invite my friends and associates into my home on Ia Terminalia to see me at feast and later, when the real revels start, witness my vigour so that my predilections be known. Closed doors are the enemy of the Empire and will seed doubt and the beginnings of rebellion in the mind of its subjects. No power on earth will save me if I try to keep my life secret. Proculus was a vain and secretive man and look what happened to him. The Praetorians hurled him from The Spire and then dragged his cooling corpse through the streets. All because he would not admit to a little buggery and this grew in the minds of the populace to become the worst sort of sexual depravity. I would rather they know who and what I like to fuck than give them a closed door with which to speculate.'

'Very wise,' Father said, nodding his head. He was joined by others making small noises of affirmation.

Tamberlaine waved their approval away, an irritated look on his face. 'I cannot afford to allow anyone to speculate on my predilections, so I must allow them to view them, such as they may be. In the end, most 'perversions' are hardly that. And my subjects want to know that I am the penetrator, not the one being penetrated.' He took a sip of his wine and looked about the table. 'I am the one who fucks,' he announced in a bland voice.

And that, I think, is one of the roots of Rume's deplorable treatment of women, my love. We can be cast aside – as well I know from Metellus' treatment of me – divorced on a whim, we cannot have any Imperial recognized control of a family. We may own no property until our husbands die (Ia forbid).

Homosexuality is of no matter and incest is cause for only the merest comment. But allow someone to put a tiny bit of flesh inside of you, man or woman, and you become despicable: the Ruman distinction between the penetrated and the penetrator is pernicious. No one respects the womb, the net of life. No Ruman respects the basket that holds food. The cradle that nurtures. They respect only the spear, they fawn upon the sword.

'And so,' Tamberlaine went on, 'I welcome you to remain after our conversation and enjoy the more fleshy activities we have planned. Nothing outlandish, I daresay. A trio of Hellene virgin boys with the sweetest bottoms you've ever seen, and a curious pair brought from Far Tchinee by our esteemed guest, Ambassador Sun Huáng who will join us later, in private, after all of these trinkets and bangles have been cleared away. The people of Kithai do not game like we Rumans game,' he swept his hand to indicate the feast, the gifts, the sprawl of indolent patricians. 'His gift, though. The girls are perfectly formed, yet their torsos are shared – heart, lungs, stomach – so that while two separate creatures, their bodies are joined. Quite fascinating, actually, and I imagine they will prove to be entertaining to those with an appetite for the exotic.'

For a moment, I looked about, searching for Lupina. Then I remembered, Lupina, Rubus, and Fuqua would have returned home, their presence at an imperial religious feast unseemly. Had Tamberlaine ordered it, Lupina could very well have been served up to the revellers later and Father would do nothing to stop him. *Could* do nothing to stop him. Surely Tenebrae would have told him of the half-*dvergar* slave. I could only hope that his eye would not fall upon her.

After the meal had finished, as a family we accompanied Tamberlaine, Tenebrae, to a side ante-chamber where he had two slaves waiting with a simple, small ash crate, clasped with a thick steel lock.

'You, Livia and Secundus,' the Emperor of Rume said, as soon as the door had closed, 'are the representatives of Rume. Within this container,' the Emperor placed his hand lightly on the box, 'is my gift and message for the Autumn Lords of Kithai. You will bear it to them. The Tchinee are a proud people. You may have to suffer indignities below your honour, and suffer hardships, but I order you to bear this message to the Autumn Lords in Jiang. Tenebrae will accompany you, along with a small force of Praetorians.'

Tamberlaine clapped his hands, two of his Praetorians trotted over to a door, said a few hushed words, and escorted a man in. He was a small man in strange white garb – a simple tunic and loose white cotton pants – clutching a long thin cane. His hair was nearly as white as Tamberlaine's himself and his features had a sharper cast to them than most Ruman's although his bearing was almost regal and he looked about the room with a detachment found only in the very old or the very highest rungs of society. In this man's case, it was possibly both.

'This is the August One Sun Huáng, our honoured guest here. He will be your guide – and, I daresay, protector – when you are in Kithai.'

Tenebrae nodded, but Secundus, Father, and I bowed, as those of noble birth know to do when presented with someone of note. Tenebrae hastily corrected himself and bowed as well.

'A pleasure and an honour,' Father said. 'I have always wished to see Far Tchinee, I understand it is wondrous to behold.'

Sun Huáng regarded us calmly. 'It is my home,' he said in a thick Tchinee accent. 'I love it but I may have become... too familiar with its charms. But I think having come here—'

'To Rume?' Secundus asked.

'Yes, having come here, it will make me see home in new light,' Huáng said.

'I don't know if that isn't the kindest thing you've said about my city,' Tamberlaine laughed. 'I imagine you've thought worse. It's a great rumpus, Rume is. Dirty and full of pleasure and nastiness and nobility of spirit matched only by its baseness.'

'Just how we like it,' Father added.

Tamberlaine cocked an eyebrow at Father, his mirth suddenly drying up. 'Yes. Quite.'

'Great Father,' Secundus said, 'It is an honour you've bestowed upon us, truly. Might I ask a question?'

Tamberlaine pursed his lips. 'You are a handsome boy, I must say.' He thought for a moment. 'Tenebrae tells me you made quite a splash in the senate the other day. I rarely pay attention to such things. Will you pursue your suit of Metellus?'

'We are in talks with him currently and it might be possible to work something out.'

'Work something out?' Tamberlaine looked curious. 'I allow the senate autonomy in their law-making to the extent it doesn't interfere with my power or designs. Yet, it's been my experience that when two parties are able to 'work something out' there is, usually, a lot of money involved. Is there money involved in this?'

'Not as yet, your majesty.'

'But the possibility of money.'

'Yes, your majesty.'

Tamberlaine was silent for a long while.

'Hmm. Rume wants for money, always,' he said. 'I expect you will render to Rume its due?'

'Of course, your majesty,' Secundus said.

'All right,' Tamberlaine said. 'Yes, you may ask a question.'

'Thank you, your majesty. The question is simple: why us?'

Tamberlaine called for some brandy and a slave quickly supplied us all with snifters. Another slave offered cigars and cigarettes which were quickly passed about and lit, making the ante-chamber stuffy and quite unpleasant.

'Why you?' Tamberlaine asked to no one in particular. 'First, your father, Snuffy here, seriously disappointed me in the matter of the Diegal girl.' The Emperor frowned for a moment. And then a wicked grin spread across his face. 'But if you had to fail, you did so *spectacularly!*' he crowed. 'I will admit that it was hard holding in my laughter when I had to tell the Medieran Ambassador that *you* allowed a Medieran princess to be eaten by elves.' He laughed, covering his mouth, like a boy who realizes he shouldn't find something so amusing. '*Elves!*' For a moment, he was overcome and slammed his fist into his leg as if trying to control himself. When he looked back up, all traces of mirth were gone and his face was awful. 'Rume must be represented by its noblest blood and since I have no progeny—' He paused then, thinking. 'Since I have no progeny that I can trust with this, I looked to my oldest friend and confidant... Snuffy. Like most of the greatest houses of Rume, you can trace your lineage back to divinity, can you not? The Cornelian clan issued from the loins of the Mater herself.' He grinned again. It flashed across his face like a carnival mask being lifted to reveal a devil underneath and then quickly replaced. 'I have no idea who could have fucked her. Mithras, possibly. Some passing deity, maybe.' He sipped at his brandy. 'Whatever the case, your blood is required. Sun Huáng here knows your rank, he knows your imperial favour—' The lupine smile revealed itself again. 'And he will assure the Autumn Lords that your blood has no cause to offend.'

Sun Huáng bowed again, gripping his cane.

'Thank you, Great Father, for honouring us in this,' Secundus said, bowing in return.

'You might not thank me when it is over,' Tamberlaine said, winking. He considered Secundus again, looking up and down his frame. 'Would you stay for the night-time revels, my boy?'

'Thank you, your majesty, but no. I have much to do before our departure.'

'A pity,' the Emperor said, sniffing. He finished his brandy and set the glass on a marble table. 'Snuffy,' he said. 'I'll expect you at the palace on the morrow. I'm sending you back to Occidentalia but not before we get some things straight about the disposition of our forces and the resources there. I'm of a mind that you've been chastised enough.'

'Yes, Great Father,' my Father said. He looked like a man in need of a drink, desperately, even though he held one in his hand. I imagined then that he would be monumentally drunk before morning.

'And I'll require that you, at least, stay for the night-time activities.'

Father blanched. 'As you say, your majesty,' he said, downing his brandy.

'A pleasure,' Tamberlaine said to the rest of us assembled in the room. 'Go with my blessing.' He turned and walked out of the room. Tenebrae raised his eyebrows, bid us goodbye, and followed the Emperor out. The black-clad Praetorians exited noiselessly.

'A pleasure meeting you,' Sun Huáng said in his stilted yet clear voice. 'I look forward to coming to know you.' He turned, without another bow, and walked from the room. In him was none of the anile fragility of the aged. There was consideration with each step, and a fluidity to his movement that belied the snowy mantle of years on his shoulders.

When Huáng was gone and we were alone except for the pair of lingering slave attendants, Father exhaled, noisily, and Carnelia went to him and placed a hand on his arm.

'I think that went well,' he said. He waited until the slaves and servants retreated and said in a hushed, shaky voice, '*That* man—' he said, pointing at the door, and we all knew it was not of the Tchinee gentleman he spoke of. 'He is pure malice, that's for sure.' He looked about the room as if seeing it for the first time. 'Remarkable. No one was crucified.'

'No, Father, we're all safe,' Carnelia soothed. She stroked his arm and beckoned one of the slaves to bring back the decanter of brandy.

Once Father had another drink in hand, he said, 'You all should leave before he changes his mind and demands you attend whatever orgy he has planned—'

'Father, I don't think you should participate—'

He made a familiar chopping motion with his hand. As you might say, my love, he was in a high dander. 'I've been avoiding Tamberlaine's orgies since before you were born, child. I plan on getting drunk beyond all recognition. Tamberlaine is many things but he wants his victims to be aware enough to know he's the one fucking them. If it gets down to that – and I doubt it will since he values youth and beauty – my arse might be sore in the morning but I'll have no recollection of the event.' He lifted the brandy snifter and drank, making almost greedy, sucking sounds. 'Anyway, he said I've been chastised enough. A public buggery of a patrician by him or one of his agents would cause serious problems in the senate and wealthier families.' He took another deep breath, calming himself by working out the situation. Or maybe the brandy situation was working on him. 'No, now that I think about it, he just wants to make me uncomfortable. He'll not shame me by making me a *cinaedus*.' He looked thoughtful. 'Secundus, the emperor is a very beneficent mood. Be thankful he did not order you to attend.'

We were all silent for a long while thinking about the ramifications of everything that had happened. Secundus picked up the ash messenger's box. As we were preparing to leave, Father said, 'Livia, did you give him that painting to mock him?'

'No, Father. It was something I was proud of and I thought he might like it.'

He gave a short bark of laughter. 'The man knows only physical beauty. Nothing in the arts would please him. If you'd dunked it in molten gold, then he would have given it some consideration, possibly.'

'He *did* give it some consideration.'

'No,' Father said. 'He gave *you* consideration. The painting was absolutely unessential.'

Secundus, Carnelia, and I gave our father kisses and made sure he was well on his way to full inebriation for the orgy before leaving. In the carriage home, Carnelia said, 'You can lie to Tata all you want, sissy, but you can't fool me. You gave that painting of the White Mountains to Tamberlaine on purpose, knowing the significance.'

'Why do you say that?' I said, raising my eyebrow at her.

'Because he's separated you from your husband! During your pregnancy! I know you. That's something you'd not let pass lightly.'

I answered her only with a smile. As you know, some things are better not to acknowledge, my love.

Three days later, after Carnelia and I performed the necessary shopping and provisioning with Fuqua and Lupina's help while Secundus and Father hammered out the details of their arrangement with Metellus, we took a carriage back to Ostia and reboarded the *Malphas*. In some ways, it felt like coming home. I've grown used to travel and developed my own internal inertia.

Father tearily bid us farewell – he'd been hungover and melodramatic ever since Ia Terminalia but insisted that 'nothing untoward occurred, children, other than a great amount of liver damage!' – and the day of our departure was no different. As

Lupina and the Praetorians organized all of our provisions and baggage (and Father steadfastly ignored Tenebrae to Tenebrae's great amusement), we embraced our father one at a time.

'Here,' Father said to Secundus, waving Rubus forward. Rubus carried a Quotidian box. 'I've included a schedule for correspondence. My Kalends is already too bloody, so we'll have to stagger the missives around the Nones and six Kalends.'

'Understood, Father,' Secundus said.

He looked at all of our faces and tears streamed down his cheeks. 'I'll be cursing you, Livia, before the day is out,' he said, sniffing. 'You're taking everyone from me.'

'You'll be all right, Father,' said I. 'Soon you'll be back in the west. When you see Fisk—'

'Yes?'

'Nothing. He knows.'

He looked at me for a long while then took Carnelia's hands and kissed her forehead and embraced Secundus warmly. 'I am very proud of you, my children. I can think of no better emissaries for Rume. Safe travels.' Blowing his nose into a pocket handkerchief, he turned and walked back down the pier to the waiting carriage, his back straight.

That night, on the turning of the tide, the *Malphas* steamed out of Ostia and into Mare Nostrum toward the Eudaemon Neck where the warm bath of our sea becomes dark and passes closely between the Ægyptian and Bedoun shores. For six days now we have steamed through these waters – quite still and steamy with nothing of the mountainous swells we had experienced on the Occidens Ocean – and now we trace the sweltering Ætheopicum coast, the waters crystal blue matched by the cerulean sky.

We are accompanied by Tenebrae and his cadre of Praetorians – clearly our guide and companion from Occidentalia, despite being an informant for Tamberlaine, is the most refined of the Emperor's private troops. These black-clad men seem brutish and dull and more interested in the *Malphas'* provender than interacting with the rest of the passengers. In addition to the Praetorians and the familiar crew of the *Malphas*, we are joined by Sun Huáng who returns to Kithai to vouch for us as we deliver the Emperor's letter. He is a strange man and quite wary of us Rumans, as far as I can tell.

We take our mornings on deck – staying below would be almost impossible in the close heat of the cabins – and Captain Juvenus has been kind enough to provide the passengers with copious deck space for sunning ourselves and whatever exercise we are able to get on the small expanse of wind- and rain-smoothed wooden planks. There are a few small tables and folding chairs so Carnelia, Lupina, and I often have coffee or tea and take breakfast in the shade beneath the front cannon where it's cooler and breezy, while watching the Praetorians and Secundus get in whatever martial drills they can without the benefit of a gymnasia. Our baby is wreaking hell on my appetites and I find myself always somewhat hungry – mostly for buttered toast and fruit – and we have been lucky to have many ports to call in for fresh victuals.

Sun Huáng spends his mornings with us on deck, as well. A young girl travels with him and a larger, lumbering man – quite powerful-looking and heavily scarred across his knuckles, on his neck and face. He presents a most forbidding aspect.

I discovered the girl's name almost accidentally. They had breakfasted near Carnelia and me until Sun Huáng stood silently and walked a little ways from where Secundus and Tenebrae (whose relationship might have suffered a blow at the discovery of the latter's position with Tamberlaine, but the blow had not sundered them) first wrestled, shirtless in the sun and later, panting and heaving, began sparring with short wooden sticks. Secundus was good with the 'sword' – practising the standard Ruman legionnaire gladuis training moves which involved a great amount of stabbing and chopping, but it soon became obvious that while Secundus was proficient, Tenebrae was adept.

Sun Huáng moved a little ways down from where Secundus and Tenebrae clacked and clattered with the wooden gladii and began a slow, methodical movement, stretching his body. First he raised his hands above his head and then performed an action that seemed almost like drawing a bow on each side, but much slower than any archer would. Then the old man moved his hands in a way that seemed like he was brushing something aside and continued to make many more slow, graceful movements, some crouching, some extending. The nearby Praetorians sniggered, and Tenebrae and Secundus had stopped to watch – which was understandable, since this was the first instance that Sun Huáng had done anything worth observing.

I turned to face the girl and hulking man who sat watching Sun Huáng.

'I am curious,' I said, speaking to both of them. 'What is he doing?'

The girl, who was maybe thirteen or fourteen and just coming into her womanhood, said in a totally normal Ruman accent, 'Grandfather is performing the Eight Silken Movements.'

'Grandfather? You are Sun Huáng's granddaughter?'

She gave a short nod to acknowledge it.

'I am Livia Cornelius and this is my sister Carnelia and maid-servant Lupina,' I said. I gestured to indicate Secundus and Tenebrae. 'The sweaty boys out there are my brother Secundus and Gauis Tenebrae, a Praetorian.'

The girl said, 'I am aware of these things but I thank you for expressing them. I am Min.'

'And your companion?' I asked, indicating the scarred man sitting quietly near her.

'He has no name.'

'No name?'

'None that we know of. He has no tongue with which to tell us.'

That took me aback. I must admit here that I know very little of Kithai and its people, and I only had only begun to dig into the books I'd bought in Rume about that far land since our journey had begun.

There was an awkward silence. Finally, I said, 'What are the Eight Silken Movements?'

Min frowned, slightly, and then stood and came to sit at our table. She offered her hand to Carnelia, who took it, and then to me. She had a dry, firm grip with rough palms. She sat down without asking.

'The Eight Silken Movements, or the Baduanjin, are a series of martial exercises that keep the body strong and fluid,' she said, looking from Carnelia to me. She ignored Lupina totally. 'The Eight Silken Movements were created thousands of years ago by the Incorruptible Master Zhongli Quan.'

Secundus and Tenebrae, seeing Min sitting with us, retrieved towels and trotted over, wiping at their shimmering torsos and laughing.

'Why, hello!' my brother said. 'I'm Secundus Cornelius and this fine lad is Gaius Tenebrae.' He pulled out a chair and sat in the sort of relaxed, languorous way that only sweaty men can have.

'Lad?' Tenebrae asked. 'You'll pay for that.'

Min extended her hand, which both men took in turns. 'I am Min,' she said, simply.

'Min is Sun Huáng's grand-daughter,' Carnelia said, her voice bright. My love, we'd been cramming sweets and meats in her

since Ia Terminalia and limiting her wine and the hard edges
of her bones had begun to soften some. Curiously, the hard
edges of her temperament had smoothed as well and recently
her company had been a great pleasure. It is possible that her
frivolity and crankiness had always been in response to an
unacknowledged hunger.

'What's your grandfather doing, if I may ask?' Tenebrae said.
'It looks very ... elegant.'

Min patiently explained the movements again, surprised that
she'd become surrounded by Rumans suddenly. Turning to me,
she said, 'The Eight Silken Movements would be very good for
you, Madame Livia. Many women, heavy with child, turn to
them to maintain their strength.'

'I will consider that, Min,' said I. 'Thank you.'

'It is a martial training?' Tenebrae asked, leaning back into
his chair. Shirtless, he was an impressive spectacle of a man –
well muscled and yet still slim and lithe. 'Ia damn us all, it's hot
here,' he said, moving his chair some to get out of the sun.

'Yes,' Min said. 'Many of Kithai's greatest warriors, like my
grandfather, perform the Eight Silken Movements when they can
do nothing else.'

'Your grandfather? A great warrior?' Tenebrae did not laugh
at her but his disbelief was evident in his tone. He towelled off
his chest and stared at the old man appraisingly.

'At home, he is known as The Sword of Jiang.'

'A swordsman?'

'No.'

Tenebrae said, 'You misunderstand me, possibly. I ask: your
grandfather is a renowned swordsman?'

Min looked at Tenebrae with a level stare. 'I understood you
quite well, Mr Tenebrae. My grandfather is called The Sword of
Jiang.'

'Maybe *I* misunderstand, then,' Tenebrae said, brow furrowed. 'Does that mean your grandfather is a swordsman?'

'He is a great warrior, sir. If that means using a sword, then he will use a sword.'

'Do you think he would be interested in a little sparring?' Tenebrae asked, sitting up.

'I think that would be a very bad idea,' Min said.

'Why?' Secundus asked, interested now.

'He does not like Rumans and would make a lesson of you.'

That last sentiment hung in the air for a while. Tenebrae poured himself a glass of water from the ceramic pitcher and gulped it down in a trice.

Secundus said, 'Come, Gaius. There is still more *armatura* to be done. We haven't worked the spear and shield yet.'

'Excuse me,' Min said, before they could rise. 'I am curious as to something. You Rumans have... as you call it... Hellfire. Guns and pistols and cannons.' She inclined her head to indicate the forward cannon at the front of the *Malphas*. 'Yet you continue to exercise with sword and spear. Why?'

Tenebrae said, 'The gun is a relatively new thing to us, and Rume was founded on the haft of a spear and the hilt of a sword. Thousands of years have not changed that.'

'Hounds bay,' Secundus said. 'Gulls dive. We cannot deny our natures. A Ruman's hand is born for a weapon.'

'And,' Carnelia added, 'Hellfire is expensive. Becoming proficient in it is for patricians and wealthy equites and does nothing for the waistline,' she said.

Min sat taking it all in, as immovable as a rock buffeted by waves. 'I think we are not so different,' she said and stood, bowing. The large nameless man rose and joined her and she disappeared inside the ship to the Kithai Embassy's cabins.

'I wouldn't be so sure about that,' Secundus said, then put his hand on Tenebrae's shoulder. 'Shall we?'

*

Captain Juvenus invited us to dinner that night in the Captain's
Mess and we accepted, graciously. A warm summer squall
sprang up and filled the air with falling raindrops, each one as
warm as bathwater.

It was hot inside the ship, too – the *Malphas' daemons* which
gave power to the dynamos and heated our meals and rooms
could do nothing to cool us in these hotter climes. The Captain's
dining room did have steam-driven rotating ceiling fans that
stirred the air, yet the air itself was so warm and moist that it
did very little to cool us. A sodden informality had descended
upon us like a malaise – men did not wear the jackets of their
suits and often abstained from ties, and the women – there
were only four of us on board; myself, Carnelia, Lupina, and
Min – eschewed the heavier confections, those with flounces and
any extra fripperies, settling for simple cotton peasant dresses
with enough undergarments to satisfy the needs of modesty. I
dare say Tenebrae and Secundus would strut about shirtless if
convention would allow them.

After we had taken our seats and Juvenus invoked Ia in a
short and simple prayer, Secundus said, 'I have bad news from
my father, Gaius Cornelius.'

Carnelia looked alarmed and Tenebrae stilled and looked at
us all at the table. Whatever this news was, he was already privy
to it.

'The Medieran Ambassador in Passasuego was murdered,
along with all his family and retainers.'

An involuntary gasp came from me. 'Passasuego? Do you
think—?'

Secundus nodded his head. 'Father – and Tamberlaine's –
agent says that Beleth was involved and that Fisk and Dveng Ilys
were in pursuit.'

I exhaled. My worse fear had been averted, but the news was still terrible.

'They have established a blockade in the Bay of Mageras and are mobilizing their fleets. We are to be on alert.'

Juvenus and Tricomalee, the *Malphas'* engineer, gave short glances to Sun Huáng, who raised an eyebrow in response. 'Kithai is not hasty when declaring war, gentlemen,' he said, simply.

We discussed the ramifications of this news for a while and waited for the first course to be served: a hearty fish soup with crusty bread and crunchy fried sardines on greens.

'Min tells us that you are a great swordsman, Ambassador Huáng,' Tenebrae said, taking a sip of his wine.

Sun Huáng looked at Tenebrae in a still, blank manner. There was no emotional content to his gaze; he simply took in the strapping young Praetorian with a frank assessment.

'I am known as The Sword of Jiang,' he said in a thick Tchinee accent.

Tenebrae smiled. 'Is that a position of honour? For instance, I am the first sword – or Primus Gladius – of the Praetorians,' he said, folding his napkin in his lap. 'I won that through trial and competition.'

Sun Huáng said, 'They began to call me the Sword of Jiang when I was a young man.' He offered no more.

'We were quite curious about your exercises this morning,' Secundus added. 'The Eight Silken Movements. Your granddaughter Min told us of them.'

Sun Huáng did not respond except to dip his spoon into his soup.

'I say, old chap,' Tenebrae said, 'I'd quite fancy some sparring in the morning. Secundus here, while quite promising, isn't really up to my level. Neither are the other Praetorians. Do you fancy a go?'

The white-haired older man sipped his soup and gave the slightest shake of his head.

'I do not want to become a nuisance, sir, but might I ask why?'

'I have seen you train. I am not inclined,' Sun Huáng responded.

The blush that spread across Tenebrae's face was like wine spilled on a white table cloth. It was almost frightening to behold the way it suffused his whole face. Secundus, looking at his closest friend, became alarmed and placed a restraining hand on Tenebrae's arm.

He said nothing, but snorted then, a sound full of contempt. There was a brittle pride to him I'd seen before in accomplished men. Having won through contest and adversity, his position was tenuous and ever vulnerable to assault or insult. Or so he felt.

Sun Huáng looked at him curiously, wiping his mouth with a napkin. In the *daemonlight* of the Captain's mess, his hair seemed almost luminous and his eyes black. Around the table, Captain Juvenus and his first mate, Engineer Tricomalee, and his assistant, all watched on, spoons stopped in their movements.

'I am on the deck every morning.'

'Yes,' Tenebrae said. 'We have seen you.' The sneer on his features twisted Tenebrae's good looks into a rather petulant aspect.

Carnelia said, 'Mister Tenebrae, might I remind you – since you are a representative of Tamberlaine himself – to remember your manners. Mr Huáng is the ambassador to Rume.'

Tenebrae blanched, and glanced at her, surprised to be admonished by Carnelia. Which is possibly why he did not take it any further. He fell silent after giving Sun Huáng a polite nod of his head, though his face remained red.

The dinner was rather stilted after that and no amount of

wine or soup could rescue the pall that hung over the Captain's table.

Sun Huáng was the first to rise to leave. He bowed to Captain Juvenus and said simply, 'Thank you for your hospitality, Captain,' inclined his head to the rest of us and left the mess alone.

Secundus threw his napkin on the table and said, 'Well, I'm knackered, though I do think I'll take a smoke on the deck, if it's not too wet. Coming, Tenebrae?'

When Tenebrae stood, Min said, 'Excuse me, Mister Tenebrae. I do not think it a good idea – as I have said – but I thought you should know something.'

'Yes?'

'When my grandfather told you where he would be, it was . . .' She paused, thinking. 'You might call it an invitation, though it wasn't that. By telling you where he would be, and when, he was allowing you a formal advantage should you wish to engage him.'

'Engage?'

'You would call it sparring I think, though in Kithai it has far more seriousness than that. Maybe a better way to phrase it would be . . .' She bit her lip. 'A non-lethal duel? Yes. That would be more correct.'

'Why didn't he bloody say that, then?' Tenebrae asked, somewhat ungraciously.

'Because he is master.'

'A master?'

'It is said in Jiang that it takes one hundred days to learn to use a sword. It takes a thousand days to master it. My grandfather has spent many thousands of days studying the arts of war and violence. To direct aggression at him is a serious thing and he must be mindful of the welfare of those foolish enough to issue challenge. He cannot issue any challenge himself.'

Tenebrae looked puzzled at this. 'So, I'm just to attack him? Even when he does not carry a sword?'

Min gave a small smile. 'He is master. The only sword he will require is the one *you* bring,' she said. Standing, she bowed and excused herself from the room.

'Strange people, the Tchinee,' Secundus said.

Carnelia laughed. 'They do know how to make an exit,' she said, and popped a bit of buttered bread in her mouth and began to chew.

SEVENTEEN

1 Kalends of Sextilius, Eleventh Hour, 2638 Annum
Ex Rume Immortalis, Near the Aethiopicum Shore,
Bay of Aribicum

It ended almost before it began.

The next morning the air was cooler, with less moisture in it, and Carnelia and I had adjourned to the deck (without Lupina, who claimed a small intestinal discomfort) to take our breakfast. We had come to the Æthiopicum shore steaming south, southeast toward the Rubrum Horn and beyond past the Persicum Sea into generally unknown waters. Æthiopicum slides by us now sedately on our port, a small, ever-shifting tan line on the horizon. Seagulls wheeled in the heavens, occasionally scattered by the ferocious dog-sized raptors the sailors referred to as Cænavia-birds. Terrifying and reputedly fiercely territorial, they did not harry the *Malphas* in any way but Tenebrae placed some of his Praetorians on guard with carbines just in case.

Captain Juvenus had warned us that these waters were filled with pirates – Æthiopicum is the hub of the slave trade in this part of the world, feeding Rume and Mediera's insatiable need for slaves – but during the day they posed no danger, due to the *Malphas'* four Hellfire cannons. At night, they could prove troublesome if they had a vessel that could match the *Malphas'* speed, which was unlikely. It would have to be *daemon*-driven and it was unlikely that anyone on this coast could afford an engineer, and doubly doubtful any fully trained member of the collegium would deign to sully herself with brigands and lawless men.

Carnelia carried a copy of Vintus' *The Teats of Fortuna* and was reading the more salacious bits of it to me with great mirth when we were joined by Min, shadowed by the hulking tongueless man and her grandfather, Sun Huáng. We welcomed them to our table but Sun Huáng, who had apparently breakfasted before coming up on deck, bowed graciously and immediately moved into the Eight Silken Movements on the smooth wooden deck. His movements, as always, were lithe and graceful yet there seemed to me an underlying ferocious strength to the man's form.

Min was blushing furiously as Carnelia read a long verse about a foolish noblewoman who is tricked into becoming a *pathicus* by a wily young soldier when Tenebrae appeared. He carried two wooden gladii, the kind Praetorians and legionnaires use to train.

Stepping into the sun where Sun Huáng performed the Eight Silken Movements, Tenebrae hailed the older man.

'Mister Huáng! Your granddaughter was kind enough to explain things to me last night,' he said, holding up the wooden sword.

Huáng slowly emerged from the movement he currently performed – one hand stretching above his head as if holding up the vault of sky, and the other as if tamping down an unruly basket of laundry – and came to a standing rest, his hands hanging loosely in front. He said nothing. He only looked at Tenebrae.

'I think a good spar will do us good, and mend any damage done by my hasty words last night,' Tenebrae said, and tossed the wooden sword into the air toward Huáng, softly, so that he might catch it. The older man neatly side-stepped the thrown sword in a movement that seemed so casual it was hard to register. The weapon hit the deck and clattered until it came to rest on a gunwale. Huáng resumed his resting stance. There was no expression on his face, no indication of his mood or temperament.

Tenebrae frowned. 'I see. "The Sword of Jiang" won't deign to sully his hands with the first Praetorian sword, is that it?' The grimace that crossed his face did not become him.

'Gaius, I do not think you should pursue this further—' Secundus said.

'Indeed, Mister Tenebrae,' I added. 'They have warned you many times. This overweening pride doesn't become you.'

He glanced at me. 'I am Ruman. As are you both! It is an insult to my person and the personage of Tamberlaine himself, since I am his representative.'

'Nonsense,' I said. 'You feel slighted and your feelings were hurt.'

'Gaius,' Secundus said. 'He's thirty years your senior if he's a day.'

Tenebrae, whose expression had grown fiercer and more incalcitrant with each word spoken to him, shook his head. 'I will just give him a tap to remember me by,' he said.

Tenebrae stepped forward, swinging the gladius forward lightly to swat Sun Huáng on the hip – a desultory movement, like a parent spanking a wayward child – but as he moved forward the old man stretched and *moved*, blindingly fast, stepping to the side of Tenebrae so that Tenebrae was moving past him in a half-lunge and Huáng grasped the younger man's sword hand, twisting it sharply. Tenebrae yelped in pain.

Sun Huáng took two steps back, holding the sword in his own hand. He came to rest again in a relaxed position, one that looked hardly martial at all.

'The only sword a master needs is the one his opponents bring,' Min said, echoing her words from the previous night.

Tenebrae looked surprised but undaunted. He flexed his hand
– the one that Huáng had wrenched to take away his sword –
and quickly scooped up the gladius he'd initially thrown to the
old man.

As our dear friend Shoestring might say, it got real ugly, real
quick after that.

Tenebrac wasted no time striking forward with his sword.
Huáng neatly stepped out of the way, his foot lashed out,
impacting with the younger man's shin as he passed and sending
him sprawling. Tenebrae drew himself up quickly, scrambling
on the deck and cursing, but he clearly favoured his right leg as
he came forward, his sword point low and weaving. In the past,
as we've watched Tenebrae at his sword exercises and *armatura*,
he'd always been quite flashy, twirling and spinning with his
wooden blades, giving triumphant little yells with each practiced
stroke. All of the theatrics were gone now. His brow was drawn,
his face grim, and all pretence of showmanship vanished.

Tenebrae lashed forward, striking, but again Huáng stepped
aside so quickly that his movement resembled a door being
jerked open and took a long lunging step to his flank so that
before Tenebrae could stop his forward motion, the old man was
close in on his left side. With the pommel of his practice sword,
he popped Tenebrae's left cheek, sending the younger man
toppling backwards. Blood erupted from Tenebrae's nose and
mouth. Secundus gave a startled yelp and went to his friend's
side. Tenebrae wiped his mouth and pushed himself into a
standing position, bleary and weaving like an axe-struck bull of
Mithras.

'That's enough, I think—' Secundus said.

'No,' Tenebrae answered. 'I'll not yield until I have at least
scored on him.'

'Gaius—'

Tenebrae put a bloody hand on Secundus' chest and pushed

him away, leaving a crimson handprint on my brother's white tunic.

I must give this to the young Praetorian; he could, if anything, take some punishment. But – and I can say this to you, my love – it was the Ruman pride and superiority pushing him on. A Ruman might be equal to every other Ruman, but no man from elsewhere is equal to a man of the Eternal City. Rume is the first among all nations and its citizens carry that with them, even to the Æthiopicum short and on to far Kithai. To their doom, even.

From somewhere, Tenebrae mustered the energy to move into a crouch and begin a more cautious stalking of Huáng. For Huáng's part, he simply stood there at rest watching the young man, the wooden sword held almost negligently. It was a curious thing. His calm demeanour almost reflected Tenebrae's aggressiveness back upon the younger man. The unassailable self-assurance that had suffused the Praetorian guard was gone now and all that was left was the gristle of pride and anger. How pleased Father would be.

Tenebrae made a feint at Huáng's leg. Huáng, in response, made a short almost comical little leap to the side and forward so that he was positioned once more to Tenebrae's side and back, behind the striking arm. The Praetorian took two hasty steps backwards, flailing with his sword, but Huáng did not press his advantage.

Moving in a low, aggressive crouch, Tenebrae circled. Blood flowed freely from his nose, making his face and jaw a gore-smeared slick and giving him an almost feral aspect. Sun Huáng did nothing except turn to face him. There was an ineffable settling of the older man's frame, almost in resignation. When Tenebrae lunged this time, Huáng parried his strike with his sword then lashed forward with his own, so fast it was almost as if the movement didn't have time to register on the eyes. His wooden sword struck the younger man directly in the sternum. Had it been a real blade, it would have exited his back and made a great swampy mess of all of his most vital innards. It was an obvious death blow.

Tenebrae pitched backwards, dropping his sword, clutching his chest. Secundus leapt to his assistance.

Sun Huáng placed the wooden gladius by Tenebrae and said, 'You may present your sword to me formally when you have recovered.'

The old man gave Tenebrae a short nod of his head in what I could only surmise was a miniature bow, turned to Carnelia, Min, and me sitting at the breakfast table, and presented a full one. He then began his Eight Silken Movements again as Secundus helped Tenebrae rise and walk below decks.

'What did he mean by presenting his sword?' Carnelia asked.

'It's a Kithai formality,' Min said. 'And a great honour. Mister Tenebrae, if he chooses to present his sword, will be offered the chance to train with my grandfather.'

'Would that mean that he'd be Huáng's apprentice?'

'No,' Min said. 'That's a more ritualized process. It would mean that Tenebrae has the proper humility to accept defeat and by doing that is able to take instruction. My grandfather then would be obliged to offer Tenebrae clear examples as to how he defeated him.'

'Examples?'

She said a near unpronounceable word. '... means martial wisdom. The only way my grandfather can make him understand how he was bested is to train him enough so that he might understand.'

'It sounds like a very formal thing,' I said.

'In Kithai, everything has centuries, millennia, of history. Much as your Rume does. There are traditions that can be broken, but the matters of war and violence are not one of them.'

'That makes a strange sort of sense. Is there a great deal of formality in the bedroom?' Carnelia asked. Min answered with a furious blush.

The next morning, his face swollen into a turgid purple mask and walking very stiffly, Tenebrae found Sun Huáng on the deck in the sun doing his exercises. This time he carried a real sword.

Approaching the old man, he stopped five paces away and slowly sank to his knees. He lifted up his sword on both palms, skyward, and said in a clear voice, 'Sun Huáng, I was wrong to doubt your skill. You bested me fairly and with great mercy, I see that now. I present to you my sword.'

I glanced at Carnelia, who sat nearby. 'How does he know to do this?'

'I told him to,' Carnelia answered, winking. 'The man is beautiful – well, not so much anymore – but he's denser than stone. He needed someone to tell him what to do.'

'That's remarkably kind of you, Carnelia.'

She waved that away. 'We're on a boat, Sissy. Tenebrae has nowhere to go and he'd been trounced soundly. If he didn't do a bit of growing up, it would make for a very tense trip.'

'Possibly it isn't just Tenebrae who has done some growing up,' I said. 'There was a time when you might have enjoyed every moment of his discomfort.'

She laughed. 'Oh, it's nice seeing him have his own arse handed to him, I grant you that. But he's a Ruman, and Secundus' lover. And I would not have our brother's heart broken by a wounded, prideful man.'

I looked at my sister closely. 'Are you sure you're well, 'Nelia? I have never heard you speak so.'

It was her turn to blush. 'Oh, sissy. I'm quite sure I'm fine.' She paused. 'I think back on our time in the Hardscrabble, when all those dreadful *vaettir* were leaping about on the backs of the shoal auroch, killing and killing our men. Scalping Gnaeus. And I think about the baby you're bearing. And now we're going to a new unknown, sailing to Far Tchinee. And then I remember how silly I've acted and I'm somewhat ashamed.'

I took her hand in mine. 'No need, dear. No need.'

She looked back to Tenebrae kneeling in front of Sun Huáng. The older man stood in front of him and was speaking in a low voice. Eventually he took the proffered sword and helped Tenenbrae to stand. They spoke for a short while and then clasped forearms in the Ruman fashion.

'Looks as if Tenebrae is serving a new master, now,' Carnelia whispered. 'I wonder how much of this he will report to Tamberlaine.' A curious expression crossed her face. 'I wonder if Tamberlaine ordered him to seduce our brother?'

That was a horrible thought. And quite likely. 'I hope not.'

'I hope the honourable Sun Huáng beats him. Daily,' Carnelia said.

'There's the Carnelia we know and love,' I said.

'There's no changing a leopard's spots.'

'No,' I said, looking closely at Tenebrae. 'There isn't.'

And that, my love, is all that I have to tell you. There is very little of the blood-ink left now and I am weary. The sea is still dark yet the sky lightens, a multihued riot of colour and striated clouds, and we've left sight of the shore. The seas have become rougher here, though nowhere near as treacherous as the Occidens, and I can see, through the thick glass porthole, the pink and purple of sky alternating with the blue-grey water. My back aches and young Fiscelion stirs within me. I hunger. I've sat here through the night, writing this all down to you. I feel as if you're closer to me when I tell it – as if we lay in bed together and I was just speaking softly into your ear the events of the last few days.

Sometimes I take out the shirt you gave me and smell it. There's something of you still in it. The ghost of you.

When the baby kicks or shifts, we are connected. When my eyes close and I can dream, I am with you. When I cut myself and let the blood, we are joined through the invisible tether.

I love and miss you.

Please write and tell me all.

Your loving wife,
Livia

EIGHTEEN

Kalends of Quintilius, 2638 ex Ruma Immortalis

NEXT DAY, WE CAME UPON the slaughtered stretcher. Strange thing was, no carrion fowl circled above, no turkey buzzards tugged at the creature's innards. The thing lay in a tamped down circle of dust. No shoal animals had disturbed it.

Fisk whistled. 'All my days, Shoe, I've never seen the like.'

'I have.'

'Let me guess.'

The elf was laid, sprawled out, bound to stakes at the ankles and wrists with what looked to be hemp threaded with strands of wispy spun silver. Its eyes were blackened as if it had *angelis* fever, its mouth open in a wail arrested in the midst of finding voice.

On its visible skin, arms and legs, were burn-marks. I'd seen them before.

'Correct me if I'm wrong,' Winfried said, staring at the corpse. 'That is a *vaettir*?'

I dismounted from Bess and approached the dead thing. With it laid out there, you didn't get the scale of the creature until you were right upon it. From crown to toes, the stretcher was at least fifteen feet tall. A big male; powerful and deadly.

But trapped. Met its end in the ignominious dust.

I fear the things. Times I've cursed them. Have done my part in killing them. But never like this. Whatever its character – and I was beginning to see that not all *vaettir* were the same – no stretcher deserved death like this.

'Been here two, three days maybe,' Fisk said, looking around. He dismounted from the black and stared at the dead stretcher. The wind tossed the shoal grasses, making them writhe and whip in the morning light. Fisk made a circle around the creature.

'Beleth made camp over here. Looks like he had a couple of fellas with him, judging by their boots.'

'How does one trap a *vaettir*?' Winfried asked.

'One doesn't,' I said. 'When stretchers are about, you hie your ass homeward or get out your Hellfire. Nothing else much to do.'

'Clearly, there's been some innovation along that front,' Winfried said, grimacing.

'Ia damn,' Fisk said.

'Last year,' I said, 'we took some patrician fools on an auroch hunt. *Vaettir* interrupted the party. Bunch of folks died but in the fracas, we managed to down one of the stretchers. She became Beleth's pet, I guess you'd call it.' I shivered with the memory.

'And those markings?'

'Beleth's work, of course.'

'What hellish thing could he be wanting from them?' Winfried asked.

'That's the question,' I said.

Kneeling by the creature, I peeled back the thin fabric covering its chest. *Vaettir* care very little for clothing and even less about modesty or protecting their incorruptible flesh from the elements but, as far as I've ever been able to tell, they love to take trophies, mementos from kills. I think the creature's shirt once might have been a homespun sodbuster's blouse or part of a dress. Woven in its hair were bits of copper and turquoise. Wound about its wrist, a golden necklace of a style known a century or two ago.

There were more intricate burn marks upon its chest and limbs. Glyphs, Beleth had called them. For an instant I remembered

Agrippina looking up at me with that unfathomable gaze. Baring sharpened teeth.

'They look like the wards and burns that Sapientia showed us on the Grantham woman,' I said. 'And those that Beleth marked on Agrippina.' I looked at Fisk.

Ignoring that, Winfried cocked her head and said, 'Like great crows, they seem.'

I shook my head. 'The *vaettir* are hard to understand, ma'am, and naturally, when you encounter them you want to liken them to something. You want to compare them to something in the natural world,' I said. The woman looked at me. Her face was drawn and, very much like the *vaettir*, she had a rapacious look about her. 'But they're beyond nature as much as they're beyond comprehension.'

When she said nothing, I continued. 'They're like crows, but they're like the bear, or the mountain lion or even the shark, too. They're fast as lightning in the anger-stoked skies. They're like vicious tricksters. They're like us, dreadful deadly creatures.' I shook my head. 'But they are more than this, too,' I said, and told her of the stretcher that saved me at the ill-fated ambush.

Fisk spat as I spoke.

'So,' she said, slowly, 'you mean to tell me that there are *vaettir* with other . . . other agendas than simply rapine and violence?'

'Bah,' Fisk said, turning away.

I ignored him. 'Yes,' I said. 'They are more than what we know. They are not just deadly, though they are that. Something else moves them.'

'I did not understand the *vaettir* even before witnessing them and now I am even more confused,' she said.'

'Then waste no more time pondering it,' Fisk said. He ranged about, stooped, looking at the ground, marking our quarry's movements. 'They're headed for Port Caldo, Shoe. You were right.'

'My three favourite words,' I said.

'Stow it, pard.' Abruptly, Fisk stood up, alarmed. 'The horses!'

A riffling sound came, like wind-whipping clothing, and a great shadow passed overhead, wheeling. A *vaettir*.

In a flash Fisk was at his black, tugging out his carbine and I had out my pistols.

'Get down, Winfried!' I said, only a moment before a stretcher arced overhead, flipping, wickedly clawed hands extended.

In response to my cry, Winfried immediately ducked and slid from Buquo's back but not before the *vaettir's* hands snatched her hat away. She cried out. Blood flowed freely from a deep cut on her forehead.

Another shadow whipped overhead, hissing, and both Fisk and I fired, leaving a cocoon of sulphuric Hellfire smoke around us. More shadows arced overhead – no telling how many stretchers were there – but Fisk and I had been in this position before. We remained low to the ground and shot anything that came close enough to sight. *Vaettir*, when they can't get human or *dvergar*, are fine with killing horses, though.

Fisk's black screamed and pitched, falling over into the dust of the shoal plains, blood pumping from its neck. Winfried, wild-eyed, snatched at Buquo's reins, tugging his head down. Bess, without any prompting from me, grunted heavily and then knelt.

Cursing, Fisk readied his carbine. When the next shadow passed overhead, he busted loose two rounds, whipping the lever action around like lightning, tracking the *vaettir* in its course.

It was the stretcher's turn to scream and whine. Off, beyond the circle of the grass in which Beleth's stretcher was tied, the *vaettir* hit the earth, hard. Fisk ran forward, levering another Hellfire round into the breach of his carbine and sighting. He was on top of the stretcher and fired, once, twice. Beyond, I could see another of the devilish things racing for him.

'Down, Fisk!' I cried, and my partner dropped.

Guns out, I fired directly into the toothy, grinning face of the *vaettir* as it came forward, directly toward me. The sinking despair

238

caused by Hellfire was matched by the knowledge that the stretcher, even though I'd placed some shots in it, was still oncoming.

Time slowed, then, in the molasses of panic. I could see the great muscled thing pounding toward me, gigantic and growing taller with every step forward. Its teeth sharp as razors and an unfathomable grin on its face, hands out like the talons of some fearsome raptor come to bear me away.

I kept the pistols between us, rising and firing and for an instant the expression on its face changed, to one of outrage, to one of alarm. My shots were finding their mark.

And then, like I'd been hit by the *Valdrossos* herself, the great monster barrelled into me, its thigh catching me in the ribs and sending me flying, senseless, pistols tumbling away and all the air in the world knocked clean from my chest.

I knew not much more but dimly heard the sound of more gunshots and felt the despair of Hellfire as *daemon* upon *daemon* were loosed.

Then I closed my eyes.

'All right, pard,' Fisk said, slapping my face lightly. 'Where'dya keep it?'

'Keep what?' I said, chest aching.

'The grog, Shoe. Cacique.'

'Waterbag on Bess,' I said.

Fisk disappeared but returned shortly, placing the bag to my mouth and letting me drink the burning, spicy liquor.

'Keeping the cacique in a waterbag? Think I'm gonna steal your hooch, Shoe?'

Shaking my head hurt. 'I'm old,' I said. 'And know all the wiles of man.' *Where did that come from?* I thought.

Fisk smiled. 'Can you sit?'

'Yes. I think so. Winfried?'

'Right here, Mr Ilys. You took a terrible blow,' Winfried said.

Her wild-eyed look had disappeared. She seemed calmer now, cantered.

'Bah. I'm fine.' When I moved, something in my side was a tad crunchy and there was pain, a whole world of it in my chest. I tamped the pain away. Ignored it. With great effort, I sat up and, after some effort (and support from Fisk) rose to my feet. I took another long pull on the cacique and then surveyed the damage around me.

'Godsbe,' said I, looking around. 'We've got two more dead stretchers here.'

'And a dead horse,' Fisk said. His face was unreadable. He turned to me. 'That's why I don't name them, pard.'

His black lay in the dirt, neck slashed and bled out, making a muddy swath around its head.

'She was a good mount, Fisk,' I said, bowing my head. 'I'm sorry.'

'Not as sorry as those who killed her,' he said, looking at the dead *vaettir* with an awful expression. 'Now go ahead and tell me the stretchers are more than just killers,' he said, and spat.

'How did they—'

'Came in close after you dropped that big bastard and I managed to hit the other two a few times – enough to scatter them.'

'Buquo can carry one stretcher, I imagine, along with you and Winfried.'

Winfried sounded alarmed. 'We're bringing them with us? The *vaettir* corpses?'

'Oh, yes. Get them stuffed and shipped off to Rume, we could make a pretty penny,' I said, thinking back on Livia's letter to Fisk. 'But that one,' I said, indicating the stretcher that Beleth had bound and marked up with glyphs, 'We need to show to our friend Samantha Decius. An engineer. If there's anyone that can tell us what Beleth is doing – or trying to do – it's her.'

Fisk nodded. 'You can ride, pard?'

I toddled over to where Bess stood. She busked me with her head and then nipped at my coat.

'I imagine so,' I said, testing the damage done to my ribs. They were barking with pain, sending out burning rings around my chest. Every breath was an agony. But I'm *dvergar* and we can push it all aside. 'I can make it to Porto Caldo.'

'Lighten the mule's load, and we'll sling this other stretcher on the back and make a beeline for the Big Rill. At the shore, we can cut saplings for a travois,' Fisk said. 'You need help up, Shoe?'

I dumped some pots and pans, an extra bedroll, one of the large sacks of oats. Bess, her head turned toward me, watched implacably as I removed all the unnecessary and replaceable stores. With all three of us pitching in, we got the stretcher on the rump of Bess, who groaned and gave me a sullen stare. The *vaettir*'s arms and legs hung down and dragged on the ground. Using rope, we bound up the corpse's ungainly limbs as best we could, so that Bess could move, but it was a precarious load.

We moved slowly for the rest of the day, and every step Bess took was a misery. I could feel my breath catching with each hoof-fall. She was a steady, indomitable beast, but had a jarring gait. By the time we stopped for the night I was in a cold sweat and half insensible from cacique.

Winfried and Fisk took watches that night, and for the first time in nearly a hundred years, I went to bed early and rose late. Whatever numen or old gods that guard the wanderers of the plains were with us, though, and the new day dawned dry and bright. Nevertheless, I'd developed a ragged cough that hurt like a bitch every time it erupted from my outraged throat.

'Shoe, you've got some broken ribs. Might be a pierced lung. Will you be able to make the ride? We push hard today, we'll make Porto Caldo by midday tomorrow.'

I pulled heavily from the cacique. Nodded. 'I'll make it,' I said, a tad too forcefully. Even speaking had its difficulties. 'You might have to tie me down, though.'

Fisk raised his eyebrows. 'That bad?'

'Bad enough.'

'All right, then, let's get started.' He took some hemp and tied me to the rings of my saddle. Bess, who must've known something was amiss, did not bite or stomp on his boots or any other such mischievousness.

After giving me a serious look, Fisk took the lead rein, and mounted behind Winfried on the massive draught horse.

'Hie,' he said, nudging the big creature with his spurs. 'Hie, Buquo.'

We rode.

We reached the gurgling waters of the Big Rill by dark and Fisk left Winfried to tend a fire on the shore as he cut four taller gambel saplings with a hatchet to make travois. The Big Rill was high and rushing and still frigid. Under Fisk's watchful eye, I stripped naked and waded out as far as I could while keeping my feet. The cold helped kill the pain, an old outrider's remedy.

'You look like a wee little bear whose hair has been rubbed thin on his arse.' He thought a moment. 'And belly,' Fisk said. Winfried, who had been only slightly alarmed by my undressing – my pain was great enough that I didn't care whether she inspected me from crown to crotch – did her best to hide her smile.

Dvergar are hairy, that's for sure, but when I can I keep my head and beard well-groomed. The rest of me? Way I figure it, it's just extra-insulation for those cold winter nights.

'No need to kick a man while he's in pain, pard,' I said, neck deep in the icy run-off from the White. I couldn't feel my feet. Nor my chest.

'Remarkable, though,' Fisk said to Winfried. 'For such a stout fellow to have such dainty—'

'That's enough of that,' I said.

'You could use a bit more meat on you, Mr Ilys,' Winfried said and I *knew* she was trying not to laugh. 'You look burly enough when clothed, but you're white as a grub naked and could use some fattening before winter.'

'The greenhorn now? Oh, damn this all to hell,' I said, and walked from the waters. I used a rough wool blanket to towel off as gingerly as I could and dressed in fresh duds, not as trail-grimed. For the moment, due to the cold waters and cacique, I was relatively pain-free.

The night was mild and the cacique bladder was quite a bit lighter before I shut my eyes.

In the morning, it was overcast and a colder wind whipped down from the White's skirts. It can get chilly even in summer on the plains.

'Any sign of stretchers?' I asked in a thick voice. I coughed into my sleeve, heavily. Black tracers swam in my vision and I felt like I was going to expire between the need to cough again and the apprehension of the pain each cough caused me. I was chilled to the bone now and no blanket or extra coat could warm me to my satisfaction.

'None,' Fisk replied. He looked haggard. I imagine he'd been up all night on watch. 'The one you dropped must've scared them off.'

'Must have 'em all out of sorts, what with—' I hacked into my sleeve, each convulsion full of pain. 'The marked up one.'

Fisk didn't respond. Winfried went about camp, rolling blankets and feeding Buquo. Fisk rigged the travois to both Bess and the larger horse. When he was through, he said, 'You want to go in the sling or on Bess?'

'I'll ride,' I said. 'Until I can't ride any more.'

'No need to break yourself over pride, Shoe. I can feel your fever from here,' he said, holding out his hands like a man warming himself over a fire.

'No,' said I. 'The travois is for the stretchers.'

Fisk pursed his lips but nodded.

It was harder to mount that morning, and in the end, Fisk had to help me up and tie me to the saddle once more.

'Drink the cacique, Shoe,' Fisk said, frowning. 'As much as you can.'

'Not much left,' I said, raising the water bag.

'Drink it.'

I did, though it didn't leave me feeling much better. We started off and at some point I passed out either from the pain or the drink, I couldn't tell you. When I woke, I was in the travois and the stretcher was trussed on Bess' back. When Fisk heard my groans, he had Winfried slow Buquo and from on high, on the back of the draught horse, he looked down on me.

'You were gone, pard. Hot as an ember to the touch. Like you've swallowed a *daemon*. Weren't gonna stay on even when I tied you.'

I couldn't respond. I was locked in some physical half-world where I had to cough but couldn't. Where fire burned me but I was never consumed.

'We're almost there, Mr Ilys,' Winfried said in a concerned tone. 'I can see the smoke rising before us. We'll be on a ferry to Porto Caldo within the hour. In two, we'll have you in a barber or doctor's care.'

'You're not gonna leave me behind, Fisk,' I managed to get out.

Fisk was silent for a long while. 'You're deathly ill. You say the word and I'll sit by your side and we'll pick up the trail once you're better.' He sucked his teeth. 'It'll be colder than Brujateton by then, though, and no telling if Beleth will still be on the continent.'

'Gods damn it, Fisk,' I breathed. 'That ain't fair.'

I cursed then, cursed my luck. Cursed the *vaettir*. Cursed the non-existent gods. Cursed Beleth.

'Go, damn you. Get that sonofabitch.'

'I will keep you informed of the hunt, pard. And you can join us when you are better.'

'Bah,' I said.

We reached Porto Caldo before the afternoon was old and Fisk had Bess stabled and my person ensconced in a cheap quay-side hotel before dark. Porto Caldo is the small harbour on the Big Rill only an hour or so ride down-mountain from Hot Springs. Indeed, when I was young, Porto Caldo *was* Hot Springs, until they found silver in the Whites.

Fisk must've gone round to tithe at the crossroads college of the Mater, for two of the mother's acolytes versed in bloodwork came by my room to examine me with cold hands and serious expressions. They made me drink a cloying honeyed concoction that would've had me swooning if I'd been able to stand upright, but merely obliterated all vestiges of consciousness. I passed out as the acolytes chanted over me and waved myrrh incense around the hotel room.

When I woke, the room was empty. My cough had eased and there was less pain in my chest. Maybe from the quality of the light or the sounds without the room, I knew days had passed. There was the clanging of a steamer's bell, and the rough hollers of stevedores moving freight onto a barge, and the smell of cooking onions coming from downstairs and horseshit, river, and dead fish from the open window.

A note sat on the bedside table, along with a piece of parchment, some herbs, and a pitcher of water, a pitcher of wine. There were embers smouldering in the room's small hearth, and a cast iron kettle above them, so someone had checked on me in my unconsciousness.

I picked up the note. It read:

2 Nones Sextilius, 2638

Shoe, my friend,
I'm sorry to have had to leave but there was nothing for it
except to go. I waited until the Mater's acolytes told me your
internal wounds would not kill you and your fever had abated. I
could not tarry here any longer.

I am bound south for New Damnation. I have taken a
steamer and the Lomax woman accompanies me. I plan on
buying a horse (or commandeering one) there and contacting
Andrae to learn if he has any more information on Beleth.

Things in the larger world are deteriorating swiftly, my friend.
Your predictions of war have proven true. As you already know,
war has been declared by Mediera on Rume. News of the
ambassador's death travelled fast, and Mediera has withdrawn
all its nationals from Rume and instituted a blockade in the Bay
of Mageras. Now, there've been two naval skirmishes on the
east coast of Occidentalia – both targeting munitions and silver
bearing vessels. All of Rume's legions are mustered and her
navies roused into their most watchful and bellicose positions.
I have this information from Hot Spring's garrison commander
who has it from on high – the information is, without a doubt,
fresh from the commander's bloody and cooling Quotidian.

The blockade in Mageras might be a boon to us in the hunt
for Beleth – it will be that much more difficult for him to get off
continent now. The other side of that denarius is that if he does
gain passage, we will never reclaim him.

We have the two vaettir with us – heavily salted. Their flesh
does not decompose at the rate of mortal flesh, yet it is fearfully
malodorous nonetheless. Be glad you are not sitting atop this
particular cargo.

Make haste, Shoe, in your recovery but do not hazard

yourself. I know your dvergar *blood gives you a resilience that lends an air of overconfidence. Rest until you are well. Once you are hale, come south immediately. I will leave word at garrisons and with Andrae as to my whereabouts.*

I remain your friend,
Hieronymous Fiscelion Iullii

I pushed myself out of bed, drank heavily from the pitcher of wine, and then pulled on my trousers and buckled on my guns. My chest hurt, yes, but it was just a niggling pain now and I would not be separated long from the hunt. Gathering what little gear I had – my money pouch remained around my throat – I went downstairs to settle up with the hotel owner and find passage south for me and Bess.

NINETEEN

4 Ides of Sextilius, 2638 ex Ruma Immortalis

I WAS ABLE TO GAIN passage on a steamer barge downstream
that afternoon, though it cost dear – a silver denarius dear
– and I had to show the papers Cornelius had provided me and
threaten to bring the portmaster before the captain of the barge,
a stout, low-slung *daemon*-fired vessel called *Gemina*, would agree
to my passage. It was the fourth day before the Ides of Sexitilius
and I was six days behind Fisk.

The barge was very similar in layout to Maskelyne's *Quiberon*,
but without the rowmen slaves. It was possessed of a squat cabin
for the captain, who was a dour man named Numask, on top
of which sat the pilot's roost. Trailing from those cabins were
the crew mess and bunks, and a couple of staterooms that could
be easily converted to more bunks. Beyond that was the domain
of the engineer, a man whose name I never learned. In addition
to the cabins, there was a large roofed cargo hold and livestock
pen, on top of which extraneous passengers were allowed to make
themselves a slow-moving camp, in the same manner as we had
aboard the *Quiberon*. Captain Numask was kind enough to supply
a rather moth-eaten canvas tent, but unlike the brusque Maskelyne,
he did not allot any of his crew or servants to assist in its assembly
on deck. So many hours into the night I struggled with the fabric
and wood contraption and my aching chest proved a great detriment there.

The *Gemina* had far fewer lascars. Those it did have were *libertini* and in general a sorry lot, idle and profane, indolent. They lolled about near the swing-stages on the fore deck, gambling, smoking, and cursing. From what I could tell, the main cargo of the ship was silver pigs and there was a heavily armed cadre of fierce-looking men, clad in the black and gold livery of the Tempus Union – a militarized delivery company out of Encantata – all speaking Brawley, guarding the precious stuff.

Once erected, mine was not the only tent on the roof of the *Gemina*. There was a pair of hard-faced female *pistoleros* escorting what looked like an extravagantly rich sweetboy and, curiously, a clutch of *dvergar* tradesmen, maybe five all told. Judging from their garb and features, they looked to be of the eastern Eldvatch clans. Like me, they had pitched their tents far down-wind of the *Gemina*'s sulphurous stacks. They regarded me warily and did not respond to my greetings given in our natural tongue. It was a large vessel, and there was ample room on the warehouse roof and much space between our tents.

After I tended Bess in the livestock hold, I returned up deck to my tent to have a dinner of hard-tack. One of the Tempus Union guards watched me with a baleful glare, as if at any moment I would make an attempt to steal a silver pig twice my own weight. I stared back at him, blatantly, too tired to do anything else. An evil smiled crept across his face, like oil on water. I did not linger about on the lower deck long enough to discover the cause of the man's mirth.

It was too easy to compare the comfort of the *Quiberon* to the dearth of it here on the *Gemina*. Indeed, as I half reclined outside my tent and smoked and watched the stars wheel overhead, the Whites pass by in a ghostly, luminous march, always aware of the thrum and shiver of the *daemon*-driven paddle-wheel, I allowed myself a short pig's wallow in self-pity. My cacique gone, my tabac pouch near empty, and once again alone beneath the vault of heaven.

And war was coming.

I might've fallen asleep. I don't know. It was late at night and a considerable time from the first hour. The *Gemina* was quiet except for the thrum of its *daemon* within and the occasional nicker of horses below me. We were anchored near the eastern shore, since night travel was perilous on the Big Rill even for the *daemon*-fired; the paddlewheel was still and all was silent. If there were Tempus Union guards alert and on guard below on the deck, I could not discern them.

When I rose to enter my tent to find what warmth and comfort my blankets and sleeping roll would provide, quite chilled from the easterly mountain wind, the moon was fat and white as a grub burrowing into the field of night above me, casting the *Gemina*, the Big Rill gurgling around us, the scrub-brush and bramblewrack on the shore, the gambel trees beyond in a sickly-strange, washed-out half-light.

Standing slowly, I shook the blood back into my feet, and stretched out the kinks in my back. A habit of old, I scanned the shorelines. The path of the Big Rill, in this part of the Hardscrabble Territories, was a snaking one, and the banks of the river to the west were eroded and quite high, twenty and even thirty feet above the surface of the water. There were many outcroppings of boulders and granite promontories, scrubbed with pine standing dark and narrow like spears pointing toward the sky.

I was about to turn away when something made me stop.

On the pine-wreathed promontory, far to the west, something came from the trees.

For a moment, I doubted my eyes, since I had been slumbering only a short while ago. There it was, a *vaettir* coming from the woods to stand openly on the promontory's peak. I thought maybe it was simply a man out in the forests at night. But the moonlight showed it as if it stood in the rays of an invisible sun, starkly visible. Its massive frame, in proportion to everything around it, gave me no doubt that it was a stretcher.

And it watched me.

Gynth, the stretcher had said. *We are kin.*

Even from that great distance, I knew this. There was a shiver of recognition within me, something that went beyond predator and prey, something that went beyond hunter and the hunted.

It had saved me once, but still I thought of weapons. I had my knife in my boot, the silver one that slew Agrippina and put The Crimson Man back in his *daemon* hand. Slowly, I eased my Hellfire from their holsters and held them, waiting.

The *vaettir* was a half-mile away and I had a river between us.

It moved, almost faster than the eye could perceive. Leaping from the promontory's peak, scrabbling from rock to rock like some possessed goat traversing a mountain-side, arcing through the air, landing in a crouch and surveying its position and then launching itself in the air again, downward, ever downward, until it stood on the rocky shore of the river.

It paused then, staring at me.

Its eyes were like black pools glittering with moonlight, and there was a strange discoloration about its face – its eyes and mouth were dark, bruised even. The creature's mouth hung open – its matching rows of razored teeth visible even from this distance – but the most curious thing was that it was dressed like some revenant vorduluk recently having pulled itself from the earth. Its clawed hands were dirty and it was dressed in what looked more like a shroud wrapping than a woman's nightgown. About its shoulders was the skin of a wolf, possibly, or a bear -- but uncured, and a mantle of gore and grime streaked away from its shoulders.

The elf looked at me, unblinking. Only the width of the Big

Rill stood between us now. My six-guns would never reach it from this distance.

Gynth, it had said.

Behind me I heard a heavy footfall. 'Hello, *dwarf*, fancy meeting you up here,' a voice said to my rear, rough and cold, making me want to turn but I dare not let my attention wander from the *vaettir*. An inch of skin squarely between my shoulder-blades began to itch.

The stretcher moved his gaze to whoever was standing behind me. I turned as fast as I could, backed away, holding one pistol on each.

The newcomer was the Tempus guard I had encountered below-decks. His grin stretched wider now, and his eyes were blacked to glittering onyx. *Daemon*held. Possessed. One of Beleth's little leave-behinds.

'Rend your flesh, I will,' the possessed man said, crouching, his arms out, fingers splayed like claws. In a flash, I saw how similar the possessed and the *vaettir* were.

Falling backward, I fired; the boom of my Hellfire six-guns tremendous in the still night. There was movement and I smelled the heavy scents of hellfire and sulphur. I was dimly aware of movement off to my right. The *vaettir* I had come to think of as Gynth raced toward the still surface of the Big Rill, arms and legs a blur. It ran over the surface of the water.

They move like light on water, I've said before, but I always meant that metaphorically. I did not know it was true.

In seconds, Gynth had crossed the Big Rill and with a thud he was on the deck and standing over me, blocking my view of the *daemon*held guard.

Gynth gave a great screech that descended into a bellow. It sent all my hairs standing on end.

The Tempus guard took a step back at the sound – there were yells and exclamations of alarm from below – and then the *vaettir* was airborne, great clawed hands held out. Gynth snatched up the guard like a doll and whipped him about in his hands.

The possessed guard thrashed and ripped like a shark plucked from the sea in the stretcher's grip, but he was no match for the *vaettir*'s inhuman strength. As they rose into the air over the deck, almost faster than the eye could follow, the elf twisted his great hands and one of the guard's arms distorted and I heard a distinct *pop* as the ball-joint was ripped from its socket. Before landing, the *vaettir* gave the man's head another quick swipe, nearly taking it off. The stretcher let the guard fall and then, at the very edge of the *Gemina*'s roof, he landed lightly on his feet and launched himself into the air again. When he landed on the surface of the Big Rill, he was already running, silvering a wake behind him.

The *Gemina* was coming to life around me, roused by my gunfire. Cries of alarm sounded and yellow kreosote lanterns and *daemonlights* were unbanked.

I approached the crumpled body of the Tempus guard, guns still out and trained on his form.

There was life in him still. The right side of his face was a ruined, bloody mess where the *vaettir* had swiped him with that terrible hand. The rest of his face was unmarred and his remaining eye fixed on me with malevolent glee.

From his chest pumped blood, black and shining in the moonlight.

From a bullet wound.

I raised my eyes from the dying thing to the far shore. The *vaettir* stood there, one hand upraised and a curious expression on its face. *Gynth. We are kin,* it had said. Thoughts of Neruda in the *Plaza de Monstruó*. Thoughts of hundreds of *dvergar* voices calling out in outrage and anger.

'I'm sorry I said your mouth looks like an arsehole,' I whispered to the thing. As I did, it turned and bounded back up the cliff, to the promontory's peak, and disappeared into the woods.

It was then the cries of the other Tempus guards filled the air and the bright, high-pitched voice of the sweetboy cried, 'Murderer! Here! Murderer!'

TWENTY

4 Ides of Sextilius, 2638 ex Ruma Immortalis

O NLY CORNELIUS' PAPERS KEPT them from hanging me. If I'd told them I was shooting at the stretcher and accidentally hit the guard, they'd have broken my hands so that I'd never hold a gun again, or worse, what with my lesser, native blood. The Tempus Union was its own militia operating by Imperial Charter within the Hardscrabble Territories and once the *Gemina* docked at New Damnation they were bloody and perfunctorily brutal. Under their own charter, they had licence to be. They frog-marched me to their nearest outpost and threw me in a cell, not without a little physical reprimand for killing one of their own. I was there five days before they started with the questions.

The lieutenant in charge of the outpost, a beefy, blond, genial-looking man by the name of Decimus Brassus, stopped the Tempus guards before they killed me, but not before I lost a couple of teeth and my nose was broken for the twentieth time in this life. Ribs cracked again like they'd never heal until the sun burnt out. But Brassus, he even gave me an anodyne – in the form of a white powder I would snort into my blood-clotted nostrils – and beer.

One day, after my nose and mouth had healed enough for talking, Brassus joined me for a little chat. It was a small cell in a small, stone hallway alongside two similar cells. As for amenities, there was a wooden chair and a ceramic chamber pot that was emptied once a day by a sour Tempus employee.

Brassus pulled the chair to him and sat down, leisurely, in general pleased with himself and the world that held him.

'A stretcher killed him, you said to the officer who apprehended you,' Brassus stated, his legs crossed, pulling a machine-rolled cigarette from a packet and tapping it on his wrist to tamp the loose tabac down. I sat on the lower bunk, watching him. He thumbed a match and drew on it heavily, inhaling, then blew smoke toward the ceiling. 'A stretcher leapt onboard the *Gemina* and then committed grave bodily harm on the late Mister Bennett? Was this before or after you shot him?'

'Before, but the man was *daemon* possessed.'

'Yes, you've said that already,' Brassus said, raising an eyebrow. 'And *that* was why you shot him.'

'There should be some marks on his body. Glyphs, wards, whatnot. That should prove I'm telling the truth!'

'Mister Ilys, it's high summer and we don't allow corpses to bloat. His body was interred in a Tempus Union cemetery not a day after the *Gemina* docked in New Damnation.' Brassus put his cigarette in his mouth and stood, walked out of the cell area and returned with a sheaf of papers. He ashed on the floor and sat back down. 'This report by his commanding officer says there were markings on his body, evidence of a new tattoo.'

'See?'

'One moment. You said that the stretcher came aboard the *Gemina*—' Here his lips gave a wry little twist. 'And the creature ran *across the surface of the river*.'

'That's right. This is the Hardscrabble Territories. You ever seen a stretcher, sir?'

He ignored that. 'And then he leapt aboard at the moment you encountered Mister Bennett.'

I nodded, fearful of how this was all coming together. I'd have a hard time buying this barrel of fish pickle myself.

'Why, then, did the stretcher not kill you?'

'Maybe it thought Mister Bennett was the greater threat?' I thought for a while. It wouldn't do to tell him the truth – and especially that I *conversed* with the damned thing – unless he and the rest of the Tempus bully-boys were going to string me up. And judging by his humane treatment of me – he wasn't party to the beating the Tempus guards gave me – I didn't think that was going to happen. 'It didn't really have a chance. Before I knew what was happening, I was caught between your Mister Bennett and the *vaettir*.'

He looked at me for a long while, face blank, smoking his cigarette.

'I'm not lying, sir,' said I.

'Mister Ilys, my problem with you isn't that I believe you're lying. Or believe you're not lying. My problem is discovering why you did what you did and who was your accomplice.'

'I had no accomplice, I'm telling you,' I said. There was a familiar buckskin portfolio tied with leather strands on the table. 'You've got my papers there from the Governor himself. Contact Marcellus. Even better, contact his spymaster, Andrae. He'll confirm some of the things I'm telling you.'

Brassus shook his head. 'Mister Ilys, were you and Mister Bennett planning on robbing Tempus Union?'

That's what this was all about. As always. As it is in Rume, so it is in Occidentalia. Money drives the gears of the world.

'As all the old gods and new as my witness, I'd never set eyes or had any contact with Mister Bennett until that day.'

He stared for a long while. Finally he said, 'I believe you, Mister Ilys, which is why you are not dead.' He dropped the tail-end of his smoke on the stone floor and ground it out with his boot. 'However, that leads to other questions.'

'What are those?' I asked.

'Why were you on that boat?'

'Heading downstream to meet my partner.'

'A man named Fisk?'

'That's right.'

'Why do you carry a near carte blanche endorsement from the governor?'

'I can't tell you that, sir,' I said, bowing my head.

'Were you on the *Gemina* to interfere with the delivery of the silver to New Damnation?'

I looked at the man. He was well-fed, though not fat, and very clean and manicured. Pink fingernails and hair that'd seen soap recently. A city man. A soft man, used to the comforts of the plate and bed and market.

'Sir, respectfully, you are interfering with something that goes beyond your little band of message-boys and delivery men,' I said. His face darkened in response.

'You are an ill-kempt half-breed who murdered one of my men,' he said, in a clipped cadence. 'It would behove you to remember that the gallows stands right outside this building.'

'I am a freeman and a member of the fifth's auxiliaries, an agent of Cornelius himself – you hold my bona fides right there – and should you hang me, you'll have to cover up your crime, because my partner – a *godsdamned legate* – will make sure Tempus Union and you personally fall out of favour with the fifth and no God old or new will be able to salvage your career after that.'

His eyes narrowed, lips pursed. 'I think we're done here, Mister Ilys.' He stood and brushed his crisp black uniform's trousers to make sure the lines were straight and there was no ash on them. 'I have tried to make you comfortable and will continue to do so, but you'll remain here until you are willing to tell us why you were on the *Gemina* and what reason you had for murdering a Tempus man. Good day.'

He walked from the cells, leaving me alone.

Dvergar live long and have even longer memories. And while I'm not full-blooded, I've been told I'm more dwarf than man. I've lived more than a century and a half, so far, and while I can feel my age, especially now, I am in no danger of re-joining the numinous spirits of my ancestors any time soon.

So the time Brassus kept me on ice was damnably boring, but it wasn't maddening. My face and ribs healed slowly. I spent my time lost in memory. At that point I had more than a century of experiences to turn over as if I were a child wading upstream against the current of personal history and picking up stones in a creek to turn over in my hands.

We *dvergar* are built for time. We come from the earth and to the earth we will return and we take to solitude like a duck to swimming. Maybe that is why we are here. To wait. For what? Maybe that is what we wait for. To find out.

If there was any discomfort in those days I was incarcerated there, it was by thoughts of Beleth.

I was tortured by the thought of the engineer making his merry way through the Hardscrabble, unmolested. At night I had dreams of the man, and in them, he would perform *lingchi* on Agrippina – even though I knew she was dead: mine was the hand that slew her – but with each cut in the *vaettir's* flesh, there was not blood, but fire. The fire of war.

It was morning, maybe the thirtieth day in the cell – and those days were *long* when I knew Beleth was loose and war on the wind – when Brassus entered and said, 'Well, this might be your lucky day, Mister Ilys. It seems someone aboard the *Gemina* that night has been talking. A sweetboy, of all people.'

He extended a rolled newspaper through the bars, then, unlocking my door, he came within. It was a familiarity he allowed himself and I did not mind. We had reached some sort of unspoken agreement: I was not going to cause him any real trouble and he wasn't going to treat me like I was an idiot. However, he did not wear a pistol when he joined me in my cell.

Sitting down on the stool they provided me, he withdrew two

cigarettes, lit them and offered me one which I took, gratefully. I unrolled the newspaper – a copy of the *New Damnation Cornicen* – and began to read.

Dwarf kills Tempus *Guard, Captured on Barge to Novo Dacia* the headline read. In a more salacious type, it read *DVERGAR GUNNED HIM DOWN*. And in smaller type below it *An Eyewitness Account of His Capture By* Tempus *Union Employees*.

I looked at Brassus who, having crossed his legs and looked supremely at ease, gestured with the hand holding the cigarette, making the smoke form eddies and whorls in the still cell air. 'It seems you are famous, Mister Ilys.'

'Hardly.'

Brassus smiled. 'True. A better way to put it is that the "witness" wishes to be.'

I turned back to the article. It read:

New Damnation – 6 Nones Geminus – Menæ Pallius

An Awful Crime

Violent as were the early days of frontier Occidentalia, nothing in recent memory equals the depravity
of the events of 6 Ides Sexitilius, where a dvergar
pistolero gunned down a Tempus Union guard escorting
cargo from Hot Springs to New Damnation. Since the
planting of the Fifth Occidentalia brag-rags in New
Damnation, our stretch of the Big Rill has become
known for its peace and prosperity. The damnable
vaettir are scarcer and scarcer with every passing
day. Yet violent incidents away from our larger
urban centres - Harbour Town, New Damnation, Hot

Springs and Passasuego – are occurring with more and more frequency, sullying the good name of our land with the rumour of wildness and outlawry.

A Hard-Bit, Scrappy Little Man

Not much is known about the murderer, an itinerant tinker *dvergar* who booked his passage under the name Dveng Ilys, but who is also known as Shoestring. One of the passengers of the *Gemina*, Sacchine Duplass, a male 'entertainer' from Passaseugo, was a witness to the crime and described the culprit thus: 'He was a hard-bit, scrappy little man with a face like a walnut and just as brown. He had a bad look to him and he avoided all of the other passengers. We berthed in tents on the roof of the cargo hold and he made sure to place his as far away from everyone else's as possible.'

Of the event itself, Sacchine Duplass was a direct witness. He described the murder thusly: 'I heard voices, rough voices, arguing. About what I don't know, but there was a lot of gambling and drinking going on the boat. I exited my tent and saw the dwarf pointing his gun at the guard. They spoke to each other again and then the dwarf shot him in the chest. It was a big sound, waking everyone on the barge. Then the little man just walked over to the guard and looked at him. The Tempus guardsmen tackled him and put him in chains.'

Lieutenant Brassus, the highest Tempus Union officer in New Damnation, told this reporter that the culprit was incarcerated in the New Damnation

Tempus Union building and that 'under the Imperial Charter granted to Tempus in 2603, Tempus Union, its landholdings and personnel, operates as a sovereign protectorate and has the authority to try and execute the prisoner if we deem it necessary.'

An Abrogation of Legal Rights?

While this reporter is glad that our beloved Hardscrabble Territories are a little safer with each successful apprehension of criminal elements, I cannot help but wonder if justice would not be better served in our Ruman courts, open to the public and with impartial advocates for each party. I am suspicious of any person, collective, or business entity who might act with impunity and separate to our lauded Ruman courts and forums, the most enlightened form of governance and jurisprudence in the known world.

The moral to this sad tale might be that you should not cross paths with Tempus Union if you want to retain your given rights as freemen under the Ruman Empire. I, for one, will be watching this issue most assiduously in the coming months. In the interim, it might be time for local advocates and magistrates to consider whether Tempus Union's charter is for the best of the citizens of Occidentalia and the Hardscrabble Territories.

When I was finished reading, I folded the paper and handed it back to Brassus, who took it and looked at me.

'So, what now?' I asked. 'Seems like it's time to shit or get off the pot.'

He smiled in response. 'Colourful, Mr Ilys. And why is that?'

'They'll be coming for me.'

Brassus' brow furrowed. 'Understand me, I would have strung you up by your neck and dragged your body through the streets except for your orders from Cornelius. Without compunction or regret. It is my task to protect Tempus Union's profits, integrity, and future.'

'Bully for you,' I said.

'Again, I wish to know why you were on that boat and what intentions you had.'

'Either I tell you and Cornelius crucifies me, or I don't and you string me up by the neck. I'll take the hanging. I hear crucifixion is mighty painful.'

'I understand your position, Mr Ilys. I wish you could understand mine.'

'I do, Mister Brassus,' I said. 'Other than the beating your boys gave me, you've been quite civil and have my thanks.' I sigh. 'Put me in touch with Andrae or one of Cornelius' contacts and they can vouch that I wasn't there to interfere with the sovereignty of your charter or to interrupt the flow of silver.'

He laughed. 'Of course they'll vouch for you! If they were trying to compromise Tempus they would not inform us of their intentions.' He sighed in turn. 'I will level with you, Mister Ilys, Tempus is embattled. Our Imperial Charter was established years ago when the political landscape was quite different here in the west. You understand that each Tempus Union representative is, in their person, part of the Imperial protectorate. Our president, Mister Aureus, is the protectorate's governor. We have no land other than small holdings within cities, our offices, but no real territory to rule. The protectorate is simply *people*. Why? Because, in a bit of legal chicanery – I can admit this – it gave us the power to legally use brutal force – even lethal force – and protect our interests without falling under the auspices of the Ruman army.'

'I remember, Mister Brassus. It was a different time, back then, wilder and more dangerous. Not to mention the threat of stretchers. Tempus did a lot of good for us, delivering messages and protecting those early settlers.'

'Yes. I remain proud of our heritage and history, even now,' he said. 'But times are changing, and there are more and more calls against that charter. If there is enough of a caterwaul, it's possible Tamberlaine will revoke it. That has kept you alive, too. Had we executed you, especially now after that damnable article, it would be tantamount to thumbing our noses at the Ruman courts here. If I execute you, it will have repercussions I cannot know politically. If I turn you over, I create a precedent of ceding rights of our charter to local Ruman law.'

'Seems like you're in a shit position, yourself.' I tsked. 'My sympathies.'

'And so, I delay in hopes that you can answer enough of my questions so that we might quietly make this problem go away,' he said. 'So I ask once more, why were you on that boat?'

I shook my head, sadly.

He nodded, tight around the eyes. 'You wouldn't consider escaping, would you?'

I laughed, 'That would solve everything, wouldn't it?'

He laughed, too. 'Yes it would, Mister Ilys.'

'Tempting, but I don't think I'm tall enough to get over the walls around this building. And, oh, there's that off-chance that some passing Tempus guard might shoot me in the back. What I don't understand is why you don't just kill me and make it look like I tried to escape.'

His expression turned near green at my words. He opened his mouth as if to speak, shut it. When he had himself under control, he said, 'You have mistaken me for a man with no honour, Mister Ilys.'

'No, I figured as much,' I said, smiling at the man. There is nothing more precious to a damned Ruman than his opinion of himself.

'Then, sadly, we remain at an impasse, Mister Ilys,' he said. Brassus uncrossed his legs and stood. 'Is there anything I can get you? Is the food adequate?'

'It's fine. I could use some tabac. And whiskey would be nice.'

From his jacket he withdrew his pack of cigarettes – Mediera's Gold – and handed them to me. 'Sadly, I cannot provide whiskey for you. A Tempus representative cannot—' his expression took a remote look, and he recited, '"Provide, transport, sell, or store any wine, beer, liquor, mead or intoxicating liquid" as that charter was given the Divangeo and Mielle companies.'

'Damnation. It's like you're more of a prisoner than I am, what with all the charters and laws tying your hands. How the Hell do you have a drink?'

'Very carefully, Mister Ilys,' he said moving to the door. 'Very carefully.'

He did not lock or shut my cell door as he left.

A week later, Brassus entered. His expression was guarded. 'You have a visitor, Mister Ilys. Would you care to receive him?'

'A visitor?'

'An official visitor.'

'Who is it?'

'A man named Reeve.'

'Reeve? 'Course I'll see him. Send him in!'

Reeve was one of our companions when we faced Agrippina in the White Mountains and learned of the death of Isabella, the Medieran noble whose death had, in essence, started the oncoming war.

Brassus left, walking a little stiffly, and in a moment, the big Northman strolled in, limping slightly, in his Ruman uniform, greave-boots, balteus with leather apron, crossed pilum cap.

'Looks like they got you running errands, Aedile Reeve.'

'Praetor now, little master. They bumped me up after the donny-brook with the *daemons* and stretchers.'

'You're in better health than the last time I saw you,' said I.

A grin split his big, generous face. He moved his arm in a tender circle. 'Broke me like a ceramic bowl, mark ye, but fitted me back together again afterwards. I breathe fine now, my arms work, and I can sit a horse so Marcellus can order me about.'

'It's good to see you.'

'And good to see ye, though ye've been in better circumstance.'

'You gonna get me out of here?'

Reeve nodded. 'That runs right alongside my orders, Shoestring.'

'How did Brassus take it?'

'He hasn't, yet. I came alone from the garrison.'

'One man?'

'That's right, a praetor, to boot.'

'Will he find that insulting? He's not a bad man, just trapped by his own honour.'

'I might be able to reason with him,' Reeve said, and winked. 'You have anything?'

I looked around the cell. I'd been there for more than a month by then and hadn't a thing other than an extra set of clothes, Tempus issue. 'No. Not a thing.'

'Then let's put the memory of this shabby little place behind ye,' Reeve said. 'Come with me.'

He walked back out where he had entered. I followed, pausing at the door. I hadn't left my cell even once in the last sheaf of days and it took a moment to force myself to cross the threshold. But cross it I did.

The outer office looked like a counting house, a wall of tall scriveners' desks flanked by a large table. Two open doors showed gentlemen's desks, nice paintings of woodland scenes and leather chairs. Armed Tempus guards stood around, jackets unbuttoned, looking at ease, and a few more clerical men, styluses in hand, all turned to look as we entered. Hands went to Hellfire. Brassus stood in one of the office doors.

'That man is a Tempus prisoner,' Brassus said.

'No longer,' Reeve said, stepping forward. 'I have come to collect the little fellow.'

'You are just a praetor. You don't have the authority to take this man. He has murdered a Tempus employee and he is in my charge.'

'No longer, I've come to fetch him.'

'You are trying my patience, sir. I did you a courtesy as a member of the Ruman army by allowing you a visit.' Brassus said. 'But removing Mister Ilys from these premises is not going to happen.'

'That's fine, then,' Reeve said. He turned to me. 'Return to the cell they gave ye, Shoe. I will return shortly.'

I hesitated.

'Thank you for understanding, Mister Reeve,'

'That's Praetor Reeve to ye, Lieutenant,' Reeve said. He made a clicking sound in his mouth and shook his head. 'It's a damn shame, too. But I will return to ye, with company.'

Brassus grew still. 'Company?'

'Surely, ye did not think the fifth Occendentalia will allow ye to keep one of their own, a favoured son, beloved by Senator Cornelius himself?'

'That is no concern of mine,' Brassus responded. 'Within the Imperial Charter given Tempus by Tamberlaine himself we are within our full rights to—'

'Ye precious charter will be good for wiping ye arse, shortly, when I return with a few mates.'

'Are you threatening me, Mister Reeve?'

'I don't make threats, friend. It lowers folk's opinions of ye when ye do. I make *promises*,' Reeve said. 'And I promise ye, I'll return with a half century of men to remove Mister Ilys from yer nice little jail cell.'

There was a moment of stunned silence in the room and all eyes went from Brassus to Reeve and back. There was an indefinable settling of Brassus' shoulders, as if some invisible weight had been lifted from him. And he smiled, showing teeth.

'You would take him by force?'

'If necessary,' Reeve said.

'Then I must relinquish him to you now.'

Reeve looked surprised. 'Just like that?'

Brassus stepped forward. 'Thank you, sir,' he said, shaking Reeve's hand. 'You have forced an issue and relieved me from any fault in this matter.' He turned to me. 'Mister Ilys, it has been... interesting... coming to know you,' he said and we shook hands in turn. 'Delvinus, bring Mister Ilys' effects, please.'

After a moment, a junior Tempus officer scrambled out of the room and returned shortly with a wooden crate full of my possessions, including my guns and money.

I went through it.

'There's something missing,' I said.

Brassus raised an eyebrow in answer. The man had expressive brows, that's for sure.

'My orders.'

'Ah, yes,' Brassus said, turning. He entered his small office and then returned bearing the leather portfolio and handed them to me.

'Here you are, Mister Ilys. All your effects returned.'

'My mule?' I asked as I began sticking knives in boots and in sheathes.

'I'm sorry, it's been sold to pay for your incarceration,' he replied. 'You can, however, retrieve your saddle and saddlebags in the stables.'

He took a step back when he noticed my expression change. I am hard to anger, yet there it was, white hot.

'I've had Bess for the last decade, and you sold her?'

'You are a murderer, Mister Ilys. As far as I am concerned, you have very few rights while in the custody of Tempus Union. Be grateful you are alive.'

'It could've been worse,' I said, doing my best to let the anger release. It was hard going. Maybe it's part and parcel of being *dvergar* – our memories are long and we hold to grievances like ticks to deer.

'It will be, possibly, for you,' Brassus said. He held a piece of parchment he must've retrieved when he got my orders. He read, "I hereby declare you, Mister Dveng Ilys, an enemy of the protectorate of the Tempus Union, having committed murder upon one of its citizens. Henceforth and forthwith, should you present yourself to any Tempus Union guard or office, or be recognized and sighted by same, you will be executed on sight and with extreme prejudice"' He lowered the piece of paper. 'Have a nice day, Mister Ilys. I will sign this after you are gone.'

Two scowling Tempus guards led us out of the offices, through the courtyard. In the stable's tack room, I grabbed my saddle under the watchful glare of the guards. My pots, pans, and other out-riding accoutrements were missing. I had to assume they all went with Bess. In addition to losing a month or more, I'd lost enough gear to make this a quite expensive sojourn. With my saddle slung over one shoulder, and my bags over the other, I walked heavily into the street beyond the walls where I smelled the first air of freedom in nigh on a month. Never mind it stank of horse dung and charcoal smoke.

'My thanks, Reeve,' I said. 'I'm glad that ended without a blood-bath, though all the gods may damn that man for selling Bess.'

Reeve chuckled, as he limped down the street, away from the Tempus Union complex. 'A bloodbath? Never any chance of that.'

I trotted as fast as I could to catch up, leather creaking. 'What? Marcellus wouldn't have pushed it any farther if Brassus had balked?'

'No idea,' Reeve said, taking off his jacket in the summer heat. 'Haven't talked to him.'

'What?'

'I've been on leave the past year, recuperating from grievous injury received in service to the Empire.'

'You mean there were no legionnaires standing by?'

Reeve stopped, cocked an eye at me. 'I like ye, Shoe, yer a good man and I'll never forget yeh saving all our skins when that *daemon*-gripped stretcher was a'rantin' and burning shit.' He chuckled. 'But Marcellus doesn't know anything about this. I just read the *Cornicen* and figured out where ye were – I've got a favourite tavern right around the corner.'

It was all too much. 'A bluff.' I laughed until my ribs hurt. 'Remind me not to play cards with you.'

'An enemy of the Tempus Protectorate, ye are. Don't thank me too much, my wee friend.' Reeve patted my shoulder and said, 'I imagine a spot of whiskey might sit well with ye, right about now.'

'I think you might be right,' I said.

TWENTY-ONE

4 Ides of Geminus, 2638 ex Ruma Immortalis

IN THE MORNING, I BOUGHT a skewbald pony from a trans-planted horse-trader from the Gaellands. He spoke very little of the common tongue and communicated mostly through hand signals and whatever facial expressions managed to get through his massive, braided blond beard. Of the mounts in his paddock, he kept offering me the ones over sixteen hands high – those that would be near impossible for me to mount – without trace of humour or mirth at my obvious dislike of the larger horses. Finally, I stomped over to one sturdy-looking little fellow, spotted chestnut, and patted his neck. Eventually, the big Gael and I settled on a fair price and I paid and tacked out the horse.

As strong as the urge was to ride out immediately, heading south to Harbour Town where I figured Fisk would be, I forced myself to ride to the garrison and visit Andrae.

I only had to wait three hours until one of his bloodless secretaries led me into his office.

'Ah, Mister Ilys! I thought you'd be mouldering in a grave by now!' Andrae said, snatching a copy of the *Cornicen* on his desk and waving it around.

'Didn't you think I could've used some assistance?' I was in no mood for sparring or verbal feints. I leaned forward, snatched a cigarette from a pewter tabac holder on Andrae's desk, and put it between my lips. I wandered over to his dry bar and poured myself a tumbler of whiskey. It had been a long night with Reeve and I was feeling a mite dry. 'It's not like I'm on an important mission to find an enemy of the state or anything.'

'Ah. Sarcasm. How droll,' he said, leaning back in his chair. 'I am a busy man with countless things vying for my attention. If you must know, I imagined that you would be dead before I could do anything. However, once the article came out and I learned that you were not dead, I did have one of my agents make sure that your friend Lucious Reeve saw it and pushed him the right direction.'

I sat down in the seat opposite him and he leaned forward and placed a box of matches in front of me. 'Seems like very little effort on behalf of one of Tamberlaine and Cornelius' agents.'

Andrae cocked his head, looking at me closely. 'A few hard realities might ameliorate your outrage at the way we handled the situation, Mister Ilys. First,' he held up one long, articulate finger. 'You are a half-breed *dvergar* and a minor officer in the Ruman auxiliaries. Should we have moved mountains to retrieve you, it would have drawn attention. Second,' he held up another finger, 'war is declared and the news of a renegade saboteur and engineer would be a heavy blow to the public perception of this conflict.'

'Gotta make sure the people are behind it,' I said, letting the sneer cross my face.

'Tamberlaine, and by proxy Cornelius, are always aware of appearances, as I think you know. While our beloved Father wields absolute power, he does so on the motions of appearance. Should the public lose faith in him – and consequently his *power and authority* – the Empire's authority and power is undermined.'

'If you look hungry, you go hungry,' I said.

Andrae pursed his lips and nodded reluctantly. 'A very simple statement to sum up an extremely complicated idea but . . . *yes*.'

I occupied my mouth with whiskey and tabac for a while, staring at Andrae. He met my gaze, unblinking. He was, all things considered, an implacable man. I did not have to like him to respect him.

I said, 'Any word on Fisk and Beleth?'

Andrae put his hands together and rubbed them briskly. Then he opened a drawer and withdrew a file.

'Since your period of recuperation in Porto Caldo in Sextilius and subsequent incarceration, your friend has been quite busy. On the Nones of Sextilius, he arrived in Bear Leg, remaining there a day. On six Ides of Sextilius, he arrived in Brunnen village where he, and his companion, a Missus Lomax, bought food and took separate rooms.' Andrae ruffled the paper. 'On three Ides he arrived at Crastus Ferry, on the ferry from Brunnen, or so my agents inform me. From there, it's not known where he went, however he did send – via your dear bosom friends the Tempus Union – a letter for you. Here. Quite a large one.'

He handed me an envelope, weathered and quite thick. It read, *Shoestring C.O. Legatus Andrae, Fifth Legion Hqrts, New Damnation.*

Of course, the envelope had already been opened. I looked to Andrae who shrugged. Inside was a sheaf of parchment, dozens and dozens of pages, with a small note attached, obviously written in haste.

5 Nones Geminus, 2638 Ex Rume Immortalis

Shoe,

Re'c word that Beleth might've bolted to Panem near the Whites in hopes of circling around New Damnation and possibly Harbour Town. He wasn't there but a whole slough of daemon-gripped folks were there waiting on us, caught us behind the livery where W and I managed to hold them off, killing two or three. Watch yourself. He's left his little playmates all over and you can't be sure about anyone. Stretchers have been acting strangely, too, pacing us on the trail but not attacking. You don't need me to tell you to watch yourself around vaettir.

Spking of vaettir, I shpped the marked-up stretcher to SD in Harbour Town, sold t'other to exporter in N Damnation. There's money awaiting you at the fifth's treasury in my legate's safebox. Inclded in this pcket is writ of introduction for you to access it. Also, incld are all of Livia's mssgs to me, please place them there. New horse took a good dunking in Lake Brunnen during the crossing and all the old letters soaked & near ruined. I'm fearful for my wife (as you will read) and want to protect her mssgs to me. I know I can trust you with this.

Tmmrw we ride to Encantata & then on to Confluence and finally Harbour Town. I do not know what keeps you, but I hope this letter finds you well. I'll leave word with SD as to my whereabouts.

I remain your friend,
Hieronymous Fiscelion Iullii

Andrae watched me as I read. Once I was through, he said, 'You have some catching up to do and I imagine you'll want to get back on the hunt.'

'What news of Beleth?'

'He was spotted in Panem, as Mister Fisk pointed out, but possibly that was an attempt at misdirection or an effort to gain something. An expatriate Medieran nobleman and gentleman farmer died mysteriously – drowned – during Beleth's time there and I cannot help but think that was not a coincidence, but I fear we will never know why. Later a man going by the name of Agares checked into a hotel in Confluence for one night only. I recently learned Agares is the name of a *daemon* that was bound in Latinum, in a small boiler room. It was Beleth's 'journeyman' piece, before joining the Collegium,' he shook his head. 'I have had no more luck finding any more *daemons* he might have bound.'

'Turns out he's not that good at it, anyway. Or so Engineer Sapientia in Passasuego told us.'

Andrae made a note on a piece of parchment, drew a star by it and circled it. I realized by saying that one thing I might have brought Sapientia within the realm of Andrae's scrutiny.

When he was through, he nodded and said, 'That explains much. Most engineers bind hundreds of *daemons* in machines, thousands if you consider munitions. Beleth? Very few.'

'He's more interested in stuffing them in humans.'

Andrae inclined his head. 'Yes, I inferred as much from Mister Fisk's letter to you. I have informed Tamberlaine and Cornelius of this possibility and made recommendations to their security. What else can you tell me about the "*daemon*-gripped", as Mister Fisk calls them?'

I ran down a short description of our interactions with them – the boy in Hot Springs, the Grantham woman in Passaseugo, the Tempus guard on the *Gemina*. I did not mention the curious help I received from the *vaettir* there. Not because of any desire to keep Andrae in the dark (well, not much of a desire, anyway) but more of a growing unease that the stretchers had some deeper purpose than killing settlers and eating young girls. There is more to their intelligence than simply hunger and instinct, I know that now.

Gynth. We are kin.

When I was through, I asked, 'Any other news?'

'You may purchase a *Cornicen* on almost any corner, Mister Ilys.'

'News of your particular stripe, Mister Andrae.'

He narrowed his eyes, thinking. After a moment of inscrutable consternation, he gave an almost imperceptible shrug and said, 'Your people are organizing.'

'You mean *dvergar*.'

'Yes. Under the guidance of a man who calls himself Neruda. Many tinkers and diggers—'

'Don't call us that. We are *dvergar* and there is more to us than just making trinkets and digging mines.'

He nodded. 'My apologies. Many *dvergar* are migrating out of the larger cities and into the Hardscrabble Territories. Some heading for Tapestry, others Wickerware, some to Dvergar.'

'Any idea why?'

'A sort of independence movement. They're calling themselves *The Vaettir*.'

I whistled. That's a statement and a half. And one from folk who've never spent time out under the shoal-grass sky. 'Why do you figure?'

'I can only assume because they feel that's more fierce than calling themselves *The Turkey Buzzards* or *Lickerfish* or some other form of life indigenous to Occidentalia. Would you fancy a re-assignment, Mister Ilys? I could use some good intelligence on what they are planning. The silver and goods flowing from the *dvergar* settlements have stopped and a half century of legionnaires have not reported in for three days.'

'A half century?' I asked. 'Marcellus must be hopping mad!'

'He is mobilizing, but cannot allocate too many legionnaires toward subduing the *dvergar* in fear of separating his forces. The Medierans are quite numerous in the Bay of Mageras and are staging on Chiba.'

I whistled. 'That ain't good.'

'Agreed. I fear this region is quickly going to—'

'Shit?'

'Yes, Mister Ilys. To shit.' He straightened the papers on his desk. 'What say you regarding the reassignment?'

'Become one of your spiders?' I feigned thinking about it. I would rather have a *daemon* squirming inside me than spy on my own people for this vile man. But I said only, 'I think I will be of better use tracking down Beleth.'

For a long while, Andrae was still. Then he smiled, showing teeth. 'Of course, Mister Ilys. I would not have you work against your conscience.' A secretary entered, bearing a stylus and wax tablet. He handed it to Andrae – I could see the fresh marks of knifework on his forearm – said a soft word in his ear, and left.

'You must excuse me. I have much to do,' Andrae said.

I left him there.

TWENTY-TWO

Ides of Sextilius, First Hour, 2638 Annum Ex Rume Immortalis, Jiang City in Far Tchinee, In the Manse of Sun Huáng

Dearest love,
We have spent the last fifteen days at sea since my last use of the Quotidian, and the steady thrum of our thrice-damned vessel is constant, a susurration at times, never ceasing. The seas grew large, waves tumultuous and higher than all imaginings. It has been so long since the *Malphas* has seen shore, I fear at times that we are lost, lost upon an unimaginably large expanse of ocean, an infinitesimal spark burning in the desolation of salt and wave. Yet Captain Juvenus assures us that we are nearing Kithai and the great port city of Jiang. How he knows this, I have no idea, though when the skies are clear and he can sight the stars, he spends an inordinate amount of time looking at the sky with a collection of strange devices whose functions have not been explained to me.

Life on board is strange – much like on the *Valdrossos* – it seems as if we're stilled and only the waters flow around us. But Juvenus tells us we travel near four or five hundred miles a day, which I have trouble believing though I have to assume he would not lie to us in jest. We should arrive within the next few days, or so I am told.

We have established our rhythms now. Mornings, when the weather permits, we adjourn to the deck, where Huáng leads us in the Eight Silken Movements – it is a wonderful way for me to remain fit while nursing our son within – and then trains with Tenebrae. And something strange has occurred – something strange, wondrous, and possibly unbelievable to you – our Carnelia has joined in the training. It happened in an odd way.

Sun Huáng who, I should say, is a taciturn man, sat down at our breakfast table and looked closely at Carnelia and me, in a very judgemental fashion.

'The things you perform while a child grows within you will colour its whole life,' he said in his halting thick accent. 'Come, come. Stand and join in the *qigong*,' he said, taking my hand. 'For your son's sake.'

When Carnelia snorted at this, his attention turned to her. 'You are sharpened. Your mind better suited to blades than this . . . indolence. Your hand suited to a jian. Come, wicked girl. Come.'

We looked at each other, Carnelia and I, and somewhat bemused, we joined in the exercises. Afterwards, having performed the Eight Silken Movements a few times, I returned to my seat but Huáng bid Carnelia to stay, which was odd.

'In Rume, women sometimes train as gladiatrix and in games and for physical contests, but rarely for war. Is it so different in Kithai?' I asked Min.

Min, who has taken to breaking her fast with us, nodded. 'In great Kithai, girls learn the ways of the flesh. The hard and the soft. The streets of Jiang, the alleys of Palikao, they are full of beggars, rapists, brutes and desperate men and women who would take what society does not provide them. We learn to fight early, and use weapons to protect our bodies and family bloodlines. It is only once we are married do we complete our knowledge of the ways of the flesh.' She blushed prettily, though I fear her association with Carnelia has increased her knowledge of the arts of the bed. Min frowned. 'It is strange, though, that my grandfather would single out your sister. An honour, surely, but maybe he sees within her something others do not.'

'All things are possible,' I said.

Min shook her head. 'Rarely. But I am puzzled by this.'

Tenebrae seemed puzzled too that suddenly Carnelia had joined him in training. They moved through stances and postures – very little of the instruction Huáng gave Tenebrae up to this point had involved sword work.

Tenebrae asked why they did not work with swords, and the old man replied, 'A sword is just a thing, no mind, no hazard.' He held up his hand. 'This is my sword.' He extended his arm. 'And this.' He touched his head. 'And this. I *am* the sword. Even when unarmed.'

The Praetorian looked puzzled but Carnelia nodded, a strange expression on her face.

It was later that morning – the morning of 1 Nones of Sextilius – a clear day with relatively calm seas and visibility – that one of the lascars began bellowing and ringing a bell. Suddenly the deck was full of men racing about, attending to the big cannons. Two of Tenebrae's Praetorians tried to bustle us below-decks but I flatly refused and moved to join Juvenus on the upper deck's lookout roost where he stood, gripping his looking glass, conferring with his junior officers and the Engineer Tricomalee.

'A frigate running the Medieran flag,' Juvenus said when Secundus and Tenebrae joined us. 'Twice-damned, possibly, though we'll test their speed and range of their swivels.'

'Is it wise to engage when we're on a diplomatic mission?' Secundus asked.

A lascar yelled 'She's turning, Captain!'

'War is declared, and we are a vessel of war, Mister Cornelius,' Juvenus said.

In the grey-blue distance, the Medieran man-o-war belched

black smoke into the blue sky, and began to narrow its profile, turning toward the *Malphas*. And then, as it turned, behind it another column of smoke was revealed.

'A brace of frigates on some bellicose errand. Do not worry, Livia,' the Captain said, placing his hand on my arm and not giving me a chance to say I was not. 'Our girl is the fleetest of ships on the seas and her claws very long.' He gave a rapacious grin, showing teeth. He was in high spirits, spoiling for a battle. He bellowed, 'Tea for the cannoneers! Swivels on marks!'

His junior lieutenants made hasty charcoal scribbles on the flat top of the railings, figuring some sort of numbers and calling them out to the cannoneers who would respond by yelping '*Mark!*' A grinding sound filled the air as men, some above and some below decks, guided the cannons in their trucks. The Captain's seconds called out numbers and continuously shouted commands, training the massive bores of the cannons on the oncoming Medieran frigates, adjusting their angles and gauging wind.

'You may fire when you are ready, Mister Gridlæ, while we have the advantage of range.'

Mister Gridlæ, a portly man with great bristling whiskers and a belly like a cask of ale barked an order. And then the Hellfire cannons erupted.

We all have experienced the dismay of Hellfire, the unease during the release of the infernal. But the *Malphas'* cannons? Hell on earth. The air shivered with the thunderous noise. The sound passed through my flesh like a tremor sundering the earth. I put my hands on my stomach – Fiscelion twisted and kicked within me. And there was the despair that came with whatever *daemon*'s release pushed the cannon shells through the air. The stench of Hell filled my nostrils and all of my muscles contracted, involuntarily, as if awaiting some blow that would never fall.

Far off across the expanse of salt and waves, geysers of water erupted, a short distance in front of the oncoming Medieran boats. Plumes of smoke billowed out from the opposing ships and then the booming report of their cannons reached us. Nearly a half-mile away, their shells fell in the indifferent foam of the Oriens.

'They are uncertain and tentative!' Juvenus howled. 'Mister Gridlæ! Respond! Rume's arm is long!'

'Reload!' Gridlæ yelled, his face engorged with blood and thick runners of sanguiducts standing out in relief on his neck, disappearing like snakes into the collar of his uniform. In a rush, cannoneers unlatched the rear of the swivels, freeing the smoking casings of the cannon shells, two teams working in tandem, one removing the spent cartridge, the other swiftly placing the ward- and glyph-encrusted next cannon-shot inside the gun itself, pulling them from a cotton swaddled crate. Inside each nestled a *daemon* ready to be loosed upon the world. 'Fire!' Gridlæ screamed.

The battery of guns exploded into smoke and sulphurous Hellfire.

Looking around, I noted the grimaces on the cannoneer's faces, the surprise and consternation of the lascars. But Captain Juvenus remained gleeful.

'More! Pour it to them, men! Pour it to them!' He turned.

Gridlæ yelled for the cannons to fire again and they answered his call.

When the monstrous sounds and infernal despair died away, the distress of the nearest Medieran ship became visible. Black smoke poured from locations on its hull other than the stacks.

Gleefully, Juvenus yelled, 'We have scored on them, boys! Again!'

After a moment, the *Malphas'* cannons boomed once more.

The sound of that outrage ripped at the sky. The far off
Medieran ship became consumed in smoke.

The engineer, Tricomalee, said in a low urgent voice, 'It is
time to turn away, Captain. Their engine room is breached and
the *daemon*—' But he could not finish.

A new sun rose on the horizon, a fire so great that even miles
distant, it burned my eyes and I was forced to turn away. For a
moment, in that bright fury, was the triumphant shape of some
massive, fiery thing clawing with glee at the heavens, freed from
its cage. And then an explosion filled the world – a release of
energy so great this language of mine is beggared to describe
it. The sound became deafening, what was left of the Medieran
ships wreathed in steam. Far off, the seas rose.

'Turn her, Ia damn it!' Juvenus screamed. 'Full ahead and turn
hard to port! Put her nose in it!'

I didn't quite know what was happening until the shockwave
from the blast hit, a wind tearing at my clothing and hair like
a hard punch. I fell to the floor of the roost, blood filling my
mouth, and cradled my stomach – our child. For a long while
I was insensible, as the air around us turned wet and hot all at
once, and the *Malphas* shuddered and moved.

Our ship began to nose downward – slowly at first but then
picking up speed – and I found enough strength to push myself
from the roost's floor and rise. We were in a trench of water and
a mountain approached us, rising a hundred, two hundred feet
into the air.

'Full ahead, or we're thrice damned!' Juvenus yelled. His
teeth were bloody and his eyes bugging but there was a mirth,
a desperate glee, matching the *daemon*'s that clawed at the sky.
A man who met danger with wildness and abandon, almost
assuredly. In that one instant, it gave me a fleeting impression
of the totality of the man – a suicidal motion, a scrabble
for meaning. Encapsulated in that one look was an implicit

acknowledgement of some fallen state from a purer one: instead of Ruman nobility, he had traded fierceness for it. That spreading terrible smile was his little attempt at banking some sort of flaw in his character. Men. They are fragile and weak, as are we all, yet they strive so hard to deny it.

A lascar rang a bell over and over. The cannoneers called each other's names.

I heard Secundus say very clearly amidst the clamour and riotous noise, 'Mater save me.'

The *Malphas* traced her course to the bottom of the watery trench, the moving mountain of water met us and, in a lurching, stomach-dropping motion, we climbed the cliff-like face of the wave. No swells, no high seas had ever prepared me for this, my love. Not crossing the Occidens, not sailing Mare Nostrum. Water began pouring over the gunwales and prow, as if the *Malphas* was a needle piercing the outraged flesh of the water. The screams of of cannoneers and lascars sounded and men were torn from whatever hand-holds they clung to and swept overboard.

We rose, high, so high that when we reached the peak of the wave, the prow of our ship passed through and beyond the face of water; salty spray drenched me and for an instant we hung in the air – a hundred tons or more of steel and iron and silver and wood. In a more personal and intimate recognition, my frantically beating heart was contrasted by our son's softly throbbing one – and then the nose of our *Malphas* fell and we plummeted down the back of the wave, wind and smoke and spray ripping at us.

It was almost more than I could bear.

A cloying steam hung in the air and my skin was tacky with the salt of this foreign sea. Strange, bloody and mangled sea creatures rose, twitching to the surface and the fins of sharks appeared shortly after and the ridged back of the more fearsome sea serpents some of the lascars called *makara* and others called *devil whales*.

When the seas calmed enough, we made survey of the destruction of the Medieran vessels. There was charred debris and bodies, but no survivors. A plume of steam poured from the ever-shifting surface of the water in a massive column that rose, towering over the *Malphas*, until it reached an altitude high enough to disperse it on a crosswind.

'What could be causing it?' Min asked, standing nearby. She was dripping wet, and looking awestruck at the watery devastation around us. Sun Huáng stood behind her, one hand on her shoulder, face impenetrable.

'We cracked the Medieran frigates with our swivels, both of them,' Juvenus said, still fierce. Still desperate.

'Yes,' said Tricomalee, the engineer. 'But only one *daemonic* vestment was ruptured.'

'Are you saying,' I said, looking at the steam and boiling water erupting from the surface, 'That you sank the ship yet the *daemon* was not loosed?'

'Precisely,' Tricomalee said. He had the bloodless, stoic reserve of an academic. His skin pale, his frame, slight – back slightly stooped. His hands, delicately articulate. He spent most of his time indoors. 'The ship has sunk to the bottom of the sea, but the devil still burns.'

'And how long will it burn?' I asked.

'Until something mars its warding. The sea will eat away at the metal and wood surrounding it and eventually . . .' He brought his hands together as if gripping an invisible ball, fingers splayed, and then he jerked them apart dramatically, making a small, hissing sound with his mouth.

'Why does the *daemon* not run rampant after it is freed?'

A wariness crept into his expression: here was a man

determined to keep his trade secrets close to his withered, under-developed chest.

'That belief revolves around munitions, that devils will be loosed,' the man said, waving his hand vaguely. 'There's a natural – or unnatural – combustion as the *daemons* enter our world. Our world and their essence is incompatible, unless within warding. Once they're free of the warding... then...'

'A release of force?' I asked.

He nodded his head. 'As we so experienced.'

'You could level mountains with such power,' Secundus said, his voice unsteady. 'Should any man have such mastery?'

Tricomalee looked seriously uncomfortable, casting his gaze about for some sort of rescue. He said, 'We should get away from this spot. If the Medieran ship's *daemonic* vestment fails, we would be caught in the subsequent explosion.'

Captain Juvenus yelled for the engines to engage, ordered us Cornelians and other Rumans, Min and Huáng below-decks until we cleared the area.

Mister Tricomalee's words were disconcerting and I resolved, my belov'd Fisk, to learn more of these infernal machines and the *daemons* that drive them.

We lost seven men – which seems so small in comparison to the titanic forces expelled in our exchange with the Medieran frigates – and the next morning of the Nones of Sextilius we held a brief, yet solemn consecration to Ia, the Mater, and the Pater Dis to lead them to Ia's heavenly triclinium, and then repaired below decks to recoup and reflect.

I have never been so terrified in all of my years, my love, and suddenly the *Malphas* seems less homely. For home means security and even in victory, our jeopardy had been great.

And I am worried. Shaken, truly, that we will ultimately pay a terrible price for these infernal devices and the terrible power within them. Each time I close my eyes I can see the brilliantly outlined *daemon* clawing at the sky. Was it rage that drove it? Or exultation at its freedom? Or glee at, as it combusted, going back to whatever Hell that spawned it? I do not know. I wonder if we have it all wrong. Maybe they aren't devils at all, just other... entities. Like Bless said, 'She wears the clothes I gave her and comes to the nuptial bed a thing of my own mind...'

No more ships have been sighted since the two frigates in the Oriens. A tight unease has settled on the ship, despite the sunny climes and the brisk winds. A separation has settled upon the passengers and the lascars – maybe it had always been there and we were just not aware of it – but there's a coldness now to the seamen of the *Malphas*, as though they blame us, to a soul, for the loss of their companions.

We keep to ourselves now, and Juvenus has suspended dinners in his Captain's Mess, citing dwindling supplies and rapidly depleted stores of alcohol. Yet I cannot but feel that he must be grappling with that terrible spreading grin, that desperate acknowledgement of his fallen state, and cannot bear the presence of those who witnessed it. That is but my surmise, yet of all here, sometimes I feel I am the only one who knows all the wiles of man.

And how I miss yours, my love. Your wiles.

I think back on the first time we

'Sorry, Shoe, old friend. Some things gotta be private.'

On 2 Kalends of Geminus, we came within sight of land, the lascars and canoneers on deck calling, 'Eous, Eous sighted!' Eous being some long-known, colloquial slang for the borders of Kithai – as some referred to as Cathay and, of course, others as Tchinee, as our grandparents first heard of it. Some of the lascars who have made the journey before – though they are not many – call the land Tandinfu, and some Sinju Matu, though there is some confusion as to whether those are names for the region – or subregions – or names for city-like dwellings. The coast was verdant and carpeted with a lush growth of trees, festooned with vines and ferns flowering undergrowth. The land's edge was traced with a line of brilliant pink sand. Due to the draw of the *Malphas* we could not get too close to the shore or the ship would founder, but Captain Juvenus was happy to lend Carnelia and me his far-looking glass, allowing us a closer view. Shadows moved in the shade of the trees; creatures unfamiliar to me, or possibly to any Western person, Ruman or Medieran. Looking through the glass, trying to puzzle out something familiar in those miasmic jungles, I had a strange foreboding. I cannot explain it. As you know, my love, I am not prone to flights of fancy. But it lingered with me throughout the morning.

It was a bright, cool day, and after I had joined Huáng, Secundus, Tenebrae, and Carnelia for the morning exercises underneath the fore-swivelgun, moving through the Eight Silken Movements three times, I repaired to a table to break my fast (for the second time that morning!) with young Min and Lupina on a repast of salted fish, rice, and candied peppers. Our son makes strange demands of my palate and I have sometimes inconvenient food lusts – milk, meat, sugar – they have all taken their turns waking me before the sun to go down to the mess where Vezia, the *Malphas'* mess-matron, greets me without smiling and presents some pastry or a cup of coffee while she then prepares a small meal for me, packed neatly in a polished wooden box. Often Lupina follows, silently, like a guardian spirit or numinous household god. In the ways that servants have, there's some unspoken connexion between

Lupina and Vezia – I often notice them glancing at each other and exchanging curious and communicative looks. But like the phantasms and ghosts we all have heard of as children, when one turns to look at the two slave women, the looks vanish. Yet Lupina is the most solicitous slave I've ever encountered, and fiercely protective of me.

There was an incident, a mere nothing it seemed, when we were moving through one of the passages of the *Malphas* – they are tight and somewhat claustrophobic. A few of the younger lascars, coming off duty, were engaged in a bit of horseplay and they barrelled into the passage we travelled down, not knowing we were there. One of them, possibly having been shoved by his companion, fell into me heavily, knocking me against the wall.

Before I could recover my wits, Lupina was there, a small knife in her hand, the point of it pressed into the trousers of the lascar, right near his genitals. Lupina said nothing, she simply waited until the lascar's unfortunate companions apologized profusely and backed down the hall, expressing over and over their sorrow at interrupting our passage. The man receiving Lupina's pointed chastisement held up his hands until the *dvergar* woman withdrew the knife. He gave a quick bow and scuttled off.

I grow quite fond of Lupina and intend to give her her freedom, once we've returned to Occidentalia. I hope she'll remain in our employ. I can think of no better nursemaid and protector than the fierce little woman.

But I dash about in my story.

The morning the lascars were calling 'Eous! Eous!' and Tenebrae, Secundus, and Carnelia clacked about the deck with bamboo sticks in place of swords, Huáng admonishing them tersely in the language of Kithai (which appears to need no translation and to be understood by tone alone, at least in regards to the learning of swordplay) I asked Min about the various names of Kithai or Cathay and its size, since no cartographer has yet been able to get a full grasp of the country's expanse.

In response, Min said only, 'You could ride for a thousand days and sail a thousand more, and not cross the realm of the Autumn Lords,' which did not suit me so I pressed the issue with the young girl.

'What does that mean?' I said. We were on the deck, watching the verdant shore slipping by us on our port. Masses of birds took flight from those far-off trees, maybe sighting the black smoke columns of the *Malphas*. They wheeled in the heavens and came toward our ship. As they neared, it became obvious that each one was nearly as large as a horse. Their flight, low over the waters and the ship, revealed vicious serrated beaks, tremendous wingspans, and greasy feathers like longknives. The sound of their passing was deafening; a fierce whistling came from their throats, and they made near-human-like cries; each wingbeat sounded as loud as a mallet striking a drum, and the rush of the wind that their wings pushed down upon us, as they flew overhead, was considerable. As too was the stench, an odour of rotten fish and a yeasty excrement.

'What are those terrible things?' Tenebrae exclaimed, pausing in his practice, bamboo stick in-hand.

A nearby lascar sneered but reluctantly ventured, 'Aepyornis. Some call them garuda or symyrrh. They will not harm us.' So he said, but he did not let his gaze waver until they had passed overhead, wheeled again, and moved downwind. Some of Tenebrae's praetorians readied their carbines, sighting the flock of gigantic birds.

Min's gaze followed the flying creatures and for a long while she stared after them as they flew, making the outlandish ruckus winging their way.

'You're too vague,' I said to Min, bringing her back to the

subject at hand. 'Surely there are units of measurement in your land, and maps. Show me how large the country of Kithai is. We have steamed for nigh on a month and travelled thousands of miles, if what Juvenus and his engineer tell us is the truth, so it is hard to believe we could not cross it with relative quickness.'

She looked down at her silk-slippered feet – just for a moment – and then she raised her head. 'It is an old phrase, ma'am, and a reflexive one. I know not how large Kithai is, but it is massive.'

'How massive? Let me understand.'

'I cannot, ma'am.'

'Because you won't, or you refuse to?'

'I cannot. I do not think anyone knows how large it is.'

I looked at the girl, closely. 'We are companions, and we have taken you into our counsels and conversations, yet there is something you are not telling me, maybe out of some sort of obstinacy, maybe from some threat of censure or consequence of censure.' At these words, Min bowed her head, a worried look on her face. Min is a curious young woman; there is a hard and superior part of her that looks at us Rumans with distaste, if not active dislike. We are as foreign to her sensibilities as she, and her grandfather, are to us. There are moments when I feel she withholds more than she gives. 'I will not force the issue, but should it be revealed that you have hidden something to our detriment and hazard . . .' I thought for a long while on my next words. 'I will not be kind. Do you understand?'

'Yes, I do,' Min said simply and looked at me steadily, her worried expression gone. 'We near Jiang, the largest city of Kithai, and should be there soon. Within the next two days.'

'At least you know that! It is good to hear. I grow tired of salted fish,' I said.

'You will know we near Jiang when the water changes colour.' Currently, the waters were the blue-green we'd experienced for the last month.

'To what?'

'The colour of mud. The Jiang river brings down silt from the farming and mountainous regions and washes it into the sea.'

Later that afternoon, we encountered the demarcation Min had spoken of, an abrupt change from wine-dark to muddy water. The point where the waters met rippled and coursed with eddies and unknown currents. On the shore, the verdant jungles of the Eous shore were gone now – we were steaming at steady clip – to be replaced by a series of small fishing villages.

'The silt is rich with minerals and other inland life. Look there.' A strange creature broached the surface of the muddy water. It seemed to have fur and long, humanoid arms, ending in wickedly clawed, webbed hands, one of which held a wriggling fish. Its eyes were bulbous and it paused in the water to look at the *Malphas* steaming by, blinking with thick membranes covering the eyes like lanterns being shuttered. It dove, making barely a ripple.

The air became richer, thicker, and I began noticing a million motes hanging there – some sort of almost invisible insect spawning from, or coming to feed from, this mineral-rich water.

Later, the villages became larger, the buildings taller and made more of stone than thatched huts and wattle-and-daub mud bricks. The brown waters we travelled became filled with sailboats Min called *chuán* but the lascars called junks. They moved through the sluggish waves prettily, each sail like an outstretched bird's wing pointing to the heavens. Other ships – xebec and hoggies, skiffs and diminutive lorcha, what looked like trawlers and sailing barges – plied the surging brown waters, letting out nets and lines. Some we passed close to and the crews on these wind-powered boats would look up at the *Malphas* with neither fear nor wonder on their angular and wind-chapped faces.

After nightfall, Captain Juvenus invited us for brandy and

tabac on deck – a nice respite from reading by *daemonlight* in
our cabins – to look upon the shore, gleaming in the moonlight,
and to witness the luminescent glow of the insects hovering in a
dreamlike fog around us.

'They call the light these creatures give off the "golden fog"
or "jinse ying", isn't that right, Huáng?' Captain Juvenus said,
looking toward the older man. He said it with a jovial, almost
dismissive tone.

'They are the thoughts of the Autumn Lords given form,'
Huáng replied, inclining his head in what could be acquiescence
or could be irritation.

'Sifu,' Carnelia said, which was some sort of term of respect
given to elder citizens of Kithai.

She said it in such a way that my interest was immediately
piqued. I'd never heard Carnelia address anyone – neither Father
nor Mother, neither priest nor praefect – with the simple, calm
respect she offered this man from Kithai. It was totally out of
character for her, but seemed honest and natural. The journey
sometimes takes us through our own internal landscapes, and
my sister wasn't immune to that momentum. Carnelia had
learned much regarding the Tchinee. In some ways, she had
been, in her adoption of the more martial of the exercises that
Huáng taught Tenebrae and Secundus on the deck, more of
a student of this country that we travel to than I had. I had
allowed that typical Ruman complacency to quell any of my
more natural inquisitiveness.

'Who are the Autumn Lords?' Carnelia asked. 'We have come
halfway around the world to treat with them and we know
so very little except that they rule this land. Can you tell us
anything?'

Huáng lowered his head, thinking. 'To understand the *qiūtiān
shén*, you must first understand the living force we call Qi.

You cannot begin to apprehend the Autumn Lords without understanding this.'

'*Chee*?' Tenebrae asked. He held a cigar in his teeth, and puffed madly, making the cherry of it burn bright, a pulsing ember in the low light of the golden fog. The *Malphas* ploughed through the waters of the Oriens steadily, and the sound of the sea constantly hushed and lulled us in the background. The low lights of village fires on the shore passed slowly as we ran, this close to the shore, at half-speed.

'Qi,' Huáng said, slowly, correcting Tenebrae in the gentlest manner. Min has, I'm thankful to say, provided me with the Rumanized spelling of the Kithai words since their writing is as impenetrable as chickens scratching in the dust. 'Is the living force – the *spirit* – that is within your body. But also in all living things and places. When you are ill, there are imbalances in the flow of Qi within you. When you fight, someone who has studied and trained his Qi, can . . .' He looked at Min for a moment, as if simply by looking at the young woman it would help him find the word he searched for. She raised her eyebrows but said nothing. 'Summon their own Qi and use it in the strike of a fist, a blow of a jian.'

One of the *Malphas*' stewards walked by, bearing a tray with a crystal decanter of brandy and a few snifters. He offered one to Huáng, who accepted, graciously, though he only but touched the liquid to his lips and then held the snifter with both hands in front of him. With Huáng, I had noticed in our daily repetitions of the Eight Silken Movements, there was an immediacy to his conversation yet a detachment from it as well. Each sentence had echoes of other meanings – perhaps unspoken, perhaps untranslatable with his poor command of the Ruman tongue. There was a duality to his consideration. It was obvious he was deadly, having bested Tenebrae to such a degree that the arrogant Praetorian deferred to the man. Made

a teacher of him. What must a person with such power feel? My
hand knows the grip of a shotgun, a Hellfire pistol, and that
is an awesome and terrifying power. But what of a man who
is deadly without any sort of accoutrement save himself? How
would that person look at the world, or his companions? Would
he simply observe – organize us into assortments of flesh and
tendons, conglomerates of bones and joints, sanguiducts and
humours – and know that any one of us, he could kill with a
touch? What a terrible thing to always see, instead of a welcome
hand or the gentle curve of a neck, the vulnerabilities of the
flesh. In that moment I found a great pity for the man. What a
horror it would be to be known simply as a weapon, as he was:
the Sword of Jiang.

He went on: 'But the master of Qi can use this force to
disrupt their opponent's. The master can sense the weakness in
the heavenly Qi raining down upon us at all times, and know his
opponents' weakness and where to strike.'

'Grandfather,' Min said, approaching him. 'Have you eaten?'
Then she said something in the language of Kithai that no one
here, save Huáng himself, could understand. The barest corner
of his mouth turned down, almost imperceptibly.

'Min, I speak now with these honoured Rumi,' he said, using
a rather outdated name for us. 'Allow yourself time to think on
the bounds of propriety and we shall speak later.'

Min looked at her grandfather – his features lined in overt
traces on her face; the small, pointed nose, the intelligent
eyes, the high brow and articulate lips – and I could detect an
undercurrent of tension coming off the girl. She demurred, but I
could tell it was a struggle for her.

At that moment one of the lascars on duty called out and we
all turned to the shore. Juvenus chuckled; he knew this would
happen, it seemed.

From the shore, multi-hued lights rose into the air to be

caught on the wind and carried out into the sea. They were coloured in reds, blues, yellows and greens, floating. Flickering.

'What are they?' I asked.

'Paper lanterns,' Tricomalee said. The thin, pasty engineer had ventured out onto the deck of the *Malphas* once the sun had retreated over the horizon. 'I was curious if they were infernal on our last voyage, so I made sure to capture one. Simply a hot-burning candle contained in a dyed-paper container. Quite clever, actually.'

'They are the *zhuìlì*. They attract the attention of the Autumn Lords toward the heavens,' Huáng said.

There was something odd about that. I am enough of a student of history to know that when a people want to draw the attention of their rulers *away* from the temporal realm instead of directing it toward it, something is amiss. But it was hard to put my finger on what, exactly, was wrong. Kithai – judging from Min and Huáng – is a culture so different from our own that possibly even their core beliefs and values are fundamentally other. And something about what little I've learned of the Tchinee culture from the Eight Silken Movements smacks of spirituality. Even the names are poetic – bordering on metaphysical. Separating Heaven and Earth. Two Hands Hold Up The Heavens. Drawing the Bow to Shoot the Sparrow. These are just a sample of the names Huáng has given the Silken Movements. They are delicate, graceful and slow. Yet they are martial as well. The movements themselves are much like a conversation with Huáng – more than one obvious thing is going on simultaneously.

'Why would you want to draw the attention of your rulers toward heaven?' I asked. Watching the passengers sip their brandies, I wished for a nice glass of wine but Lupina – ever solicitous of my, and Fiscelion's, health – had prohibited all alcohol and I acceded to her commands. 'And how does an understanding of Qi – which, honestly, puzzles me – lead to an understanding of your Autumn Lords?'

Huáng considered me. I stood with my hands on my stomach, feeling the life contain within. Huáng, mirroring me, held his snifter as though he were heavy with child.

'They are . . . things of pure Qi,' he said.

'They have studied this . . . magic? It seems as though that would take a lifetime and not leave much time for the administration and rule of a land as large as Kithai.'

'The August Ones attend to the . . .' he paused, thinking. 'The administration of our land. I am honoured to be counted among their number. The Autumn Lords, they do not concern themselves with the . . .' Another pause as he searched his considerable memory for the correct word. Min hovered nearby, wringing her hands. I couldn't understand her anxiety. Much like his movements, Huáng's language tended toward the precise, despite his not so firm grasp of our vocabulary. He understood the grammar and structure quite well. 'Chores of daily maintenance.'

'It occurs to me that is the primary focus of rule. An attention on the matters of state. A focus on trade, the security of the nation. Not paper lanterns.'

Min stepped forward, standing by her grandfather. 'Our culture is hard for Rumi to understand and so some things will make little sense to you. After all, your nation is young and ours was old when yours was being born.'

'Rume has existed for almost three thousand years.'

'But not quite,' the girl said with a tight smile. 'Grandfather, you really should eat.'

He held up one hand, the long fingers only slightly curved. Her eyes narrowed and her lips pursed.

'The Autumn Lords are fierce, as you would expect from their . . .' He said a word in the language of Tchinee. 'Their mastery of Qi. They conquered our people thousands of years ago, in a time of great upheaval.'

'So theirs is a military rule?'

He shook his head. 'No. They are . . .' Again he said a string of words I couldn't understand. 'When we arrive, you will be brought before them and will understand.'

'I find it hard to contain my excitement,' said I, earnestly.

'Tell me, Master Huáng,' Juvenus said, slurping at his brandy. 'During our last trip to Jiang, our guide kept speaking of the illustrious Sun Wukong. Is he one of the August Ones?'

'Sun Wukong?' There was a moment – just the barest sliver of an instant – where I would swear Huáng was surprised. But he covered it well. 'He is a legend. Nothing more.'

'What were the guides saying, Captain?' Secundus asked.

'Oh, the usual. Wukong is a trickster king, a thief and a rake, a lover of men and women and father of orphans. They call him the Monkey King.'

Min said, 'A myth. The poor make up stories to ease the burden of their situation.'

'It was a passel of nonsense,' Juvenus said, chortling. 'But I rather liked his style.'

'I would hear more of this Sun Wukong,' said I. 'What is the legend?'

'A tale told to children,' Min said. It was a subject she did not want to discuss. So, naturally, I wanted to discuss it.

Huáng, however, said, 'Some say he is a god that walks among men, others a . . .' He said a word to Min.

'Capricious,' she said in response.

'A capricious being. He steals from the rich . . .'

Juvenus laughed and Tenebrae joined him. '. . . To give to the poor,' Secundus said, grinning.

'You have it, exactly,' Huáng said, smiling too.

'We have our own legends of the noble thief, Iulius of the People.'

'Maybe our cultures aren't so different,' I said to Min.

Huáng said, 'But he is not a god and not very nobility... noble. He is – was – simply a man who concerned himself with tearing at the...' Another pause, thinking. 'Order of our world.'

'They said he lived in a graveyard, in a necropolis,' Juvenus said around his cigar. 'And served a dark master, a vorduluk.'

'A drinker of blood?' Carnelia said. She giggled. For a long while in her teens, she'd been quite fond of the hyper-sexual three sestertius thrillers, all depicting women ravished by handsome vorduluk.

'Yes, that is the tale. The *Chiang-shih* and his nest of rats.'

'Yet this Sun Wukong seemed quite beloved by those folk who spoke of him. Not some servant of a dark thing,' Juvenus said.

'He is a double person,' Huáng said. 'Two men within the same body. One man, he wishes to do good. The other man...'

He did not need to finish.

'You sound as if this is a real person, a person of your acquaintance,' said I.

Huáng remained still. He had the aspect of someone trying very hard not to allow himself to move. 'I do not know this man who calls himself Sun Wukong.'

Silence then. There are those moments within social groups brought together out of necessity or circumstance rather than real friendship – moments of dislocation and awkwardness when the conversation dies. And it did.

The floating paper-lanterns hung prettily on the golden air, drifting out over the *Malphas,* and colouring the deck with their red, blue, yellow, green glows. A gong tolled somewhere on land, over and over, hollow and forlorn. The rising coloured globes stopped ascending and within a short while the Eous shore grew dark. Carnelia finished her brandy and accompanied me to our berth. I was tired and hungry again.

'I don't trust Min,' I said, simply, after we had disrobed and were applying lotion – Carnelia to her legs, me to my stomach. 'And I'm beginning to think she maneuvred Tenebrae into his duel with Huáng.'

'Well that backfired, did it not?' Carnelia chuckled. 'She seems a little shite, sissy, and I did not appreciate her words on Rume one bit.'

'Yet you are now a pupil of her grandfather,' I said, teasing. But only a little. With sisters, all teasing is rooted in truth.

'Lupina says that food and exercise are the key to putting on weight.' She flexed her calf muscle. 'See, I could rip a gladiator in half, should he come to my bed. I will be fit for any marriage Tata arranges.'

'Carnelia!'

'Oh, sissy. You're pregnant. Surely, that didn't happen spontaneously.' She laughed. 'You're blushing! I shall mark this day in my journal.'

'That's enough.'

Later, that night, I lay in bed and my thoughts, as always, came back to you, my love. My thoughts always come back to you.

The next morning our on-deck exercises and training never began. We entered the mouth of a wide, muddy river teeming with boats of all kinds, flitting about on the surface of the water, bells clanging, lascars and fishermen shouting, as the *Malphas* steamed in through its gaping maw. Dredges hauled muck from the river's bottom, keeping the main channel of the River Jiang clear so that larger ships, like the *Malphas*, with deeper draughts, could still have passage. Along the banks were countless, modest buildings nestled between small piers

and wharves each with a stone base disappearing into the
brown waters and the open passages of thousands of narrow
canals disappearing away into the distance; beyond them, the
scalloped backs of pavilions and towering pagodas looked like
ebony bones in some natural philosopher's study – rigid spines,
vertebrae stacked one on top of the other. In the sky, paper kites
with long, flowing tails swooped and dashed about over the city,
like raptors hunting smaller birds. A pall of woodsmoke hung
over it all, though here and there I saw the smoky columns of
daemon-fired stacks. The Jiang citizenry clambered onto roofs
and scaled walls to look at the *Malphas*, where it steamed
past – I daresay very few Tchinee had seen the might of Rume
expressed in so grand and fierce a vessel.

A whistle sounded and the *Malphas'* lascars scurried about
the deck, dropping anchor with a deafening metallic clamour,
while the thrumming engines were banked, quieting. Juvenus
and Tricomalee came on deck, followed by Huáng and Min, and
they all observed very closely a squat, blocky *daemon*-driven
paddle barge looking very much like a turtle shell, pluming
black smoke from two stacks. Elaborate detail was given to the
exterior of the barge; it was gold and black lacquered, ornately
carved with skeins of what appeared to be mosaic work on
the hull and ringed in shining panels that appeared to open to
reveal either guns or ballista, possibly, to snag renegade ships.
A clutch of brightly robed men and women of Kithai stood on
the deck-roost, all facing the *Malphas*. When it came alongside,
one of the gentlemen of Kithai bellowed a series of phrases in
the Kithai language, though the tone and air of command with
which they were delivered made clear their meaning: 'Prepare to
be boarded.'

Carnelia, Secundus, Tenebrae and I joined the *Malphas*
officers and Huáng and Min on the observation deck. Huáng

was saying, '. . . it is Ting Huáng, the August One Who Minds the Port.'

'Is he your brother?' Captain Juvenus asked.

Huáng seemed puzzled. 'No, why do you ask this question?'

'Because you have the same patronym?'

'I do not understand what that means,' Huáng said. 'Ting Huáng is the August One Who Minds the Port. I am Sun Huáng August One That Confronts the . . .' He paused, looked at Min. 'Rumi.'

Min laughed.

'What is funny?' Carnelia asked, eyes narrowed. She stepped near the girl – possibly her training with Huáng making my sister more assertive, more belligerent – and Min responded by turning to face here with one eyebrow raised, as if daring her to lay hand on her person.

'My grandfather is as quick of tongue as he is of hand,' Min said. A growing smile – not a kind one – spread across her face. 'And he edits himself. He is not 'August One That Confronts the Rumi,' he is 'Sun Huáng, August One That Confronts the Foreign Devils.'

Juvenus spluttered. 'Ia's nuts! The gall.'

'That's a pretty title,' Secundus said, grimacing. 'I don't fancy it at all. And here we've welcomed you into our society as an old friend and family member.'

Huáng bowed to Secundus. 'I am sorry for my granddaughter's words. Our relations are tense, between Rume and Kithai. For many years, I was August One Who Commands The Glorious Armies of Autumn, but after the incident at Shang Tzu, where your Rumi ship *Belphagus* fired upon the August Master of Imports' ship, sinking it, my . . .' He stopped, looking about. 'You might call it a title . . . was changed, by word of all the August Ones. They were not pleased.'

'Wait a moment,' I said. 'Are all August Ones named 'Huáng'?'

'One puts aside one's family name when he takes up service to the Autumn Lords.'

'Yet you're still the Sword of Jiang.'

'One is a reputation, the other is . . .' He questioned Min. She responded with 'Birth.'

'A right of birth,' Huáng finished. 'Please accept my apologies. I find great honour in your acquaintance.' He, quite formally, bowed to each of us.

'That's a good chappie,' Juvenus said, tucking his hands into his belt over his belly. Like most Rumans of noble birth – and I think Juvenus was distantly related to Marcus Claudius, I made a mental note to ask Carnelia, she would know – all his umbrage at the disparagement of Rumans quickly evaporated in the face of obeisance. But I do not think he grasped the man bowing before him, or the country that formed him. For we *are* devils. Or the agents of their spread. The Ruman engineer first bound the daemon, first made an implement of war with the infernal thing hundreds of years ago. And that knowledge was guarded and made secret yet the Hellfire – as is its wont – spread and others captured its strength. 'That's quite fine. You're a good sort,' he pointed his chin at the turtle boat. 'What of these gentlemen?'

Min said, 'They will want to search the ship – and view the crew and passengers to ensure that no Ruman disease enters the city of Jiang.'

Tenebrae bristled at 'Ruman disease' and Carnelia actually settled into a stance that I'd seen her take on the decks: a fighting stance.

Huáng barked one word that pierced us all – for a moment I could believe in the magical Qi he spoke of – and then gave Min a long, vituperative tongue-lashing in their native language. Her eyes grew large, she covered her mouth, and fled the deck when he was finished, sobbing.

Huáng, who normally was so composed, seemed rattled. 'My apologies,' he said. 'To make amends for the insult my grand-daughter has given you, please accept my invitation to take rest at my . . . house.' He shook his head solemnly. 'Min will not be there. She has proven troublesome and I am sending her to reflect upon her insults to our family's honour.'

'That's very kind of you, Sun,' I said, looking toward Secundus. As the male heir of the Cornelian family, it was his duty to accept or decline. 'But isn't that a bit harsh? She is young, and our countries are, if not at war, at odds. What she said wasn't as offensive as all that,' I said.

'She has not just offended you. She has offended our honour with her mean spirit and pettiness.'

'We accept your apology,' Secundus said, formally, giving a deferent bow to Huáng. 'It would be an honour to continue to train with you, as well.'

Tenebrae, standing near Secundus – always standing near Secundus – nodded his head enthusiastically.

'Then so it shall be,' Huáng said, and bowed once more.

Tin Huáng, the August One Who Minds the Port, was a rotund, moustachioed man clad in ornate silks and topped with a curious little cap, also silk, that much resembled a Truscan cabasette, or nightcap. His face was swaddled in loose skin and lined with merry wrinkles. He boarded the *Malphas* with a few advisors – both men and women – and approached Captain Juvenus and the rest of us where we waited on deck.

He said something, pouring out angry and harsh-sounding words, indecipherable to all but Huáng. Huáng answered him.

The dialogue went back and forth between the two men, Tin questioning harshly, Sun answering in his mild, calm way, until Sun Huáng turned to us and said, 'He wants the crew and all passengers to assemble on deck, only then can his inspectors go through the hold.'

Juvenus snorted. 'Unacceptable. I am on orders from Tamberlaine himself; no Ruman ship is to be boarded, willingly or no.'

Huáng's mouth tugged downwards in the barest hint of a frown, and he spoke to Tin once more. Finally, they seemed to reach a conclusion and Tin turned to leave.

'Captain Juvenus, thank you for the journey and your hospitality. Tin Huáng has decreed that he shall take the Cornelians and their retinue in his ship, where they'll remain in quarantine. He states that the *Malphas* must remove itself a distance of no less than one hundred *li* from the Kithai shores. Beyond the striking range of the guns.'

Juvenus cursed, long and with great imagination. 'I'm ordered to remain in the mouth of the Jiang River, sir, to ensure our envoy's safety.'

Secundus turned to Juvenus and placed his hand on the older man's arm. 'You are also ordered not to cause another international incident, are you not? We are bridge building and that requires concessions.' Secundus' tone was reasonable with a hint of pain. Juvenus looked at my brother and then made his decision.

'All right, but I don't like it,' he said. 'Come with me to my cabin so I can give you a signal.'

'A signal?'

'Ia damn me to perdition's flames to be buggered by devils if you think I'm going to let you traipse off into Far Tchinee without some way to let me know you need rescue or assistance. I'm not going to return to Rume with that hanging about my neck.' He turned to the rest of us. 'It has been a pleasure, lords and ladies, delivering you to Jiang. Now I suggest you make haste and get your assorted shit together and prepare yourselves for search.'

We all thanked him for his generous service and after hastily packing our belongings quickly found ourselves on board the Tchinee turtle boat, looking down-river as the black form of the *Malphas* steamed out of Jiang and back to open sea.

TWENTY-THREE

Kalends of Geminus, 2638 ex Ruma Immortalis

After a perfunctory physical examination by the August One Who Adjusts the Energy Flowing Within and an inspection of our belongings by fastidious men – who had a heated discussion over my Quotidian but did not confiscate it – we were allowed to disembark the quarantine ship and enter the swelling city of Jiang.

Jiang is a queer place, by turns elegant and jumbled, beautiful and horrific. In this way it is much like Rume but without the engineer's influence on sanitation. On the pier, the city stood before us, tall and expansive and teeming with activity. Jiang itself is situated on the Jiang River in a pan-like valley, flat and lined with waterways and canals (though I think there was very little water mixed with the sewage) through which numerous gaily painted (and dung-stained) boats, narrow with shallow draughts, make their way; stretching away from the canal district are swiftly rising hills, upon which stand a multitude of buildings. One gets the impression, upon first viewing it, of congestion and over-population – a million ribbons of smoke rise into the sky, the streets are small and cramped. More scalloped buildings stand there, growing taller the further away from the river they are. In the canal district their roofs swarm with peculiar, featherless flying things with leathery wings like bats but larger, the size of cats, or small dogs, making a cacophonous din and shitting absolutely everywhere. The milling citizens – pedestrians, mothers with children, merchants, delivery men – all walk about with umbrellas. We were lucky that Tin Huáng's palanquins had a supply of intricately decorated ones. Only a portion of the decorations were smeared with faecal matter.

'The little lóng . . . little dragons . . . live near the wharf and canals and not on the hills. The wharves are better for eating of rats and the cats that prey on rats. And the dogs that prey on both.' He smiled. 'Small fish swallowed by big fish swallowed by many smaller fish. But away from the docks, the air is not so full of dragons or shite.'

'They're not really dragons, are they?' Secundus asked. 'My father would . . . well, shite himself if he thought that there were wyrms in the world and he hadn't witnessed one.'

Carnelia sniffed. 'He might be interested until he caught a whiff of their scat.' She wrinkled her nose. It had a harsh, ammoniac smell. 'Father loves the ideal, not the reality of things.'

Huáng smiled but it was terse and he quickly gestured toward the line of waiting litters.

Each palanquin was born by two men, wearing wide conical hats that were large enough to shelter their whole bodies from the intermittent splatters of faeces, and we were swiftly borne out of the canal district into more residential and industry minded areas. The rain of lóng faeces slowed. Before us, great stone walls loomed, heavily fortified and lined with archers (presumably to kill flocks any of the little dragons that flew near and offer protection from vermin of the human sort, the poorer classes and the disenfranchised) and we rode through gates so large they could allow the *Cornelian* – or the *Valdrossos* at least – to pass underneath with room to spare and came at last to an immense boulevard that was half market and half processional *passegiata*-cum-park. It was constructed of massive white flagstones with amply bricked sluiceways to take runoff downhill to the canal district. Statues of towering, stylized yet grim-faced figures, also carved of white stone, eyes closed and hands tucked into alabaster sleeves, lined the way. Clustered at their feet, countless stalls sold rice and meats and vegetables. There were numerous nationalities on display – I noticed Medierans and Galls and Numidians and a few Bedoun – but they were but a tiny fraction of the whole multitude. A few men and women walked about in western suits and not all of them were of Kithai. Floating paper lanterns hovered overhead and musicians played atonal melodies that never seemed to resolve to a central key but simply wandered across the musical emotional ranges. Many buildings lined the thoroughfare – some in the scalloped, rising fashion of Kithai and others in more western form. There were no signs but many of the silken flags and banners draping the facades bore the images of coins or baskets, books and parchment, cuts of meat and spools of thread, fletching and lanterns, and one building – a building that would look more at home in Passasuego than Jiang, obviously of Medieran design – bore the image of what could only be taken as a Hellfire pistol.

While not as pervasive as in Rume, the signs of the use of Hellfire were there, in the smoke stacks, the turtle quarantine ship and its guns. Rume has expanded and maintained its power for the last two centuries because of the infernal and the rise of engineering, and it does not share its technology lightly. Yes, knowing something exists and can be achieved is a powerful prod – the Medierans in turn developed their own infernal technology, as well. Of course, this is all known to you, my love.

As we were passing through a less populated area of the great thoroughfare, we found ourselves and the palanquins surrounded by a gang of young men, dressed in loose-fitting

brown clothing and boots and button caps. Many had iron
rods in their hands, fixed with spikes; others bore shovels that
did not look as though they'd ever turned dirt. One man, older
than the rest with a fierce beard and hawklike eyebrows – quite
impressive they were, sweeping like wings to his temples – bore
a sheathed sword in his hand, one of the straight, thin ones that
I have heard our Sun Huáng refer to as jian.

Huáng himself barked an indecipherable order in Kithai, the
palanquin bearers set his down on the massive cobbles, and he
exited, standing tall and holding his cane. He approached the
hawklike man and they had a long, angry-sounding debate.

It looked as if it would end in some sort of violence. As I
watched Huáng, the cant of his shoulders, the way he held his
body, an ease imbued it. It is hard to describe, my love. It was as
though at the moment of incipient violence, Huáng resolved to
commit to something and that was a great relief to him, and he
relaxed. He became still and, looked absolutely non-threatening.
The other man, however, became alarmed. He took a step
backwards, gave a terse bow, and then said some words to his
men and they passed us by, give terse little genuflections to each
palanquin.

'What was that all about?' Secundus asked, being in a litter
closer to Huáng.

'They are Monkey-boys.'

Tenebrae said, 'Monkey-boys? Do they have something to do
with this Wukong fellow Juvenus spoke of? The Monkey King?'

'They are his followers.'

'They seemed a tad belligerent,' Secundus said.

Huáng nodded. 'They are rebels.'

'Rebels?' Secundus said. 'Do the August Ones have some sort
of police force?'

Huáng thought for a moment. 'We have a . . .' He looked

around, thinking. 'A militia. It keeps peace in Jiang. Outside Jiang, we have troops. Army.'

'What was that at the end?' Tenebrae asked. 'They seemed to reconsider their bellicose position.'

'My home is but a short way. We should go,' Huáng said, ducking his white-crowned head and getting back in his palanquin. 'My home waits.'

Eventually, we left the market and thoroughfare behind, rising higher. The cobbled lanes were still busy, but a hushed sort of expectancy accompanied our passage, and many of the citizens stopped in their labours or occupations to watch us until we moved out of sight. It was a strange and uncomfortable journey.

When we halted, it was before another stone wall, far enough away from the port and canals for the air to be sweet and the neighbourhood to have taken on a more sylvan aspect; soft, drooping trees stood swaying in the breeze, horses clopped along down the cobbled path, passing elegant houses and walled estates with apple blossom trees peeking over walls and songbirds chirping merrily inside the demesnes.

Two orange painted wooden doors – thick and roughly carved with curving geometric designs at the peak – creaked open on massive iron hinges. Huáng stepped forward and said, 'Welcome to my home.' He gestured for us to enter. 'It will be a long while before Tsing Huáng, the August One Who Speaks for the Autumn Lords, will summon us to the Winter Palace. He now tours the outer regions. When he returns, we will bring you before the Autumn Lords to make your entreaty.'

A bevy of servants, mostly young men and women, trotted up in a deferent jog – a curious, shuffling gait that I only understood when I saw they wore slippers rather than shoes or boots – and escorted us through a walled estate that would rival any patrician's villa in Rume or Cumæ. The path led us forward through manicured foliage, across ornately carved and lacquered bridges, over fishponds filled with brilliant orange and white spotted fish. Following a footpath, we came upon a lovely miniature pavilion hidden in a little grove of trees with spreading yellow and red leaves, a species I have never before encountered. Beyond that was the manse – I cannot call it a house; villa doesn't suit it – that had graceful yet sweeping points on the tiled roof and seemed a more squat, considerably wider version of those scalloped buildings we witnessed on our journey through the streets of Jiang. We were led inside, where more opulence assailed us. Golden doors and finely wrought statuary of what I thought must be mythical creatures, though the existence of the little lóng made me realize that some could truly exist. Apes in clothing with intelligent faces, insects that bore weapons, furred creatures that half-resembled dogs but were shaped more as bears. Birds with long curving beaks like swords, fish with jagged mouths that no western fisherman has ever seen.

As we stared at the strange opulence the atrium offered us – Carnelia stood entranced with a painted fabric wallhanging that depicted a fierce woman holding a sword and keeping a phalanx of what could only be described as monsters at bay, each creature having wickedly angular eyes, claws, and fangs – a servant came to stand by each of us, even Lupina, who entered the manse last as she organized our baggage. Within moments they were tugging at our sleeves and saying, 'Sígueme, porfavor.' Secundus and Tenebrae shot me dark looks at the utterance of Espan, the Medieran language. The signs of the Medierans were everywhere.

Through gestures and pidgin Latin, we made the slaves to understand that we were sisters, Lupina our handmaid, and we wished to share a sleeping chamber. Much attention was brought to my belly, smiling Tchinee women clustering about, the many servants touching me there with light hands and giggling, though what amused them I still cannot say.

Huáng bid us be comfortable in our new quarters. His servants would bring our luggage, and someone would come round to notify us to supper. One of his stewards had brought him a parchment and he disappeared, still reading the glyph-like writing of Kithai that covered it.

Our room was massive, with towering ceilings covered in moulding that was so intricately wrought with relief sculpture and designs it would take a ladder and a month to puzzle it all out. In an alcove was an elaborate and fussy blackwood bed with three sides covered in flowing silk and the other standing open – a bed for lovers, if the lovers stood fifteen feet tall. Multiple mattresses were covered in satin brocade and the yellow coverlet – the Autumn yellow, I later learned, the colour of Kithai's rulers – was embroidered with flaming red lóng and puffy white clouds. The room had a rich, varied smell and Lupina wrinkled her nose as she picked up one of the many pillows strewn about on the floor and in low-slung blackwood chairs. She sniffed and said, simply, 'Stuffed with herbs,' and walked to the door to the room and tossed it out.

There was a flawless mirror – so flawless I was stunned by my own reflection and, on closer inspection, the pallor and blemishes on my skin from the long, near-closeted journey on the *Malphas* – flanked by shiny black lacquered armoires, each festooned with golden ornamentation, for us to store our clothes. We settled in, swiftly, while Lupina took all of the herb-stuffed pillows and neatly stacked them in the hall.

More servants entered, one a beautiful young woman, black hair pulled back in a severe bun, who motioned to us, saying only, '*aquí, maestra*' in a thick accent. She approached a wall (every inch of it decorated with filigree and relief carvings) and pressed a section that depicted a young robed woman standing by a pool. There was a click, and the wall moved, revealing a door which swung open. Inside was a small pool set in the white stone of the floor. I could smell woodsmoke and char, and from another adjoining room two heavily muscled men entered, bearing between them a copper pot that Lupina could fit in, and poured boiling water into the pool. A few moments later, another two men entered and repeated the process, exiting hastily. There was a stillness in the women servants while the men were in the same room. When they were gone, the pretty young maid turned an ornamental flower on the side of the pool and more water poured in, diluting the steaming hot water.

After placing the petals of a yellow flower in the water and pouring scented oils, the servant dropped her robes and stood before us naked. She was quite comely and the bath looked and smelled so inviting after the long journey that Carnelia and I disrobed and joined her in the water, while Lupina scowled and loitered about until I told her she had to bathe and only then would she disrobe and join us.

It was quite a merry little gathering in the pool and at some point a carafe of spicy wine appeared – I did not see whoever brought it – and even Lupina relaxed. Afterwards, we dressed in clean clothes and strolled the estate, walking on its beautifully manicured footpaths, listening to the songbirds roosting in the blossoms of the trees, watching the fish sluggishly swim the artfully designed ponds. When the sun fell, we were summoned to dinner with Sun Huáng. In another massive room we dined. As opulent and elaborate as his manse was, his dinner (like his manner, his style of dress, his economy of movement) was simple. There were steaming bowls of rice, lightly vinegared and sprinkled with sesame, grilled meat tossed with vegetables, and a light fish soup followed by a pudding of some sort for dessert. It was delectable and the perfect repast and we all praised the quality of the victuals to Huáng. He seemed pleased, though he did not show it, but when questioned about the Monkey-boys, he answered in the tersest fashion. I daresay he was distracted, for throughout the dinner his stewards would approach him silently, touch his shoulder with great respect, and either whisper in his ear or hand him folded parchment that he would read and hand back.

After dinner, we walked the grounds again, this time to watch the release of the coloured paper *zhuìlì* into the sky. Here, in the Jade Yu, was where the wealthy and August Ones lived, and so the light display was very grandiose and quite lovely. In addition to the lanterns, there were some sort of combustible embers that rose into the air to explode like patterned flowers of fire.

'I say,' Tenebrae said, looking up as a loud boom swept through Huáng's garden, his upturned face coloured pink and green by turns as the fire-flowers burst overhead, casting coloured light on all below. 'Are those sparkly things *daemons?*'

Huáng shook his head. 'They are made of *yanhuó,* smoke and fire. It is a compound known across Kithai. The... recipe the gods gave to our ancestors before the Autumn Lords came. The *yanhuó,* it is made from the shite of little lóng, charcoal, and other ingredients that occur throughout Kithai. It is a common thing,' he shrugged, slightly, as if to indicate the *yanhuó* was worthless.

'So this occurs every night?' I asked Huáng, gesturing to the sky. It was hard to believe that this sort of event, so beautiful, would occur with such frequency.

'No,' he said. 'Some nights the sky remains dark, if the Autumn Lords move in the city.'

'Move?'

'Moving. With the people.'

That was curious. 'They take that much interest in the citizens of Jiang?' I said. 'I had assumed they were some sort of religious order, that almost all of their time was consumed in contemplation of the magical force you mentioned. This Qi.'

'They are always concerned with Qi, always,' he said. 'I cannot...' He shook his head, slowly. 'I do not have the words. Our masters are not... happy.' His face soured and I could tell now he regretted sending Min away, however rude and offensive she could be. 'That is not right. They are fear.'

'Fear? Do you mean fearsome?'

'Yes? No? I think so.'

'So, the Autumn Lords are fearsome. What do they do when they interact with the people of Jiang?'

'They take those with the most Qi.'

'How does one tell who has the most Qi?'

'It is a simple matter if you can... direct yours.'

'Where do they take them?' I asked. The lack of answers regarding the Autumn Lords was beginning to chafe.

At that moment, a massive explosion of sparking golden flames showered overhead, crackling. Afterwards there was a flurry of chatter in the Tchinee language, and servants scurried up and beckoned us away. Huáng never answered me.

The next morning, after waking and a luxurious breakfast in our room, Huáng's servants beckoned us to the garden where the August One Who Confronts the Foreign Devils was in the garden, moving through the Eight Silken Movements. Secundus and Tenebrae were already there – Tenebrae had found some excuse to remove his tunic and was showing off his chiselled physique – and we joined them happily. Afterwards, I walked the garden with Lupina in the morning light, admiring the lovely flora and fauna, thousands of unknown flowers and budding plants, trees which have no counterpart in Latinum or even Occidentalia. Carnelia and the boys clattered about with their bamboo sticks, working on their swordplay under Huáng's watchful eye. In the afternoon we had a sumptuous meal of pork fried with peppers and vegetables and dipped into a sweet sauce, steamed rice, and more of the delectable rice pudding. The food here, while simple by Ruman standards, is flawless in its freshness and simplicity. Young Fiscelion grows happy and strong within me.

At night we dined again, lightly, and watched the *yanhuó* and *zhuilì* rise into the sky, speechless. In addition to the coloured lanterns floating above the city, the horizon was streaked with rising pinpricks of fire that exploded with deafening booms and flashed with bright coloured lights.

This has been our daily routine since we have arrived and nothing has broken the reverie of this schedule. Carnelia looks healthier than I've ever seen her and comes to bed smiling and content, though sore. Huáng has presented her with a jian, a long absolutely plain sword with only the barest hint of a guard and a leather-wrapped sheath.

'It's rather plain, is it not?' I said, looking at the sword as Carnelia held it and made some experimental thrusts in our bedroom.

Carnelia frowned. 'It is perfect. Flawless.' She struck a pose as if a scorpion and lashed out. I was half alarmed and half delighted. My sister has always been a wonderful mimic of human motion – when she was younger all she had to do was but witness a dance once to be able to reproduce it beyond my ability to recognize any flaw. 'Huáng has taught me the movement needs to be simple, direct. Economy in everything.'

I laughed. ''Nelia, you are delightful.'

She frowned. 'This is no joke for me, sissy.'

'You said that about learning The Festus Progression.'

'I was a silly little brat then,' she said, her face tense. 'I need you to understand this, sissy. This training...' She chewed her lip slightly. 'What I am learning now resonates on such a deep

317

level in my soul that I am frightened at the intensity of it,' she whispered finally. 'Please do not belittle it.'

''Nelia, I . . .'

'I know I have been an idiot. A frivolous spoiled child. But this . . . this is—'

'Important for you,' I said.

'Yes.'

'I respect that and am happy for you,' I said and was surprised to see tears standing in her eyes. 'So, tell me why this sword is so wonderful.'

She wiped her eyes and smiled again, excitement suffusing her face. 'Look at it! Finest steel. Simple as a killing thought!'

'It looks rather like a metal stick.'

'It is intentionality made physical. Huáng says there is no sword, that the sword only exists in your mind and the metal you hold becomes filled with Qi and thus becomes a part of *you*.' She went on for a long while, lecturing me, repeating and recounting the things she'd learned, all in a rush, and I must admit, because I was full of food and Fiscelion kicked, I did not retain much of it. Eventually she sheathed the weapon and came to embrace me before bed.

And so our days pass somewhat dreamily, waiting to be called before the Autumn Lords and this Tsing Huáng who speaks for them. I want the day to come swiftly, so that I might return to you all the sooner, but if we must wait, I cannot imagine a more pleasant place to do the waiting.

In our wonderful period of expectant languor, there has been only one incident of note that I should convey to you, my love. One evening, as we finished a lovely dinner of some sort of sea fish that neither Huáng nor his servants could convey the name of, a gong began to peal outside the manse and then was taken up across the rest of the city, a thousand gongs tolling in varied rhythms across the valley, over the Jiang River.

Huáng bid us finish our dinner and when we were finished, he stood. 'Tonight, there will be no *zhuìlì*. I bid you to go to your rooms and be comfortable.'

'No *zhuìlì*?' Tenebrae said. 'I'd grown quite fond of them. Wonderful way to cap an evening.'

'No lights,' Huáng answered. 'Not tonight.'

'You said the *zhuìlì* ritual is cancelled when the Autumn Lords move among the citizens, is that right?'

'Yes,' Huáng said. 'And it is our custom to keep to our homes then. Good night,' he said, and turning, he removed himself from the dining hall.

The servants beckoned us to come – their normally smiling and genial expressions absent, their movements hasty.

'There's something strange here,' I said to Secundus, who held Tenebrae's arm in his. While the boys were assigned separate rooms, they rarely slept apart, I noticed. 'Keep an eye out this evening. Huáng said the Autumn Lords are moving through the populace and that puzzles me. I do not know what is happening, but I need your vigilance.'

'Of course, sissy,' Secundus said, letting loose Tenebrae's arm and coming to embrace me. 'We will watch.'

'We have come to Far Tchinee and it is not so foreign as we thought. But I am not at ease. Be watchful. Be wary.'

His smile faded and he held me out at arm's length, considering me. 'I see that you are concerned.' He took my hands in his and squeezed. 'I will remain on guard, my dear,' he said, and allowed his boyish smile back.

'And I will as well, Livia,' Tenebrae added.

'She only needs me to watch out for her,' Carnelia said. 'Since I carry the *biao*.'

The boys groaned. Secundus said, 'You're never going to let us forget, are you?'

'What's this?' I asked. 'The *biao*?'

'I have the stone,' Carnelia said, pulling an object from beneath the neckline of her top. It was a river-rock, smooth and polished, fastened with a simple black leather cord. Of all the objects I'd seen in Huáng's manse it was the simplest, if one did not count Carnelia's *jian*.

'What does it signify?'

Secundus groaned again. 'She scored on us both while sparring. And Huáng awarded her the *biao*.' He grimaced. 'But she'll have to give it back in the morning.'

'Tomorrow's another day!' Tenebrae said. And then he laughed as well.

The servant girl escorting us, the one we've taken to calling Delia since she reminded Secundus of a cousin of ours who died very young, tugged my sleeves and said, 'Aquí, maestra, aquí' with a tense face and so our conversation ended and we retired to our rooms.

It was with some alarm that I noticed on this evening, when normally we'd be enjoying the coloured lights of the *zhuìlì*, Delia and the other servants shuttered the windows and all the doors. When they left, I heard an audible *click* as if some mechanical tumbler had fallen. Going to the door, I tried the latch and found it locked from outside.

'Locked, sissy,' I said to Carnelia. I normally try not to state the obvious but she wasn't paying much attention to me.

My sister looked up from where she sat. She'd had a strenuous day, this day, scoring on the boys. She lounged in one of the blackwood chairs, her legs spread apart and her arms on the armrests.

She waved her hand. ''Pina, please tell me there's some wine in here,' she said.

'We're locked in, Carnelia!' I said, trying to get some sort of response from her. Sometimes she could be just like my father.

She only shrugged as Lupina poured her a glass. 'So?'

'Why are we contained here? We've had full run of the grounds until tonight!'

'I don't know, sissy.' She yawned. 'And quite frankly, I'm buggered.' She shifted her arm in its socket, wincing. Then she felt her breasts as if searching for an elusive pain. 'He made us perform one hundred leverages from the ground today. My teats are unfortunate indeed,' she said, making a joke on the title of *The Teats of Fortuna*.

I raised my eyebrow at that but Carnelia was too busy drinking wine.

'I can see it now,' said I. 'My sister becoming a great throbbing brute.'

She grinned and scratched at her crotch, theatrically. 'I'll show you throbbing, girl,' she said in the thickest voice she could manage. Then she erupted into giggles. 'Oh, sissy, I'm exhausted. We can find out in the morning.'

In a very short time, she was in bed asleep. Lupina watched me from the pallet of pillows (those not stuffed with herbs) she slept on at the foot of the bed. We had entreated her to join us in the great blackwood bed since we could all easily sleep there, splayed out as if crucified, and still not come a foot within reach of the other it was so large, but she balked.

Lupina instinctively knows when we need assistance and I do not know what I would do without her. She's there whenever I have any of the cravings or intestinal discomforts that pregnancy visits upon women; she's ready with cloth or drink or an arm whenever my body has needs requiring them. She rubs down Carnelia's sore muscles at the end of each day and brushes my hair and manages my wardrobe. I have come to dearly love the dour little woman. There is more to love than enchantment and personality – loyalty and consistency become seated in the heart as well.

'Wouldn't be right, ma'am,' Lupina said.

'Nonsense,' said I. 'Don't sleep there when you can be far more comfortable with us.'

'No, ma'am. Comfort can dull you.' She looked about the room. 'All this is comfort. It sucks us in, it does. But these folk ain't our kin or friends and all I hear from the servants is the beaner talk.'

'Espan?'

She nodded. 'Them Medierans been kicking in this stall before we got here,' she said and I had to agree.

But on this night I told Lupina I was sleepless and needed some privacy. And so, against her natural inclination, she climbed into the big blackwood bed and went to sleep with Carnelia, while I paced our room, hands on stomach, wondering at this strange and unforeseen incarceration. A stillness fell upon the manse. No servant stirred, no wind brushed the eaves. I fancied I could hear the wicks of candles hissing, spitting. Against Lupina's wishes, I helped myself to the dry, spicy white wine that the Tchinee favoured and ate some of the honeyed rice cakes that Delia, in her halting pidgin Espan, conveyed were good to swell children in their mother's bellies. When I was sated (and growing uncomfortable with the food sharing space with young Fiscelion) I tried to pace again but my feet were swollen and achy. My hands felt as sausages.

Our physiognomy visits such indignity upon us when with child, my love. And it is all your fault. You have my love, you have all my affection, and you have my ire too, for you spurted this child into my belly. And it is a cracker of a beast, this boy. He swells my extremities and plays havoc with my appetites.

I was considering my fat sausage fingers and ankles when I heard something above. The room Carnelia, Lupina, and I share has a set of lacquered windowless double doors that resemble the Gallish ones that are so much in fashion now. Yet these are constructed of solid wood, with the exception of a small panel

that would swing open if unbolted to provide an unobstructed
view of the garden or, if in dire straits, anyone who might be
trying to gain entry, unwarranted. The thumping sounded once
more on the roof and ceased but I heard an excited explosion
of song from the nightbirds that roosted in the drooping trees
of Huáng's garden. In my mind's eye, I imagined a large lóng
landing on the tiled roof above our heads and then lighting
to try to make a meal of some of the lovely birds that made a
home on the manse's grounds.

I went to the 'Gallish' doors and slid open the panel and
looked out upon the private garden, bathed in moonlight.
There were only high and wispy clouds in the ocean-deep blue
of sky, and I could see no evidence of a little lóng from the
Jiang quayside frolicking in the trees or menacing any of the
garden's night-birds, nor did I see evidence of the fecund little
things on the pavestones leading away from where I stood.
By craning my neck, I was able to see the outside bar on the
door and considered reaching through the portal to see if I
could lift it and venture outside, but just as I lifted my hand,
something caught my eye. On the far side of the garden, past
the blossoming trees, where the stones of the outer wall stood
in relief against the grey rising hills beyond and the night sky, a
figure stood. A lone shape, draped in what appeared to be silks
that ruffled in the night air and one of the odd, short caps that
the people of Kithai favoured, which look somewhat like a silken
version of an upturned pot.

It was a large man, long of limb and lean as a willow, and he
stooped some, as if withered by age. He had big knobby wrists,
elbows – his joints were oversized – and when he turned in the
light so that his profile was visible, I saw he had a fine brow and
a sharp, long nose that Hellene sculptors would love to render in
undying stone.

Yet something was wrong with him, as well. His head turned

this way and that, as if searching for something, and he often raised his head as if scenting the wind. And there was the puzzlement of the manner in which such a stooped man might gain the top of the wall.

I was about to call out to him when he crouched, loped across the top of the wall like some preternatural jungle creature, and launched himself into the air and disappeared beyond my sight.

A wholly curious incident and one that gave me some thought.

And so we remain here, waiting. The nightly *zhuìlì* have resumed and Carnelia and the boys' training continue apace. Word has come that Tsing Huáng, the August One Who Speaks for the Autumn Lords, has finished his inspection of the outer provinces and has begun his journey back to Jiang though it could take him weeks to reach the city.

I continue to miss you and curse Tamberlaine for separating us. In some ways, my body grows into this wonderful thing, a glowing ember containing two souls, and I often feel a sublime contentment suffusing me and then . . . I become hungry. Or catch a glimpse of myself in the mirror and notice something has happened to my nose – it has become enlarged, slightly, widening, and Lupina says that is a sure sign of a healthy boy though Carnelia disagrees, saying that since time immemorial the Truscans in old Latinum state that a widening nose is a sure sign of a girl. And so they merrily argue about it because, probably due to the strangeness of our surroundings, an old argument is as comfortable to them as worn pair of slippers. And I do not mind.

And yet.

I miss you.

At night I hold up my hand and trace the scar that marks us. Through that scar we are joined. Sometimes, I feel like there is a

tether between us, flowing between scars. Wherever I may roam,
it connects us two – I am you and you are me.

I love you.

Ever your wife and partner,
Livia

*Kalends of Geminus, Sixth Hour, 2638 Annum Ex
Rume Immortalis, Jiang City in Far Tchinee, In the
Manse of Sun Huáng*

Dearest Love,
Do not be worried, I am well. As is our child, still growing
within me.

Very little has occurred since the Ides of Sextilius and my last
letter. However, Sun Huáng brings word that Tsing Huáng has
finally returned to Jiang and we shall be presented before him
and the Autumn Lords very soon. This news has sent Carnelia
and the boys into a fit of depression, since their training with
Huáng and life in this lovely manse has been idyllic and almost
dreamlike. Everything here is luxurious and comfortable – the
food, the appointments, the servants, the grounds. Even the
quality of air. The day is filled with refulgent light, a million
motes hanging upon shafts of sun, and insects swim through
the air like undersea creatures. The trees blossom in the garden,
mirrored by shade-loving flowers below. Streams gurgle and swirl
among the footpaths, tracing their course and filling the air with
a lulling sound.

Delia and the other servants dote upon us, and me especially,
bringing little gifts of sweets and dainty bits of meat steaming
from the kitchen. They make much of Carnelia's long hair and
delight my sister with intricate and ornate methods of braiding it.

Secundus and Tenebrae are obviously in the grips of a great love affair – and I am happy for my brother, though I still cannot entirely trust the man who is so very deep in the pockets of our Emperor. Yet, for the moment, they are happy. Kithai custom, however, frowns upon the love between two men (or women) and so in hopes of remaining circumspect and inoffensive to either our host or the August Ones (through vicious rumour), Tenebrae and Secundus do not overly show any physical love for one another except in the most comradely manner, a fierce hug or embrace after a trying sparring session or bout of *armatura*. Yet all of the signals are there – they are in love, or as close as one can come in such a fallen state in which we live.

On twelve Kalends, Sun Huáng took us on a small jaunt out of the city of Jiang to witness an event that is still hard to describe. We rose early, at the insistence of Delia, and found ourselves bundled into palanquins and hustled out into the morning air, through the city. As we entered the great thoroughfare, Monkey-boys watched us yet did nothing, though I noted one running off as if our appearance was exciting to him. We passed down to the Jiang Bund where a pleasure barge awaited us on the quayside. It had a canvas awning streaked with white marks of lóng dung, as all flat surfaces in the Bund are, but other than that, it was quite opulent and *daemon*-driven. Before the sun could rise too high we were steaming upriver, watching the Bund fall away and passing out of Jiang itself and breakfasting on soft-boiled eggs and sweet rice wine and green tea for me.

We entered a flat landscape where the river widened so much that the farthest shore was hard to discern. We hugged the north-western bank, close to the many fields and thick, congested clumps of brush and tangled vegetation. By mid-day, we came to a village that looked quite prosperous with stone

buildings, a large scalloped pagoda of some sort, and a heavy
stone wall with a kind of ballista set at intervals along the
top, manned by Kithai men in armour. Its wharf teemed with
commercial boats and river-vessels – barges, fishermen, water-
taxis and what appeared to be a paddle-driven ferry carrying a
clutch of the small, woolly Tchinee ponies I'd seen in the market
and the by the wharf at our arrival (though I have witnessed
some draught horses in Jiang itself). We disembarked – this
Bund was suspiciously lacking in any little dragons, so umbrellas
to protect us from raining excrement were not necessary – and
followed a stone road toward the centre of the village. Sun
Huáng informed us the village was called Uxi, which felt strange
on my tongue when spoken, as do most of the names in Kithai.
On foot we entered the market square, led by Sun Huáng and
some of his advisors and two other August Ones who remained
unnamed and watched us though they pretended not to.

In the square, a group of women were alarmed, and there
was a clangour of high-pitched voices and shrieks. It was quite
a ruckus, so loud and frantic that Sun Huáng placed himself
between us, the August Ones in our company, and the bevy of
outraged women. And outraged they were. Some ripped their
hair, some beat on their chests, eyes streaming.

'What is the matter here, sifu?' Tenebrae asked, using Huáng's
honorific.

'A child is ill unto death, I believe,' he shook his head and
barked out an order to one of his attendants. The man scurried
forward and began yelling.

'What's he doing now?' I asked to Carnelia. She had worn her
jian this morning and looked rather fierce, I should say.

She shrugged. 'I imagine he's announcing the presence of Sun
Huáng, the Sword of Jiang.'

'You can understand their language well enough to translate?'
I asked, a little awed.

'Ia help me, no. But I heard his name and the rest of it . . . it is what I would do.'

I looked to Huáng. The old gentleman held his *jian* – looking very much like a plain bamboo stick – in his hand like a badge of office, a fascis held by lictors. The crowd quieted and parted.

We passed through the women and village folk. Some of the braver ones called out plaintively to Sun Huáng as he passed and his face clouded but he took no further action.

'What was that all about, sifu?' Secundus asked.

Huáng shook his head. 'There's some trouble with the children and the mothers are upset.'

On the steps of the great pavilion, a clutch of magistrates, prosperous farmers, and local businessmen greeted us. They stared openly at us Rumans, some of the men tittering behind their hands, some of the women examining the boys brazenly, with appraising stares. In a long and formal ceremony we all exchanged small gifts (Huáng had provided us with them – paper toys, pinwheels, kites, candles) and everyone had a short glass of rice wine save me. As our party drank, one of the farmers brought forth a kid goat, bleating constantly. Huáng and the local people of import rose, and we rose with them and walked out of the village into the terraced rice fields that bordered the white-stone road.

We came to a pillar of stone on the side of the road, embossed with a curling and sinuous scaled design that brought to mind some of the representations I'd seen of lóng at Huáng's manse. I looked upon our destination. The rice field in this paddy was different than the others we had passed on our walk here. It had a wilder look, and tufts of red grains grew in wild patches and weeds were thick on the edges where the other fields had a manicured aspect to them.

'We have come to witness and give offering to *shé*, the great *Nāga*,' Huáng said, smiling. 'Carnelia, Secundus, Mister

Shadow,' Huáng said, a quirk to his mouth. It was the first time I heard him refer to Tenebrae as such, but the nickname did fit him. 'Observe the movements. Take them inside yourself.'

'What is *shé*, sifu?' Carnelia asked.

Huáng nodded toward the unkempt and flooded rice field. 'You will see.'

The man leading the goat rolled his loose pants legs up to his knees and waded out into the water. The ripening grains, turning from green to golden, parted as he made his ungainly way out into the muck. It soon became apparent that the sodden earth of the paddy sucked at his bare feet, his movements became a great labour. The goat bleated furiously, tugged along behind.

Some of the villagers – the more prosperous-looking ones – said some words in unison as the man who had led the goat into the field began his hustle back to where we stood by the white stone marker. One of the well-fed women clad in silks dashed a ceramic container of rice wine onto the stones of the road, shattering the container.

One of the larger tussocks of red grain – some sort of milo or blademeal – shivered and thrashed. An expectant hush fell upon the gathered, and something black came into the rice field. It moved with a muscular, sinuous grace. A serpent of tremendous size, easily thirty or forty feet long and as big around as a barrel. Black as midnight, its scales gleamed in the sunlight as it cut through the field toward the goat. Behind its massive triangular head, it had a ruffle of scales around its neck that bristled like feathers.

The goat thrashed and cried out in human-like screams, seeing the black serpent approach. Thank Ia, the *shé* was direct and precise. It came within ten feet of the goat, coiling around itself like a spring, then lashed out striking, its maw open. The movement ripped the goat from its tether. The bleating ceased.

The *shé* lifted its head to the sky, working its mouth open to get the goat down its gullet, then made some undulating movements in its throat to allow the carcass to pass.

When the goat had disappeared, the *shé* raised its gleaming head, turned toward where we stood on the stone road, and stared at us balefully, a long red forked tongue probing the air.

The village folk bowed in a genuflection to the creature. Huáng watched it steadily, his sheathed sword in hand.

Then the *shé* lowered its head and moved away, back toward the tussock it came from.

A palpable sigh moved through the gathered Tchinee, and they drank more rice wine and chattered in their language.

'Why do they feed the creature, Sun Huáng?' I asked. 'It seems as though it would be a great danger, this near the village.'

'Possibly you have answered your own question,' Huáng said slowly. He thought for a moment. 'The *shé* terrorized this region, all the way to Jiang, until the Autumn Lords came many thousands of years ago. The *shé* is a pure creature of Qi and so the Autumn Lords hunted them for this. *Nāga* is the last. She has no mates, she has no . . .' He cast about. I was forcibly reminded that Min was no longer with us and wondered where she was and what she was doing. 'Paramour? Is that the Ruman word?'

'Yes,' I said.

'She has no paramour. And so, we bring her food until the Autumn Lords decide to take her, too.'

'That's very sad,' I said, looking toward the tussock. 'I can't imagine what it must be to be absolutely alone in the world.'

Huáng grew still. 'It is death, Madame Livia. Death before its time.'

'Why did you ask us to watch how it moved, sifu?' Carnelia said.

'Because when you release Qi... when you strike... it is good to think like the *shé*. To move like her. This is why I brought you here.'

Understanding crossed Carnelia's face and Tenebrae – Mister Shadow – gave a little 'ahhh' of realization.

'We study creatures of the earth,' Huáng said. 'Training is repetition and following these...' He turned to look out at the tussock that hid the great serpent *Nāga* one last time. '...outpourings of animal Qi allows us to see, like opening a door. A way of being. Always new. Does this make sense?'

'Yes, sifu.' And it did. Sometimes, when the common speech failed him, you had to see between the words.

We Rumans walked back in silence. The village leaders were gregarious and chatty, seemingly buoyed by the rice wine and the success of their offering. When the road entered Uxi, most of our Tchinee companions peeled away from the group, waving goodbyes and calling out indecipherable farewells. In the square, there was considerable confusion. The women who had been in distress before were now possessed by a terrible and violent outrage. A great pushing and pulling mob had formed, blocking the way back to the Uxi Bund where our pleasure barge awaited. We passed through, warily, and when we approached the Bund a great hue and cry sounded from behind us and the figure of a boy raced down the street. The lad was in that awkward phase of development when his body had suddenly stretched on entering puberty, and all his limbs were long, his joints knobby, yet very thin. As Father might say, 'the lad's balls had dropped' but not by very much. He had a curly head of hair – exceedingly rare among the Kithai I'd seen – and he was smooth of skin and clean of face.

Except for the blood. A brilliant gash traced its way from his temple down his jawline. Blood discoloured his tunic, which appeared to be silk and fine, though now ruined. His mouth, smeared with blood, was open in a black hole of terror or alarm, his eyes wild.

Behind him came the mob, tossing rocks, flagstones, ceramic vessels, all clattering to the cobblestones or shattering on the walls of the buildings surrounding us. They chanted a phrase over and over again. 'Chiang-shih! *Chiang-shih!*'

A metal brace or lead pipe whanged off the back of his head and he went stumbling, pitching forward onto his face and falling in a jumble of gawky limbs.

I reacted without thinking, that is clear. Holding my belly, I ran as swiftly as I could to interpose myself between the boy and the mad crowd of women. Carnelia cried out, behind me. I felt some thrown thing smash into my shoulder. A rock caught me on my brow, rocking my head back. But I was incensed and furious and felt no pain. This invulnerable fervour had overtaken me though my sister tells me my hands never stopped cradling of my stomach. I stood over the boy.

The women – pressed together in a clutch – stopped in the street, surprised to find a foreign devil between them and their prey. They chattered and screamed in fierce voices and I watched as the short-lived expression of surprise on the lead woman's face was soon replaced with rage and she raised the rock she held in her hand and chucked the damned thing at me.

Then Huáng was there, a naked blade in one hand, its sheath in the other, his white hair in a wild clot around his head. He yelled, giving one tremendous bellow that echoed off the walls. The mob stepped backward. Huáng, looking relaxed, stepped forward.

Grabbing the boy's arms, I helped him to his feet. Lupina was there, then, scowling, and helping me, with Carnelia not far behind. We retreated, toward the Bund and our awaiting barge.

Looking back, I saw the mob had recovered from Huáng's magical bellow. One woman shied a rock at Huáng, who neatly side-stepped it. A large woman with a cleaver advanced, urging her companions to accompany her.

In a quick movement that seemed so simple it barely registered on my eye, Sun Huáng severed the cleaver and the hand that held it. The woman's mouth opened and closed, soundlessly, like a fish's plucked from a stream. The crowd became quiet.

Huáng said something in a low voice, the now bloodied sword held loosely before him.

Another rock was tossed, and it clattered onto the stones to the left of Huáng, but the mob had lost the fervour or madness that gave it cohesion. The burly woman whose hand had been chopped off emitted a high-pitched keening, gripping her stump, which gouted blood. With dark looks the women of Uxi village began to retreat and disperse.

'Come,' Huáng said, backing away, sword still in hand. 'To the Bund. Now.'

With Lupina at my side and both of us taking one of the boy's arms, we made our way back to the barge and in moments were steaming down the muddy river back to Jiang.

'What in the blazing Hells were you doing, sissy?' Carnelia asked once we were back on the barge. 'You're pregnant! There's more to think about than yourself!'

Carnelia was furious, face flushed, waving her hands madly about.

'I wasn't thinking,' I said. 'Sometimes that happens.'

'I can't *believe* you!' she said. Secundus and Tenebrae watched on, content, seemingly, to allow my sister to harangue me. Lupina, who tended to the gash on the boy's forehead, frowned at me and nodded as Carnelia spoke. Huáng, on boarding the barge, went to confer with his secretaries, who had remained behind. 'You're acting Ia-damned selfish!'

I tried to hide the smile but could not contain it. Carnelia forced me to sit and began daubing with a wetted handkerchief at the cut on my forehead where the rock had broken skin. There was some blood and a painful, swelling knot there – and my shoulder was sore – but for all that I felt remarkably well.

'It's not funny!' Carnelia screeched. She extended an accusing finger and waved it right under my nose. 'You are responsible for a baby! A Cornelian! Father would be so... so...'

'Angry?'

'Fucking livid, that's what. Stop grinning!'

'It's just I've never seen you like this, 'Nelia.'

'Well,' Carnelia bit her lip. 'Get used to it. Especially when you act like a lunatic. Who here is supposed to take care of you when you do stupid things?'

'Huáng didn't seem to have any trouble,' Secundus said, placing a hand on Carnelia's shoulder. 'No harm came of the incident, sister. And Livia has always gone her own way—'

'She's got a *passenger* now, brother,' Carnelia said, putting all the scorn she could in her voice. 'She can't be foolish and think it will *only* affect her.'

'You're right, sissy. I will be more careful.'

'Bloody right you will,' she said, huffing and blowing back the hair from her eyes. But her next words were softer. 'You could've been seriously injured, not to mention the baby.'

'I say,' Tenebrae said. 'I'm not sure she was ever in any real danger. Did you see Huáng? Ia's balls! How he moved! I was a fool ever to challenge him.'

'Yes, you were,' Carnelia said. 'But we knew that beforehand.'

Tenebrae and Secundus laughed, in the easy camaraderie reserved for those who share a common pursuit. For a while they discussed Huáng, the profound brilliance of his swordplay and martial prowess, until the man himself returned.

'Let us speak with this outcast,' he said, looking toward the

boy who lay quietly on one of the barge's padded benches as
Lupina tended to his wounds.

Huáng stood over the boy – young man, really, but he had an
unblemished innocence about him. Looking at him critically,
Huáng let loose an explosion of words that I could not
understand. Secundus and Tenebrae looked at each other with
incomprehension. Carnelia, hawkish and intense, only regarded
the boy.

The boy said and did nothing, except blink. His large eyes
were shuttered by eyelids ending in long lashes, giving him an
almost Hellene sweetboy appearance. He remained mute, and
looked upon us with wide eyes.

'The boy seems simple,' Tenebrae said. 'Perhaps the stoning
the women gave him knocked what little native intelligence he
had out of his head.'

'The question I want answered,' said I, 'is why were they
stoning him in the first place?'

Carnelia cocked her head. 'They were chanting something.'

'Chiang-shih,' Huáng said.

'What is '*chiang-shih*'?'

Huáng took a deep breath and held it for a moment. He
looked older now. He'd always seemed youthful, if wizened, but
now he simply looked old, the wrinkles at the corners of his
eyes dashing away from what those eyes had seen over the course
of his years.

'A drinker of blood.'

'What?' Carnelia said, hands clutched before her. 'A
vorduluk?'

'I do not know this word. A *chiang-shih* is a thing that
consumes Qi – mostly in blood. But it will eat flesh if it must.'
He reached forward and touched the boy's forehead, looking at
the gash. 'Other *chiang-shih* take the jing.' He waved his hand
negligently at his crotch. 'The pearly essence. It is all Qi.'

'These vorduluk take the lifeforce?' I asked.

'Yes. They take jing, which is of the body Qi. Does that make sense?'

'Seems to,' Secundus said, helping himself to the wine. Like our father, when the conversation became difficult, he would turn to wine for truth, or succour.

'They are monsters of myth. Whenever something happens to a child in the villages, women cry *chiang-shih*,' Huáng said. He looked at the boy closely. Reaching out, with one hand he took the boy's chin, not roughly, and turned his head back and forth, and observing the lad's face. The boy kept his mouth closed, and tight. 'The women of Uxi were upset, but I fear the boy is the . . . focus? Yes, the focus of their discontent. I am doubtful that he is the cause.'

After a long while of peering at the lad intently, Huáng said, 'For the time being, I will take him under my protection and he will be a companion of the Rumi. We have seen Madame Livia's affinity for him. Is this acceptable?'

'And when we are gone?' I asked. 'What will happen to the boy?'

Huáng considered the question. After a pause, he said, 'I cannot tell what native abilities or talents the boy might possess, other than that of angering village women. Let us have our company, and us his, and decide together. Possibly, he could make a page for you, Secundus, or become a Praetorian, Mister Shadow.'

'Or find some sort of employ with you, Sun Huáng. We two saved him. I won't allow him to be cast aside.' These strange maternal instincts had been stirred in me.

'Yes. Let us see what abilities and Qi he possesses.'

'Curious thing, this Qi,' said Tenebrae, the issue of the boy settled. 'We seem to encounter it quite a bit in conversation without having a full understanding of it. Is there some book or treatise . . . a pamphlet even . . . that has more information on it in the written language of Latinum?'

Huáng nodded. 'While Min was in Rume, I instructed her to transcribe the—' His brow furrowed and a lock of white hair fell. He brushed it back. 'The title would be, roughly, 'A History of Kithai.' It was presented to Tamberlaine as a gift, with the double-headed concubine. It had a large section on Qi.'

'I don't imagine there's any copies, then,' Secundus said, mulling over a silver goblet of spiced white wine. He puckered his mouth as he sipped. 'I will confer with my father via the Quotidian. It is possible we can have him – or one of his secretaries – give us the information regarding Qi on the Ides.'

'I will instruct Min to provide another copy,' Huáng said, frowning. 'From her cloister.'

'That would be wonderful,' I said. A thought occurred to me. 'The Qi. When we use these infernal devices . . . they take our Qi, is that correct?'

'Your physical form of it. Your jing, if I'm not mistaken.' He nodded his head. 'I witnessed your Ruman Emperor Tamberlaine using one, once.'

'And you said the Autumn Lords are "creatures of pure Qi".' Huáng nodded his snowy head.

'And vorduluk, these 'chiang-shih' consume it?'

'Yes.'

'How are these things connected?'

He smiled. 'Qi is life. There are hungry ghosts. There are hungry men. Mothers that eat their young. It is a monster of a world that we live in and *we* become monsters to survive,' he said. It all came out in a rush, so his pronunciation was terrible and, now, as I write it, I'm filling in where Huáng flubbed our words and declensions. But the sentiment was obvious.

'I am trying to understand, yet sometimes it still seems like magic to me,' Tenebrae said. 'All this talk of Qi.'

'Shut up, Shadow,' Carnelia said. 'Sifu is talking.'

Huáng smiled at Tenebrae. 'You are Ruman, and it would take many sheaf of days to get you to lower your practical nature and embrace the idea of Qi.'

The boy sat up and looked about, blinking. He had huge eyes, for a young man, and almost preternaturally fair skin. Huáng beckoned a serving woman and set her to washing his face and hands, cleaning the wound on the back of his head. Interrupting her work, I probed at it with my fingers, delicately, and though it seemed much less of a wound than it appeared when he received it. The skin was barely broken.

The boy stared at me with wide, open eyes and lightly placed his hands on my stomach. He said nothing, made no noise.

'I will make sure the boy is well, and safe, Livia,' Huáng said, softly. 'There is no worse thing than to be alone in the world.'

I didn't truly understand why he said that, but my heart clutched, and I thought of Fisk, so far away. I did something then I had not done before. Many times, I had seen Carnelia, Secundus, and Tenebrae bow to Sun Huáng when entering the *armatura* pitch, and he would respond in kind. I, however, being a Cornelian, and emissary of Rume, have always felt that it was a sign of submission to do so and at least one of our party should remain unbowed. Yet here was this man, this old man, full of knowledge and wisdom, and who in all appearances had remained honest and true to our mission and cause. I felt a great warmth for him then, and I know not if it was the inner currents of my jing or Qi or whatever in my body – or young Fiscelion's – but, rising, I bowed to Sun Huáng with as much respect as I could.

He returned the bow.

Again, I acted on impulse. I took his hand in mine, I kissed it. It had the liver spots that many aged have – my grandmother Livia, whose name I bear, always spoke of them as mistake marks, as if each big one, her first husband, her affairs, her second son, were writ upon flesh. Yet, taking his hand, looking at it, feeling the texture of his skin, the strength beneath, at that moment I found him beautiful, this withered bit of lightning made flesh. At first he was tense – this, I think was one physical interaction he was wholly unprepared for – and then he relaxed and I drew his hand to me. I placed it on my stomach, where the boy's hand had just been. He laughed, a soft breathy sound, and said words I did not understand. For a while we stood there together, him feeling my stomach twitch and convulse. Young Fiscelion popped him a good one right in the palm and Huáng's eyes widened and he laughed, a merry, musical laugh. When he did that the years on him fell away.

When I released him he smiled at me and placed his hand again on my protruding belly and I did not make him remove it. For all the talk of Qi, and jing, he seemed to want to know the wellspring of lifeforce.

'You are a delight,' he said. 'And hard as quarry stones.'

'I am Ruman,' said I.

'And I am an August One of Kithai,' he said, bowing to me, again.

'The August One Who Confronts the Foreign Devils.'

'Yes,' he said, his face pained. 'I am he.'

We returned to Jiang and settled back into our daily routine there. The boy is now accoutred if not like a little lord of Kithai, then a lord's page, and he wanders Huáng's manse as if in some dream, silent and unspeaking. Tomorrow or the next day, we will be taken before Tsing Huáng who is the August One Who Speaks for the Autumn Lords and if he deems us worthy, we will parlay with the rulers of this land and present the chest that Tamberlaine has instructed us to bear here.

I am near bloodless now, having refreshed the sanguine-ink slurry once already.

Know that I love you and miss you and

I remain,
Your loving wife Livia

TWENTY-FOUR

15 Kalends of Sextilius, 2638 ex Ruma Immortalis

I WAS FIXING TO LIGHT out from New Damnation for Harbour Town, putting my hangover and the last month behind me, when I received the note. Written in a fine hand.

The Tempus *Union sold your mule to Mister Mortuus Caccoups, a trader from Carthago Delenda Est. I give this to you because you seemed somewhat lonely when last we spoke and I thought you might miss your wife – Sincerely, A*

A real card that Andrae was.

I didn't know where Fisk was – his last letter mentioned Panem and Confluence and finally Harbour Town, so I decided to truck on to Carthago Delenda Est – the fancy name for Carthage, known to residents and neighbours as Fishstink – a minor little sea village not far west of Harbour Town on the shore of Gulf of Mageras. So I booked a passage on a steamer – took my share of the stretcher money from Fisk's legate's chest to tide me over – made sure there were none of the Tempus Union assholes on board and then headed down the Big Rill and from Encantata was able to buy passage with an old woman waggoneer who let me off in the general vicinity.

I found Bess in a stable not too far from the shore where the sound of the waves wasn't enough to mask her hawing. Her coat was nappy and demeanour brisk, but she brayed when she saw me and I kissed her on the nose and rubbed her canescent cheeks until she tried to bite me and I tried not to think about Andrae's jibes.

Her owner didn't want to sell, even with my orders from Cornelius – 'A forgery!' he cried – so I crushed one of his testicles with a knee-strike, stuffed a silver denarius into his pocket, managed not to kill his burly son with a knife (a fine piece of work, that, avoiding his vitals), and lit out expecting a pursuit. They must have thought better of it.

So it was not until the 3 Ides Geminus that I arrived in Harbour Town to look for Fisk. At the Collegium of Engineers, a studious looking young gentleman told me where I could find Samantha Decius, now chief engineer in charge of munitions. She'd set up shop at 32 Victrix Way.

Harbour Town was unlike most Ruman colony burgs in its layout because, like Passasuego and Hot Springs, it was first a Medieran settlement. It is said that the Medieran soul burns with all sorts of undeniable desires – for sex, for art, for poetry – and consequently, they're absolute shit in the organization and execution of city planning. Rumans, on the other hand, think with their high-heads, not their low ones.

Harbour Town was a jumble of neighbourhoods, carious with alleys, riddled with thoroughfares that went nowhere and ended abruptly. But Victrix Way was in a warehouse district near the western piers, on the western side of where the Big Rill emptied into the Bay of Mageras, and it was there I took myself to find Sam.

There were Ruman legionnaires everywhere though none bothered me until I found number 32 – a massive stone building that might've been a warehouse except for the sturdy construction. It was even larger than the Passasuego engineer's collegium. Two great, oxen-fed brutes guarded the front entrance with Hellfire carbines and pistols. Along the roof of the building, which was nondescript and bland – just as most Rumans like them – I could see sharp-shooters with the tell-tale silhouettes of rifles. I gave my name, presented my portfolio, and waited until one of the bully-boys escorted me to Samantha's office.

I've seen enough engineer and summoner's chambers to know that Samantha's was an exception. While Sapientia's was neat but overfull, Samantha's was pristine and almost devoid of all clutter. It was a windowless chamber (as nearly all of the engineers' chambers I've ever been in save Beleth's were), lit by *daemonlight*, with bare stone walls. A worktable of rich stained wood, mahogany or some other dense tree, centred the room, surrounded by cushioned barrel-chairs. In the corner was a secretary's desk, its parchment, quills and inkwells, wax tablets and styluses immaculately arranged, and the wall flanking the desk was covered entirely with neatly labelled storage cabinets and drawers.

Samantha herself sat at the table, a secretary near her, and they were discussing something in low tones when I entered behind the legionnaire, who positioned himself by the door as I approached her. Spying me, Samantha smiled, a big genuine smile of welcome, and stood. Once plump and ruddy cheeked and rather plain in the way that soft men and women can be, she now showed the toll of her new elevation in the engineering world at the order of Cornelius, and the stresses and workload that accompanied it. She had lost weight, copious amounts of it, but instead of her becoming some ingénue, her skin was loose and waxy, her teeth yellow, her hair thin and brittle, and she was hollow eyed.

'Shoe!' she said, coming around the table to embrace me. In the past, I would've been buried in her big, matronly bosom, but now there were hard angles and ribs there. Her clothes – dungarees, an engineer's apron with deep pockets filled with awls and quills and styluses and whatever other tools the engineers used in the pursuit of their craft poking me in the sternum, a fine cotton tunic tucked into pants – hung loosely on her frame. 'Don't look at me like that, Shoe,' she said with a hurt expression.

'Sam . . .'

She shook her head. 'Yes, I look atrocious.' She held up a long, calloused hand. She had always been a strong woman, of personality and physique, and her blunt, craftsman's hands and bright, supremely intelligent eyes were still the same. 'Spare me. I have no time for worry that I am ill. I am not. I am but sleepless and busy and no advice can change that.'

'Do you like chicken?' I asked.

She seemed taken aback by the question. 'I guess so.'

'I will fry some for you. You need to make the acquaintance of fried yardbird. It'll sort a multitude of problems for you.'

'Yardbird.' She narrowed her eyes. 'Like what problems?'

'You ain't eating enough, that's for sure, and once you eat a half-a-bird, you'll go right to sleep, which I imagine you'll sorely need.'

'Chicken,' she said, incredulous. A woman who, now that Beleth had turned traitor, was in charge of the munitions production of the western front of Occidentalia in the Hardscrabble Territories. But more than that, this was a woman who dealt with the raw, undirected forces of the infernal itself on a daily basis.

And I spoke to her of yardbirds.

'They'll stick in the yard as long as they know they'll be fed,' I said, moving my head in the pecking manner of a rooster or a hen at their feed.

Sam laughed. 'You can always surprise me, Shoestring,' she said.

'You're the one with the big surprises, Sam. Most of 'em doozies.'

'Come. Wacher?' Sam turned toward the secretary, a lovely blonde girl in her teens but, judging by the amount of doodads and writing utensils in her apron and the intelligent questions in her eyes, a good companion for Samantha. 'Will you please fetch us something to drink and eat?'

Wacher nodded and scuttled out and we settled down. She returned swiftly with cheeses and cured meats and smoked fish and sliced pleb loaves and a glass pitcher of wine as dark as coagulated blood and a matching pitcher of water as clear as air. Sam poured merely a finger of wine and watered it until it was pointless to drink. I poured wine, picked up the water pitcher, tapped it against my glass and replaced it. We drank.

'You're here for Fisk.' A simple statement.

'Yes, ma'am. He would be with a woman. Winfried. A fierce one, and grievous wounded at the loss of her husband and brother.'

'I've met her. They came here nigh on a month back and left a message for you with me.' She took a drink of her 'wine' and retrieved an envelope from her desk. It read on the front – SHOE. The wax seal of Fisk's legatus badge was unbroken.

Nones of Geminus, 2638 ex Ruma Immortalis

Shoe,
About time. We've taken lodging at a boarding house near the century garrison – you'll know it by the razorback hog on its sign and the word Ingenuus below. If we are not there, I have left instructions with the widow Balvenus, the lady of the house, to welcome you to and allow you to bunk down with me. You can stable your mount at the garrison, it is but a hop, step, and jump away from the House Ingenuus.

Heard word of Beleth, or someone who sounds suspiciously like him, sniffing east around Dvergar. Our mutual friend Andrae has sent word that his agents confirm that Beleth's interests have moved in that direction and, if you missed it after your recovery, much of the fifth and the third legions have mobilized and begun moving south where we are most vulnerable from attack by sea, since Mediera has blockaded the Gulf of Mageras.

Things move apace and I'm ready to have you back by my side, old friend.

Fiscelion

After reading, I thanked Sam, handed her the letter so that she might read it, and helped myself to the tray, making small sandwiches and washing them down with strong red wine.

'What is Beleth up to? Fisk brought you up to speed, did he not? Of all people in the Territories, you know Beleth best.'

She nodded and looked concerned. 'I am troubled by the marked *vaettir* you found on the plains. The body has gone bad, but I had an artist – Undreas Fesalian – make detailed drawings of the glyphs on the body.'

'Sapientia said Beleth had a thing for possession.'

'Indeed. He was not the strongest physical engineer, which is one of the reasons I was his assistant.' She smiled again, weary, and it barely touched her eyes. 'But he was ridiculously talented in the manipulation of *daemons*. Sometimes I wondered . . .'

She paused, thinking. The way her eyes slid off me, looked at some far fixed distance away, through wall and stone – it was the look of someone who pondered a troublesome question over and over, like a glass-smith polishing a creation until the surface was unblemished and clear.

'What?' I said.

'That he might have been—'

I caught the thread, tugged. 'A *daemon* himself? That is an interesting thought.'

'Not a *daemon*, but possibly infested with one. He spent years in Kithai studying. And when he returned, they say, he was different.'

She shook her head, dismissing the idea. 'No. It's preposterous. It would mean that all that time—'

Easy to dismiss such a heinous idea when it means the snake was in *your* trousers the whole time. It *was* an interesting idea, and something to be seriously considered.

In some ways, it was more terrifying to believe that Beleth might just be a human beast, a devil born of man.

She stood, went to the wall with the desk, opened one of the drawers there and removed a sheaf of parchment and returned to the table. She tossed them on the table in front of me. 'Take a gander, Shoe. I've made some notes.'

I riffled through the drawings, all of an elongated torso. Had it been of anything else, I'd have thought that the artist had the proportions off.

Over the heart, a curious glyph that seemed to have concentric circles of words burrowing down into a smaller size into illegibility. On another sheet, I found a larger detail of the circular writing. It had an old familiar phrase, one I'd heard before in Beleth's chambers when he bound the Crimson Man to Isabelle's hand. The writing said *in girum imus nocte et consumimur igni* in the old debased tongue of Latinum and looped around on itself a few times then went on to say more indecipherable things. But I did see two words I recognized.

Loci and *Belethus*.

A note beside it indicated it was a *genius loci* glyph. It read, 'B's use of the *genius loci* glyph – unusual. He's brought a Ruman idea to *SUBORN* the infernl into a foreign bdy. Inventive & fucking crazy as licking lead.'

I whistled. 'This is a world of shite. He trying to hop into a stretcher?'

'I am still grappling with the fact he managed to do it to the woman in Passasuego .' She slowly picked up her wine and took a sip. 'It's quite astounding.' She frowned, 'I have sent messages to Sapientia for information regarding the possessed woman—'

'Grantham? You have any idea if she ... made it?'

Samantha shook her head. 'I have no information on that score. It's a terrible thing to do to someone.'

'Beleth doesn't give a damn. He'd murder a family if it meant he'd belly up to a steak dinner.'

There was pain then in her eyes and I figured I knew the reason why. She hadn't seen the monster in her own company. Either she'd been blind to it or she hadn't *wanted* to see.

'I am coming to understand this,' she said. 'And at some point, I will have to deal with him.' The way she said that was ominous.

'Well, let's find the sonofabitch. Has Andrae contacted you?'

She looked puzzled. 'Andrae?'

I waved that off. 'Tamberlaine's spymaster in New Damnation. If you don't know him, he hasn't. Have *you* had any word of Beleth?'

'No, I haven't, other than from Fisk and now you. I communicate with the head of the College of Augurs and Engineers once a month, though it will be quite a while before I do so again.' She held up her arm, exposing a fresh gash on her wrist where she had let blood.

'You have any idea why Beleth hasn't fled the Territories? He's had ample opportunity.'

She pursed her lips. 'Possibly because of the stretchers. He needs to be here, maybe, to continue his research on the effects of warding and glyph on their physiology.'

I nodded, seeing it. But it wasn't enough. I said as much.

'He's pushed Rume to war with Mediera – as if we needed more pushing – with his slaughter of the Medieran Ambassador in Passasuego,' Samantha said slowly, sussing each word out as it was spoken, as if testing the validity of the idea behind the sounds.

'Go on.'

'That means he wants something from either the Rumans or Medierans, even if it's vengeance.'

'He wants vengeance, it'll be on Fisk and the Cornelians. He did not like being put off his feed and on the run. He said as much when we had our chat at the Pynchon.' I thought about it. 'But bigger things are moving. After my wound from the big stretcher, I took passage on the *Gemina* – a barge heading down the Big Rill – and one of Beleth's *daemon*-possessed party favours was on board. A Tempus Union Guard.'

Samantha grew still and her expression soured. 'That's not good.'

'No. But – I've not told anyone of this – a stretcher appeared. Looked like he'd just dug himself out of the ground, from a grave, and he had on a woman's dress. He called me "gynth" which means—'

'Kindred.' She nodded. 'I am not wholly ignorant of the *Dvergar* language, Shoe. Like you, I was born here in the Territories and here I remain.'

'Of course, Miss Samantha,' I said. I should've known. Like most folks who make it to adulthood here in Occidentalia, those that do miss very few tricks. Very few. 'And then the stretcher snatched up the guard leaping into the air and brought him crashing back down on the deck.' I held my hands open, as if wondering and offering it to her all at once. 'The damned thing saved me.'

'That *is* bizarre. I remember you saying once that the *vaettir* would trade with *dvergar*, a long time ago.'

'I have memories of *vaettir* – usually singly, but sometimes in pairs – coming to the outskirts of our village, carrying huge haunches of bloody meat. We would bring out knives, or old clothes or fabric, cheap baubles – and they would leave the meat and take what was given and bound off, like they do, without any mischief. But sometimes, they would kill or taunt or terrorize, as is their wont.' I scratched my chin. 'Though, thinking about it, I never saw those that traded with us commit any crimes against the *dvergar*.'

'I am thinking,' Samantha said, slowly, 'that there are more than one stripe of *vaettir* and that some have enough intelligence to deny whatever dark nature churns within them and to work toward a goal. But what are those goals?'

'Got me, Sam.' It's real easy to ignore that which you don't understand. And the actions of Gynth had me stumped. He'd saved me twice now. 'I think only time will tell. In the meantime, there's Beleth to consider. Is there any way to determine his location? You know . . .' I waved my hands about in the air and said, 'Dominus ominous and all that.'

Sam laughed. 'Dominus ominous? Uh, no, Shoe, summoning doesn't work like that.'

'You would know, I imagine.' I picked up my glass and drained it of wine. 'Truly, what do you think Beleth's doing?'

She thought for only a moment. Then she nodded. 'He won't like the discomfort of war and he's probably self-aware enough to realize that. He's working to end the conflict as fast as possible, with the most clout, power, and wealth for himself when it's all over.'

'That's right,' I said. 'But he can only do that if he remains a player here, in the Territories,' I said.

'Bingo,' Sam said.

'And that means eventually, he's got only two places he can set up shop. New Damnation. Or here.'

I thought about it. 'Won't be New Damnation.'

'Why not?' Sam asked.

'No places to bolt other than the river. You think Beleth is going to endure another midnight run like he did at Passasuego? No, the man will want a quick and easy escape, so times get desperate. He loves the integrity of his neck,' I said.

'Yes, you have the right of it, I think,' she said.

'And that means he'll be here in Harbour Town, or nearby. It's the seat of munitions industry in Occidentalia, there's the port, and it's got the Medieran stronghold of Chiba in the Gulf of Mageras and many people of Medieran descent in the population, sympathetic to their cause,' I said. 'He is *here.*'

'That seems like a good working hypothesis.'

'So,' I said, reaching for the pitcher of wine. 'How do I find him?'

'He'll need silver. Fisk and his companion, Winfried, have ridden east to investigate the rumours of a new silverlode near *Dvergar.* Beleth wants silver. Mediera wants silver. Even rumour of a new silverlode will draw him out of whatever hole he's hiding in.'

I shook my head. 'He'll be wary.'

'He's always wary. Fisk told me he investigated in the city, but could not find hide nor hair of Beleth.'

I sucked my teeth. 'Fisk is my bosom friend, Sam, but there's one thing he ain't – a snoop. Being an effective snoop requires an abject quality that highborn folk – even of Fisk's stripe – don't possess.'

Sam laughed again. 'Shoe, now I remember how much I enjoy your company.'

'I do what I can, ma'am.'

'So, he'll want for silver, that's a given. People in our profession go through quite a bit of it and if he doesn't have large amounts of cash—'

'He'll have to take it in other ways.'

'Yes. And he'll want for charcoal too, and a bellows, a small one, to melt the silver for whatever wardwork he's doing.'

I frowned. 'That's too general and impossible to track.'

She raised a hand. 'But Beleth trained in Tchinee, remember? And he picked up habits there.'

'Please tell me that you've got something for me.'

She smiled. 'In Kithai, all "fire gardening" is done with a very special salt – one that goes through a process of purification and bleaching and is mixed with the silver during smelting.'

'And he's kept up this practice even after leaving Kithai?'

'He did while I was his assistant.'

A boon, then. A piece of luck. 'And there'd be merchants selling this kind of salt here?'

She shrugged. 'I have no clue. It is the first I have thought of it. There's a small Tchinee neighbourhood near the wharfs. You could look there.'

I stood. 'Thank you, Sam, you've been a huge help.'

'Don't try to confront him without Fisk or me. He's far too dangerous.'

'I can handle myself, Sam. Remember Agrippina?'

'You can handle yourself, yes,' she said. 'But it's debatable if you can handle Beleth.' She rose, came around the table, and embraced me. 'Good hunting. Send word to me when you find him. I still have the *daemon* hand and . . .' A frosty glint came to her eyes. 'I for one *know* how to handle him.'

TWENTY-FIVE

14 Kalends of Sextilius, 2638 ex Ruma Immortalis

G OODS CAME TO HARBOUR TOWN one of three ways – from
the sea, on vessels full of crates and barrels tended by dusky
men and women from far shores, all kissed by sun and weathered
by rain and wind; on paddleboats down the Big Rill, hauled by
Brawley-speaking stevedores and riverfolk, thick-chested and randy
and whiskey-bound, all willing to fight and fuck, in that order;
and finally by wagons driven by sodbusters and merchant men and
women who braved the west, the stretchers, and other hard men
and *dvergar* and indigenous life itself to put down roots into the
recalcitrant soil of the Territories when they weren't rolling about
on wagon wheels. The mechanized baggage trains never made it
down far enough to bring in goods by rail, unlike Fort Brust and
Dvergar.

Yet the curious thing about seamen and women, more than those
other tradesfolk, they put down their roots like weeds seeking water
in hardscrabble – every place they find port, a village springs up
with the character and culture of the founder. In Harbour Town,
there was a Tchinee quarter, a Little Mediera, a Higalle district.
You could find dislocated Northmen in almost any tavern, Galls
and Hellenes in every shop, Tuetons, Numidians, Ægyptians, and
Bedoun in the markets and squares – some hawking goods, some
acquiring them, some gathering intelligence for far-off govern-
ments, some in transport of taxable goods, some smuggling wares.

It was uncouth, hilarious, aggressive. Restless.

One helluva town.

The salt Sam told me about had a peculiar name, yófuyán – I had her write the word down on a handy scrap of parchment – and was known by the bluish tint of it. The blue – one of the most pristine of colours to the Tchinee, or so Sam told me – could be faked by a minuscule amount of dye added to a rolling drum of regular salt, or, for the real stuff, primatura, it came from the salt itself, carved in blocks from some secret deep cave wall deep inside a unknown mountain in Far Kithai. The blue salt of yófuyán was accreted in the making of the world, and ran like a sanguiduct down from the Tchinee cave where it was found into the heart of our earth.

So I toddled off to the widow Balvenus' boarding house, made my introductions and dropped off my kit, strapped on my silver longknife and cinched up my gunbelt, and stabled Bess at the garrison, two streets down the way. The whole neighbourhood reeked of horse sweat and manure which, truth be told, are not bad smells. Not wholly.

I walked seaward, toward the Tchineetown. The closer to the shore, the louder the seagulls' calls sounded in the steamy morning air, the fresher the wind. The clanging bell of a *daemon*-fired steamer as it lowered its swing-stages and came to pier. Cursing in Hellene, and Gallish. The smell of garlic and stewing meat coming from an open door. The bright carmine splashes of sacrificial blood and flowers on the crossroad stones outside a neighbourhood collegium, a brace of bully-boys, arms crossed, glowering at me as I passed. Feral dogs sniffing along alleyways, chased by hungry mongrel children, knives bright in their grubby hands.

I came to Tchineetown from the North, along the Via Maceda, and was welcomed by the ornately painted wooden dragon sign marking the entrance to the little community within a town, its lacquered face festooned with the bright Tchinee ideograms that pass for writing in their neck of the woods. Stopping in a small teashop filled with wizened Tchinee patrons, each one staring at me warily if not with some real animosity, I approached the shopkeep.

'What do you want?' the withered old man asked, cocking a jaundiced eye at me. He wore a long embroidered tunic with half-collar and we stood about the same height. As half-*dvergar*, I'm often greeted with some immediate dislike solely on account of my blood and stature, but with this old man, I sensed he disliked all of mankind equally and did not discriminate in his hatred. And that made it fine by me.

I withdrew the parchment and read the strange word. 'Yófuyán? Blue salt?'

'No,' he said. 'This is a tea shop. Green tea,' he said, slapping the surface of his counter. 'What do you want? Big or little?'

'Trying to find where I can buy this here blue salt. You know where?' I said.

He looked at his patrons, who were watching us parlay. He said something in the clanging, bizarre language of Tchinee and waved his hand viciously at those seated in the shop, sipping tea from small white cups. Eyes were hastily averted.

He leaned in close. 'What do you want? Big or little?'

'Big.'

'Five sesties, gold.'

'Five?'

He wagged his finger. 'Good green tea. If you don't want, there's the door.'

'Three.'

'Pfui!' He made brushing motions with his fingertip.

I coughed up the money and he chuckled. 'Look for Mistress Jade. She keeps a shop round yonder corner with a painted sign.' He held up his hand. 'Open hand. One emerald in palm.'

'A sign has an open hand with one emerald in the palm. Got it.'

He made the brushing movement again. 'Make tracks, mister.'

'Nothing doing. Where's my tea?'

I made my way to Tchineetown. Sandwiched between the warehouse district and Little Mediera, the Tchinee neighbourhood possessed a copious amount of wagon traffic clattering down its narrow streets. Stone and wood buildings, built in the Ruman style – three stories tall and blocky, with no windows on the ground floor and spacious atriums inside – were placed close together in an airless mash. In Harbour Town, there were few squares and fewer parks. The town had grown by necessity, not intention, and the result was a congested snarl of streets and neighbourhoods – businesses stood alongside merchantmen's houses, schools were placed alongside factories or counting-houses.

In Tchineetown itself, most of the storefronts had obscure signage I could not read, though some had Ruman numerals on them – more than likely for taxation purposes, because if there's one thing I know about Rume it's that no barrier of language has ever stopped it from collecting taxes – but most of them I could figure out by just looking. A butcher (cleaver), a baker (a rolling pin), a haberdasher (glove), a hat-maker (conical hat), a farrier (hammer: easy one, right next to the stables), a wheel-wright (a wheel), a barber or doctor (the sign displayed an intricately painted nude man with his heart displayed and focus points and strange current-like lines all about his person), a brothel (rooster crowing on a field of red – but it was the whores sitting in windows on the second floor and the strong scent of cheap perfume that clued me into the sign's meaning), and many more.

Yet, of all these, Mistress Jade's sign was the hardest to find and then discern. It was small, and half-hidden behind a flurry of signage for some services I couldn't understand except for a seamstress – the needle and thread being nearly a universal emblem for that task. Mistress Jade's was half the size of these other signs, all wooden, but hers was enamelled in some way, making it slick and bright in the morning light, as if it was wet. The sign bore a painted woman's hand with long clawlike nails and in its palm was a large green gemstone.

I rapped at the door, it swung open swiftly and I was met by the sight of a large man who'd had his nose broken at least once a day for many years. His face had the knotted, lumpy look of sculpture created by an artist with little talent. He was large, but not overly so. He was fat, but still muscular. A man of appetite matched by exertion.

'What duya want?' he asked in a low grating voice. He looked me up and down and sneered.

'Mistress Jade,' I said. I didn't intend on taxing him with the detail of my visit and I don't think he would've understood anyway.

'She ain't here,' he said. 'Make tracks, dwarf.'

I pulled the piece of parchment. 'I've got a task,' I said. At the man's dumb look, I said, 'A task, man. *Work*.'

He nodded and snatched the parchment from my mitt. His brow furrowed as if he were extruding shite rather than discerning script. Obviously, the man was illiterate, at least in the writ of Latinum.

'Blue salt. Yófuyán.'

The bruiser nodded and disappeared into the shadowy interior of the building, shutting and bolting the door when he left. I waited on the street as morning passers-by gave me curious glances, some smiling, some with menacing stares. The sun rose above the roof and coloured the street in bright light. The air became hazy.

The door rattled and I heard the bolt being thrown. The lumpy-faced Tchinee man opened the door and said, 'She'll see you now,' and gestured for me to enter. I did, swiftly.

It was dark inside, and cluttered. The shop's interior was filled with fragrant pots and urns, cups and vases and ornate boxes and chests. My eyes teared, the smell was so strong – sweet and acrid and sour and smoky and shitty all at once. There was very little light and what there was came from a high, near-ceiling grated window lining one wall, and a lantern on the other.

Lumpy led me through the warren of spice crates and casks of oils to a simple wooden door. He knocked, once, and threw it open. Inside was a sun-drenched little atrium, teeming with flora, ferns and oily leaved plants I'd never seen before, with great white blossoms with yellow centres. A fountain tinkled merrily and it was cool here. At a small table sat a woman, dressed in silk, her hair in a bun. She looked young – no more than twenty-five – and very pretty. On her left hand she wore sharp, silver claws. She beckoned and I approached.

'Ah, a visitor!' she said. The accent was there, but very faint. 'I am Mistress Jade. And you are?'

'Dveng Ilys, ma'am, man of the fifth legion.'

'Mulo tells me you want yófuyán. Why would you want yófuyán? I do not know you, but I know you are not a man of fire.'

That was an interesting thing to call an engineer. But appropriate.

'No, ma'am. I'm not. I don't actually want any blue salt, but I would like to know if anyone else, any Rumans, have bought some from you recently.'

Her eyes narrowed and I revised my estimate on her age. She was very well-preserved but was more likely in her thirties than twenties.

'I have had no Ruman customers recently. Only old ladies of Jiang wanting to put some iron back in their old husbands' spines—' She winked. It was glib, too glib, really, for such a short exchange.

'You've had no one come inquiring about it?'

She shook her head and clicked her silver claws like a Medieran dancer clacking together castanets. They made a bright ringing sound above the tinkling of the fountain.

'No, I am sorry,' she said. 'Mulo? See our friend out.'

Mulo came and stood beside me.

I didn't intend to press my luck. I allowed Mulo – indeed there wasn't much I could do to stop him if you didn't count using Hellfire – to lead me out.

Once on the street, I made my way around the block and found the alley that ran behind the block of buildings that Mistress Jade's shop was in. Yes, *dvergar* are short, but our hands are knotted and strong and climbing stone comes almost second nature to us. One of the buildings in the alley was built of rough-hewn granite, and it was an easy matter to climb up and settle myself on a ledge with a full view of the alley.

I didn't have long to wait. After an hour, Mulo came into the alley, ducking his head through a small door and, despite the day's sun and heat, drew a cowl over his face and tromped off, away from where I sat on the high ledge. I scrambled down and followed him.

He led me a merry chase through Tchineetown – though he didn't know I was following him, I'm sure. We passed through wharfside, through warehouses and supply dumps for the fifth, past the shipyards and into a workman's neighbourhood full of shanties and shacks and then into a rather well-to-do area where the houses turned to villas with walled gardens and guards. Mulo approached one, spoke with the guard there, and then handed him something – I must assume a note – and he turned and tromped back the way he came. I was, luckily, wary enough to have ensconced myself in a privet hedge near a villa wall before Mulo passed, but I could smell the man as he walked by.

When he was gone, I marked the house – 12 Via Dolorosa – and found a good vantage where I could watch the comings and goings easily without being spotted. Again, my *dvergar* heritage lends me abilities others have not. I ducked behind a row of bushes and dug myself into the mulch there. There wasn't too much horse manure.

I watched the house. The sun grew high in the sky and then passed beyond the other villas, casting the street in shadow and finally went down. There was a breeze from the ocean, salty, and the cries of seagulls still filled the air and the clang of barges moving down the Big Rill to dock wharfside could be heard. The sound of hammers and sawing. The clopping and passage of horses and occasionally a wagon would pass with men and women chatting. No one left 12 Via Dolorosa.

My stomach was rumbling violently and night had fallen when the figure left the villa I watched. I started with surprise as a small donkey came from the courtyard with a cloaked rider on its back. Maybe it was the sensation of looking into a mirror and seeing myself reflected there. The rider was *dvergar*. Male, judging from the width of his shoulders, the square blockiness of his build.

I followed him out, down Via Dolorosa to the east, across the Pons Milletus, over the Big Rill and past the shanties and barges, dredges, scows cobbled together on the pilings below in a make-shift floating village that most folk in Harbour Town just called the Tethering, or some, Bargetown. The *dvergar* rider took his time, walking the donkey – indeed, most donkeys did not enjoy the spur and let you know it, as if the great umbrage of having a rider was enough. Urgency was crossing some asinine line.

The Pons Milletus is a wide stone bridge, standing quite high over the river, to allow for riverboats and sea vessels to pass underneath, coming in from the bay upstream. With the advent of *daemon-fired* ships, less draw is needed to let ships pass there, and so the drawbridge and towers near the middle of the pons had fallen in to some disrepair. Though occasionally a ship with a mast or tall stacks required the bridge to be raised.

Beyond the Pons Milletus, you enter the market and main resid-ential areas of Harbour Town. There's natural rise there, where the ocean, possibly in the dim mists of history, was higher, washing away the shore and leaving a small cliff upon which the wealthy could build their homes. The most desirable domiciles in all of Harbour Town were there, in a tidy clot of red-roofed villas and luxurious shops and sylvan parks so that they might enjoy the breeze from the Bay of Mageras and view the sun's light shattering into millions of shards on the sea without the smell of shite or goat stew steaming with spices or *daemon*-fired stacks to bother them. Below them, much like in Passaseugo, the more plebeian classes lived, wooden tenements standing steaming, lantern light pouring oily smoke into the air and casting pale yellow onto the cobblestones.

A fleeting, niggling awareness. A motion at the edge of my vision. Like a bird, even, flapping above.

I turned to look, into the night, upward. There was not enough star or moonlight to lighten things. But something paced me, on the rooftops. Something fast. Something ruffling with speed.

I did not have to strain too hard to think what it might be. I touched a palm to Hellfire sitting at my waist.

It could be an errant stretcher (which was very doubtful, since Harbour Town had been settled for a long, long time) or, all the gods and numen forgive, one that Beleth had suborned into his service by some infernal means.

I pulled my guns, looking into the sky. The skyline. The roofs.

There was noise and a dog barking into an alley. Beyond that, stillness. Nothing.

I watched, and waited, half-hunched over in the middle of a Harbour Town street, peering into the night for something that wasn't there. After a long while, I holstered my guns, and trotted to catch up with the rider I tailed.

But it was full night now and the streets were dark. We did not go to the Bluffs, where the rich lived. We did not go toward the bay, where more piers and wharves stood against the tide, and fishing boats moored, knocking hollowly in the surge. *Daemonlights* were unshuttered at intersections, tended by the crossroad college bully-boys as part of their sacred duty to Ia. The *dvergar* rider kept his head down and continued on, never looking back. And I followed.

Past the soft hills of the Higalle, where the homes and architecture took on an easier look, more wood and plaster, less Rumanesque stone. The streets were lined in trees, no gambles here, since the Whites were far to the west. Here stood live oaks dripping with moss and catching the *daemonlight* in ghostly grey-green streamers. Beyond that through Brawleyville and its warrens, where the lower-bloods of the Galls, the stevedores and labourers and craftsmen made their home.

And then the streets turned to dirt and gravel and the lights fell away and it was dark, with only hearthfires and small lanterns in homes casting light. I was panting from the exertions of the day. The *dvergar* rider's donkey was slow but steady and I had spent a day beneath a bush, without food, chasing someone who quite possibly had nothing to do with Beleth. I don't know what drew me onward. We had entered the outskirts of Harbour Town, where tenements and shacks gave way to farms, and little clusters of daub-and-wattle huts like most homesteaders and sodbusters lived in here in the Territories. In Harbour Town, they called it Tinkers Heath, sometimes, if they called it anything at all. It was a scattered *dvergar* settlement, since *dvergar* don't like to cluster together too close in cities. Their houses are too easy to raid and burn, and a dispersion of the populace makes most menaces troublesome for the interlopers.

The rider turned down a lane, braced by small farmsteads, to a cluster of small outbuildings. One was brightly lit, with a sprig of holly on the door.

From the interior, I heard many voices, most of them male and deep, and all speaking in *Dvergar*, my mother's tongue. There was the scent of wood-smoke on the air, even in the warmth of summer, and a faint hint of roasting meat.

I stopped in a yellow pool of light from a kreosote lantern. A figure appeared silhouetted in the doorway. A *dvergar* woman, who gestured hurriedly for me to enter, calling softly in my mother's tongue.

'Come, now. Come. It's about to begin.'

I entered the low-slung building. It was a cottage, really, mud-brick with a low ceiling and a great pot with some sort of stew being stirred by a young *dvergar* girl over the woodfire, her ruddy face beading with sweat. The room was one of those countless sodbuster meeting rooms – half bar, half communal hall – with long, rough-hewn tables with matching benches, lanterns, and a counter serving as a bar at the far end of the room. The tables were filled with twenty or thirty *dvergar* men and women, all sombre, all serious, yet a certain electric expectation filled the room. An excitement. I could see it writ large in their faces, bright eyes, alert gazes. Many made note of me, and looked me up and down brazenly, whispering to their companions. I bore the only human – or in *Dvergar, svietch*, meaning 'short-lived' – blood in the building. All the rest were native to Occidentalia.

A man broached a small cask of beer, began passing out pewter cups full of the brown, rich ale. I found one in my hand and the woman who had beckoned me in took my elbow and said, in dvergar, 'Come brother, sit. It will begin shortly.'

I scanned the crowd for the rider, curious if he'd marked me. Many people stared, some with open curiosity, some maybe harbouring suspicion or fear, I could not tell. I made my way to a table near the back, away from the fire, with room to sit. I drank quietly and listened to the talk.

'They'll call for us to take arms, now,' an older woman sitting at the table said. She had a craggy, unforgiving face that had seen two centuries of hardship, at least. She knew the land before the Rumans and Medierans came. 'And I'll take up the blade, my brothers and sisters,' she said nodding.

'Praverta, we have no idea why we've been called tonight,' a younger man said. He had a wide beard and a rather thin narrow face for a dwarf. 'I think you're wishing for blood rather than wanting to preserve it.'

'Ruman blood I'll take,' she said, holding out one grizzled hand palm down over the table and lowering it in a strange slow-motion movement, as if she was slamming her hand down. But with such deliberation it had a terrible finality to it. 'If Neruda would but call to action.'

'There's more to motion than just motion,' the man said. 'It must have direction.'

'Don't quote Viquesco to me, pup,' Praverta said, narrowing her eyes. They were shrouded in heavy brows and wrinkled lids. 'He might be here to spread Neruda's good words but his are always "wait, watch, and be ready".' She sniffed with disdain. 'I remember Wickerware. I remember Tapestry. It always ends in blood. Either ours, or theirs. This time, I would it be theirs.'

A moment then of awkward silence. I thought of when a man named Bert reminisced so loudly about his rapine of Tapestry and its women. I thought about the *thwock* of the lead ball impacting his cheek, his jaw. How blood poured from his lips and teeth flew.

I thought about my wife Illina, whom I spent almost a human lifetime with.

Praverta, obviously the fiercest at my table, looked at me and said, 'So what brings you to us, *dimidius*?' A *dimidius* is, according to the Rumans, a thing of halves. Like me. It was a double insult, truly. The name, and using the speech of Latinum, rather than *Dvergar*, which I had been obviously following.

You can live your whole life on the outside and when you find yourself among those who should be your own, you'll still be on the outside looking in.

I said in *dvergar,* 'Matve Praverta, I come as a leaf blown on the wind.' An old phrase, and an innocuous one.

'I don't like the look of this one,' she said to the others, her lips puckering into a wrinkled, sucking hole. 'He's got the look of informer about him.'

'Too much *svietch* blood,' the younger man said.

'There's more of Rume about him than *gynth*,' another woman chimed in.

This was getting out of hand.

'I have spoken with Neruda,' I said, the *dvergar* words coming easily. And the lie. But I tempered it with truth. I can be eloquent when I want. 'I have seen him. He too is ...' I twisted my face around the word. '*Dimidius*. But you would hang on his every word and follow him yet not trust me? Your mettle is soft and your wine watered.'

Praverta pursed her lips and sniffed. She didn't like me tossing Neruda's parentage in her teeth. 'You will be watched, half-man,' she said, simply, and then fell silent, except for the slurping of her beer.

We waited. A man brought around clay bowls of soup and I gave him a copper sestersius for the effort and he smiled, while the rest of my table-mates looked furious. Eventually, the woman who had greeted me at the door called for silence and said, 'My brothers and sisters of the mountains – my *vaettir!* – we have come together to hear the words of wise Neruda.'

There was a murmur but it died down after a moment and she went on. 'But there is news now, and one of our *vaettir* is here to convey the words of Neruda. I shall let him speak.'

I hadn't taken much notice of the door behind the counter where the ale had been served. From it came a burly *dvergar* with a neatly groomed facial hair – waxed moustache and tapering blond beard – and blaring white teeth and blue eyes. We're a dark race, normally, if fair skinned, and he was one of the *vanmer* – a product of two *dvergar* with blue-eyed, blond-headed blood far back in the roots of their family veins. It was a mark of purity, the *vanmer* claimed, and favour of the gods. Usually, though, they were just pretty boys and women pursued by countless suitors. Give me a dusky lass, like my Illina, and I'll be happy.

He came and stood in front of the assembled there, raising his hands to quiet the growing murmur.

'Hail, kindred,' he said. He used the word *gynth*. 'I come with news from the father of *vaettir*,' he said, not naming Neruda outright. 'There have been some efforts by the Rumans to take our father captive, to silence his voice, to still his busy hands. In Passaseugo, they raided his workshop. In Wickerware, they stormed our father's house in hopes of finding him in bed, but he was gone.'

The murmur of the crowd rose and fell with his words. The anticipation thrumming through those gathered was near palpable. Yet they kept their agitation under control. It was the quietest outrage I've ever felt.

Praverta said, loudly, 'So, what are we to do? Are we to just go back to our labours?'

The *vanmer* man shook his head. 'No. I bear a message for you all from Neruda himself. He says, "Every stone waits for the chisel to bring out its inner being in sculpture. Every piece of wood holds a tool within it, dormant, waiting to be carved and brought into the world. Every pig of iron or steel contains within it the blade, unforged. So too does time contain the moment we have waited for. That moment must present itself, make itself manifest. You will know it when it arrives".' As he spoke, many in the crowd grumbled and stirred. Praverta, her rheumy old eyes bright, cursed under her breath. "Continue with your labours. Forge weapons, store food. When the time comes, you will know it by its imperative. Each of you will know it because it will be mirrored inside of you".'

The *vanmer* fell silent and bowed his head in a bit of theatrics I found distasteful. 'And then what?' A man called from a nearby table. 'We'll "know" this moment. This I can accept. And then what?'

'Do what you need to do, my brethren, to survive and no more. Listen to me! Of this Neruda has been perfectly clear. *Vaettir* are for independence in Occidentalia! Not for revenge. When the moment is ripe, you will know when to move. To come east to the Eldvatch. The *vaettir* will find you there.'

'Why not go now?' A woman bellowed, outrage filling her voice. 'I've served these masters all my life! I would go to be with my kin!'

'Aye!' another man called. There was a chorus of agreement. 'We could make our stand against the Rumans! We could take to our hills and warrens! Take to the Eldvatch where they'd never find us!'

The blond man shook his head. 'Store food. Forge weapons. Soon Rume will have more than a passel of *dvergar* with swords and arrows to contend with. War is declared. If you, our people, begin abandoning cities – their masters, their owners – in droves, Rume will send legions before we are ready!'

'They sent a century! And we defeated them!' the florid man called in response, his voice hoarse. 'We will defeat any they send!'

'You did not witness the battle, my friend,' the blond man said softly, a pained look on his face. 'We lost far more than we gained. Neruda . . .' He paused, the words failing on his tongue. 'He is a great man, a leader, a thinker. He is no general, though, and our people were slaughtered. We lost four *dvergar* for every Ruman legionnaire that fell. We have no Hellfire.' He shook his head and made a chopping with his hand. 'No. We cannot match them, might to might. We must be clever. We must be wily.' He paused. 'We must be . . . *vaettir*.'

The room fell silent, thinking on this. The silence drew out.

Finally the man said, 'When the Medierans move, all people will know. You will know. Bring your weapons and food – especially your food – east. When there's war, farms and fields and granaries will burn. Rumans, Medierans, and *Dvergar* will starve alike. Yet we are prepared. Are we not?'

There was a murmur of assent, though half-hearted. In the general demeanour of all those assembled, there was a scarlet streak, a lust for blood, as if they wished this messenger would have told them to take up their knives and swords and cleavers and rush into the streets of Harbour Town and begin cutting down the first Ruman citizens and soldiers they saw. It was madness. They could not withstand the might of Rume, or the fierceness of its legionnaires and lascars and vigiles. They could not withstand Ruman Hellfire.

Yes, this *vanmer*, and Neruda himself, had the right of it. Wait, watch, and when the bottom drops from the bucket, take food and weapons and flee eastward, back to home.

Neruda's messenger moved among the people, then, his oration over, and said kind words to people who grasped his hands. Soft words with platitude and no news of Neruda's location. Eventually the crowd began to filter into the yard, and then slowly back down lanes and cobbles to Harbour Town. I marked the cloaked rider by the braying of his donkey and easily tailed him back to the domicile on Via Dolorosa.

After watching the man enter the building, I considered my aching feet and the soft bed at widow Malvenus' house and turned to go. It was then that two shadows dropped from the roof and something smacked the back of my head. I pitched forward, reeling, my arms out, falling to the flagstones of Dolorosa Way. I barked my chin on the ground, hard enough that even with my bristly cushion of a beard, I felt my jaw giving way. But old habits are bred in the bone – and *dvergar* skulls are thick – and I executed a clumsy forward roll and felt something in my side, where the shoal stretchers bowled me over, give. I howled some then.

Black-eyed, grinning men came within my sight, flexing their hands. *Daemon*-gripped.

The larger of the two, a massive Brawley, drew back his meaty paw of a hand and brought it across my face, wiping my consciousness from me.

TWENTY-SIX

13 Kalends of Sextilius, 2638 ex Ruma Immortalis

ROCKING. SWAYING. IN A CARRIAGE. The clop of a horse's hooves on flagstone, then dirt, then flagstone, rhythmic. A woman's cooing. The sound of crying, incessant. I was on the floor, the smell of dirt and horseshit filling my nose. Gunnysack over my head.

'Cease that child's infernal squalling, woman, or I can replace you easily.'

Beleth's voice.

'Master, the child wants its mother.'

'Give it your teat,' Beleth said.

'Yes, master.'

I stirred, trying to determine the extent of my injuries, my situation. I was bound. Trussed like a hog for the slaughter.

Something pressed on the gunnysack, mashing down hard on my nose and mouth.

My awareness, like a fading circle, diminished.

And I was gone.

'He is bound, yes?' Beleth said as I came awake.

There were hisses and grunts and I felt the cutting pressure on my wrists increasing to a point where I thought I might cry out. But I would not cry out.

A *daemonlight* lantern was unbanked and I became aware of my surroundings. My head throbbed something fierce where the big bastard had struck me. I was in a large space, with rough wooden floorboards. The gurgle and surge of waves on pilings, and the smell of salt and dead fish. A pier maybe, or a seaside warehouse. There were glass windows high above, where I could see the dark blue of the night sky filtering in. The cloud cover had passed and now the sky was strewn with stars and stained with the milk of moonlight.

Two black-eyed men watched me, grins like pools of oil on their faces. One had drool seeping from the corners of his mouth and his hands were brown with dried blood. None of it was mine. Yet.

And then Beleth stepped forward, into the light, wearing a nicely cut, brown tweed suit. He'd grown a beard and shaved his head – a small concession to being a fugitive – but the avaricious, hungry eyes remained the same.

'Mister Ilys! How wonderful to see you again,' Beleth said, cheerful. He walked away, taking the light, and picked up a small wooden crate with one hand, brought it back and flipped it over and sat down on it. 'Would you like a smoke?'

I nodded. Tracers swam in my vision and my face felt like auroch liver. My chest hitched, too, where the stretcher I killed had cracked my ribs.

Beleth pulled a pack of Medieran machine-rolled smokes from his pocket, popped one out of the pack and took it into his mouth. He thumbed a match, drew heavily on the cigarette, and then, leaning toward where I sat, tied against what felt like a wooden column, reversed the cigarette and placed it in my lips.

I said around the cigarette, 'Why don't you get your puppets to do the job for you?'

He smiled, broadly. 'Ah, my little soldiers,' he said, crossing his legs and placing his hands on his knee, lightly. There was something about the way he said 'little.' 'They are good at rough jobs. Sniffing out blood. Killing.' The two *daemon*-gripped men watched me closely. One of them, the fellow who looked as if he were a riverboat man, panted like a large dog.

'Little?'

'The smaller the *daemon*, the easier to control,' he said. He tapped his temple with a forefinger. 'But they've got less going on up here, Shoestring.' He paused. 'May I call you Shoestring?'

'Why don't you take these ropes off me and you can call me whatever you want.'

He smiled. 'Mister Ilys it is, then.' He did a prissy little thing then with his lips, as if he was amused but was thinking about how to go about expressing it. 'I trust you've been well since last we met?'

'You've led us on a merry chase, that's for sure. How was your departure from Passaseugo? Comfortable?' I said.

His face darkened. 'Ah, you mock my love of creature comforts.' He grinned again. 'Creature comforts!' he exclaimed, nearly merry. 'That phrase takes on a whole new meaning now.'

I drew on the cigarette, blew out smoke. One of his *daemon*-gripped men was working his jaw as if he had a piece of gristle in there or he'd taken too much cocoa leaf tea. Damnation, I hope I never encounter a *daemon* that's got a jones for the cocoa leaf.

'Don't rightly get you. But who ever did?' I said.

'Indeed, Mister Ilys. Indeed.' He picked an imaginary fleck of lint from his pants and then smoothed them. From above came a rattling sound and dust filtered into the circle of light thrown by the *daemon* lantern. Beleth looked up. 'Hmm. Probably a rat or some miscreant feline stalking the same. However, we do not take chances. You,' he said and then followed it with a word in Tchinee I didn't understand but which sounded harsh and ugly. 'Go, find whatever made the noise, kill it, and dispose of the body in the river. Indicate with a single word if you understand your orders.'

The drooling man turned to Beleth and worked his mouth as if it had turned traitor. 'Yeeersssssshhh.'

The man stood and, with a great haste, trotted off into the shadows of the warehouse.

'You see?' He sniffed. 'Dullards, these lesser *daemons*. But good hunters.'

'Yes, good hunters.'

He smiled. 'As you are yourself, so it seems. Twice you've bested my little leave-behinds, which, quite frankly, astounds me. You do not look so fierce.'

'I had some help,' I said, not feeling the levity I was trying to project into my voice. 'What did you mean by creature comforts, since we're all cozy?' I shifted my weight, trying to get where blood could get back in my hands. Judging by the lack of hard spots on my body – I was shirtless, too – they'd stripped me of all my pointy things and blades.

'Ah, questions, questions. You have some. I have many.' He shifted in his seat. 'I do not have time for the Lingchi, Mister Ilys, nor the inclination. So I offer you this: I will answer your questions as long as you answer mine. If I feel that you're being dishonest, I'll simply cut off a part of you.' He waved his hand. 'The answers to your questions, the carrot. The slicing? The stick.'

He stood, took off his suit jacket and draped it over the crate he'd been sitting on. He rolled up his shirt-sleeves and walked out of view, returning quickly with a leather portfolio that had an ominous heft, judging by the way he held it. He set it down on his jacket, unbuckled the leather clasp, and withdrew a shining silver knife. He removed a whetstone, spat on it, and began honing the blade with a supremely practiced hand.

'In the spirit of goodwill,' Beleth said, placing the silver knife and whetstone down. 'I will answer your question before I begin with mine.' He barked another phrase in the language of Kithai and clapped his hands. I heard, from behind me, something move. Something large. Something heavy. I could feel the vibrations in the wood. 'My creature comforts have taken a rather specific turn,

Mister Ilys,' he said, smiling, holding the knife. 'I've been told I'm quite literal.'

The thing came into view. Half shrouded in shadow, at first I thought it was simply a large man, until it squatted down on its hams to leer at me. It was a big bull stretcher, nude, dick hanging down, its torso covered in runnels of blood from the intaglios of glyphs there, big clawed hands open at its sides.

And its face.

There was a terrible animation to it. Its eyes were fiercely black, like shiny obsidian; its lips bloodless except for the blood spattered on skin. Its smile, otherworldly. I had seen a smile like that once before, on Agrippina's face. Yet, while hers was infused with a terrible malice and glee, this one was of hunger and greed. As I looked at the creature – the scent of dirt and waste and blood pouring off its incorruptible flesh – it curled back its lips to show me teeth.

A *daemon*-gripped *vaettir*. All the old gods and new, help me.

'I see you understand what I have achieved here.'

'I see that set of teeth on you sure ruined the perfect arsehole,' I managed to get out. 'I see what you are.'

He frowned and looked serious. 'No, Mister Ilys, I do not think you do. And it will matter very little in a short while,' he said. He came and stood near me, took my ear between index and thumb and pulled it away from my skull. 'Where is the *daemon* hand, Mister Ilys?'

It took me a moment to recognize what he was talking about. I said, 'Isabelle's hand?'

'The very one. The one with Belial stuffed inside it.'

'Samantha has it. She keeps it locked away, she said,' I answered as truthfully as I could. I am not a vain man, but a hat will sit funny on your head if you've only got one ear to prop it up there.

Beleth did not respond. The *daemon*-gripped *vaettir* panted and leered. His clawed hands flexed, as if he dreamed of shredding flesh, my flesh. The other *daemon*-gripped man edged away from the stretcher. Seems *daemons* have some sense, after all.

'Where is she located?'

'What, you don't know where Sam is? That doesn't seem like something you'd let slip your—'

He tugged on my ear. I felt cold steel at the point where pliable flesh met my cranium. 'Remember, Mister Ilys. I want to know if *you* know.'

'Thirty-two Victrix Way. Huge warehouse, warded to the nines. Guarded by engineer goons toting Hellfire. You're gonna need more than even this big bastard to get to her, sorry to say.'

'Why are you here?'

'You nabbed me and brought me to this dump.'

There was a burning sensation and pain and suddenly Beleth held something in front of my swimming eyes.

'A sliver of you, my little friend.' It was the top part of my ear, a little half-moon of it. 'But, since you're such a stickler for precise thoughts, let me rephrase. Why are you in Harbour Town?'

No need to pause on this one. And the ear, what was left of it, I wanted to keep. 'Hunting you.'

Beleth chuckled. 'On your own recognizance?'

''Course not,' I said. 'Cornelius wants you.' More than likely my life would be forfeit if I told him Tamberlaine's interest in the matter. If Beleth was in bed with the Medierans, that information wouldn't be sensitive, but it would be a bloody nose to the face of Rume and the Medierans would no doubt bandy it about. They probably would anyway, but at least my name wouldn't be attached to the information. 'The governor took you burning down his boat kinda hard.'

Beleth's face grew stern. Like Samantha, he'd lost some weight in the last months. Neither looked better for it. He had an angry tautness to him when he ceased forcing himself to be jovial.

'From what my sources tell me, you were with Cornelius until recently. That is so?'

'Yes,' I said.

'You're bosom friends with his mongrel son-in-law, the one that bedded Livia?'

'He ain't a mongrel,' I said.

'Surely they kept you nearby for their counsels?'

I said nothing. He jabbed with the knife, and it sunk into my cheek. There's the surprise of having a knife sticking in your face and then there's the pain of it. Hard to tell which is worse. I would die here, I knew. But I am old and that knowledge was like a child's clap in a large hall. I'd seen this man work his deadly game with bound creatures before – the *vaettir* Agrippina – and surely he thought of me as even lower than her. Of the indigenous people of Occidentalia, stretchers are at least accorded fear. We *dvergar* get only contempt.

'Surely they kept you nearby,' he said.

'Yes.'

'What are the intended dispositions of the legions?'

'I don't know.'

He withdrew the knife from my cheek. The sensation of a knife-point exiting a wound is one of inversion – increasing pain and increasing relief. He squatted, slowly, keeping the blooded blade in front of my face. When level with me, his brown eyes considered me coolly. There was no anger, no mirth animating his face. There was nothing.

'Mister Ilys. Shoestring. I must insist. You know the stakes. For me. For you.'

'The fifth stays in New Damnation.'

'And?'

I looked at him. 'Does it really matter? I tell you, I'll be crucified if I survive. But I doubt you'll let me live, so what's the point?'

'Pain.' He sniffed. 'Whole landscapes of pain for us to explore together with no easy death at the end.'

'Yeah, I figured that much,' I said. 'You ever seen a crucifixion?'

He laughed. 'I like you, Shoestring, despite myself. And the exigencies our situation demands. Had I time, I would try to convince you of joining—'

'You?' I shook my head. 'You have to believe in *something* to convince folks to follow you. Sad, but true.'

His face once more became a mask.

'All right, then. Pain it is.' He walked over to his leather portfolio and began running his fingers over the instruments there. Lovingly.

From overhead, there was a scuffle and thump. The bull *vaettir* stirred and worked his mouth full of jagged sharp teeth, craning his massive neck to look up at the ceiling. 'What was that, Mister Ilys? Were you with someone at your congregation of dwarves? An accomplice?'

'No. I was al—'

Still holding the silver knife, he took three steps toward me and brought the pommel across my jaw, hard. My head twisted violently to the side and my mouth filled with blood. 'Quiet,' he said, shushing me. 'I want to hear.'

Another thump and dust floated down into the lantern light.

'Something's not right—'

There came the sound of breaking glass, shards fell around us. And then a sucking wet meaty sound as the body of the drooling *daemon*-gripped man fell to the floor of the warehouse. Blood and streamers of bodily fluids streaked away from the point of impact.

'Ia's blood—' Beleth breathed and then craned his head toward the ceiling where the building's windows stood. A shadow moved into the rafters of the warehouse, far above. There was a hissing sound, and a cough. And suddenly a hulking figure dropped to the floor on tree-trunk legs, arms spread and claws out, and with one great hand snatched up the other *daemon*-gripped man and wrenched his head around so that the face was turned backwards, facing me. It held the man like a child, an infant. With a twist, he slung the man at the *daemon*-possessed stretcher, who fell back with the blow, crowing like some furiously basso bird of prey, stumbling into Beleth, sending both sprawling, the leather portfolio tumbling. Various bladed and pointed things rang as they scattered over the wooden flooring.

From the floor, Beleth yelled out, 'Get the damned thing. Kān! Kān!' He drew his thumb across his throat.

The *daemon*-possessed *vaettir* leapt forward but the other one – yes, for an instant it caught my eye in the gloom of the warehouse and the spark of recognition leapt between us: it was Gynth! – was already moving, dashing forward, hands out. Each long finger dagger-like. The *vaettir* moved like light. It moved as I thought an Indus tiger might – pure viciousness, strength, and intelligence married in incorruptible flesh. In the air, it snagged the *daemon*-gripped *vaettir*'s throat with its hand as it flew and, barrelling forward, wrapped its arms and legs around the other elf's torso. The two things went tumbling off and away into the dark of the warehouse. The wall shuddered. There were indescribable vocalizations – either from the pits of the *daemon*-gripped's gullet or my ally stretcher, my gynth – that made my skin ripple. The building shuddered with an impact as the two things fought in the dark, slamming against a wall or support piling, just out of sight.

There was a long moment of silence when all I could hear was Beleth's panting and the creak and groan of massive creatures straining against each other in the dark.

There's an old phrase out here in the territories: Some days you eat the bear, some days the bear eats you.

By my foot, a bit of shining silver. I put my heel on it and drew my leg back.

There was another jumble of movement in the darkness and then the two creatures were back in the flickering lantern light, streaked with blood and sheened with whatever might pass for sweat on such things. Hellish, their contortion; like some oiled nightmare. Difficult to tell where one creature left off and the other began. But as they struggled, and my eyes grew accustomed to the speed with which they moved, things became clear. The *daemon*-gripped *vaettir*, nude and tattooed with glyphs, held Gynth from behind, his massive arms snaked around and over the other's face, his legs wrapped around its waist. They had inverted positions. Gynth twisted viciously and wormed a corded arm up through the hold the other had on him, and went into a flying roll, out of sight. Another great shudder in the building and an audible grunt, and one of the struts supporting the ceiling came down in a shower of dust and splinters and a great *clook* sound.

The metal under my heel seemed to be a surgical knife of some sort. I almost dislocated my leg to get it back to my hand.

Beleth had scrambled up, blood streaming from his nose and two long gashes streaked across his face, pouring blood. Gynth must've raked him during a lunge, or the *daemon*-gripped man Gynth had flung had. Regardless, Beleth's odds of winning the next Hot Springs Belle of Beauty Award were approaching Zip City. He looked around wildly, then snatched up the silver dagger and wheeled to face me.

I was rising by then, the silver blade in my hand and the hemp cords that bound me unravelled at my back.

I crouched, hands out, sporting metal. This son-of-a-bitch would feel something from me.

'Mister Ilys, I—'

'Call me Shoestring,' I said. 'We're about to get real cozy.'

I came forward, blade slashing. Beleth made a desperate sound in his throat, halfway between a yelp and a strangled utterance, turned and simply ran, with surprising speed. I began to tromp after him but my legs cramped from being bound – and I stumbled. Off in the darkness there was a huge bellow, two inhuman voices rising in unfathomable language, even, possibly, different languages.

The two *vaettir*, locked in mortal combat, careened into view. Gynth, still arrayed in stolen funerary garb, his face buried in the crook of the other stretcher's neck, legs wrapped around its waist, while the other creature tore at him with big clawed hands. They crashed into a post, locked in furious combat, and the wooden post gave way under their mass and they tumbled in a heap on the floor. The whole building groaned, the air filled with falling dust, and a sharp cracking sounded all around, like trees being felled.

There was a moment then, when I had a choice. I could pursue Beleth with no clear assurance I would catch him, my physical conditioning at the moment suspect, or I could do what I might to assist Gynth and discover why such a creature as this *vaettir* would assist me. Thrice now. I chose to help the *vaettir* for, I was surprised to find, I did not want him to die.

It is a decision I have mulled for many, many years now. Had I the chance, I would not do things the same way.

The *daemon*-gripped stretcher made a keening sound deep in its throat as Gynth wormed his face back and forth – he had sunk his jagged teeth into the flesh and thrashed his head about. The other *vaettir* frantically shredded Gynth's arms, shoulders, and back with his claws. The contest was becoming one of endurance, rather than frenetic leaping and lightning fast attacks. The two creatures strained against each other – I could almost hear their tendons stretching and creaking. The surgeon's blade in my hand would never be enough. My eye fell on Beleth's abandoned leather portfolio. I scrambled over as quickly as my cramped legs would allow. Flipping it open, I found a long silver dirk as thin as a leaf and light as a feather. I snatched it up and turned back to the stretchers, locked in a vicious embrace. All at once the black-eyed stretcher's legs thrashed and suddenly they were inverted, Gynth on the bottom and the other on top. His back was to me now and there was no better time for me to make my move.

I came forward, crouched, knife in front of me. Something – my breath, a footfall, some unknown *vaettir* sense of life – must've alerted the creature because as I came close enough to plunge the dagger in its back, it began to thrash again and leverage itself up, drawing Gynth with it, wheeling about. Its terrible eyes fixed on me.

Gynth, realizing the advantage, began whipping his head back and forth, driving it into the cheek of the other creature with meaty *smacks*. The *daemon*-gripped stretcher howled.

I stepped as close as I could and drove the dagger in. Blade flat, between the ribs. It was hard – only in plays and mummer's farces do blades slip into flesh easily. All life wants to protect itself. The stretcher's muscles clamped around the blade. His body turned, clenched, and ripped the knife from my hand.

But the damage was done. Blood burbled up from the wound and Gynth seemed to gain strength from the other creature's injury. He slipped a gore-slick arm around the front of his enemy and brought his elbow across the temple of the *daemon*-gripped one with a resounding *crack!* In the instant of stunned inaction that followed, Gynth had snaked the hilt of the knife from the other's side and began plunging it over and over into the creature's chest like a robber in an alley. The sound that came from the mortally wounded *vaettir*'s throat was unlike anything I'd ever heard before – a rising and falling in pitch, all at once – and the sound carried a horrendous rage in the rising tone and an ineffable sadness in the descending one. Possibly it was the two creatures dying as one that gave its final vocalizations such a dual nature.

Gynth did not let it linger long. When his opponent had no more energy to fight, he plunged the knife in its eye and it shuddered once and then fell still.

And suddenly I was alone with dead bodies and a blood-drenched *vaettir*.

'Well,' I said to the thing. 'You look like hammered shit.'

TWENTY-SEVEN

13 Kalends of Sextilius, 2638 ex Ruma Immortalis

T HE SURVIVING *VAETTIR* STOOD, glistening and bloody in the yellow lamplight. He dropped the silver dagger to the floor.

On his palm, strangely unbloodied, a growing welt like a burn where the silver had scorched him.

Gynth leaned back, his back cracking, and twisted his head to the side. It was such a *dvergar* gesture that I was surprised – a motion most men and some women will make after strenuous labour.

'Ia damn,' the *vaettir* said in what passed for it as *dvergar*. *Svringin doon.*

Not stopping myself, I laughed.

Gynth looked at me. His face dripped with blood, his chin and neck slick with it, and only some of it was his. Mouth open, teeth like snarled standing stones, he seemed a creature of pure malice and fury. But his words.

'Ia damn,' he said.

'No shit, partner. No shit.'

I bent to collect the knives, noticed my hand was sore, too, where the surgeon's blade handle had touched me. Gynth lifted his hand, I lifted mine, and we looked at each other.

'Don't know why you're helping me. Your kind always been keen on killin' and deadly games.'

'Gynth,' he said. *We are kin*. He looked at the *daemon*-gripped

383

vaettir he had killed. He said, '*Vordrull*.' The *dvergar* word for abomination. His bloody mouth curdled around the sound.

'Beleth fled,' I said, looking to the door. 'If we hustle, we could find him. You know, you got the running and leaping stuff down.' Gynth shifted then, flexing his clawed hands, dripping with blood. And for that moment, I was reminded what a thing he was. An elf. The most fearsome predator in Occidentalia. And here I was chatting to him as if he were some housecat.

From above, and the walls, something snapped – the sound of breaking wood – and a groaning sound filled the darkened warehouse.

I was shirtless, shoeless, clutching a portfolio of silver weapons. Another *crack* and groan.

'It's time to go, hoss,' I said to the *vaettir* who seemed to be collecting his wits, looking about with a dull expression. If he hadn't been a stretcher, I would've thought it was shock and exhaustion.

From above, something gave and a large joist plummeted to the floor with a terrible percussive impact and a tremendous sound and the floor shuddered and gave way beneath it. I felt myself tossed away as the floorboard I stood on rose, buckling. The rafter punched a hole through the wooden floor and wooden splinters big enough to pierce my whole body were sent flying into the gurgling water below.

Gynth had thrown himself back – such a massive creature and wounded, but preternaturally fast – and from the edge of the lantern light, our eyes locked and there again was the frisson of recognition, acknowledgement. Connection. Somehow, when he called me gynth I had to believe him.

Like a racing snake in the hardscrabble, he whipped about and lashed away, up the far wall and back through the window by which he had entered earlier bearing the body of Beleth's *daemon*-gripped guard. The warehouse's ceiling groaned again from Gynth's weight and another rafter fell, making the hole in the floor considerably wider. Salted air and the stink of fish and pitch filled the space. The roof – in an alarming lurch – shifted.

Time to go.

I put my body into movement, heading in the direction that Beleth had fled. Finding a door, I exited into the street, half-naked and not knowing where I was or truly any other thing than simply being lucky to be alive.

The vigiles found me by *daemon*-light in the early morning under the Pons Milletus and laughed when I told them to take me to Mistress Balvenus'. But something about my demeanour stilled that derisive noise, and I was glad for that. Maybe it was the blood upon me. Maybe it was the strange leather portfolio full of silver instruments. Maybe it was me. I don't know.

Mistress Balvenus, her great bosom heaving, greeted us at the door in a nightgown. The sky was lightening, and she ushered me in and tended to my wounds herself, binding what was left of my ear and dressing my cheek where I'd been both struck and stabbed, and wrapping my hand in gauze and salve. She was not giddy, or foolish, or wanton – she simply saw what my body needed, and gave that succour. There was no whiskey but she had strong port wine and brandy and I was occupying my sore mouth with a glass of it when I saw Fisk entering the room.

'Ia's blood, Shoe. What happened here?' Fisk exclaimed, rushing forward in alarm.

'There's some cacique in my room. If you fetch it, I'll be happy to tell you the details,' I said. He looked alarmed, but went to get the maguey juice and handed me the container. I took a long pull – my whole face felt afire – and after Fisk asked for some privacy and closed the door to the side parlour where Mistress Balvenus had been tending me, I told him the story, the whole story, from the point I woke in Porto Caldo until then.

He interrupted me in points and looked sick when I told him of Gynth.

'You're telling me that some damned stretcher saved you? Three times? Followed you into town?'

'Seems like. The only explanation.'

'I don't believe it.'

'It doesn't really matter. There's a dead stretcher all marked up with those engineer's glyphs sitting in a half-collapsed warehouse near the Pons Milletus. Send some vigiles down there to retrieve it and take it to Sam. She'll be able to verify I'm not lying about the *daemon*-gripped bastard.'

Fisk whistled. 'I believe you, Shoe. I do. But it goes against—'

'Everything?'

He nodded.

I drank some more cacique. 'Where the hell have you been?' I asked. 'And where's Winfried?'

'She's been wounded and is in the care of a medico near *Dvergar*. She has money and Buquo and will re-join us here when she is well.'

'What happened?'

'We were out near the *Dvergar* spur. Small scouting expedition and had rumour that Beleth was out that way.'

'Looking after Cornelius' silver interest, were you?'

'A man in Panem, an important man, a man with a Quotidian linked to one of Tamberlaine's spies, told me that a child with black eyes held a knife at his throat and questioned him about a group of *dvergar* calling themselves *vaettir*, and making a home out east on the far edge of the Hardscrabble.'

I thought about it, putting myself in his position. 'That makes sense. How'd the man live through it?'

'He's got a twitchy son toting Hellfire.'

'Ah.'

'Beleth would be as interested in silver – and who controls it, should some *dvergar* guerrillas take control – as anyone.'

'Point taken,' I said.

I rubbed my face, testing the extent of the damage there. All things considered, it wasn't too bad, but the cacique was talking to me now. 'I meant to tell you earlier, Fisk,' I said, recalling the meeting with the gathered folk of Hardscrabble descent in the Plaza Monstruó. 'But I didn't think it was much of your concern at the time.'

His jaw hardened and he looked at me closely but said nothing. He was in the weathered blue uniform of the fifth, neat but had seen some travel, with his legatus badge prominent on his chest and both six-guns at his hips.

After a moment, he stopped eyeing me and with an infinitesimal shrug, seemed to banish whatever thoughts he'd been having. His brow furrowed.

'Shoe, what did you say about crying? "I woke to an infant crying", you said.'

'That's right. We were in a carriage, and they were taking me wherever they were taking me.'

'Why on Ia's green earth would Beleth be in the company of an infant?' Fisk said, rubbing his stubbled jaw.

Many ideas came to me then, and none of them pleasant.

Fisk hopped up, straightened his gunbelt. 'I need to get the vigiles and Sam.'

I pushed myself straight, despite the cacique I'd drank.

He tried to push me back down, but I was forceful.

'I don't need you, Shoe, if you've gone dissolute on me,' Fisk said.

'Cacique? Mother's milk.'

'I'd hate to meet your mother.'

'Let me get some clothes and a knife or two.'

'You lost your guns.'

I shrugged. 'We'll get them back from Beleth momentarily.'

He blinked, drew one of his, and handed it to me. 'I'll get my carbine.'

In moments we were on the street outside Mistress Balvenus'. I wore my itchy second shirt and unpatched old boots, my trousers tied with twine and the Hellfire pistol tucked inside a weathered satchel.

'You look like a panhandling dwarf, Shoe,' Fisk said, sucking his teeth.

'At this point,' I said, 'I *am* a panhandling dwarf, pard.'

'Come on, friend,' Fisk said, trotting across the street toward the garrison stables.

Mounted on Bess, it was a quick ride to the nearest vigile barracks and Fisk, brandishing his legatus badge, corralled a team of the bright boys to head to Pons Milletus and recover the bodies there and bring them to Samantha's workshop, providing them the address.

'How will we know the building, sir? You haven't given us an address.' The vigile, an alert, rat-faced little man with an olive complexion, seemed bright enough, but a stickler.

'Look for the half-collapsed warehouse,' I said. They gave me some strange looks – I did appear derelict – but rounded up a wagon and jogged off.

We trotted through the streets of Harbour Town, heading toward the western wharf district and Via Victrix. Fisk, riding his new horse – a lovely mare, piebald, with clean lines and a fine alert demeanour – had the opportunity to consider me.

'What's with the *vaettir*, Shoe?'

'The big ones or the little ones?'

'The ones that sent a century to their graves.'

'A half a century, or so Andrae says,' I responded.

He waved a hand. 'Don't matter. You know of them. You been—'

'Compromised?'

'Yes.' He nodded gravely. 'Yeah, compromised.'

'I've spent my whole life compromised, Fisk.' I looked at him, hard. 'Always on the outside looking in.'

'Bring me a small lyre,' he said, 'So that I might play you a sad song.'

'You can be cruel when you're of a mind,' I said.

'How deep are you in with them?'

'Not at all. In Passaseugo, I found myself in the middle of some sort of rally. Neruda spoke. He's a man of the Hardscrabble, Fisk, and I think you'd like him.'

'How so?'

'From what I could tell, his idea is – other than disliking the Ruman boot – that our Hardscrabble Territories have created a breed of man that should truly be independent.'

'So he's a revolutionary?'

'Struck me as more of a philosopher.'

'You're taken with sophists now, Shoe? Fuck me with a rake.'

I laughed. Shook my head and after a moment he laughed too but it was short and died quickly. 'It's not like that, pard. You'd understand his position. He's a likeable man.'

'I don't doubt that, Shoe. I'm sure Tamberlaine likes many men he's crucified.'

'That right? And now you're his legate. So, who's been compromised, then?'

'I believe you still get your bread buttered from the gold of the fifth.'

'Lay off, Fisk. You're looking for something in me that isn't there.'

He cursed then, under his breath. This tension between us had never existed before – we'd always had an understanding. He had his cracks, and I had mine, and we didn't go shoving wedges into the other's. From a pocket, he drew out a tabac pouch and a paper, rolled a cigarette in one hand, a trick I'd never learned, not for lack of trying and being a hundred years older than Fisk. He thumbed a match and cupped the flame against the wind and drew the smoke deep into his lungs and looked for a moment like he'd hand me the smoke, as he so often had in the past. But he didn't.

'Come on,' he said, kicking his horse forward and not looking back. 'Let's see what Samantha has to say.'

We arrived at Sam's and had to wait before her Hellfire-toting bullyboys could bring us into her workroom. Sam was indisposed, they said. By the time they'd let us in, the air was warming and I'd begun to sweat and the ache of all of the previous night's indignities had sunk in. Sam greeted us with wine and warm words – though she winced looking at my battered face.

She embraced Fisk as an old friend – we'd all been through Hellish events together and that tends to create bonds that remain after most others fail – and beckoned us to sit and tell her what had transpired.

I ran over events quickly, skipping what I didn't think necessary. She stopped me and questioned me intensely regarding the *daemon*-gripped *vaettir*.

'Did you see the markings on it?'

'He was marked up pretty good. We've sent vigiles to retrieve the body.'

'Good,' she said. She hopped up and trotted over to the wall full of cabinets and drawers and grabbed some papers and came back. She was wearing a white cotton robe, cinched at the waist with a leather belt that held a dagger, some tools, pouches full of unknown things – maybe cotton bolls or ink or silver shavings. Behind her ear was a stylus – forgotten, of course – and she wore oculars on her nose, absentmindedly. She placed the parchment in front of me and said, 'Does any of this look familiar?'

The drawings were very similar to those she had showed me before, but this time were of the full torso of a *vaettir*, done in an almost flawless hand. It was as if Winfried had used the inferno-graph to take the image, it was so accurate. However, it was signed at the bottom in an illegible scrawl indicating it was done by a man or woman's hand.

The renderings captured perfectly the fierce aspect of the *vaettir* and, even sized to fit on the parchment, the scale of the creatures. Whoever had drawn this image included a bowl, a dagger, and book in the image, showing how greatly the elf dwarfed the items.

Its jaw lolled open in death and its eyes had the vacant, milky gaze of statuary. Its chest was riddled with glyphs and intaglios of scarring, all etched on the paper in scarlet ink.

'That all seems right,' I said, pointing at the creature's left shoulder. 'And here.' Its abdomen. 'But this is all wrong, though I can't tell you how it is,' I said, indicating the right shoulder with my finger.

Samantha rubbed her lower lip and nodded, thinking. 'He's modified the locus warding to something else. You can't remember any details?'

'No, it was dark in the warehouse, and I was bound.'

'You look the worse for wear. Let me get you some wine.' She poured some – her secretary was absent – and offered us both cups. I downed mine quickly, but Fisk ignored his.

'I'm almost as curious about the stretcher that's been assisting you as I am this *daemon*-gripped one. I would not have thought either was possible, if it was anyone other than you telling me of these events.'

'It's true,' said I.

Samantha's eyes brightened and she actually rubbed her hands together. 'Fascinating,' she said. 'What else can you tell me about Beleth?'

'He seemed a little wasted,' I said. 'But as smug and bloodthirsty as ever.'

'He did not always wear that so openly,' she said. 'He seemed to all the world simply an engineer—'

'You can't be blamed for not knowing the depths of his mendacity,' I said. And she nodded wordlessly.

'He had an infant with him,' Fisk said, abruptly. 'Why would Beleth have an infant?'

'What?' Sam said, shocked. 'An infant? Surely you must be joking?'

I shook my head. 'They had me in a carriage. A woman with a Medieran accent gave succour to a baby.'

At that moment, Sam's whole aspect changed. Her face went pale, her mouth opened and then closed silently. Her wine glass fell to the floor, shattering.

'Oh my—' she said.

'What is it?' Fisk asked. 'I thought that sounded bad.'

Quickly, she stood. 'Help me,' she said, and raced over to her desk and began dumping papers into a leather satchel.

'What's going on?' I said.

'No time,' she said. 'Oh, gods help us, no time—'

'Sam! What's going on?'

She stuffed more papers into the bag. 'Beleth. He's going to summon something.'

'What?'

'Something tremendous.'

'Can we stop it?'

She gave a helpless laugh. 'We don't even know where he is. He has an *infant!*' She looked shaken to her core. 'We must flee Harbour Town.'

'Hold on. Hold on,' Fisk said, making patting gestures with his hands. But Samantha had dashed to the wall and began pulling a cord there. In a moment her secretary, Wacher, came into the workroom.

'Saddle two of the best horses and sound the alarm. We have to get out of here,' Samantha said.

'What? Why do we—'

Sam made a chopping gesture with her hand. 'Just do it.'

The secretary nodded, looking terrified, and dashed off.

Fisk grabbed Sam's arm to slow her mad dash, to calm her, maybe, and she looked down at his hand and then at his face. 'Let go. There's no time for discussion,' she said clearly and without rancour. He let go. She slung the satchel over her shoulder and then walked to the centre of the room and kicked aside a colourful Bedoun rug that lay there. There was a small but very ornate skein of wardwork carved into the stone of the floor and then laced with silver so that the scorch marks were still visible. At the centre of the warding, a keyhole. She withdrew the key from a chain around her neck, inserted it in the keyhole and turned. A metallic clack sounded and suddenly the stone rose and kept rising with an odd silence, as if on greased pneumatic cylinder. When it was waist high, a small chamber in the stone became exposed – this too encircled in warding and hidden behind a webwork of silver beads suspended in a fabric. It was a clever thing, the beads, forming a ward of pure metal, guarding the opening into the stone and fixed at the corners, but Sam whipped out her knife and sliced it open, cutting easily through the fabric. Reaching her hands inside, she grasped something and pulled it free. A box, also warded to the nines.

'Your old companion, Fisk,' she said. 'This building is stone, and so completely warded it would take a titanic *daemon* to breach the walls by force – as far as I know. But Beleth might have some trick up his sleeve and he wants this back.'

'The *daemon* hand?' Fisk asked, pale.

'The Crimson Man, Belial himself,' she said, nodding. 'And he's coming with us.'

She swiftly twisted the key again and the secret compartment began lowering itself again. 'Come,' she said, heading to the door. 'It's time to go. We may already be too late.'

There were bells ringing now, and many engineers in smocks and white robes running about, yelling at each other. One lovely young woman in a stained smock appeared in front of us, wild-eyed, saying, 'Is there some breach? Is there an irrevocable *breach?*'

Samantha swept past her. She said, brusquely, 'Best act like it and evacuate. On my orders, Pavia. *Now.*'

The young woman began to sob and rushed away, calling for a man named Artuo. We raced down warded hallways and past doors festooned in glyphs and finally came to the atrium.

'Our mounts are out front,' Fisk said.

'Head north on Via Portus, straight from the front of this building,' Sam said. 'Wait for Wacher and me at the Campus Salaria. You know where I'm talking about?'

'Yes,' I said.

'Go,' she said, pointing. 'Our stables are around on the side. We must hurry.'

I opened my mouth but she waved her hand in my face and said, 'Stop talking! Go!' Then she turned and she and Wacher fled down another hall.

Fisk looked at me, gritting his teeth, and said, 'Let's high-step, Shoe,' and trotted off.

At the horses, Bess chucked her head and brayed, as if she knew her normal drag-ass gait wouldn't suffice today, and she kept up with Fisk's horse without her usual grumbling and grousing. The citizens of Harbour Town looked at us warily as we blew down the cobbled lanes, horseshoes making a terrible clatter on the stones. Bess frothed and Fisk's new horse blew air explosively from its nose and worked its frothed jaw around the bit when we climbed the rise to the Campus Salaria on the northern edge of the city. From there, the Via Portus became dirt and headed north through an unnamed neighbourhood of wooden shanties and shacks until it hit the bluffs that rose above the Big Rill's delta.

The sun shone bright and warm, and from where we sat the smell of the sea came to us without the stink of city dwellings. There were legionnaires working through their *armatura* on the Campus Salaria ground, marching, drilling, while centurions bellowed inventive profanities at them. Across the Via Pontus was a small market where matrons – some with children, some of the younger ones more obviously gravid – worked through bins of potatoes and cabbages; beyond them, a butcher was slaughtering a hog which squealed unmercifully as they hoisted it up by the hind legs then put the tin tubs below it to catch the blood. It stopped squealing abruptly and the only sound then was of women murmuring and children laughing, the curses of the centurions and the pattering sound of blood as it filled metal tubs.

'What do you think of this?' Fisk asked. He was tight, and that meant he was angry and disgruntled. Toward me, toward the situation. I couldn't tell.

'I don't know. Never known Sam to be mistaken.'

'You *sure* you heard an infant squalling?' Fisk asked. 'You'd been knocked out. Sacked.'

'I'm sure.'

Fisk spat. He twisted another cigarette as his horse moved sideways beneath him. This time, he lit it and gave the burning smoke to me and began to twist another. A small thing, but I couldn't express how much it reassured me.

We smoked and watched the Via Pontus.

'I'm sorry if I doubted, Shoe,' he said. 'I can be an ass.'

'That legate's badge might've gone to your head.'

He snorted. 'Hardly. The only reason I wear it is, for me, it's become an emblem of my connexion to Livia.' He raised his arm and opened his hand. The nuptialis sectum – his wedding wound – was fresh. He'd used the Quotidian recently.

I thought of her, then, so far away.

'She is well?' I asked.

'Livia is. Much has happened. Things with her are—' He looked pained. 'Strained. Once we are away, I will give you her letters.'

I nodded.

We could hear them coming before they came into view. Samantha, Wacher, and a few other engineers – along with a couple of burlymen guards toting Hellfire carbines – they raced along the Via Pontus until they came to the square outside the Campus Salaria. Sam had a harried look, and Wacher cut protective glances at her.

'We must keep on,' Sam said, pulling her horse beside ours. 'There's no time to rest.'

'These cobblestones are shite for hooves, Sam,' Fisk said. 'We keep riding, hell-bent, we'll end up—'

'Hell-bent is exactly what's about to happen, Fisk. If it doesn't, I'll gladly give you the silver pig we've got with us. It would be worth it.' She looked back at the lower levels of Harbour Town, extended her hand, and pointed. 'Look there. Out upon the bay.'

Summer sun shattered upon the swells. Seagulls wheeled and cried with desperate voices. The light was brilliant, and glaring. But shadows were visible.

Ships.

Big steamers pouring *daemon* burn into the sky. Some with sails. Some with ominous-looking black things on their prows. Cannons, maybe.

'They're not moving,' Fisk said.

'They wait. We must *go*.' She looked at her entourage. 'Come. With all haste,' she said and wheeled her horse about and galloped north without looking to Fisk. As an engineer – it was true – she was incalculably more valuable than a legate, no matter how well connected, and so did not have to defer to his elevated rank.

'Ia damn it, Shoe,' he said. 'There's a whole city down there and they're just running away. At least the garrison commander should be notified.'

Sam and her posse diminished, down the Via Pontus. I looked to the sea from our vantage. I turned to Fisk.

'Feel free, partner. I'm not one to gainsay your lead,' I said. 'I think I'll follow Sam, just to keep an eye on her. All this might be a joke and we can laugh about it—'

A shift, a tilt in the world.

The earth shook and suddenly a blazing sun erupted from below us, in the centre of Harbour Town. All of the Via Pontus, Campus Salaria, the market, the buildings became brilliant with light and harsh in shadow.

'*Ride!*' Fisk screamed.

I began to kick Bess, but she had already jumped into motion. I flailed backwards but kept my saddle.

There was a rumble and an unknowable sound, beyond the ability of human or *dvergar* and even stretcher to understand. A wind began to blow. But backward. Toward the light, as if we were being sucked in.

Bess scrabbled against the cobblestones. We flew down the lane, now made brilliant in the light.

Then the light died and there was a thunderous sound. Flames. The sound of fire roaring like all the world was aflame.

I turned, craning around to look behind as I rode.

Monstrous.

A *daemon* towering above the city, titanic. Rising and wreathed in flame as the friction of entering our world caused the waves of shock to radiate outward and unimaginable heat to pour off it.

Fisk spurred his horse on, rising in the stirrups. Bess gave a hooting sound, so hurried that she couldn't haw properly. I might've been screaming too, I don't know. In front of us, the cut in the bluffs that allowed us up the rise and the limestone markers and

397

the wall that was the northern terminus of Harbour Town. Behind us, roaring and hot wind.

Our mounts hit the cut, barrelling and at full steam. Fisk jerked his reins to the right and yelled '*Here!*' pulling his horse into a washout in the side of the bluff. It wasn't much. Bess came in behind, slamming into Fisk's horse's rump and spilling me to the rocky ground where I landed on my back, in a heap, just in time to witness the hot wind and fiery air whoosh into the gulley leading to the top of the bluffs overlooking Harbour Town.

I could feel my face becoming tight, skin burning. Bess' tail began to smoulder and then caught fire. It was almost impossible to see, now, the air was so dry. The roaring we experienced before grew louder, and there were words in it, words no *dvergar* or human had ever heard before, nor any since, gods and numen save us. It shivered through my integument of flesh to bone. I could feel it in my teeth, behind my eyes.

Then Fisk was there. How I knew this I could not tell. I felt water on my face.

When I could open my eyes, the roaring had diminished, and Fisk was dumping the last of his canteen on Bess' smoking rump.

'Ia's beard,' Fisk said. 'That Beleth son of a whore wants for a killing.'

When the hot wind had died away enough, we took stock. I had burns over half my face, skin bubbling, and on the backs of my hands. Fisk was burnt, but less than I had been – he'd dropped and hunkered down on the ground the moment he saw me fall, though the back of his neck was raw and some of his hair had been burned away.

Bess took the worst of it, poor girl. Her tail was gone and the little nubbin of flesh the tail had grown from was blistered along with her haunches. She was hawing bad, now, and I had to take her chin and rub her nose for a long while to quiet her before she would move.

We walked out and up the gulley, eyes streaming, and the whole world seemed wreathed in a yellow, noxious smoke. Leading Bess, we stumbled to the top, where the wind tore the smoke away into the pines. Standing not far away was Samantha and her posse, looking down on Harbour Town. She glanced at us as we approached. Her face was hard, unforgiving.

'Of all the things he must answer for, this is the worst,' she said.

Harbour Town was aflame, an inferno. The *daemon* was gone, but the city lay in ruins. No building had escaped unmarred, even the stone forums and temples.

'Look there,' Samantha said, pointing beyond the rising smoke and ruinous view below us. 'They are coming.' The flotilla of ships in the bay had moved closer to shore. 'They'll wait until the fires die out and then—'

'This area will be swarming with Medieran soldiers,' Fisk said.

'And Beleth is still out there, somewhere,' I said.

We watched the city burn. In the warehouse region, there was an explosion, rising.

Samantha smiled. 'He couldn't wait.'

'What's that?' Fisk asked.

'Beleth. He wants the *daemon* hand back. He couldn't wait for the fires to be extinguished before he tried to get it.'

'Why not?'

'Medierans.'

'How do you figure, Miss Decius?' Fisk asked.

'Every thief will lock his own doors,' she replied. 'Beleth is untrustworthy. So he cannot trust anyone else. He had to get to my workshop before the Medierans did.'

'How?' I said. 'It's a godsdamned furnace down there.'

'Of all the buildings in Harbour Town, that one would not have been affected. He possibly came to it by boat, maybe from the shore. I don't know.'

'And the boom?' I asked.

'A little present I left him,' she smiled, a cold, furious expression. 'If it didn't kill him or his minions, then he'll be seriously crusty for a while.' She watched the city and her smile died. 'Oh, gods.'

Elsewhere in the ruin, other smaller explosions sounded, no doubt bound household and industrial *daemons* being freed from their warding as silver and iron melted, stone cracked, wood splintered. The fabric of Ruman life was unravelling. The stink of brimstone was something fierce. Yet better that than the thousands of citizens down there cooking in those Hellish fires.

'We'll need to get to New Damnation,' Samantha said, voice catching. 'Marcellus will need to field the fifth, send messages east to mobilize the eight, thirteens, and whatever other forces are available.' She turned away from the destruction and I noticed the tears streaming down her cheeks.

So much death. So much destruction.

Every soul that remained in Harbour Town was dead, or soon to be. Thousands upon thousands of souls. The weight of that knowledge was almost too terrible to bear.

Fisk drew me aside and said, 'We should go east.'

'East? Why?'

'Silver.'

'What can two men do to protect silver interests?' I asked.

'You mean, what can a man and a *dvergar* do to protect silver interests?'

'Neruda.'

'If any of us can speak to him, it'll be you.'

'I told you I have no connection to the man. I just ran into a folderol he'd orchestrated.'

'You do have a connection.' He paused. 'Blood.'

For an instant I thought back to my rescuing *vaettir* saying 'gynth.'

'Godsdammit, Fisk. It's like everyone thinks they got a piece of me.' I shook my head. 'We should go to the legion.'

'No. There's a new silverlode near *Dvergar* – that is a surety. Been there myself. If the Medierans are controlling the mouth of the Big Rill and the bay, then soon they'll push north to reclaim Hot Springs and Passaseugo, if they can get that far. Past the fifth. But if we move quickly, and broker a deal with this Neruda fella, maybe we can keep them from the silverlode in the east. Doubt they know about it yet but they will, eventually.'

'You're not doing this just because you've got an interest in the silver money that lode will give you?'

'Ia dammit, man! *War runs on silver!*'

I thought for a while. Seeing something in me give, Fisk said, 'So, you'll go?'

'Yes,' I said.

Fisk nodded. He approached Samantha, who had been lost in her own reverie for a moment. Her secretary and attendants looked on, dazed. Fisk spoke to her in a low voice. She looked surprised, argued for a moment. I could see in her face the instant Fisk revealed the existence of the new silverlode near *Dvergar*. Then she nodded. They spoke for a bit longer. Eventually, they came back to me.

Samantha said, 'I agree with Fisk. If there's some chance you can secure a treaty or bargain with the *dvergar* and protect the Ruman interest in that new silverlode, you must do it.'

'You just want to make sure your silver don't run out.'

She shook her head. 'I don't care about money, or silver. I care that those things keep the fabric of our country – of the *Hardscrabble*, goddamn it, Shoe – together. Money brings security. Silver brings guns. I shouldn't have to explain this to you,' she said, looking at me in a way that made me uncomfortable.

I spat. 'I already told Fisk I would go.'

'Yet you still need convincing,' she said. 'I'll notify Marcellus what's happening and requisition another one of these Quotidians – or two – so that I can communicate with you.'

'Still don't have to like it.'

'Would you stop with the grousing?' Fisk asked. 'It's like you and Bess are the same damned creature.' Bess, hearing her name and in extreme pain, hawed loudly.

'And,' Samantha said. 'I think it's time to give you back this.' She dug in her satchel and withdrew the warded box that contained the hand that held the Crimson Man.

Fisk paled. He did not reach for it.

'You should keep hold of that, until you can destroy it,' he said.

She looked at him, sadly, the drying streaks of tears visible on her face. 'No,' she said. 'I can't destroy it, nor can I banish the devil inside it or I would have already. And I won't use it. It's time it goes back to you, its original bearer.'

'No,' Fisk said. 'I won't take it.'

She turned and extended her hand to take in all Harbour Town. 'This power was used against us. You've borne the Crimson Man around your neck. We know you can withstand him, for a while at least. We may need his strength in this coming war.'

'He stopped Croesus' men from using Hellfire in Hot Springs,' I said.

'Fat lot of good that did, Ia damn you, Shoe. He burnt down the city anyway. He didn't need Hellfire.'

'We might need him,' Samantha said again. 'An army with the Crimson Man riding at the fore would be unstoppable.'

'I won't.'

'You must,' she said, holding out the warded box containing a young girl's severed hand.

Fisk looked at it a long while, working his jaw. Finally, he took the box. 'Ia damn you both,' he said.

Samantha looked out at the smoke pouring into the sky from the inferno of Harbour Town. 'He already has.' She turned her horse about and nodded at her attendants. 'We'll ride to Marcellus and tell him of your plan. If I were you, I'd make haste. The Medierans are putting their ships into position and will be swarming this place within hours.' She looked at Fisk. 'And they'll send folks to follow us – and you – make no mistake. So it's better we split up.'

Fisk looked about how I felt: overwhelmed, shocked, saddened by the outrageous loss of life, and a tad pissed off about the situation forced upon us. He nodded and I found myself doing the same.

Sam held up one hand in a fist, showed us her teeth in what was either a frightening smile or a grimace, turned her horse to the north and rode off, her entourage close on her heels.

Fisk looked at me. He dug in his shirt, pulled out a sheaf of parchment tied with twine. 'It'll be a long while before we rest,' he said. 'For when we do, my friend.'

I took the papers – written in the fine, spidery script of the Quotidian – and secured them in my satchel, next to Fisk's pistol on loan to me.

Fisk said, 'The whole world's gone to shit, seems like.'

The smoke was thick, and the wind had shifted, pushing it toward us. I did not get to respond.

Coughing, we kicked our mounts into motion and rode on, east and north, in a world made Hellish by fire and flame.

TWENTY-EIGHT

Ides of Geminus, 2638 ex Ruma Immortalis

My dearest Fisk,

All is well with me and young Fiscelion. I am healthy and if not happy, then hearty – I've been packing on weight. Rice, honeyed cakes, and pork seem the staples here. But there are also puddings and iced creams and fried delicacies, from strange vegetables to obscure or unrecognizable meats, most delicious. It seems the cuisine of Kithai sits well with me. And when I say sits, it is regionally appropriate – my rump, my thighs, my stomach, of course, that great growing globe of our son – I understand gravidity.

Thanks to the Eight Silken Movements, I remain limber and mobile – though the idea of running now seems preposterous, great bits of myself moving all at once in opposing directions.

At times I find myself repulsed by smells that once had pleased me, or made me ravenous. The scent of a flower, like the water lilies that bloom on the edges of Huáng's pools in his garden, can make me nauseous. Yet horse-dung has a rich, interesting scent that my nose seems to want to puzzle out. Fried fish or squid or other delicacies make me salivate, yet the breaded strips of pork I cannot stand.

The other morning, Delia came to our room and drew me aside and in Medieran bid me to follow her out into the garden. The boy we rescued from the stoning mob tagged along, as he's

wont to do. He follows me about like some lost puppy, without
the animation. The women have taken to calling him *yōulíng*
which Delia explained in her halting Medieran meant *Fantasma*.
Ghost. Between the boy and Tenebrae and their quirky names,
we have quite a spooky menagerie.

But on this day, I allowed myself to be drawn aside, not before
ducking into my dressing area for a few minor accessories,
one of them Hellfire. Strapping it to my leg under my dress
felt familiar and foreign at the same time – I had to let out the
straps a couple of notches to make it fit.

Why did I want my Hellfire this day? I can only say it was
intuition and I had been thinking very much about what
Carnelia had said to me regarding the incident of the boy. My
recklessness and myopia.

Outside, as I followed Delia through the garden, I noticed
the sky was clouded and great flocks of the lóng passed far
overhead, out of range of the Jiang archers lining the walls of
this neighbourhood, and, thank Ia, not in an expulsive mood.
She led me among the bridges to the gate and when I balked
at passing through them – Huáng had made it clear not to
wander as Rumans about the city – two of Huáng's men awaited
alongside two litters. One of them presented me with a lovely
embossed piece of parchment which read, 'To Livia Cornelius
of Rume from Sun Huáng – My apologies for not speaking to
you in person: I am away on affairs of the Autumn Lords this
morning. Chuienlani has asked to take you to a revered place
on the city outskirts so that the life growing within you will
continue to grow strong. It is a location that possesses much
Qi. I have provided you with two guards and litters. You need
not accompany her, if you do not wish. She is simply a servant
and they can be frivolous. But, since this was a matter of female
concern, and she is a trusted employee of my house since

childhood, I have honoured her by facilitating her request. I remain at your service – Sun Huáng.'

Delia looked at me expectantly and smiled prettily when I nodded my acquiescence. Fantasma stood bemused, staring at the sky. Men appeared and took up the palanquins – Delia, the boy, and me in one and the two guards in the other – and trotted us down streets and through messy little neighbourhoods of multi-coloured laquerwork and white stone, moving slowly up the hill. Eventually we passed underneath a large forbidding wall ringed in armoured guards, some of whom seemed to be carrying spears and swords and others who held what looked suspiciously like Hellfire, and passed out into some woodlands, though the area was still very populous, small little hamlets far off on hillsides connected by paths where woodcutters walked with axes and fieldhands trudged to their fields, hoes and shovels over their shoulders.

The palanquin bearers eventually brought us to the ridge that overlooked Jiang and we spent some time looking out at the river snaking itself through the countryside below, but the day had grown warm and I felt some discomfort from the heat and we pressed on to this 'blessed' location that awaited us. A few leagues farther, we came to a strange declivity behind a copse of trees (tall narrow trees that for all the world looked like swords standing pommel down) and into a kind of raw, open place in the earth.

Once the litters were placed on the ground, we exited and Delia tugged my sleeve to lead me down toward a white rubbled area. The guards looked on impassively. Fantasma floated behind us on soft feet, with huge, unshuttered eyes, his face placid.

On the path down, we passed two women, each one heavy with child. They hailed us in some ritualized manner I could not understand. At the end of the path, we came to an open space, where a single stone statue stood, and on it was carved a beautifully simple aspect of a radiant mother, cradling an infant. Beyond the statue, a white pit. As I looked on, I could see another woman – equally pregnant – disappearing into the pit as if she was taking steps downward.

'Come,' Delia said, tugging my sleeve again. And I allowed myself to be led. My curiosity was getting the best of my natural wariness.

Fantasma made to follow me but Delia touched his arm and he stopped. She shook her head gravely and said 'Wūdiǎn. Impureza.' He looked at her, bemused. That morning the serving women had dressed him in the cotton robes of a servant of the house and he looked a page to a lord, maybe. One of the more delicate and cloistered servants of rich men. His expression remained totally blank and I worried for his mind. It seemed as vacant as a passing cloud.

The steps led down into a pure whiteness. The smell of the open earth was strong here, scented with the smell of powdered stone – a smell you never know you've smelled until, well, you smell it, my love. I took the stairs down and was surprised that Delia did not accompany me, but when I looked back at her she shrugged and waved me forward. At the bottom of the declivity was the woman I had seen earlier, dressed in simple Tchinee garb, hair pulled into a tight bun, a colourful silk scarf fluttering behind her. She stood before a wall of the white stuff that made the whole of this place and was digging in the stuff with one of her hands while the other rested on her full stomach. She did not react as I approached her.

One hand covered in the white fabric of the wall, she brought it to her mouth and began to eat of it. Watching her, her mouth rimed in the white of the earth, something welled up in me and I don't know if it was the stress of not being with you, my love, the weight of this child I bear, the burden of my familial and political obligations, or something else. Like the world we live in, my body has begun a war with itself, a new nation calving away into its own entity. I have lost control – I am like a leaf borne on the wind or a bit of wave-tossed flotsam on the sea, without my husband, my body turning traitor and host to a foreign thing.

I reached out and clawed at the wall, took a handful of the clay-like white dirt. I brought it to my mouth, and ate.

Afterwards, the grit of the soil in my teeth and gums, I walked from the pit wondering what had just occurred but Delia smiled and clapped like a schoolgirl and said, 'Buena, buena, maestra! Buena!'

I felt light and airy as one of the *zhuìlì* floating above the city. I do not remember the journey back except for one occurrence. The litter bearers took a different route to the city, and we entered not from the northern gate, but a western one. The clouds had thinned and the sun made all of Jiang a refulgent, steamy cauldron. It was as if I could feel my hair curling with each moment, the moisture catching in every fibre.

The afternoon sun cast long shadows away from us, and as we entered the city the clang and clamour of life there filled the air: the cries of vendors matched by shrieks of lóng wheeling high above, the sound of hammers falling on timber and metal, the stately clop-clop-clop of beasts of burden, the sizzle and scrape of rice stalls and smoked meat sellers, the cry of children in happiness and pain, laugher. Weeping. Overwhelming smells of sewage and spices and smoke and sulphur. Heat. Moisture.

And then everything fell away, and I might have dozed off as I am wont to do in the afternoon, Fantasma pressing into my side as the palanquin rocked back and forth like a child's bunting-bed. I woke as our small entourage passed among stone shapes and buildings and there was no smell of shit, or spiced food or burning wood, but the faint whiff of death, and mould. All

was quiet except for the far-off cry of the little dragons hunting
seagulls upon the currents of air.

I looked about and off to our right was a silent city of
standing stones, thousands of them on a rising hill – some of
them wreathed in flowers and piled with little bottles of water
or rice wine or ceramic plates of little cakes. Between the stones,
I saw a man standing still and watching us. An older man,
white-haired, and for an instant I thought it was Huáng. I called
for the palanquin bearers to halt and they did after a moment
and I walked out and away from the litters. Delia remained
behind, looking frightened and called, 'No, maestra, ciudado los
muerto!'

But there was someone there. I had tasted the earth earlier,
the pure white earth, and now we came upon this necropolis in
the heart of Jiang. I felt dislocated and centered all at once, as if
this was where I was supposed to be. So I waved for Delia to be
silent and beckoned the guards who lumbered along behind me
slowly as I walked up the rise among the gravestones. The boy
Fantasma walked dreamily by my side for a short distance.

There were people here, no doubt vagrants filching the
offerings to the dead, the rice wine, the honeyed cakes. But
all was silent and as I strode up the hill among the markers,
I felt my earlier weights and concerns falling away, the fret of
our mission, the focus on our son and his health even in my
womb, my blooded connection to you, Fisk. I was fine, not out
of control, fully possessed of myself, as if I'd created a fortress
within me where I could live and not let the obligations and
pressure of life weigh me down.

'You are far from home, miss,' a voice came, shocking me
out of my reverie. Again I had a moment's thought it was Sun
Huáng speaking to me, for the voice had a similar cadence and
timbre. I wheeled about, looking for the source of the voice, or
my guards. The guards were nowhere to be seen. The speaker,

though, stood a few paces from me, a wizened old man in smudged grey robes with a black-lacquered cane. His white hair haloed his head in a tangled clot but his eyes were bright and merry.

'As are you, if you know my language,' said I.

He gave a little laugh, as if he was generally pleased with my response. 'I am home, miss.' He smiled, an expression that cast his face into a beatific wrinkled mess and walked over to broken stone and sat on it. He patted the space next to him. 'Though I have been to your land, once, when I was very young. It is how we learned your tongue, my brother and I.'

'Your brother is Sun Huáng?' I asked. 'This is not a . . . a turn of phrase?'

'We shared a mother long ago, but not fathers.'

I considered this. If Sun Huáng and this man were brothers, they had taken near opposite paths through life. What could have happened to cause such a division?

As I thought, I noticed Fantasma standing a few paces away, still and staring. There was a look on his face I could not place, as though more thought and consideration moved behind his gaze than I could see, like invisible currents in the sea. The boy never lolls about with an open mouth so at times he appears considered. The old man gestured to the boy and said something in Tchinee and the Fantasma moved away, out of sight.

'What did you say to him?' I asked.

'I told him we wished to speak in private.'

It was remarkable that this old man's request was obeyed by the lad. For the time he'd been with us, Fantasma did not respond to direct instruction and only wandered about dreamily. If given a task, it was more likely than not to be abandoned. If directed toward a location, he was likely to drift away. I observed him closely and could find no trace of the maliciousness the

women of Uxi accused him of, yet I feared for the soundness of
the young man's mind.

'Where are my guards?'

He looked about the sepulchral space, over standing stones
and graves thick with the language of Kithai. He waved his
hand. 'Somewhere around here, I'm sure. It is easy to get turned
about among the stones.' He patted the seat beside him again.
'Come, let us talk.'

'Who are you?'

'My name is Sun Wukong.'

I paused. Looked about once more for my guards. Eventually,
with some effort, I dug in my dress and pulled out my sawn-off
and thumbed back the triggers. The old man's eyes widened.

'I am no fool, sir. And as I've been reminded lately, I've got
a passenger that wants protection.' I went and sat down beside
the old man, keeping the barrels pointed in his direction. 'I have
heard your name. You are spoken of with great mystery. And
some reverence.'

Sun Wukong opened his hands – I could see they were spotted
with liver marks but for all that they looked powerful and clever.
'I cannot help what is said about me.'

'Huáng said that—'

Sun Wukong laughed, a rich laugh, full of wisdom and years
of mirth. 'His tongue is made of steel, and very sharp. Mine is
but the flesh of mankind.'

'That sounds pretty but is not very clear,' I said. The white
earth I had eaten had changed me somehow, made me more
fearless and hard, all at once. Though I had never been too
fearful or soft in the first place. 'I require clarity when I speak to
others.'

He laughed again. 'You truly are a Ruman,' he said. 'Moreso
even than your brother.'

'Have you been watching us?'

'There is not much in Jiang that passes my notice.'

'And your Monkey-boys?'

He gave a slight inclination of his head.

'What do you want with me?' I asked.

'To know you. To see your intentions.'

'I am here as an emissary to the Autumn Lords.'

He snorted. 'The Autumn Lords?' He placed a finger on the barrel of my sawn off and pushed it a little, not hard, so that it wasn't directed at his stomach. 'You will learn the nature of our Lords of Autumn.'

'Why don't you just tell me their nature?'

'They are creatures of Qi.'

'That is what Sun Huáng said, too. I am still not sure I understand what this Qi is. Can you explain it?'

'I am old and have not the years left in me to make you see, though I can tell I would quite enjoy being your teacher.' He patted my knee in a grandfatherly way, totally ignoring the Hellfire weapon there. 'Let me ask you a question, miss.'

'I am a married woman.'

'It's not a proposition,' the old man said, and then winked and I couldn't help but laugh. He grinned at me. 'Everybody wants something. Sun Huáng. Your brother. The emperor Tamberlaine. What do *you* want?'

It was unvarnished and simple yet it was hard to answer. I sat silently for a long while. 'A healthy son. A return to my loved ones. Safety.'

Sun Wukong looked at me closely. 'These are all good things.' He stood. In some way, I could tell from his expression, I had said what he wanted to hear. 'I am simply a small and aged man. But should you require my help, come here and call for me and I will give you what aid I can.'

'Why should I trust you?'

'You shouldn't, this is true. You should trust no one, in the

412

end.' He smiled. 'Or, since you are a good judge of character
– this I can tell – you should trust each living thing to act
according to their own nature.'

'I don't know you well enough to know *your* nature,' I said.

'Shame, that. Something we'll have to rectify.' He laughed and
then scrambled up over a shelf of fallen stone and leaped to the
top of a marker, as spry as a goat on the mountainside. 'It is at
this point I must ask you to turn over all of your money.'

I snorted, and pointed the Hellfire directly at his chest.

He looked sheepish. 'My reputation is that of a man of the
people. While I have enjoyed talking with you, you are *most
definitely not* of *the people*. And so, that means, I must rob you.'

'You can try,' I said.

He cocked an eyebrow at me. 'What if I was to tell you that if
you do not give me all your money, the lovely handmaiden or the
boy that rode with you here will die.'

'You're bluffing.'

He whistled and shadows began moving through the standing
stones and graves. Men and women. Rough and armed. The
Monkey-boys. They shifted about and then, almost at once, they
blended back amongst the stones.

'I do not think you would kill an innocent.'

'How do you know they are innocent?' Sun Wukong said.

'How do you know they are not?'

He did a quirky little movement and it took a moment for
me to realize he was dancing. 'No one is innocent, my dear, no
one is safe. No one is innocent, my dear, no one is chaste,' he
chanted in a little sing-song voice. 'No one is pure, my girl, no
one is blameless. No one is—'

'I'll give you the money if you stop singing.'

'All of it?'

'All I have on me,' I said.

Sun Wukong bowed. As he leaned forward, he dropped into

413

a roll – an outstanding feat for a man of his advanced years – and before I knew it, he stood before me again with his hand outstretched.

'That is acceptable,' he said, his eyes glinting merrily.

'It's technically not robbing though.'

'The Monkey-boys of Jiang dip their fingers in extortion, too. Should I start singing again?'

I rummaged in my dress and withdrew my purse. He snatched it from my hand.

'We thank you, miss,' he said.

'Trust people to always follow their own nature,' I said.

'Consider this an object lesson.' He tucked the money away. 'You have my word. Should you be in need, come here and I will help.'

'You'll just rob me again.'

He winked. 'Technically, it was not a robbery.' He scrambled up and away from me, stopping in a V caused by the collapse of two standing stones. 'Remember,' he said, and disappeared.

It took a short while to find myself back at the palanquins. The guards were there and in a state of high agitation, along with Delia and the boy, Fantasma. Of them all, only Fantasma seemed nonplussed about my absence. The guards bustled me into the litter and drove the bearers home at a brisk trot.

Because the culture of Far Tchinee is so different and unexpected, I did not tell Sun Huáng of the events of the day for two reasons: the first was I feared the guards might be put to death for their inadvertent transgression, or at least seriously reprimanded, physically or financially, and I could not see as it was their fault; the second was because I worried about his reaction to my discovery about his relation to Sun Wukong. At some point I would broach that question with him, but not now. That did not mean I wouldn't ask some questions.

That night, at dinner, Sun Huáng had returned and seemed

in a good mood. We dined on fried bits of fish covered in a spicy brown sauce with vegetables, on rice, and a delectable soup made from the grasses found on the high-plains far to the north and stewed in some sort of creature's stomach over a fire. Carnelia, Secundus, and Tenebrae chattered on about the events of the day's training and asking Huáng questions regarding armatura or mastering their art of martial exercise and movement and Huáng gave them instruction, yet his eyes continued to return to me.

'Today, Sun Huáng, we stopped at a necropolis in the western part of Jiang,' said I, watching his face for some reaction. 'It was a beautiful place, yet solemn and a little lonely. Afterwards, I recalled you mentioning that the robber Sun Wukong lives in a place like that. I am fascinated. Can you tell me more of this Sun Wukong?'

Huáng's eyes narrowed, and he cleared his throat nosily. 'What would you know?'

'Surely, like an August One, no one becomes a famous robber overnight.' I took a drink from the water in my glass. 'What can you tell us of his origins and his history?'

'Nothing,' Sun Huáng said. 'His story is a fabrication, full of half-truths and lies. He claims to be for the people, yet he lives in a city of the dead.'

'This necropolis had many standing stones with offerings at their bases. What is the story behind those?'

Sun Huáng drank some rice wine, wiped his mouth with a napkin, and then slowly considered his words. 'The *Sicheng*, or city of revered dead, is a place of great Qi, where we remember and honour the great energies cast into the world by our ancestors.'

Secundus said, 'Sifu, does this mean you worship your dead?'

'No,' he said after a long moment, his eyes never leaving mine. 'We revere the energy they passed into the world. Each person's Qi rises and mixes with the ebb and flow of the world's. Only those of exceptional Qi are remembered in *Sicheng*. The fathers of families, the matrons that gave birth to many notable children. Accomplished men and women. Warriors and poets.'

'And August Ones?' I asked.

'Of course. The August Ones are the first among men and women. But they are so far below the Autumn Lords as to be mere . . .' He thought. 'Animals.'

For a moment I had to consider if Huáng was struggling with our language or if he was being guarded. Or both.

'When will we be brought before them?' Secundus asked. 'I have been enjoying your hospitality and training so much, I fear I've been lax in expiation of my familial and national duties.'

Huáng turned to look at Secundus, letting a shallow smile touch his face. 'I am sorry, it will be a bit longer. Ting-thiam Huáng, the August One Who Administers Trade, had a problem with the Manchus and needed Tsing Huáng's assistance and so he was called away. You must wait a bit more before you can go before the Lords of Autumn.'

Secundus shrugged and Tenebrae seemed to relax. Carnelia looked at me and then back to Huáng, as if she was caught between two extremes. And maybe she was. Finally, she said to me, 'It won't be long, sissy.'

'And how was the reason for your trip? Did you take part in the *tǔ mù* – the ingestion of the pure?'

I laughed. 'If you meant, did I eat the white dirt? Yes, I did.'

Carnelia made a curious sound in her throat and said, 'Sissy, why didn't you take me with you?' And then after a beat, 'You ate *dirt?*'

Secundus said, 'I say, Livia, are you going native or something? Performing Tchinee rituals and the like?'

'I have seen you bowing to Huáng, brother.' I said, 'Going native? No, I think not. Of all of us here, I am the one most eager to complete our task and re-board the *Malphas* and put this place behind us. I would bear my child with my husband, or at least knowing I would soon be with him.'

'Then what's this *tǔ mù* business our host is referring to?' Secundus said.

'From what I could tell, it's something pregnant women do. They go to this quarry, I think, and eat the white dirt there. For the health of the baby.'

'Preposterous. How could earth help an unborn infant?'

Huáng raised a hand. 'Secundus, every day you train to learn to channel and express your Qi, yet you cannot believe that the earth itself might do the same?'

Secundus looked thoughtful for a moment. 'I guess it is reasonable, expressed like that.'

'So that would mean,' Carnelia said, 'Livia was consuming the earth's Qi! Like some vorduluk?'

Sun Huáng shook his head. 'All of life possesses Qi. The pure earth Livia ingested is known as the white jing of the earth. Its essence.'

'Its "pearly" essence?' Carnelia said, arching her eyebrow. 'Oh, Livia.'

'Stop it, Carnelia.' I said, not interested in her silliness. I shrugged. 'When I found myself at this wall, smelling the earth, I felt a twinge almost like a craving. I cannot explain it, but I took it up and ate the dirt. From what I could tell, the women of Kithai have been doing it for hundreds, if not thousands, of years. It should not hurt me.'

'No,' Huáng said. 'It will not hurt you. And Delia is a trusted servant of my house. But you must remain wary.'

'I am always wary,' I said. 'I trust only that everyone will act according to their nature.'

Standing, I excused myself. Huáng watched me as I walked from the room.

*

Fantasma continues to puzzle me. He's a lean, rangy thing, with sharp calloused hands, the likes of which you see on street urchins or prostitutes. But his skin is flawless and his features almost girlish. When you look at him, the immediate appearance is of youth, but should you sit at a table with the lad nearby and close enough, flooded with morning sunlight, he seems older. He has very little pigment to his skin. He would seem an idiot, but he is tight lipped and never speaks – I have never heard him utter so much as a word – so he has not the slack-jawed appearance of the addle-brained. Though his eyes do have the cast that most people from Kithai possess, it is far less pronounced than his countrymen. And his mess of black hair, sometimes curly, sometimes straight when wet, gives him a constantly shifting appearance.

But more than all this, he seems dislocated, like his mind is not here. I have never seen him eat – though I know he must. Once, when I sat with Carnelia in the garden, taking a strong cup of the dark tea they serve us here in the afternoon, he wandered up to us, face blank, with a rather large blue feather caught on his lower lip.

'Look, Livia, the cat has caught the canary,' Carnelia said.

I considered the lad. On this afternoon, his hair was lying straight on his head, shaggy and wild. With his blank features and placid demeanour, he did seem more feline than I would have liked and he turned those blank eyes toward me. Carnelia reached out and plucked the feather from his lip, yet he did not flinch or blink. A strange lad, altogether, I thought then, like those soldiers who come back from whatever front they fought and laboured on to discover their enthusiasm for the world they fought for has withered away within them in its absence and everything in life is monotony at its best and, at its worst, a thing of dread.

On the day after meeting Sun Wukong in the Jiang necropolis, I was asked to take lunch with Sun Huáng and was quite surprised to find Min with him. We met in Sun Huáng's study, the walls crisscrossed with shelves that looked like wine racks, and where each bottle might have sat was a heavy scroll with wooden spindle. Incense burned on a small statue of what looked to be a bear and a man standing together, there were flowers filling the air with their luxurious scent and mixing with the smoke, and the afternoon sun spilled in great luminous geometrical shapes on the wide expanse of stone floor.

Huáng greeted me as warmly as his reserve allowed, took my hand, and by my leave lightly touched my stomach, almost as genuflection to the child growing there – or maybe the Qi swelling it within me. The distance of the night before, when I was prodding him with the proverbial stick, was gone.

'I have allowed Min to re-join us,' Huáng said. 'For I cannot bear to be gone from her too long, and . . .' He thought for a moment. 'She has convinced me of her regret in her treatment of you.'

Min emerged from a side room, having been waiting for this moment.

Dressed in a simple and straight gown, Imperial blue with yellow and pink flowers embroidered into the fabric, a high collar that showed off her slender neck, and her hair freed from its normal severe style, she looked very much sincere as she bowed to me and presented a formal apology: 'Livia of the Cornelians, please allow me to apologize for my previous words and actions. I was acting not only out of childishness, but a foolish and slavish devotion to Kithai, not recognizing that the rising tide raises all boats. It is only through mutual respect for our countries that we can come to some accord.'

I considered the girl. Her eyes were wide and clear, the pupils very dark, and I could not discern any disingenuousness nor dissembling. However, I did not trust her words. Sun Huáng watched her with a blank expression worthy of Fantasma, and he remained very still as only Huáng can remain, seemingly at total rest yet with an expectant air about him.

'It is important for us to remain true to our beliefs while not being slavishly devoted to them,' I said. But, my dearest Fisk, Sun Wukong's words echoed again in the chambers of my mind – *trust everyone to act as their nature dictates*. Eventually Min's would be revealed if given world enough, and time. 'On behalf of the Cornelians, I thank you for your apologies,' I said. 'And will convey your well wishes to my brother, Secundus who, while my junior, is the titular head of this expedition.' I laughed. 'After all, we foreign devils have thick skins. Indeed, I think you might have offended your grandfather more than you could have offended us. Though I do not speak for all of us.'

Min bowed again and turned to Sun Huáng with an expectant look on her face, as if waiting for his approval. He gave the barest incline of his head and then Min smiled, brilliantly. With less stiffness, she turned and withdrew a large scroll from one of the crosshatched nooks and presented it to me.

'Please accept this pamphlet regarding Qigong and the map of its currents both in Kithai and within the human body.'

I took the scroll and inclined my head toward the girl. 'Thank you, Min. It is very kind of you and I hope it will help us to understand this magical force you all have spoken of so often.'

Min bowed her head. 'Qi requires some belief to perceive its movement, and so Rumans and other people from the Occidens have trouble in its apprehension.'

'Indeed. I have much difficulty in its apprehension, much as I do with the aspects of Ia or the existence of the numen or other things that cannot be proven. But I thank you for it and am glad to have you once again in our company.'

Huáng cleared his throat lightly and said in his halting

speech, 'Tsing Huáng, the August One Who Speaks for the Autumn Lords, has called us to come before them. Three days. In the Winter Palace. And Min will be important then, Livia. She speaks the Rumi tongue as well as anyone and will be our valued translator.'

'The Winter Palace?' I asked. 'I've heard it mentioned before but why is it called that? Is it in Jiang?'

Huáng shook his head but it was Min who answered. 'The Winter Palace is situated just to the north and east of Jiang, on the old Spice Road. It was once a city itself, called Kinsai, but it is abandoned now. It is there so that the Autumn Lords will finally move toward cold and winter and rebirth so that they might find new vestment and not dwell too long in the fiery grip of Autumn. For too long have they been clad in the raiment of fall and harvest.'

'New vestment?' I asked. 'I do not understand what this means. Please explain.'

'You know of Qi. Those people of great Qi can move from one state to another as easily as changing one's garb. And the Autumn Lords are beings of great Qi.'

I frowned. 'This seems, as they say on the streets of Rume and Ciprea, hollow words from empty sleeves.'

'Apprehension of the Autumn Lords, like Qi, is difficult, Livia,' Min said.

I had grown tired of the obfuscation regarding the Autumn Lords and wished to be done with smoke and mirrors. The fey, oblique ways the people of Kithai dealt with straight-forward questions had begun to gall me. Yet, in the spirit of our reconciliation with Min, I let it lie.

My back hurt and Fiscelion was kicking with a vigour typical of the morning, pre-lunch. Breakfast seemed so long ago. I may have been, my dear husband, a tad cranky. This is something you have been spared, my moods, for I have always been even-keeled but now, as Fiscelion approaches, I know not which way my mind or heart will jump with any given thing, any random stimuli. The other morning, in the sun-dappled garden, I found myself crying as I watched the boys and Carnelia at their desperate martial labours. There was something so plaintive about Carnelia's face as she practised striking with the armatura sword, something that reminded me of when all the world was new and my mother and father were still married and we possessed an innocence forever lost to us now. But there it was, the lustre of it, on Carnelia's face, the way she looked with adoration on her brother and Tenebrae and most importantly on Huáng, whom they call *sifu* in deference and even obeisance. For so long I thought she was lost to that, to innocence and pleasure and everything new. Her face looked soft, full of light, and I loved her very much in that moment. And so, I found myself crying, caught in a shaft of light at a little bamboo table and chair, glad no one paid enough attention to me to notice.

Except the boy, Fantasma. He watched me with black eyes like pools, head cocked like a bird's, his jaw working in and around in his mouth. It was a disconcerting thing, finding him standing there by the footpath to the ponds, staring at me, shoeless. When I turned to fully face him, a lóng or some bird on the wing cried out and he craned his head upwards to find them in the sky and then wandered off.

I wonder about that child. At times he seems to have some sort of reason, some faculty for higher thought, and then he wanders off to stare at flying creatures or insects caught like motes in light.

But today we are packing and Carnelia orders Delia and Lupina around with much delight in her authority over them while my stomach – the great precious expanse of it – is in an uproar. I have enough strength to let blood and write this missive to you. I am upset because you are not here – and I am upset because I am not there. I bear you some anger, and my father and above all Tamberlaine. It is the wiles of man – of *men* – that have put us apart and you, all of you, bear some guilt in this. Women are too easy to push aside when they become more than simply silent childbearers. We are messy, yes, gloriously messy and from this mess spills life and in that we make you all, men, afraid.

But I shall not end this on that sour note.

Be careful, Fisk, and remain well so that when I return to you we can forget the sorry days that spun out in the interim.

I remain your faithful wife –
Livia

TWENTY-NINE

Fisk,

I am weakened, my love, so very weakened. But Fiscelion has come into the world, bright, bloody, squalling. And so very small. Our son is born. I must make this as short as I can because I have lost some blood and am so very tired. Carnelia let blood on my behalf and now, face furious and fierce and protective, watches me from the chair in our stateroom on the *Malphas*, holding our screaming child. He will not stop. It is hard to marshal my thoughts. Juvenus has given me some sort of drink that makes the *daemonlight* waver and throb and pushes back our child's wails and makes everything bright and streaked, as if light itself has become molten and smeary.

The swivel guns boom overhead intermittently, and despair – that peculiar despair that emanates from Hellfire that washes over us with each gun's report – ratchets Fiscelion's cries into new heights. I can barely think. I must move to somewhere more conducive to this letter and tell you what I have to tell.

The day after my last missive to you, my love, through the Quotidian to you on the Ides, we had packed for a short trip – three days, nothing more, as Huáng assured us the trip would take but a half-day at most by carriage, and we would be brought before the Autumn Lords on the day after that. On the

appointed morning we made ourselves available in the courtyard
of Sun Huáng's manse. An elaborate lacquered bamboo
carriage, absolutely massive, drawn by three sets of horses
champing and chuffing air through their moist noses, stood
waiting for us. Inside the carriage itself was a clever roof-hatch
and ladder that allow those riding on the inside to climb up and
onto the roof and sit on benches there to enjoy the breeze and
watch the city and country-side pass by. There were two armed
men at the reins of the carriage, both with Hellfire visible at
their waists though seemingly of Medieran design. And there
were two more at the rear carrying what looked to be ornate
yet deadly blunderbusses, each one festooned with ornate and
intricate warding and decoration. Where one left off and the
other began, it was hard to tell, though I fancy that Samantha
Decius would quite love to find one in her possession.

Our group carried Hellfire, of course, though not enough
should we be braced by a large group of ... Of ... I know
not who. I seemed to doubt that Sun Wukong's monkey-boys
would bother us but the people of Kithai and Jiang were and
remain an unknown quantity and there could be any sort of
fractious cadres of men and women – brigands, blackguards,
and shitheels. But looking on our group now there were far
more swords in the mix. Carnelia had her lovely jian tucked into
a sash at her waist and I had a moment's remembrance of her
as a girl in the atrium of our villa on the Cælian, dashing about
with a cat's tail from the pond and jabbing at servants and
slaves, cat's tail dander flying, shouting in her high-pitched voice
'I am Iulii of the People!' and giggling madly. Secundus and
Tenebrae also wore rougher swords, not as fine, though both of
Kithai design. Sun Huáng carried his cane – which was all the
man needed, truly – and Min too had a jian every bit as fine as
Carnelia's.

On the carriage ride Carnelia, Secundus, and Tenebrae

climbed up to the roof and rode there, chattering like roosting lóng – while Min and Huáng rode their own personal mounts, finely accoutred, with opulent saddles with long stirrups that guarded the entire leg and ended in near boots that made each horse easy to mount; a very clever saddle that had an girth system that used the neck and back legs as bracing through leather straps so that the saddle and rest of the extensive tack were firmly attached – and I was left in near solitude with only Fantasma and Lupina for silent company. The Kithai carriage had sliding rice-paper windows that we threw back, letting in fresh air and allowing me some breathing space. Fantasma tended toward somnolence in confined spaces and often his body would loll against mine or Lupina's (though hers less frequently) and my mood had swung, like an internal, invisible pendulum, toward a cranky lethargy as it is wont to do for long periods sitting. The countryside looked much the same as it had when we went to witness the goat offering to the *shé* outside the village of Uxi: terraced hills of rice paddies, small clutches of well-tended buildings huddling together, rough-spun farmers and farmwives trudging about on well-packed earthen paths, carrying water or baskets of rice or flagons of drink. Beyond the fields, woods covered soft hills and far, far beyond those, the barest blue intimations of mountains and cold. For us westerners, Kithai was massive and obscure, the veiled continent, and in most ways less was known about this land than, say, Ombra Terra, for at least Rumans and Medierans had placed that island country and the dark clouds always looming over it. Its borders had been mapped, if not the landscapes contain within. But Kithai was most unknown except to those Tchinee who had travelled its breadth.

I was forcibly reminded of this as we neared P'ing-Yüan, the Winter Palace. For a short while, it seemed we were following a burbling river (one of the many tributaries that flowed into the

Jiang) upwards into a forested rise, and then we were among the ruins, crumbling stone, collapsed roofs, choked with vines and reclaimed by ancient growth. The smell of burning incense and woodsmoke and the rutted trail through the ruinous land were the only indications of any sort of habitation here and it was with some surprise that we came upon the Dōngtiān Gōngdiàn, if I have transcribed that correctly – the Winter Palace of the Autumn Lords.

The land opened up, Huáng's horse nickered with agitation and pranced sideways, and the carriage slowed. From above, I could hear Carnelia and the boys nattering on, making exclamations of delight and amazement. I called for a stop and exited the carriage, tired and cramped and unprepared for what I was to see.

The scale of the Winter Palace beggared the senses. It was as if some great, horned, ridged turtle had climbed from the sea, out beyond Jiang, and, streaming water, lumbered here to die and within the great shell of the creature a palace had been created with thousands of halls and doors and rooms. It was a scalloped affair, with the ridged roof an angry collection of spines and spires and hard bristling points of white stone. Tamberlaine's palace could fit inside this building a score of times and have room to spare. The white stone towered overhead and the stairs themselves leading to the front gates were long and shallow and took a mile – at the least – to rise up to the entrance. On the stairs, I could see, were houses larger and once finer than the Cornelian estate on the Cælian, and around those houses, sat like discarded children's toys in the shade of Dōngtiān Gōngdiàn, I could see the minuscule figures of guardsmen in yellow sashes and blue uniforms.

'Ia's balls,' Tenebrae said, bristling some. A man will become angered if his sense of self-importance takes a blow. And indeed, the Winter Palace was built to cow mankind – of this there is no doubt. Whatever overweening ego built it millennia ago, it was to glorify a single man by making all other creatures seem insignificant. 'That's one hellacious jumble of stone.'

Secundus scratched his chin. 'Wasteful. Why over-build something to this scale? It's folly.'

Min drew her horse alongside the carriage and Huáng joined her. 'It *was* folly, this is true. When this dwelling was built, all of Kithai was under the rule of Yu Xia – a good Emperor, and a beneficent one. That was the year of the great storms, when the sun became black in the heavens, and the first of the Autumn Lords appeared. Yu Xia built this building as a kingdom within his kingdom, where all would be safe indoors, at night.'

'Safe? From whom?' Carnelia asked.

'The Autumn Lords, before the seasons settled on them and they became drowsy.' She waved her hand forward. 'We have quite a ways to go and the Great Stair is not easy.'

Tenebrae said, 'So, the Autumn Lords came to power as an invading force?'

Min shook her head. 'Things will become clearer, but the Autumn Lords are beings of—'

'Pure Qi,' I said. 'We have heard this before. But what does it mean and how can a nation of people follow leaders that they have to protect themselves from?'

Min gave a sour laugh. 'I have been to Rume, Livia. People always have to protect themselves from their leaders.'

'That's not what I meant,' I responded. 'The people of Kithai have to stay indoors at night!'

'The August Ones came to an agreement with the Autumn Lords.'

'How?'

'That knowledge has either been lost to history or concealed.'

Min and Huáng dismounted and we made our way slowly up the steps. Secundus and Tenebrae carried between them

428

the chest we'd brought from Rume. It was not heavy but they
began sweating, for the day was warm. The steps themselves
were carved from living stone and were worn with the passage
of millions upon millions of footsteps over thousands of years.
As we approached, I realized that the little clusters of houses
along the way to the front entrance of Dōngtiān Gōngdiàn were
more in the nature of a small village, rather than individual
domiciles – such is the scale of the Winter Palace. A village
can sit upon its front stoop and not be noticed. There was a
clutch of buildings, built upon one of the evenly spaced terraces
leading up, where the stone gave way to earth and opened up
onto a grassy field truncated four or five hundred feet away by
a retaining wall. There were horses and some odd woolly beasts
grazing there. The homes themselves were of stone and wood,
very sturdily made, with heavy shutters. We passed this little
hamlet and continued on. The sun passed behind the peak of
the Winter Palace's roof, casting us into shadow as we craned
our necks to get a better idea of the enormity of the building.

'Gods and *daemons*, I've never seen the like,' Secundus said,
looking about. 'I thought the stone was pitted and carious
by wear. It is not.' He pointed to a column. 'There is a great
twining dragon around that one, and all those marks...' He
squinted. 'I believe they are spearmen, doing battle with the
great beast.'

Huáng said, 'Yes, like much of our world, artists want to
focus on the details.'

'In this case, it was an Imperial edict,' Min said, a trifle sadly.
'The Autumn Lords can become bemused easily and that was
the hope in these frescoes and decorations. It is rumoured that
at one time, a hundred men were employed to keep the exterior
details painted in bright colours, almost lifelike.'

'To draw their attention, as with the *zhuìlì*?' I said.

'Yes. Yu Xia was fabulously wealthy and had many artisan

slaves who spent thirty years crafting the exterior of this place.'
She shook her head and pursed her lips, as if tasting something
sour. 'Ten thousand slaves died building it, a terrible waste of
the people.'

'You speak of them as if they're gold, or silver. A commodity,'
I said.

Min cocked her eye at me but did not react to my tone. I *was*
cranky. My feet were swelling with each step and I needed to
take a seat and cool them off with some water – would that we
were in Huáng's garden, where I could dip them in a burbling
brook.

'It is a strange thing to think of them as such, but all of
humanity is a resource,' Min said. 'I hope not one that is
squandered.'

'You sound like a Monkey-boy, Min, talking about the
nobility of common man,' Huáng said in an even tone, but I
knew him well enough now to discern that his tone was near
dripping with scorn.

'Grandfather,' Min said, 'I will, of course, defer to your
wisdom on this matter, but should we not value the workers, the
fieldhands, the craftsmen? Too many taken and there'll be no
rice on tables, no wine in cups. There is honour in wielding a
shovel or an awl as much as a sword, is this not true?'

'Of course, as long as one strives for excellence in this. But
what you say sounds like something Sun Wukong might—'

Min gave a small bow. 'I will cease speaking, then,
Grandfather.'

'That is not what I want. I simply wish you to be . . .' He
paused. 'Precise. Each word is a sword strike and what you say
reveals who you have trained with,' he said and looked at her
closely. She became tense, agitated. Something passed between
them then, though it remained unspoken.

We continued on until arriving near the front entrance. The

doors standing there were wood wrapped in burnished bronze, and five elephants standing on each other's backs could not reach their height, nor, if they battered the door with their bony skulls, could they have budged them. It would take a legendary dragon of old to open these doors, or siege engines. Or one swivel gun.

A small garrison – large enough for thirty to forty men – hid in the lee of a column and a pair of the men stationed outside, watching the steps, ran forward and made obeisance to Huáng, once it became clear an August One stood before them. Huáng exchanged some words with them and the superior officer, judging from all the golden bangles and braids on his uniform, barked an order at a subordinate.

'Tsing Huáng is being notified of our arrival,' Huáng said.

'Sifu, can you give us any idea what we can expect?'

Huáng remained silent for a bit, marshalling his thoughts. 'He will offer tea. We will accept. Food will be served. He will attempt to determine who is in charge of you Rumans.' He raised his eyebrows and looked between Secundus and myself. The point was not lost on me. 'Then Tsing will begin negotiations and it is then you will offer the present from Tamberlaine,' Huáng said, gesturing toward the ash chest with the gleaming steel lock.

Secundus said, 'You have the key, still, TennyShadow?'

'Of course,' Tenebrae said. There was an anxious air about the man and I think he might have flinched when Secundus called him "Tenny" but, my love, all of writing is done in reflection, and I colour the past knowing now what I know.

'Then what, sifu?' Carnelia asked.

'After you and Tsing come to some—' He thought, searching for the word. 'Some... accord... and Tamberlaine's message is opened, he will bring you before the Autumn Lords.'

'Why would we not deal directly with the Autumn Lords?' I asked. 'Can they not make decisions themselves?'

Huáng shook his head. 'They are beyond that sort of thought,' he said.

'So, in truth, you and all the other Huángs – you're their caretakers. *You* rule, not the Autumn Lords.'

Huáng bowed his head. 'Of course. I thought this was understood. The August Ones rule and keep the Autumn Lords docile. This is our way.'

I think I already knew then, but it was hard. About many things. A growing dread was upon me and part of it was the weight of Fiscelion swelling within, part was my outraged body swelling without. But some of it was the unanswered questions, the August One's oblique answers, the near mythic otherness of the Autumn Lords. I found myself furious, with Sun Huáng, with Tamberlaine, with the stupid look upon my brother's face, the self-satisfied complacency that animated Tenebrae's features. But Carnelia? She looked at everything as if she were a child taking in her first draughts of sense: vibrant colour, riotous sound, towering vistas. And that quieted if not quelled my mood.

The blue- and yellow-clad Tchinee guardsmen trotted back, all accoutred with Medieran Hellfire weapons, but none pointed at us. In the Territories when we – Carnelia, Secundus, Gnaeus, and my father – had first arrived in New Damnation from Novorum to experience the wild Occidens and the hardbit Hardscrabble Territories, we toured the fifth's garrison and I had heard a stout centurion whom you probably know, my love, by the name of Miklos Kohl, haranguing his men on 'trigger discipline'. He was quite a bear about the whole thing: 'Fools and sots, you do not wet your prick until the cunny is primed, do you? Do not waste Hellfire! Place your stinky finger in the cunny only when your gun is ready to fire. So it is with Hellfire.

Straight lines. Assume every weapon is loaded! Never mar any
warding or cover your bore with anything you do not intend to
be destroyed! No diddling the trigger guard until you have made
up your addled brain to fire, Ia-damned fellators!'

These poor Tchinee guardsmen did not have proper trigger
discipline.

If there's one thing that gives Rume primacy, other than the
natural strength of its children, it is its rigor in process. Every
legion is drilled in martial procedure and tactics, each soldier in
armatura and Hellfire trigger discipline. Centurions like Miklos
Kohl make it so.

Behind them came a flowery man, not fat, not thin, yet soft
around the edges, save his eyes and hard mouth. He was young,
at least in initial appearance, and he wore yellow silk robes,
split at the legs, so that the hilt of his jian and pistol stuck
out like diphallic erections at Ia Terminalia, and a hat in the
'button' style that many men of Tchinee favoured. He greeted
Sun Huáng without smiling and stood in the ineffable manner
of all lordlings, holding their bodies in such a way that makes
all other men seem inconsequential – never meeting their peer's
eyes, holding their bodies at an angle, crossed arms, speaking
over the others. I disliked Tsing Huáng almost immediately.

Sun Huáng spoke to Min and she bowed first to Tsing and
then paused to listen as he spoke for a long while. When he was
through, she said, turning to us, 'The August One Who Speaks
for the Autumn Lords, Tsing Huáng, bids you welcome to the
Winter Palace and Kithai and wishes to take tea with you, if you
would do him the honour.'

We all bowed and made sounds of acceptance, though Tsing
had already turned and stridden away, pulling a comet's tail of
guards behind him. We followed, passing through the entrance
beyond the towering bronzed doors, into an area of sunlight,
a veranda beyond the wall, luminous from clever openings and

mirrors high, high above in the palace's roof and teeming with lush flowers and fragrant plants that seemed to shy away from us as we hurriedly passed through, following Tsing Huáng. Walking through galleries with fabulous and foreign statues and frescoes – one depicting a bearded dragon the size of a warship wrought in lacquered wood and painted to the last detail, ferocious and lovely and bright – through dark columned spaces and echoing empty chambers that seemed cavernous and foreboding. Our footfalls were ominously loud on the marble floors.

The Winter Palace was beyond any definition of a building in Ruman culture, it was more like an abandoned roofed city. Some of the rooms we passed through were heavy with dust that only intermittent traffic swept clean paths through. Many of the painted columns were scaling, the once-bright colours dull and peeling away. In some halls, open sky showed through ragged holes in the ceiling, making bright, insubstantial pillars of dust-choked light in the midst of the space and casting its margins into shadow. The guards and Tsing Huáng picked up their pace there, and I was huffing and puffing trying to keep up as we threaded our path through boulder-sized bits of fallen roof. It was labyrinthine, massive, and utterly foreboding.

Eventually, we came to a great room, a space larger than any I've ever been in before. Above our heads hung thousands of *zhuìlì* floating dreamlike in the closed air. In the space of the cavernous hall, the paper lanterns seemed like bits of windblown trash arrested mid-flight – desperate and small, casting ineffectual coloured light like some child's bedroom toy.

There was a wall bisecting the great room, tall enough that it would require a ladder to scale, and the top of the wall stood adorned with countless rusty implements – spearheads, blades of all sorts, trowels, spikes, bent daggers, nails – packed so tightly and artfully it seemed like the maroon bristles of an

anemone or the hackles of an angered dog. The wall itself held
another mosaic representation of a great lóng, and looking at
it, I thought of my father and his love of all the myths of the
great wyrms. As an inveterate hunter, he would find no prize
greater than that creature, save maybe the *shé* Nágá. He would
be disappointed in the vermin lóng shitting everywhere in the
city of Jiang.

There was a golden door, barred, and it was manned by a
contingent of Hellfire- and sword-bearing guards. Tsing and his
retinue escorted us into a smaller building – another building
within a building, a good three hundred feet away from the
wall – a raised construction crafted mostly from rice paper in
bamboo or wooden frames, and it was there we settled in and
took tea, a deathly dull affair. Tenebrae and Secundus looked
relieved to set down the ash messenger's box from Tamberlaine
and even Lupina and Carnelia appeared to be relieved that we
had finally ended our passage through the palace. Fantasma
seemed unfazed. Sun Huáng had wanted to leave the boy behind
in Jiang, but he came along at my insistence. We had saved his
life, together, Huáng and I, and it did not feel right to put him
aside. And truly, for all his dreamy wanderings, the boy was
self-sufficient and not any labour.

Yet. I felt uneasy and discomposed. My feet hurt and the
strangeness of the Winter Palace niggled at me, and I was not
able to remain at ease enough for deep, analytic thought. And I
was hungry.

Servants appeared; some bearing candied fruits, nuts, and
other delicacies; others bearing ceramic bowls of steaming
fragrant lemon water for washing our faces and hands. Tsing
Huáng beckoned us to sit in front of him – he had taken his
place on a rather simple and spare raised dais of gleaming black
wood, and perched himself there like some great raptorial bird
settling into its eyrie, his legs wide, his hands on his knees so

435

that his elbows jutted out aggressively. We settled in low-slung couches arrayed in a half-circle around the dais. I felt that for someone who was technically an administrator – a Huáng, He Who Speaks for the Autumn Lords – and someone coming to a meeting with emissaries of a country at least as powerful and bellicose as his own, elevating his own status was a mistake. While I give no credence to the idea that the Cornelian clan can trace its lineage back to the Mater herself, or Tamberlaine to Pater Dis, it is still something to come from a sovereign nation of such power as Rume and be seated below an administrator, a Praetor – a jumped-up Quaestor. But, my love, I was cranky and, as I have said, disliked the smug man almost immediately.

Soon servants brought an ivory tray with ornate jade tea cups – big blocky things – and Tsing Huáng went through the process of brewing the tea and making rather a spectacle of pouring for us. The tea – a green liquid with a slight bitter taste – did nothing to cool or ease me and I was rather pleased when another servant came round with a bottle of rice wine. I took a cup of it under Lupina's disapproving stare.

After the tea was cleared away, Tsing Huáng said, through Min, 'Who will speak for Rume?'

Secundus shifted in his seat and opened his mouth to speak, but I said, 'The Cornelian family will speak for Rume.'

Min dutifully repeated this to Tsing Huáng in the Kithai language. He questioned her closely and she indicated me and Secundus when she replied. Tsing nodded.

He thought for a long while, then said, 'This is acceptable. I have had correspondence with your master.' We waited and he pulled a small scroll from his sleeve and spoke again. (I will, my love, leave out the mechanics of the conversation.) 'On 6 Ides of Nyarus, in the year 2636 by the Ruman reckoning, the Ruman warship *Hellaphor* fired on two vessels of Kithai – *The Imperial Beauty of Evening* and *The Ship of A Thousand Colours*

– destroying them. Three hundred and twenty three sailors of the navy perished, including Ngo Dyong Huáng, The August One That Commands The Autumnal Fleet, and his family and retinue. Do you have any contention with this statement?'

Secundus glanced at me and said, 'No, we have no contention with that statement.'

'The cost of those two ships is placed at two hundred thousand yín each, not to mention the loss of life.' As she translated, Min's voice hardened, as if she was either conveying Tsing Huáng's extreme displeasure or was becoming perturbed herself. Our history with the girl made it unclear. 'From Rume and the Emperor Tamberlaine the Autumn Lords demand a formal apology to be cast in stone and placed in the centre of Jiang for all to view.'

Secundus said, 'We understand this demand and will consider it closely.'

'In addition,' Tsing Huáng said through Min, 'we will want monetary recompense.'

I raised my eyebrows. 'How much did the Autumn Lords have in mind?' I asked, my voice neutral.

Tsing waved and a servant trotted forward, bearing a different scroll. A larger scroll. A much larger scroll. The servant brought it before us and began to unroll it. On the left were the strange ideogrammatical signifiers of the language of Kithai. On the right of the scroll, in a great unending column, were figures in the speech of Rume and identifiable numbers. High numbers.

After both Tenebrac and Secundus unravelled the scroll to the end and read the final damage – somewhere north of ten silver talents – Secundus' jaw tightened and Tenebrae looked dazed.

'And,' Min said after a flurry of sounds came from Tsing Huáng, 'the Autumn Lords require the instruction of Rume's Engineers. You will provide ten of your finest firegardeners – these men and women of the Hellfire – and send them to us to live for a period of no less than five years, so that we might learn their secrets and implement their lore.'

Tchinee had had their own summoners and engineers for at least a thousand years, but it took Ruman ingenuity and innovation to make it a deadly science.

The expressions around the room looked quite grim. Even the boy Fantasma seemed to notice the mood and watched Tsing quietly but with some concentration.

'And in return?' I asked. 'What will you concede to Rume?'

'It is recompense for the crime of Shang Tzu. You will assuage your – and Rume's – guilt.'

'And then you'll ally with us?' Secundus asked. 'You will make a binding treaty not to take up arms against Rume on land or sea or assist those that do?'

'That is what we must discuss.'

'Then let us begin,' Secundus said.

After Min had translated for Tsing Huáng, he dismissed Secundus' last statement by waving his hand. 'He Who Speaks for the Autumn Lords says the day has grown late and he is tired from his travels. He bids you to be escorted to the Chambers of Waiting Dawn for the evening to rest. On the morrow we will have a discussion, you can present your message from the Ruman Emperor, and then you will be brought before the Autumn Lords.'

Secundus frowned and Carnelia, grown impatient from all the waiting, *harrumphed* a little. She had her lovely jian and was fingering its hilt avidly. The guards had allowed us to keep our weapons; I had my sawn-off on my leg and it was, I admit, contributing to my discomfort.

'That sounds fine,' I said, standing. At my movement, Tsing Huáng faced me. He might have been surprised at my actions, I could not tell. But I wouldn't wait for his by-your-leave. 'Come,

come, family. Friends. Let us retire.' I looked at Tsing Huáng
and said clearly, 'Instruct your men to lead us to our chambers.'

After Min translated, his eyes narrowed and he pursed
his lips, looking at me closely. Tamberlaine might be able to
threaten and intimidate, but I've stared down *vaettir*. I am of
Rume. This man would not cow me.

Also, I wanted a bath.

So I met his gaze until he gave an almost imperceptible
nod. A score of liveried guards trotted over and we all made
our way out of the walled hall and back a few chambers the
size of villages until we came to a stair that rose into the dim
heights of the ceiling. There was a litter-bearer for me, and
one for Sun Huáng, and I gratefully piled into the cushioned
seat and allowed them to bear me up. We came to an opening,
streaming with golden light, and into the bright air of a late
afternoon that smelled of jasmine and was full of the hum of
insects. The roof of the Winter Palace held little mansions and
keeps – some crumbling, some standing proud – all wrought
of the same stone as the building and created in the scalloped
style so common in Jiang and Kithai. Someone, centuries ago,
had brought uncounted tons of soil from the ground far below
and created a rooftop ecology here, around the Chambers of
Waiting Dawn. There was soft grass and wispy flowering trees,
ponds with cattails and a fragrant herb garden filled with
greenery and another plot for the growing of vegetables. The
guards led us to the building and we found our rooms. It was
a bare building – the stone was intricately carved but there was
a dearth of furnishing here, unlike the opulent cosiness of Sun
Huáng's demesne. The great rooms were empty except for a
table and heavy wooden chairs, a gallery with tapestries and
simple stone benches, bedrooms dwarfing their single beds and
tables. The Chambers of Waiting Dawn were built as though
giants had lived here, left long ago.

Carnelia, Lupina, and I bathed in a cool sunken tile pool
in a gazebo surround by bamboo and broad-leaved ferns, and
then, once clothed again and feeling refreshed, joined the boys
and Sun Huáng and Min (who did not bathe with us) for a
light dinner. I helped myself to another glass of the wine and
Carnelia and the boys got a little inebriated, pouring enough of
the rice spirits down their gullets to make even the most hard-bit
legionnaire dry and dispirited in the morning. On the bright
side, drinking the rice wine did not make Carnelia's teeth go
roan. I retired to bed when they drunkenly decided to take up
their armatura and practise in an outer gallery.

Quietly Lupina and I made our way back to our assigned
rooms, passing through a bare but lovely gallery that looked out
over the gardens. *Zhuìlì* filled the sky above the Winter Palace
with their light, like low-hanging stars. On the grass below,
surrounded by falling blossoms, stood a robed figure, very tall,
wearing a Kithai button hat. He stood there, staring up into the
sky, watching the coloured lanterns drift lazily on the eddies of
wind. There was a strange bemused lull to the man – for it was
a man – and I was reminded forcibly of the dreamlike states that
the boy, Fantasma, fell into. At first I thought it was Sun Huáng,
or possibly even Tsing, but the man's arms were longer than
both and he had a rangy, angular look to him.

'Is that Huáng?' Lupina asked before I could shush her. I
do not know why, but in that instance, I felt disturbed by the
unknown man's presence and uneasy at the thought of him
discovering us here, watching, from above.

The figure started, and shifted, bending his knees and
extending his arms in almost a crouch. He craned his head
around on a long, gimballed neck, searching.

I put my hand on Lupina's arm and drew her back, away from
the gallery's balusters into the shadows, out of the light of the
stars and the *zuhìlìs*. But the figure loped toward the building

out of our sight, moving faster than I would have thought anyone could move. Pushing Lupina back, I dug under my dress and came up with the sawn-off; I thumbed back the hammers with a soft metallic *click* in the night air. We put our backs to the stone wall.

Down the gallery, a black-robed figure vaulted into the space there, casting a long shadow on the wall. His fingers were long, sharp, and flexing as if a large cat readying itself for a pounce. He moved fluidly into a crouch, softly and quickly moving down the gallery toward us, disappearing as he passed through columns' shadows, and reappearing in the pale moonlight.

Lupina gripped my arm tightly, and I shrugged her away, readying myself.

As he neared us, I could hear a sniffing sound and with alarm realized he was smelling for us. A high keening sound issued from his long neck, like an infant that's touched a red-hot stove. Twenty paces away, he stopped. Craned his head. Turned slowly to face me.

My love, at this time I thought of you, of our son. How I could be like you. I thought how you might act in this situation.

I stepped from the shadows and levelled my Hellfire at the man's chest.

In the light, I could see him better. He was wasted, thin, black-eyed and mouth open, and his chin was mired in gore. Sharp teeth. He was very tall.

A *vaettir*, my love. An Ia-damned stretcher.

There is no churn to a stretcher's features before they move, no twitch, no jerk, no change of expression. As you well know. They simply *change* states. Perfectly still. Moving. And so it did: leaping forward, hands out, bloody mouth open, and its robes whipping behind it. The sound of the sawn-off in the gallery echoed, booming, and its forward movement stopped. It flew backwards as if being jerked by a tether. The keening sound rose into a scream and I could smell the thing – incense, perfumes, an acrid hint of urine – blanketed now by the smell of brimstone. That old sinking sensation of releasing the *daemonic* filled me, yet I thumbed back the other hammer and raised the gun again.

The *vaettir* whipped and thrashed on the floor and then, screeching again, vaulted upright and flung itself out and away, over the balusters and into the air of the garden, the dark robes furling behind it like bat wings, ruffling. I raced to the rail, sighted down my barrel but it was moving too fast and I did not waste the shot.

In moments, Sun Huáng burst onto the gallery, moving like lightning toward where Lupina and I stood, Min fast on his heels. Tenebrae, Secundus, and Carnelia followed behind, swords bared. The guards followed after, trailed behind by the boy, Fantasma, blinking and looking lost.

'What has happened here?' he said, breathless. It was the most discomposed I'd ever seen the man.

I remained silent for a long time. Lupina looked at me closely, eyes narrowing. 'A man. On the gallery, waiting in the dark. For a moment I thought it was—'

'What?' Huáng asked, face intense.

'Nothing,' I responded, shaking my head. Secundus and Tenebrae seemed very puzzled. 'I fired once but he moved too fast and fled into the garden.'

Huáng went to the balusters and looked down. He deflated some, then, and put his free hand on his back and winced. 'I will send guards into the garden to see where this intruder might have gone. Possibly it was a brigand or thief looking for a trinket to steal.' He sagged and looked tired in the moonlight. The *zuhíli* were gone, scattered on the wind. All was quiet. 'I am not too old for speed, but I am too old not to feel it afterward.

Good evening.' Min took his arm and escorted him back down the gallery.

When Huáng and Min were gone, I said to Secundus simply, 'Stretchers.'

Of course there was argument and discussion, but by the end I had convinced them – with Lupina's help – that what I'd seen was truly *vaettir*. Tenebrae speculated a long while on why the stretcher would be wearing clothes and a hat, since most of the ones we've witnessed in the west were clad in skins and the cast-offs of their victims. We came to no answers then, but agreed there was more to these creatures than we understood. For a long while, we discussed the possibility that it could have been a tall *daemon*-possessed man and, truly, I could not answer with any definitive proof it was not except I didn't *feel* that was the right answer.

In the morning, they brought us back before Tsing Huáng, but this time we did not take tea in the rice-paper building. Descending from the brilliant sun-ripened world of the roof into the Winter Palace below felt like entering a crypt. The dragonback wall gate was open and we passed through into the other half of the great chamber. While I was rested and young Fiscelion quiescent within me – indeed, I felt quite buoyant and hale, my hands and feet swollen no longer – the events of the night before weighed on my mind as we made our way beyond the spiky partition. Again there was a hall within the hall, and this time the guards stopped us before entering and, with brusque hands, took our weapons – removing pistols, *jians*, and knives and placing them in an ante-chamber on a silk-lined table lit by guttering candlelight. They did not, however, take my sawn-off, which was strapped to my leg. Something regarding my condition prevented them from searching me, a sort of vestigial sense of propriety. The head guard, a weasel-faced man with sparse facial hair and a squint, looked at me closely, taking note of my stomach, and waved his men away.

The building beyond the dragonback wall was strange – stranger than any other we'd been in. Here there were artisans painting, and sculptors moving larger stone works with block and tackle. The building seemed more like a theatre than the hall of rulers – there was what we Rumans would consider an atrium, every inch of which was illuminated by lanterns and candles so that the oily smoke from them rose and pooled in a high open space ringed in lesser galleries. A great set of red double doors stood closed, with guards outside, and waiting in the atrium were numerous people that were not guards but seemed more likely to be performers, dressed in blousy, bright silks like acrobats might wear and accoutred with strange devices I could not discern the usage of.

We were led on silent feet up a set of lush carpeted stairs into a side room – Tenebrae and Secundus once more carrying the ash messenger's box from Tamberlaine. The room was massive and golden and centred on a long table with a map of Kithai at the centre of it and brilliant with numerous *daemonlight* lamps and lanterns, casting a buttery-yellow glow that seemed different from Ruman engineers' *daemonlight*. The map was intricate and I guessed it would be worth thousands of sesterius to any man or woman of military mind back in Rume, but it was so detailed and large it was hard to take in all at once. It was a map for those who knew the land. Tsing Huáng greeted us through welcoming hand gestures and bade us sit and take our rest. Min, looking at her grandfather, took her seat next to Tsing to better translate his words for us, and Sun Huáng positioned himself on the other side while Tsing Huáng's slaves and servants bowed and brought cushions.

Of the Ruman contingent, we sat together, first Secundus,

then me, Carnelia, and Tenebrae. Lupina waited, standing, watching the room and Tsing Huáng's guards with a frown. All nobles have servants and so Lupina was not remarked upon and had clutched Fantasma's hand to keep him from toddling about, and for the moment the young man was calm and quite manageable. I examined the art in the room, various paintings of battles and farmlands, dragons and warriors, and a series of finely wrought ceramic busts set in alcoves in the room's wall — each one a man resembling Tsing Huáng. Possibly his ancestors; most likely former August Ones That Speak for the Autumn Lords.

Tsing said through Min, 'Now we are to the business of treaty.' He snapped his fingers and one of his servants hustled forward with a scroll while others moved through the room, around the great map table, with drinks and light foods to break our fasts. Another servant brought a sheaf of parchment and an elegant brush and inkwell. Tsing Huáng handed the scroll to Min and said something in Tchinee.

Min looked to us. 'Tsing Huáng asks that I read aloud his proposed terms of treaty and then you may discuss.'

Secundus and I indicated she should continue. She did, reading in a slow voice much of what had been discussed the day before.

Once she had finished reading Tsing Huáng's terms, Tenebrae said to Secundus, 'The Emperor has authorized me to accede to monetary demands. To an extent. These terms fall within those limits.' He pursed his lips. 'He will be more upset about the apology on display in Jiang than the money itself, though the money smarts.'

Secundus rubbed his chin, thinking. He turned to Tsing Huáng. 'We need assurance you will not take up arms against Rume in the future, or assist its enemies by granting them resources or passage.'

Tsing spoke to Min and she said, 'You mean the Medieran King, Diegal.'

'Yes,' Secundus said, simply. 'We are here to procure a treaty so that the world doesn't erupt into war.'

After Min had translated that, Tsing Huáng laughed. 'It is doubtful there is much you can do to stop it. But treating with us now is a good beginning.'

'We have noticed you have had some dealings with Mediera,' I said, pointing at the guards stationed at the door, Hellfire rifles held loosely, pistols holstered, jians tucked into their belts. 'Those are not Ruman make.'

'Yes,' Tsing said. 'Until now, Rume has proven reticent to sell its munitions. Despite our long history of firegardening, we do not have the physical engineering capabilities that Rume or Mediera possess and so it remains an esoteric study, fit for the few initiated in its secrets.'

'And that's what it boils down to,' I said. 'We need assurances you will not assist Mediera and you want our technology and engineering.'

Tsing Huáng looked at me very closely as Min translated for him. When she finished, a tight smile touched his lips and he gave me the barest intimation of a nod.

'The Hellfire and engineers, that is easily quantifiable. But for your part,' I said, 'and Kithai, what do we have other than your word you will not assist Mediera?'

Tsing laughed as Min translated. 'Indeed! All treaty-making is based on trust.'

Tenebrae shifted in his seat and, from around his neck, removed a chain and key and tossed it in front of Secundus. It clattered to a stop, drawing all eyes. Tenebrae looked somewhat pale, and discomposed. 'I think it is time to open it, Secundus.'

'Why are you shaking, Tenebrae?'

Tenebrae, for his part, swallowed heavily and then gave a

nervous laugh. 'Secundus,' he said, and there was the totality
of their relation in his expression. As long as Tamberlaine's
box remained locked and the message unread, they were free to
be friends and lovers. Tenebrae's wrists remained unblooded,
the Quotidians silent. Both he and Secundus could forget that
Tamberlaine was his master and great father, as he was all of
ours. But his sacred duty as a Praetorian was to safeguard the
Emperor's designs. Once the ash box yielded up its contents,
those contents might not make Tenebrae and Secundus rejoice.
Some ineffable puff of air locked tight inside the box, the air of
Rume, might be anathema to their relationship.

Tenebrae is not a likeable man – he is a handsome man, and
an aggressive one, and an able one – but I felt for a moment a
great sadness for him. He looked at Secundus with such fear and
self-loathing, the pain twisting across his face almost too much
for me to bear.

Secundus placed his hand on the key, lifted it, and opened the
box.

From inside, he removed a small piece of paper embossed
with the Imperial signet, an eagle bearing a flaming sword in its
claws.

Secundus read in a flat, emotionless voice, 'From Tamberlaine,
Emperor, Lord and Master, Best and Greatest, Ruler of Myriad
Kingdoms, Wielder of the Secret of Emrys, Sacred God of the
Latinum Hills – a Message to the Autumn Lords, Rulers of Far
Tchinee, Kithai, Cathay, or Whatever Else You Wish to Call
Yourselves.'

Min's voice was low, translating Secundus' words, an incessant
drone filling the room as my brother spoke.

'My greetings. I am sorry I cannot be there myself to conduct
this meeting. As Emperor, it is often my duty to look unpleasant
realities in the face, to accept the hard truths of rule.

'The hard truth in this situation between Kithai and Rume

is that there is no foundation upon which a structure of trust can be built. Regarding the Shang Tzu incident, mistakes were made by Rume. Possibly mistakes were made by Tchinee and its emissaries. Right now, trust is what we need between our two nations so that an accord can be reached.

'So, it is my thought that I bind myself to you and bind you to me. My son and heir Marcus Aurelius will take to wife a Tchinee woman of noble birth, chosen by you with the input of Sun Huáng, who knows me. He will sire children upon her so to join my family with yours. Furthermore, I hereby declare that I have formally adopted Secundus, Livia, and Carnelia Cornelius. From this moment forward they are my heirs – in addition to Marcus Aurelius, who retains primacy – and are in direct line of succession to the throne after my first-born son. Of the women, choose between them. The younger is unattached, and the elder is obviously fertile. All previous bonds of marriage are hereby dissolved and dismissed.'

Secundus paused. I felt as though I had been shot. My stomach cramped. There was a stunned silence. Secundus remained quiet. The parchment shook in his hand. He did not look away, but a great struggle warred within him.

'This is my offer, and I hope it falls on reasonable ears. Everything I do, I do for the continued safety and prosperity of Rume and her citizens. Sincerely—'

Secundus dropped the parchment, letting it fall toward Min and Tsing without finishing it.

'I did not know,' Tenebrae said, opening his hands, helplessly. 'I was instructed to only open the box in the presence of the August Ones. How could I have known?'

'Then why did your hand shake?' Secundus asked.

'Because I had reason to fear.'

Secundus turned away from him. Carnelia stood, looked about the room, sat down again. I was silent for a long while.

Tsing Huáng watched us avidly, an oily smile on his face. Sun Huáng looked uncomfortable.

I focused on my breath, in and out. In and out. Fiscelion shifted and kicked inside me. I felt my mind going away, unable to focus on any one thing for too long.

'Wine,' Sun Huáng said, and then he repeated it in his own language. Servants bustled forward, bringing ceramic bottles of the pale rice wine.

After a long while, Tsing Huáng broke the silence. 'Your Emperor doesn't understand the situation here. While his offer is very kind, we must consider it very closely.' He bowed to us. 'Shall we continue? Sun Huáng said you had issue with the figures for the two ships?'

Secundus seemed to shake himself out of his reverie. In the course of a single letter, he'd become second in succession to rule the Ruman Empire. And, my love, Fiscelion swelling in my stomach, is also in that line of succession.

Know this, love: we are wed, our blood is joined by the wound we both bear, and no force on this earth can put us asunder. I am, and will remain, your wife. As will become clear.

Tsing Huáng had sense enough not to push us Cornelians – though the smirk on his face made him even more unctuous and greasy than usual. He was the snake in the garden grass, already triumphant.

'Let us discuss figures and your somewhat... specious... valuation of the two ships,' Secundus said, setting his shoulders. His ability to set it all aside awed me, the turmoil within me was so great. His face, still smooth with the softness of youth – he is just twenty-four – seemed a mask, hiding a greater confusion and anger.

Picking up the scroll with the figures Tsing Huáng had presented us with the day before, he ran down the list. 'Item one – you have valued an unspecified cargo at 10,000 yín, which converts to something around 3,500 denarius. What was this cargo?'

Tsing Huáng's eyes narrowed and he clapped loudly for his secretary, who rushed forward. Secundus, Tsing, Min, and the secretary put their heads together and began discussing money in quiet tones.

Carnelia looked at me, tears welling in her eyes. I moved down the table from where I sat to join my sister, ignoring Tenebrae.

'Oh, sissy,' she sobbed, putting her head on my breast. 'How could he?'

'Tamberlaine?' I asked. 'Very easily.'

She sniffled for a bit. 'That terrible, terrible man. How could he just dissolve your marriage like that? You are pregnant!'

The fury that had been building in me rose some. 'Father plays us as pawns. Tamberlaine plays our whole family.'

Carnelia's eyes widened in realization. 'Tata is childless now.'

'Nonsense. He has us.'

'But we've been "adopted".'

'Against our will. I refuse to believe we're powerless in this situation.'

'So, if this man—' She waved her hand at Tsing Huáng. 'If he decides to take you as a bride, you'll fight?'

'I will make that decision when I must. As will you,' I said, brushing back her hair. 'Tamberlaine offered this without knowing the situation here with the Autumn Lords and the real rulers, these August Ones.' I shrugged. 'They call us "foreign devils", sissy. I doubt they're jumping to wed and bed you and I.' Looking about, I noticed something. 'Where is the boy?'

Carnelia sat up. 'Fantasma? I saw him twiddling about near that tapestry a while ago.' A thick wooden door, carved as two carp wheeling underwater, stood open.

I stood. 'I will fetch him,' I said.

'I will come with you,' she said.

'No,' I said, waving her back. 'I need to clear my head.'

I walked around the table and approached Min, asking if there was a water-closet behind the carp door. She nodded, giving me directions. I went through the open doorway, entering a long arched hallway, stone-floored with a red runner carpet that gave the impression of a tongue dashing away down a long gullet. Each wall was replete with images of dragons, birds, insects, flowers, flora, fauna, dogs, cats, men and women, and other more hideous creatures, *daemonic* faces leering with tongues caught between gnashing teeth and avaricious eyes. Faded tapestries hung limply, stirred by no breeze, their colour leeched away. After passing a stone bust of who I could only assume was another of the August Ones Who Speak for the Autumn Lords (this one notable because it was a woman, and lovely) I found the door with a moth and moon motif carved into it and with great effort wrenched it open and performed my ablutions in the lavish, candlelit silken washroom.

Afterwards, I was puzzled. I hadn't seen Fantasma, and worried he'd wandered off in one of his dreamlike states, staring into lantern light or tracing frescoes with his index finger. I turned away from the room of negotiations and walked deeper into the building within a palace.

Following the throat-like hall, I found it curved to the left and into the deep guts of the building. My feet were silent on the carpeted stone, and a hushed expectancy filled me. It was as if I were internally performing one of the Eight Silken Movements, or the whole world was, drawing in a great breath and pausing before the moment of exhalation. The release. The silence drew out with each step forward. I put my hands on my stomach.

Eventually, I came to a crossing of passages in the throat of the building, and there, thirty paces to my right, stood the boy, Fantasma.

He stood above a pair of the Tchinee guards crumpled on the floor. His face was smeared with blood, and the rich red stuff dripped from his lower jaw as if he'd been buried deep in gore. In bloody hands he held a *jian*, obviously pilfered from his victims.

My heart sank. I'd been a blind fool. I had wanted to believe that the boy was an innocent and the village women superstitious fools. But I was the fool instead. The boy was every bit of what the women in Uxi had believed.

Seeing me, the thing in the shape of a boy raised his head and his glittering gaze fixed upon me. His mouth spread apart in a grin, showing two rows of sharp teeth.

As I dug frantically at my leg to retrieve my sawn-off, Fantasma turned and raced down the hallway, holding the pilfered *jian* off to the side, angled away from his body. He moved like an arrow, a lance, a striking bird. His movement was almost too fast for my bewildered eye to follow. In a blink, he was out of sight. I chased him, running as fast as my thickened body would allow, my gun in hand.

My mind raced. Why would Fantasma lurk in our midst, docile and only now show his true face? Why kill now? I thought of how we found him. Monkey-boys. I thought of Sun Wukong, and how Fantasma had followed his order. How they had watched us. Sun Wukong.

The passage made a hard left and narrowed. The ceiling pressed in more tightly and the walls possessed less ornamentation and frillwork. The buttery *daemonlight* lanterns stood farther apart, lit at fewer intervals. This area, lined in doorways, seemed a more functional area – there were scents of herbs and spices, and behind one door I could hear two women chattering excitedly and the clatter of wood and straw on flooring. I imagined brooms being swept across stone.

I could run no more. I walked as fast as I was able down the corridor, until I found one door standing suspiciously open. Looking inside, I could see a very narrow passage, the width of a single person and devoid of *daemonlight* lanterns. Yet the passage was illuminated dimly by what seemed to be openings along its right side. I entered, holding the sawn-off in front of me.

Twenty paces in, I came to the first opening. It was a rectangular inset, vertically aligned, and too small for a person to pass through. Leaning in, I put my face to the opening.

A massive hall hundreds of feet across was bathed in buttery *daemonlight* below, full of golden statuary and carmine wall hangings. I was somewhere high up near the vaulted ceiling. Countless *zhuìlì* hung in the air, caught in languid rotation as if trapped in a sluggish eddy. On a raised dais stood ten thrones, each one tremendously tall, and upon each of the ten thrones sat long, bony figures – *tall figures!* – clad in flowing silken robes and absolutely motionless. From my great vantage, it was hard to make out details of their features. Below them, acrobats wheeled and turned somersaults and the faint strains of music from a clutch of players reached my ears, faint yet unmistakeable. Some of the throned figures had their faces tilted upwards, toward the floating lanterns, and others watched the acrobats vacantly, unmoving.

Abandoning the window, I moved as quickly as I could down the tight passage. It curved to my right as if hugging the arc of the vaulted ceiling. I came to another inset window and peered through it. Closer now, the Autumn Lords were easier to make out. One of them seemed to be staring directly at me, but surely that was only a coincidence. And where was the thing we had called Fantasma?

I was about to pull away from the opening and go on in search of the creature when suddenly, below, one of the throned figures surged into movement, hopping from its seat and falling upon one of the acrobats, mid somersault, amid cries of 'Chiang-shih! Chiang-shih!' As the Lord flew through the air, I was reminded of the attack on the Chambers of Waiting Dawn gallery the night before. He landed squarely on the acrobat, bearing the poor girl squealing to the floor, and bit at her neck with what I could see now were sharp teeth. And his size! Only with the Autumn Lord on top of the Tchinee performer did I realize how much larger he was.

The Autumn Lords were *vaettir*.

My stomach sank such that I felt as though my descent to hell had begun, my love. Worse than the firing of swivel guns on the *Malphas*. The whole centrepoint of the world had moved.

Guards rushed in as acrobats and musicians scattered. There was a great chatter as they surrounded the silken Lord that feasted on the acrobat's blood. The girl's screams died and the guards, bearing crescent-bladed poleaxes, surrounded the *vaettir* and waited. The other Autumn Lords remained still – watching *zhuìlì* bob on the arteries of air, bemused. They were stuporous, in a languor. I realized these creatures were old, ancient, and tired of the world. The most innocent of things could attract and fix their interest. Hence the elaborate and colourful ornamentation, the paper lanterns and fireworks, the barred windows and doors. The people of Kithai worship the Autumn Lords as gods made flesh, but they fear them too. And well they should.

After a long while, the *vaettir* lord unfurled itself from the acrobat girl and slowly staggered back to its seat, blood dripping from its open mouth. It sat back down on its throne and tilted its head back, staring at the brightly lit ceiling and *zhuìlì*, and stilled. Two guards picked up the body of the girl. The others backed away from the dais, calling out for the acrobats to resume their gyrations. They did so, tentatively at first and then regaining vigour as if spurred on by desperation or fear. Most likely both.

Horrified by what I saw, my mind turned back to the boy. I turned and, holding my gun in front of me, followed where the passage led, passing more windows and coming to a small opening large enough for a man to pass through that led to some sort of suspended scaffolding alongside the vaulted ceiling's circumference, for maintenance and replacement of the hanging *daemonlight* fixtures. There was a small wooden door there, standing open, as obvious as an arrow.

I took a step out on the scaffolding, suddenly vertiginous. At least a hundred feet above the floor, my heart froze and I found myself immobile. I could not move forward, only back out. There was a boom from outside the room and more yelling. Looking around, I spotted the thing that we called Fantasma, crouched not far from me, looking down at the scene below, the *jian* held loosely in its hands. Sensing I was there, it turned its face to me slowly, still grinning. The blood on its jaw had dried and its visage struck me as pure malevolence and mirth. It was the mirth that truly frightened me.

It turned back to the scene. The guards below were running to the great doors that stood barred. There was yelling from without the room, and more banging. Something was happening beyond the confines of the hall.

With a high-pitched keening – a laugh, I realized – Fantasma leapt from his perch before I could take aim. Indeed, I had almost forgotten I held my shotgun, so stunned and alarmed I'd been at finding myself on such a high and exposed precipice.

Fantasma arced through the air, snatched a *daemonlight* hanging lantern and swung farther out into the room, changing trajectory and releasing, pulling into a ball, arm out and sword flashing, and landing with a hiss on the dais with the *vaettir* Autumn Lords.

With one fell movement, so fast I had only the impression of what happened rather than any true visual experience, Fantasma lopped off the first lord's head, leapt up onto the back of the next throne and drove the *jian* deep inside the next *vaettir's* body cavity through the hollow of the neck.

The Autumn Lord that had feasted on the blood of the acrobat took the sword through the eye. The next lost its head.

The guards began yelling, screaming in high jangling phrases. There were more bangs and deep booms from outside the hall – someone was trying to get in and from the alarm being raised, it did not seem Tsing Huáng's men and the guards of the Winter Palace had sent them an invitation.

Fantasma had slain eight of the *vaettir* lords before any of them could be roused enough to engage with the assassin in their midst. The first of the remaining Lords screeched horribly and leapt out of its throne toward Fantasma, matching speeds, yet the thing that had once seemed to be a boy whipped about like a snake, and the Autumn Lord's arm had detached from its body, spraying blood. And it was curious, my love, that I could feel such emotion, joy even, at seeing the Autumn Lords perish, even though it was by one of their own hands.

The last Autumn Lord changed tack, leaping up and backward, snatching at one of the carmine wall hangings with its clawed hand and then quickly hauling itself up the wall like a lizard scaling the face of a rock. Fantasma howled, mouth bloody and jagged; dashed forward and ran sideways along the wall, so quickly its forward momentum did not allow gravity to take hold, until it too reached a long tapestry and scaled up the wall as well, faster than imaginable.

The Autumn Lord vaulted away from the wall hanging and grabbed the *daemonlight* globe hanging from the ceiling. For a moment I did not understand what was happening, it was all moving so fast as the *vaettir* climbed higher.

But it was coming to me. If it reached where I stood, the *vaettir* lord would kill me in passing, a single blow, wrenching my head around backwards with one powerful twist of a clawed hand, or just tossing me from this great height. When it passed, I would die, this I knew.

Fantasma pursued, armed with a wicked grin and a bloody sword.

Swinging back and forth from the light, its silken robes hung like a bell ringing, the Autumn Lord gained momentum and then released, flipping through the air. It landed on the scaffolding with a great shudder and in a wild instant I feared the wooden platform would shear away from the stonework of the wall and both of us would plummet to the floor.

It must have been thinking the same because it did not move immediately. It just rose to its full height – ten, maybe eleven feet, *oh so very tall* yet not as tall as the stretchers in Occidentalia.

When it turned, my gun was up and out, centred on its chest. Even so, it was almost too fast for me.

I pulled the trigger.

As the despair of Hellfire filled me, the silver and holly shot of the Imp round was travelling several hundred miles an hour, such dizzying speed that the Autumn Lord, in all its alacrity and ferociousness, could not outrun or dodge. The shot exploded in its chest, blowing it backward and off the edge of the platform, where it wheeled blindly and fell, clawing and screeching.

Fantasma landed then on the scaffolding, a lesser thud. I was awed that we had lived in such close confines with the creature, this leering vicious thing. How many times had this 'boy' rested its head on my breast? Placed its hands on my stomach as if awed by the life contained within? Was it only the hunger of the *vaettir* that stirred it and gave it life?

Again, it smiled at me, its blood-brown lips peeling back

from its teeth. It raised the gore-slicked sword in a mockery of a salute and flipped backward into the air as I fired my second and last Hellfire round at Fantasma.

I did not wait to see if Fantasma dispatched the remaining Autumn Lord.

I ran.

Secundus and Sun Huang were already up and pacing the room when I returned, the latter barking orders at serving men and women. The booms were audible even through the walls of this building inside a building. They started when they saw me and Secundus raced over. My alarm must have been writ large on my features.

'What's wrong, sissy?' Carnelia asked.

'There were two guards. Dead,' I said. Yes, Fisk my love, I am able to lie with some facility at times of stress. I could not let them know I was the hand that shot the Autumn Lord. 'And some banging and booms from rooms deeper inside the building.'

Tsing Huang exploded with a flurry of foreign sounds and Min responded in kind. Tsing hopped up, trotted to the outer door – the one we had entered through – and, collecting all but two of his guards, dashed off, away.

Once he was gone, I said, 'We have to leave. Right now.'

'What?' Tenebrae exclaimed. 'Why? Where is the boy?'

'Fantasma is no boy. He is—' I thought about him, his actions, his movements. 'He is *vaettir*. I know it sounds strange. I know!'

They exploded with questions. I held up my hands. 'And there's more. The Autumn Lords. They are dead.' I didn't explain to them that they too were *vaettir*. I thought that if we lived through the next few moments there would be time enough for stories.

'The Autumn Lords, they are dead? Truly?' Sun Huang said, his face grave and intense.

'They are. Slain by Fantasma. It was—' I struggled for a word. 'Brutal. But there's more. There was yelling and loud noises from outside the hall of the Autumn Lords. Someone was trying to get in. Guards maybe. I don't know.'

Sun Huang tugged at his bottom lip. He cocked an eye at me. 'Did you have anything to do with their deaths?'

'No,' I said. 'No.'

He said nothing for a long while. Then finally, he said, 'Livia is right. We must flee. The Autumn Lords were the balancing point for all of Tchinee society—'

As I opened my mouth to respond, the floor shuddered and there was a deep boom somewhere off in the building.

Sun Huang said, 'Come. We must go. Swiftly. I can get us out of this building, but beyond, in the Winter Palace itself, it will be much more difficult.'

Out in the halls, the white-haired old man led us swiftly down passages and corridors I had not seen before. At one point, he halted and said quietly, 'Wait here. Come with me, Shadow,' and after a few breathless moments, they returned nearly staggering under the weight of our guns, knives, and swords.

As our party took up our weapons, Sun Huáng said, 'Someone is in the Winter Palace. I heard guards yelling for reinforcements. We cannot trust that those we encounter here will be allies. Indeed, you as Rumans will all certainly be considered suspicious.' He bowed his head. 'Yet, I have agreed to be your host – and protector – and I will let no harm come to you as long as I breathe, should even my kin come to molest you.' He waited, watching us, letting that sink in, that he was willing to kill his countrymen to keep us safe. A rare man, Huáng.

'Come, we must flee.'

Down stairwells, through smaller cramped passageways – much like the one leading to the scaffolding catwalk – we hurried until we came to a small wooden door, heavily barred. After a moment, with both Secundus and Tenebrae helping, Sun Huang unlocked the door and we exited the building into the tremendous confines of the Winter Palace.

Sun Huang listened quietly for a span of time before leading us into the dark. The sound of metal on metal, screams of the dying, and the occasional report of Hellfire sounded in the hall. My terror lay stuck in my throat like a palpable thing. We passed through the dragonback wall gate, running into a group of rough-looking men, not in the livery of Tsing Huáng or any other August One, that I could tell. They bellowed harsh words and tugged at weapons at the sight of us.

Sun Huang moved like light flashing. With a quick sidestep and lancing movement of his hands, his sword was free of the scabbard and flashing out at the guards.

'Behind me!' he said, slashing the nearest guard across the face.

I fumbled for my sawn-off but realized I'd emptied it back in the hall of the Autumn Lords. Tenebrae, not heeding Huang's command, jumped forward, firing his Hellfire pistol into the guards and slashing with the *jian* that he held in his left. Two guards fell away, though others could be heard yelling as they approached. They were not going to let us leave unharried.

Sun Huang moved through them and I understood why he was named The Sword of Jiang. It was as if he was dancing, yet his movements were simpler than any dance. He moved like a martial seer might, already knowing how his opponent would attack. This man, he speared through the belly; this man, pierced through the thigh in a major sanguiduct; this one struck through the throat. The ground grew black and shiny with blood; the air filled with the scent of faeces and fear.

Carnelia drew her sword, as did Secundus.

'Don't be fucking idiots,' I said, grabbing their shoulders and tugging them back. Lupina held a large cooking knife and looked for all the world as if she knew how to use it. I imagine you don't come of age in the Hardscrabble Territories if you can't protect yourself. 'If you have Hellfire, get it to hand and stay by me.' I took two steps back.

Tenebrae, for his part, was quite deadly. And Min whirled about like some deadly dancer, felling men twice her size with parries and snake-like strikes. Between Tenebrae and Min, they accounted for a good number of the ruffians before they drew back to recoup and call for aid.

'Monkey-boys,' Sun Huang said, looking closely at one of the dead. 'The Palace is under attack. Fantasma was of our party. By now Tsing will have set his guards to either kill or capture us. We have not much time. We must reach the Garden of Windows before they can. Otherwise, we will be trapped inside the Winter Palace. Go,' he said, pointing. 'That way. Min, you lead. Shadow and I will trail.'

'I would fight with you, sifu,' Carnelia said, raising the *jian* he'd given her.

Sun Huang touched her cheek softly. 'I know you would, child. And well. But you must remain safe. I would not have you in more peril.' When he drew his hand away, there was a smear of blood on her cheek. 'Min, lead,' he said.

'Follow me,' said Min, and she moved into the dark beyond the torches and *daemonlight* on the dragonback wall.

We hurried interminably through the dark. At times I thought I could go no farther and during those times I would call for a stop and our group would obey, though I could tell Min was as impatient as Lupina was solicitous. She had taken to standing very close to me and at any moment of instability the dwarf woman would take my arm and drape it over her shoulders, bearing as much of my weight as she could.

After what seemed like hours, we came into the Garden of Windows – that sun-filled room with lights and mirrors in the roof, full of ferns and greenery. There it was that Sun Huang and Tenebrae caught up with us.

'A large group,' Tenebrae said, panting and breathless. He bled from a cut on his arm but otherwise seemed fine. Sun Huang's robes were spattered with blood, none of it his own. 'They come quickly. Too many for us. We killed as many that we could identify as having Hellfire as we could. Go to the steps before the main entrance and we'll make our stand there. Carnelia, you'll finally get to use that beautiful thing.' He pointed with his chin at her sword.

A hundred guards burst into the Garden of Windows before we made it to the entrance steps, howling and chattering and calling out.

As we took our positions behind Sun Huang and Tenebrae, the contingent of guards rushed forward. Sun Huang shouted at them.

Min, who also had drawn her *jian*, said, 'He tells them he is the Sword of Jiang and is not afraid of giving death. Or receiving it.'

The guards drew back. Secundus, lifting his pistol, began firing. The guards rushed forward, some with the crescent-bladed poleaxes, some with swords, some with bludgeons. Sun Huang flowed between them, blade flashing, leaving toppling bodies in his wake. Tenebrae, his Hellfire ammunition exhausted, engaged with three men bearing swords. More guards swarmed around them, and Min and Carnelia began striking.

Then there was the sounding of horns and from behind us, at the top of the steps near the entrance to the Winter Palace, a hooting coming from many throats. Turning, I looked behind me, and streaming down the steps were men clad in brown shirts and trousers, wearing ridiculous button hats, hefting clubs and daggers and spears.

More Monkey-boys.

Min yelled over and over at the Monkey-boys, pointing at Tsing's guardsmen. They rushed around us, not attacking us, and fell upon the remaining palace guards with a furore.

They entered the fray, hooting loudly, flailing about with drunken grace, rods falling, clubs swinging. The guards fell back, and Sun Huáng and Tenebrae harried their heels, felling more with sword strikes. The battle seemed to prolong, to stretch, to seem infinite – though, thinking about it now, I know it was only a matter of minutes. In my head there was such a clangour, it was deafening, but part of me understands what a small, pathetic little conflict it truly was, a mere skirmish between threadbare and ill-trained men. With the exception of Sun Huang and Tenebrae.

It was then I heard his moaning and at first I thought Tenebrae might have been grievous wounded. But then Carnelia began screaming as well and reason fled.

On the steps lay Secundus. He had taken a spear to the chest. My brother is dead.

Ears ringing, a numbness came upon me and my sister's screeching fell to silence and the white noise of men went away and I walked like a ghost to my brother's body and took his head in my hands and smoothed his hair and prayed that his soul was judged fondly by Pater Dis and welcomed into the great feasting hall of Ia.

In the end, Lupina had to pull me away.

Sun Huang told two Monkey-boys standing nearby to bring Secundus' body and we turned and climbed the stairs and walked out into the light of day, onto the grand entrance to Dōngtiān Gōngdiàn, the Winter Palace.

*

Even in the shadow of Dōngtiān Gōngdiàn, the day was bright in comparison to the dark interior. On the great step to the entrance, someone waited.

Sun Wukong stood with a grim look on his face as we made our way into the light, surrounded by Monkey-boys and bearing my Secundus' body.

'Hello, Li Jing,' he said to Sun Huáng, bowing. 'My brother.'

Sun Huáng did not bow. He stopped and remained still, holding his sheathed *jian,* and squinted his eyes at Sun Wukong. 'Hello, brother. It has been many years since anyone has referred to me by that name.'

'It is fitting, then, I be the one to remind you of it, now that the name given you as a Huáng of the Autumn Lords has become meaningless.'

Sun Huáng bowed slowly, crossing his hands over his heart as he did so. Even with his *jian* in hand, he did it elegantly. 'You have taken from me everything I am.'

'I am a thief,' Sun Wukong shrugged, grinning. 'But I never take more than my victims can bear.'

'Sun Huáng was all I was. I was a simple man and, I think, doing good for our people.'

'Truly all you are, brother?' Sun Wukong said. 'You still hold your *jian* and the world still knows you as the Sword of Jiang. The other name, the slave name, wasn't becoming of you. You can continue to work on behalf of the people.'

I followed the conversation in a daze. Carnelia had ceased wailing and Tenebrae looked lost. Lupina guided me to a stone where I could sit. Li Jing – it would take me a long while to think of him as this – shook his head. 'There was stability with the Autumn Lords. Now, every Huáng will be scrabbling to consolidate power. You've doomed us to civil war. Tsing Huáng will most assuredly take control of the army and—'

'Ah, here Tsing comes now,' Sun Wukong said, raising his eyes up to the roof. From the upper reaches of the Winter Palace, a figure moved, crawling across its face like an insect, or reptile. It moved faster than one might think possible across the intricately carved surface of stone. As it closed on our position, it pushed itself into the air with a great heave, flipping over and over and landing before Sun Wukong. The figure bowed and placed the severed head of Tsing Huáng at Sun Wukong's feet.

'Excellent work, Tizio,' Sun Wukong said, prodding Tsing's cheek with the toe of his boot. Tsing's eyes stared vacantly into space.

'Fantasma!' Min exclaimed.

'Yes, my niece. You have grown lovely. Come give your great-uncle a hug.'

She did not move.

'You have killed *my* brother!' I said. It popped out of my mouth before I could stop it. 'You and this . . . this thing,' I said, pointing to the *vaettir.* I spat at his feet. 'Nothing you can do to undo that. And Rume—'

Sun Wukong came to stand near me. 'I am sorry, Livia, for your loss. The Monkey-boys were not to harm you—'

'You caused this! Your pet murdered the Autumn Lords, making us your accomplice!'

He looked at me for a long while and something in him sank, seeing the expression on my face. 'I fear I have done great good here today. And great evil. I am so sorry for your loss.'

Fantasma turned to look at me. Its face was blank – no smiling or triumphant slaverous grins now. His face was brown with dried blood. It said something to me in the language of Kithai.

'The chiang-shih says "I am no pet",' Min reported.

Fantasma barked another phrase, and pointed to Lupina, who stood clutching my arm.

'What did it say?' Carnelia asked, wild-eyed. She ripped her *jian* from its scabbard and with a bound was at Fantasma, lunging. The sword took the creature in the side, but it was fast and vaulted away and came to stand ten paces to the side. It looked at the blood coming from its wound and then back at Carnelia.

'We took you in, you bastard,' she said. 'It was all a lie. And now Secundus—' A fury took her over and she raced forward again, toward Fantasma, but he was too quick for her and leapt high, coming to rest on top of an ancient stone marker on the side of the steps like some great raptor.

It said something again pointing at Lupina. Min who remained quiet for a moment and then she said, 'It said, "I know you of old. We are kin".'

Lupina said, 'The Hell we are.'

'Come,' Sun Wukong beckoned. 'My boys will keep the guards from spreading this news to Jiang. We have horses waiting. We must return these Rumans to their ship. It would not do for the Ruman navy to begin firing their tremendous devil guns at our city. You have a way to signal?'

Tenebrae went to Secundus' body and removed a necklace from around my brother's neck. After putting it on, he clutched at his chest – at his heart – and nodded.

'Then follow, all. The time of the Autumn Lords is over and what will come, will come.' The old man turned and began the long journey to the base of the great steps and the road back to Jiang.

Sun Wukong and his pet *vaettir* left us when we reached Jiang, bidding each of us farewell in turn. Li Jing had turned pensive on the ride back and only grunted in response. We stopped at Sun Huáng's manse long enough to gather belongings and flee to the Jiang Bund. A throng of Monkey-boys escorted us.

At the wharf, Li Jing commandeered a junky and set us in it.

Once out in the bay, Tenebrae cut his palm with a folding knife and dripped the blood on the signal, which began to glow, shudder, and rise. With a jolt, it shot high into the sky, leaving a trail of brimstone-scented smoke behind it and, at some etheric height, raced south out over the Nous Sea, toward the *Malphas*.

And then it was gone.

That is the end of my tale, my love. Except for this.

The *Malphas* steamed into the bay. On board, the gunners and lascars stood at attention as Juvenus greeted us. 'We've been paced by a score of Kithai warships since coming into this Ia-damned muddy bay. One had the temerity to fire upon us with ballista. They are following. We need to move quickly.'

'I would put this accursed land behind me,' I said.

Tenebrae wordlessly nodded. Turning, he barked orders at lascars to take Secundus' body below deck. Carnelia gripped her *jian* and glared about with an awful look upon her features

'Agreed,' Juvenus said. 'These damned Tchinee are taking a decidedly bellicose stance, the idiots. Mr Gridlæ could use some range-finding practice.' He snorted, making the whiskers on his face cant and shift. 'Your quarters await you,' he said. Spying Secundus' remains he cursed. 'Ia damn these bastards all to Hell,' he said and stomped off to see to his charge.

Li Jing cleared his throat. 'I must leave you now, my girls,' he said, looking at Carnelia, Lupina, and me.

'No, sifu,' Carnelia said. 'Come with us. I would have you with me, always,' she said.

The old man smiled. 'I am tempted more than you know.' He shook his head sadly. 'But my brother is right. There is much work to do here now that the Autumn Lords are no more. Wukong and I can be a strong factor for peace. And order. Without us, there will be war.'

'There may be war, anyway,' Carnelia said. 'Secundus—' Her voice broke and she struggled to get herself under control. 'Secundus was Rume's emissary. And now he's dead.'

Li Jing frowned and drew her into an embrace. 'All the more reason for you to go, my student. You must let your Emperor know what has happened here.' He sighed and looked to the city of Jiang and the shore. 'Kithai is not your enemy. Now, I must make sure it does not destroy itself. Go with my love and great affection and sorrow,' he said. He turned to me. 'And you . . .' He turned to me.

But I did not notice. My water had already broken and the first of the convulsions had begun.

Fiscelion Secundus was born on the crest of a wave, and came squalling into this world. We're born into pain, and we live in it. It makes us strong for what comes after and what we must do while we are here.

I love you my husband, with all my heart. Our son will grow strong in the waiting days as we travel home to you. I will not return to Rume. I will not bend the knee to Tamberlaine. I will see you soon, before fall turns into winter in the Hardscrabble.

Ever your loving wife,
Livia

THIRTY

WE MADE OUR WAY EAST, toward *Dvergar*. The skin on my face had blistered and peeled and Bess was cantankerous and ornery as all get out. Between the two of us, we made a sorry pair, pus-weeping burns and all. Behind us, the smoke of Harbour Town's destruction still rose in a tremendous cloud, two days later. It hung in the sky and even with our backs to it, its presence felt like a blow about to fall upon us.

We took on water and a little hardtack at a small sodbuster farmstead on the westernmost edge of the Hardscrabble and I took rabbits when I could with my sling, but out here, in this arid flatland, the rabbits were meagre and small and no herbs grew to sweeten the pot.

Fisk had taken to outriding, even at night. The *daemon* hand he once wore round his neck, even though it was in its case, stirred in him a great agitation and he found it hard to rest.

The fire was low by the time I'd finished Livia's letter and I sat there smoking, watching the embers glow and spark, deep in my thoughts about the kindred of *dvergar* and *vaettir* and the idea that there was a child of Fisk and Livia in the world now.

When I'd come to the end of her message, I will admit my heart fell, and I offered up to the numen and old gods of wind and stone a prayer that Secundus' spirit would join with theirs and become part of the great breath of the world. He was a good lad, and I miss him still.

The dawn was lightening in the east when I heard the sound of hooves.

Fisk came into camp, dismounted, and snatched up the rest of his kit.

'Shoe, we got company,' he said.

'Who?'

'Who you think? Beleth. Riding at the head of a pack of Medieran horsemen, all of them carrying a bit of damnation with them.'

I cursed for a while.

'All my backtracks and manoeuvring aren't working. They're onto us. We've got to ride and ride hard. Make for *Dvergar* and hope your Neruda fella will grant us safety.'

He didn't need to tell me twice.

It took only a few minutes to tack up Bess and pack my gear.

We rode just as the morning sun broke over the gunmetal blue-grey line of the Eldvatch Mountains.

'Ia damn it, Ia damn it all to Hell,' Fisk said, over and over, as we rode.

Acknowledgements

My thanks to Sensei Tanner Critz for speaking with me about the history and philosophy of swordfighting in Eastern Cultures;

My thanks to Sensei Chris Perry for his friendship and guidance in the martial arts;

I am very glad to have found a community to be a part of in the Gouitsu Dojo.

Thanks to Max Gladstone for some translations of phrases into Romanized Chinese;

My thanks to Andrew Liptak for an essential reference to a naval battle of the Spanish-American War;

My thanks to Myke Cole for his steadfast assistance and support, his encouraging words, and for keeping the streets of NY and the east coast maritime waters safe;

Many thanks to Pat Rothfuss for his kind words, support, and facial hair grooming advice;

As always, thanks to my wife for supporting me in my labors, both during the day and at night. Without her, Occidentalia would not exist.

Turn the page for an excerpt from the sequel:

Infernal Devices

1

Kill Their Horses

I can show you what is left. The ruins of Harbor Town, in Occidentalia. Of Novorum. Of Rume, the immortal city, herself, if you wanted to walk among those charred stones, if you wanted to see what the machines of war, the machinations of man, and what Hellfire can wreak. And, maybe, someday, when you are ready, we will take you so you can learn. And by learning, rule. – Dveng Ilys

'Ia damn it,' Fisk said. 'Ia damn it all to hell.' His horse, the new one, had froth working out from under the saddle-blanket and champed the bit furiously in her mouth. Fisk wore a pinched expression – he was irked. Like most men accustomed to the rigors of the Hardscrabble, he liked to do the chasing. Not be chased.

'They're what?' I asked. 'A half day behind? This godsdamned place has a million hidey-holes we can bolt to,' I said, sweeping my arm to take in the cracked and sundered expanse of the eastern reaches of the Hardscrabble. The bright, brittle sky became hazy at the edges, this late in the Summer, and the heat was on us something fierce. Bess barked and coughed occasionally, due to the burns on her rump from the titanic blast of Hellfire that destroyed Harbor Town.

And now the Hardscrabble, and soon the rest of Occidentalia, would be lousy with Medierans. Like the ones pursuing us – Beleth and his new mustachioed friends.

'Half-day, yes,' Fisk said. 'Maybe more. But he had some daemon-gripped stretchers with him, leaping this way and that. If he sets those damned dogs on us, we'll be in a spot.'

'We can't keep this pace forever,' I said. 'Don't have enough water and too far from anywhere or anyone who might give us succor. We could make for the Bitter Spring, maybe.'

Fisk thought for a long while.

'We'll rest the horses for a bit, over there, in the shadow of those rocks. Then we'll push hard on to the The Long Slide, and wait.'

'You're getting sly in your old age, Fisk,' said I. 'An ambush?'

'That's about all we can do, unless we discover that half-century of legionnaires toddling about the Hardscrabble.'

'Don't hold your breath,' I said.

We rested the horses in the shade of a crag of sundered rock as the sun rose. I stripped Bess of tack and saddle and tended her wound as best I could – water, maguey sap slathered on her arse, and kind words. She blew hot air through her nose and nipped at my breeches with yellow-green teeth, her stubbly mane bristling. Fisk tended his own mount and we gave them what water we could though there was scant water to spare.

The brutal sun rose in the sky and the shadow where we rested the mounts narrowed and shrank so that we ended up pressed against the rock-face, moving to stay out of hammer-blow light. Weariness passed over me, and all over my body the injuries and insults pricked memories – burns on my hands, ears, and back of my neck recalled the incandescent flame of Harbor Town's destruction; the throbbing knot on my scalp where he sapped me, Beleth and his daemon-gripped stretchers; my abraded wrists, where they bound me – Gynth, the vaettir, fighting, saving me; my hunger and thirst, the taproom of militarized dvergar. Beyond that, and before, I could not recall then. I passed a hand over my stubbled head where the hair was almost burned away.

Everything's gone to Hell. And my old carcass was just a mirror of it.

Not much shadow, by then. Even the horses seemed to feel the growing tension as pursuit neared.

'This is Ia-damned ridiculous,' Fisk said, finally, his boots on the line where rock-shadow met brilliant Hardscrabble. 'Let's go.'

Bess and Fisk's mount weren't ready to move in the heat of the day, but our urgency swayed them, though Bess hawed something fierce. I loved Bess dearly, but she was still willful, like any beast, or offspring, possessed of abnormal intelligence where parents simply want for a docile and accepting child.

When I had her tacked out, I took the saddle and she chuffed hot air and chucked her head in annoyance or agitation from the chase, I could not tell. Her smarts were hard to fathom.

We lit out, taking it easy. Taking it easy, urgently. No canter, but alternating between trotting and walking, over the Hardscrabble. It was a matter of hours before the Long Slide hove into view and then a matter of hours more before the ascent was well made.

'You thinking what I'm thinking?' I asked Fisk as we took the rise. It was a strange

'We wait here for them, there's no other approach except up the Long Slide or miles around.' He looked back behind him, over his horse's rump. Far in the heat-warped distance, something moved on the horizon. Horses, maybe. 'We kill as many as we can. If he's got daemon-gripped with him, kill them first and then, once it's just us . . .' He paused, thinking. 'Just us men, well, we know what to do then.'

I assumed he meant more killing. 'We need water. We can't hold out pinned down here for days on end.'

Fisk nodded. 'If it comes to that, then, you'll ride on to the Bitter Spring. But it won't come to that.' He looked at me closely. 'You let the stretchers and the daemon-gripped get right on top of us, Shoe. Close enough for a kiss,' he said, pulling his carbine and checking the rounds. He thumbed each one's warding, checking the integrity. He'd restocked his supply, recently, in Harbor Town – possibly the work of Samantha or one of her junior engineers. Some paltry comfort there, that she was here with us now, even if it was solely through her handiwork.

I laid out my six-guns and began unloading and reloading them.

Almost to himself, Fisk said, 'Yes. You kill the stretchers and daemon-gripped my friend. And I'll kill their horses.'

A Thousand Tomorrowless Days

It is the stillness of the mountain lake you must find within you so that at the moment the moon rises, its face is mirrored in the waters. Then action is equal. The still will always master the restless. – Sun Huang, The Sword of Jiang

The Hardscrabble: the tawny gold of the dirt from which sprang the dvergar and vaettir, emerged from some fathomless, impossible origin; the countless skeins of bramble wrack veining through the gulleys and mountainside, the impassable brakes and soars of gamble and ash and keening pine, traced now with the passage of native creatures – shoal aurouch and turkey buzzard and licker fish suspended in eternal movement, to rise and fall, to eat and be eaten, in a steady progression of a thousand tomorrowless days; now comes the tread of man, first the Medieran boots flickering across the Hardscrabble plains, then northmen for a year or day, for a blinking moment and again Medieran for years following the mapless miles of the Occidentalia wildernesses; blood, the piping hot blood of the creatures hunted and harvested by man, dvergar, and vaettir alike, spilling into the dust to be joined by the blood of Medieran and Ruman and northmen, watered with blood, drenched in the hot stuff, at the clawed hands of vaettir, and the swords and guns of men. Dispossessed, too, the land: the dwarves held it, and the stretchers hunted it, ravenous ghosts, not knowing the bounty and treasure they had and with the coming of the Ruman, Hellfire in one hand and whiskey in the other, lost it; dispossessed of land and identity too, not knowing where to belong and only realizing it maybe when the Rumans, when *we* gave them something to fight against. Dispossessed of home and hearth, but never the vaettir, never the stretcher, the genius loci, the leaping lord. It is he that is the possessor of the land, and the West, and while he might die, he will never relent of it or be dispossessed.

Dispossessed I am, now, too. We sail to Rume.

I have no home but where Fisk is, and he is lost to me.

Juvenus, pale-faced and sweating, entered our stateroom after a polite knock. He'd put on his suit and even worn a tie, though we'd become inured to the sight of the man sweating in shirt-sleeves. The Nous seas grew high with towering swells and the weather had turned cold, but the innards of the *Malphas* were always hot. Hellish hot.

I greeted him as Lupina fed young Fiscelion and Carnelia stretched, sore from her *armatura*.

'Miss Livia,' the captain said. Behind him stood two lascars bearing carbines and frightened, taut expressions. He cleared his throat and scratched at his arm. The bare white of a fresh bandage peeked from the cuff.

'How may I help you?' I asked. I pointed at his wrist. 'You come to me freshly bandaged, and not by my hand, so I assume you have had use of a Quotidian and have received a message and that it bodes ill for us.'

'I am here,' he said, clearing his throat and tugging down his cuff to cover the bandage, 'To relieve you of your Quotidian device, madame. By order of Tamberlaine himself.' He looked uncomfortable and his voice pitched toward nervousness, if not villainy.

'And what reason did he give?' Carnelia said, straightening. She had sweat plastering her hair to her neck and was dressed in the loose, flowing garb that Sun Huáng had insisted they – lost Secundus, Tenebrae, and her – train in. Carnelia placed her hand on her *jian* that she'd negligently sat upon the dresser. The two lascars shifted their weight.

'He is Emperor and our Great Father,' Juvenus said. The words were wrote, and came from him like stones falling from one's mouth. 'He need not explain himself to me.'

'I am of noble blood as he,' Carnelia said. 'Cornelians can trace our history back to the gods, just as Tamberlaine.'

Juvenus lowered his head. The muscles popped and worked in his cheek. 'I am sorry, Livia, Carnelia. I am sorry. You are to be placed under guard until we reach Rume. This is his command.'

'Is Tenebrae also placed under guard?' I asked.

Juvenus paused. 'No, he is not.'

'I see. We are to be corralled home to become pawns on the knightboard of Tamberlaine once more.' I went and took Fiscelion from Lupina and kissed his fat cheek. He cooed. 'Are we to be confined below decks?'

'No, madame,' Juvenus said. He gestured to the lascars standing behind him, white-knuckling their carbines. 'You will have an escort should you want to venture about.'

'Guards you mean,' I said.

'Escorts. You remain my guest and will receive all due honor and civility that the *Malphas* and I have to offer,' Juvenus said. 'I am sorry it has come to this.'

'You are sorry,' I said, thinking of how the folk of the Hard-scrabble used that word. 'I have never seen someone as sorry.'

Juvenus, bowing his head, said, 'Please send me a message if you have any needs and I will make sure they are addressed.'

'Wonderful,' said I, though I can only imagine that my tone

belied my words. 'Thank you. You may go,' I said, waving a hand toward the passageway behind him.

He stood there a long while, looking agitated and sheepish. Eventually he screwed his courage up to say, 'But you have not turned over your Quotidian. I cannot leave until you do.'

Handing Fiscelion to Carnelia, I retrieved the argent-warded box. It smelled of sulfur and blood and woodsmoke and when I handed it to Juvenus, I felt heavier rather than lighter because of it.

When Juvenus was gone, Carnelia began cursing and clenching her fists, maybe because she felt some great furor at being controlled once more by the patriarchs of Rume or maybe because she knew that by forcing us to return to Rume Juvenus was consigning me to my sundered marital bond, Fiscelion bereft of a father. I did not know. Lupina watched implacably, sucking her teeth.

'Sissy,' said I. 'We must come to an accord.'

'What? And let them do this to us, again? Let us be corralled like beasts? I think not,' Carnelia said. Her neck was flushed red, as if the anger in her belly grew and moved through her like fallowfires across the shoal grasses.

I approached her and lowering my voice, said, 'I do not know if they will stoop to eavesdropping on us, but I say to you now I will *not* submit. *We* will not submit to Tamberlaine. I will not remain in Rume. The emperor has said I am divorced, but I am not here,' I struck my breast with a fingertip. 'And I will get back to Fisk and Occidentalia.'

'I will stay with you, sissy, unto the ends of the earth,' Carnelia said.

I embraced her then, which was made awkward by Fiscelion being held between us, and he squawked and made infantile coos and gurgling noises.

'Oh, sissy, how you have changed,' I said, looking at her. There were lines at the corners of her eyes, and a fierceness in her disposition that was marked and new. She had always been fierce, and wild – but before, it was the fierce outrage of uselessness, of the possessed and now she was like me, dispossessed, divided from a home, her fierceness had meaning, and usefulness. And she had her *jian*, her talon. And her wits, which had never been inconsequential, but the pettiness had fallen away and left something altogether remarkable.

She smiled, but it did not touch her eyes. 'And what of this accord?'

'We must wait and watch for a time to escape. I doubt we will be allowed off ship at the Ætheopicum port when they take on fresh water, wine, and supplies. And so, we will find ourselves at the Ostia pier before the Ides to be returned to the society of our father and the rest of Rume.' I touched her hand. 'We must appear entirely content with our situation until the moment we must move. We will dote and exclaim over our father, as he dotes and exclaims over Fiscelion, and do whatever Juvenus asks with absolute aplomb and grace.'

'Ah, what a bitter role,' Carnelia said. 'Where's the fun in playing nice? I would spit in their faces. Or,' Carnelia said, whetting her finger in her mouth and then drawing circles in the air with it as if it were a sword, 'Better, prick them with my sword, sissy.'

She smiled, and it was not wicked, but avid and predatory.

'Yes, sissy,' said I. 'I know you would. I hope you will not have to.'

Carnelia was quite for a long while, thinking of it. Fiscelion reached up and played with her hair with fat, pink hands and gurgled.

'We must raise no suspicions of our intent,' I said. 'And be compliant.'

'And, mendacious.'

'Yes, mendacious. Yes, coy. Yes, docile, if we are to have a chance,' I said.

'Too much of my life have I been so,' Carnelia said. 'I do not want to be so again.'

'Would it ease the chafe of having to be so to know you will be working toward that break?'

'A little,' Carnelia said, and wandered over to the settee, where her hand found the *jian's* hilt as if of its own accord.

'Can you do it?'

She thought for a while. 'Livia, once you denounced Rume and parentage and everything else in front of our father, and tossed it all into his teeth. I watched you then with a little girl's grubby heart, only thinking of my own pleasure and ease. But when you said those words, something stirred in me that I didn't know was part of my make-up. And I was jealous and envious and terrified for you all at once.'

'I remember,' I said.

'It has taken me a long while to get to that place, myself. But I am there now, like you, without home and without destiny except that which I make and I will not give that up lightly.'

'So, you will be compliant until it is time to not comply?'

Carnelia withdrew her sword and held it up so that it caught the *daemonlight*.

'I will,' she said, looking at the blade and turning it this way and that to catch the light as she once might have a mirror.

Writing becomes habit. Over the long months separated from Fisk, I've become used to taking down a history of my events of the day, my thoughts. And now the Quotidian has been taken from me, it is to myself I write, instead of my love. Indulgent. Indulgent and necessary. A much less bloody endeavour, altogether, and I have not yet decided if that is a good or bad thing. Sometimes, when I write, it is like whispering my secrets into great Occulus of the Caelian, the eye of Rume peering toward the heavens, the hushed voices of its visitors echoing strangely. Other times, it is like a cough, a reflexive exhalation – all my love, my hate, my worries, my concern for Fiscelion the Younger – all exhorted in a mad rush of words that I pen down.

There are nights, though. There are nights when young Fiscelion snuggles with Carnelia or Lupina in our state-room, and on numb feet I go onto the deck and stand on the prow, in the shadow of the swivel guns, the salted-air heavy and cold, the *Malphas* rising and falling on the swells, as the lascar guards watch me silently, gripping their carbines. I ignore them as best I can. I would scream but for the observers and the accord Carnelia and I made. Off in the distance Rume awaits, and there's no turning away from it. No amount of bribery or wheedling could change Juvenus from this course.

At times, Carnelia joins me, on deck, under the stars, with her *jian*, and she makes the arcane moments, the tracery of air, the turnings and jumpings of Sun Huáng's swordplay until she is slathered in sweat and panting. Once Tenebrae appeared on deck, a wooden gladius in hand, as if to join Carnelia, but the look she gave him was so frightful he paused and then went back below-decks.

We both have our armatura of grief.

ABOUT GOLLANCZ

Gollancz is the oldest SF publishing imprint in the world. Since being founded in 1927 Gollancz has continued to publish a focused selection of bestselling and award-winning authors. The front-list includes **Ben Aaronovitch**, **Joe Abercrombie**, **Charlaine Harris**, **Joanne Harris**, **Joe Hill**, **Alastair Reynolds**, **Patrick Rothfuss**, **Nalini Singh** and **Brandon Sanderson**.

As one of the largest Science Fiction and Fantasy imprints in the UK it is no surprise we have one of the most extensive backlists in the world. Find high quality SF on Gateway written by such authors as **Philip K. Dick**, **Ursula Le Guin**, **Connie Willis**, **Sir Arthur C. Clarke**, **Pat Cadigan**, **Michael Moorcock** and **George R.R. Martin**.

We also have a strand of publishing in translation, which includes French, Polish and Russian authors. Gollancz is home to more award-winning authors than any other imprint, with names including **Aliette de Bodard**, **M. John Harrison**, **Paul McAuley**, **Sarah Pinborough**, **Pierre Pevel**, **Justina Robson** and many more.

The SF Gateway
More than 3,000 classic, rare and previously out-of-print SF novels at your fingertips.
www.sfgateway.com

The Gollancz Blog
Bringing you news from our worlds to yours. Stories, interviews, articles and exclusive extracts just for you!
www.gollancz.co.uk

GOLLANCZ
LONDON